COME FORTH
IN
BLOOD

COME FORTH
—IN—
BLOOD

Matthew Heilman
& Ryan Henry

STYGIAN
PRESS
PITTSBURGH, PENNSYLVANIA

Book Design and Cover Illustration by Craig Hines,
based on an image © DepositPhotos

Character Illustrations by Ture Ekroos

Edited by Kimberly Henry

PUBLISHER'S CATALOGING-IN-PUBLICATION DATA
Names: Heilman, Matthew, author. | Henry, Ryan, author.
Title: Come forth in blood / Matthew Heilman; Ryan Henry.
Description: Pittsburgh, PA: Stygian Press, 2021.
Identifiers: LCCN: 2020925460 | ISBN: 978-0-9785591-4-4 (Hardcover)
| 978-0-9785591-5-1 (pbk.) | 978-0-9785591-6-8 (ebook)
Subjects: LCSH Vampires--Fiction. | College teachers--Fiction. | Universities
& colleges--Virginia--Fiction. | Paranormal fiction. | Horror fiction. | Noir
fiction, American. | BISAC FICTION / Horror | FICTION / Thrillers /
Supernatural | FICTION / Occult & Supernatural | FICTION / Noir
Classification: LCC PS3608 .E55 C66 2021| DDC 813.6--dc23

First Hardcover Edition
ISBN: 978-0-9785591-4-4

Published by Stygian Press
www.StygianPress.com

Printed in the United States of America on acid-free paper.
23 22 21   LSI   0 9 8 7 6 5 4 3 2 1

We hope this passes a "Craig Test."

No sacrament can teach the dead to bear the sight of day.
Gottfried Augustus Bürger
Lenore

†

*I searched everywhere for a proof of reality, when all the while I understood
quite well that the standard of reality had changed.*
Algernon Blackwood
The Willows

†

*She fell as a wreath of snow before the sun in spring.
Her bosom heaved in death; her soul came forth in blood.*
James MacPherson
Fragments of Ancient Poetry

1

Belgium, December 1944

UNTEROFFIZIER MATTHIAS BARTSCH STOOD IN LINE, SHOUL-der to shoulder with the captured panzergrenadiers. He shivered in the biting cold. Slick mud clung to his lowboots and covered the hem of his woolen greatcoat. The air was thick with the smell of burning diesel, propellant, and scorched flesh—vapors from a vicious firefight that had concluded moments before.

Victorious American soldiers paced up and down the line, surveying the row of prisoners. Clad in drab utilitarian uniforms, the Americans jeered and spoke in loud angry voices. Some were looting the dead. Others tore through the pockets of their German prisoners.

A non-commissioned officer of indeterminate rank prowled between the captives, pistol in hand. He stopped before the senior German officer and began shouting. Oberleutnant Schnell answered him in broken English, shook his head, and pointed to the breast eagle on his tunic. The NCO jabbed Schnell in the chest with the barrel of his sidearm. He continued screaming at the oberleutnant.

Although Matthias kept his eyes forward, he noted that the Americans were collecting the paybooks of his comrades. They weren't bothering to inspect them.

Another enemy soldier foundered in the mud of the crossroads. He slogged back and forth across the ruts and tank tracks, a Browning automatic rifle cradled in his arms. The GI muttered something about Germans shooting Allied prisoners.

"These bastards are gonna get what's comin' to 'em." The ruddy-faced machine gunner kicked the shattered treads of a disabled *Schützenpanzerwagen*. The damaged half-track, still smoldering, had been pushed into a nearby ditch.

Matthias tried to make sense of the chaos unfolding around him. He inadvertently stumbled two paces forward.

A group of American privates moved to surround the tall, broad-shouldered medic. One of the enemy soldiers closed in on him. The American's eyes were wild from the lingering rush of combat. Unteroffizier Bartsch could smell tobacco and stale chocolate on the soldier's breath. The private clutched his M1 tight against his chest. His finger caressed the trigger guard.

"Get back in that goddamn line." The private nodded at the conspicuous brassard around Matthias' left arm. "Ya think wearin' that Red Cross is gonna protect ya?"

"Das verstehe ich nicht." Matthias forced the words through his chapped, bleeding lips.

"You're a dead man. Whaddaya think of that, ya heinie shit-heel?"

"Mein Englisch ist nicht so gut."

The American didn't understand him, yet Matthias could sense resentment in his enemy's words.

"Hey, Grayson. He's a medic. We can't execute him. It's against the rules of war."

"Get a load of this clown. Rules of war? You're as crazy as a shithouse rat, Miller. How long you been over here?"

"Three weeks."

"Goddamn replacement. I've been nose-to-nose with these bastards since Normandy. So let me set you straight on somethin'. There ain't no rules of war. The krauts shoot our medics all the time." Grayson sneered at Miller. "This big dummy's got a bullet with his name on it. Just like the rest of these fuckers."

With a trembling hand, Matthias opened his greatcoat. He reached into his left tunic pocket to procure his neutrality papers. Grayson stepped forward and slammed the butt of his rifle into Matthias' wrist. The medic cried out in surprise and pain. Strong hands reached under his collar and ripped the dog tag from his neck.

Matthias doubled over and clutched his forearm. One of the American privates wrenched the steel helmet from his head. Locks of greasy blond hair fell around his eyes to frame his gaunt face.

"I got my first souvenir. It's a real pretty one, too. All whitewashed and everything. I'll bet there ain't a soul in this division that's got a kraut pill-pusher's helmet."

"Luttrell, get rid of it." Grayson shook his head. "You plan to lug that fuckin' thing all the way to Berlin?"

"Hell no."

"Then pitch it, will ya?" Grayson pointed away from the line. "Roosevelt didn't send your sorry ass overseas to collect scrap metal for the war effort."

Still bent double in agony, Matthias clutched the leather medic pouches on his belt to steady himself. He began to retch as Private Luttrell kicked the helmet across the road.

"*Steh auf!*" A voice cried out to the right.

Out of sheer instinct, Matthias obeyed and stood at attention. An American sergeant approached the cluster of privates. The GI, clad in a tanker jacket, slung his Thompson submachine gun and approached the privates. His helmet was cocked haphazardly on his head, shading his grimy face.

"There a problem here?" The officer stole a glance at his wristwatch. "You get this one's papers yet?"

"No, Sarge."

"Goddammit." The sergeant spun on his heel to face Matthias. "*Wie heißt du?*" He spoke in near-perfect German.

"Bartsch. Unteroffizier Matthias Bartsch. *Sanitäter. Ich bin ein sanitäter.*"

"What's this kraut sayin', Zimmerman?"

"It don't matter, Grayson." Zimmerman answered in a rough Brooklyn accent. "We got our orders."

"Sarge," Miller said. "This one's a medic."

"Your point, kid?"

"I tried to tell 'em we can't shoot him. It's against the Geneva Convention to—"

Sergeant Zimmerman tore the Red Cross brassard off of Matthias' left arm and shoved it in his jacket pocket. "I don't see any medics in this line." He paused to glare at his subordinates. "Do you?"

None of the privates replied.

"You three keep goin'. Round up those paybooks and dog tags. The lieutenant wants this to be quick so we can get back on the move." Zimmerman glanced down the rough road. "Battalion S-2 says there's more enemy armor comin' this way."

"Sure thing, Sarge."

The privates shuffled away, cursing and complaining in their native tongue.

Zimmerman pushed at the lapels of Matthias' greatcoat and held it open. He surveyed the tunic underneath. His eyes fixed on a red ribbon stitched into a buttonhole. "Bartsch. *Hast du in Russland gekämpft?* Stalingrad?"

Matthias remained silent.

"Wie hast du das verdient?" The American ran his index finger over a black wound badge pinned to the medic's tunic.

"Ja." Matthias pointed to an irregular scar on his throat where he had been struck by a Russian bullet. A sudden gust of wind nipped at his face, chilling his uncovered head.

Zimmerman dug a grubby hand into Matthias' tunic pocket and removed his paybook. The short man thumbed through the battered booklet and glanced at the Sutterlin script. The weather-beaten pages provided a summary of Matthias' service in the German army. A photograph slid out from between the pages to land in the mud below. The sergeant stooped to pick it up.

"Ist das deine Frau?"

Matthias nodded.

The sergeant placed the photograph between Bartsch's anemic fingers and walked away with his paybook.

The grenadier standing next to Matthias whispered with a trembling voice. *"Sie werden uns erschießen! Schau mal was sie mit unserem Soldbücher tun!"*

Matthias followed the surreptitious nod of Grenadier Fuchs. The privates who had searched them dumped the collection of paybooks into a compact pile. An American corporal swung himself out of a Jeep with a jerrycan. He doused the documents with gasoline. The corporal withdrew a small matchbook from his pocket and lit the pile of tattered paybooks ablaze. Cardstock, paper, and celluloid photographs evaporated into the gray winter sky.

An American lieutenant barked an order, and the privates rushed to form a line parallel to the surrendered Germans. Young replacements in ill-fitting helmets and baggy field tunics fumbled with their M1s. On the officer's command, they jammed fully-loaded clips into their waiting rifles. Fuchs began to pray.

Matthias Bartsch—the twenty-six year-old medic who'd managed to survive three winters on the Eastern Front—looked at his young wife's picture one last time. As he returned the photo to his pocket, he raised his head to face the jagged line of enemy infantrymen. Their rifles were poised to fire. Matthias pursed his lips and stared into the barren trees beyond the eager executioners.

The Americans' firearms flashed and pounded in succession, but Matthias stood fast. He pushed his chest forward as .30 caliber rounds tore through his wool clothing and pierced his skin. Feeble moans rose above the thunder of the guns as Matthias and his comrades fell to the ground.

The gunfire ceased.

Matthias dug his forehead into the mud and pressed his burning chest against the frigid earth. In a final stroke of irony, one of the bleeding panzergrenadiers called for a medic. The sharp clap of an M1 put an end to his pleas. Matthias clenched his teeth and gasped for breath.

As the ringing in his ears subsided, Matthias heard the nearby Jeep's engine roar to life. Above the din, two soldiers conversed.

"I shoulda kept that helmet. Maybe I could grab another one or look for a Luger. That officer over there's—"

"Nah. Take these dog tags."

Matthias heard the clink of aluminum disks changing hands.

"When you're an old man, you pull 'em out and tell your grandkids you killed a buncha krauts in the big war with your bare hands. Gutted 'em with your bayonet or somethin'. Any way you cut it, you're Fenton-by-god-Luttrell of Poquoson, Virginia. Goddamned war hero."

Raucous laughter erupted from the nearby Americans.

"Come on, you ignorant son of a bitch! Shove 'em in your pocket!"

Matthias fought for breath. His blood was already congealing in the bitter cold of the Belgian winter. He remained still as he heard heavy footfalls pass by. Booted feet kicked at the bodies littering the ground. Any surviving prisoner that twitched or cried out was subsequently shot.

Matthias heard footsteps behind him. The barrel of a .45 pistol jabbed at an exit wound along his upper thigh. The pain of each prod was unbearable, but Matthias fought the urge to move or make a sound. He had fallen so his mouth was pressed against the sleeve of his overcoat. When he exhaled, no trace of breath was visible.

The pistol barrel was abruptly removed and the footsteps shuffled toward the dead man next to him. Matthias remained motionless until he heard the last of the Americans lumber away, their boots heavy in the mud.

Unteroffizier Bartsch opened his mouth and gasped for breath. Even the slightest movement was painful. He opened his eyes to stare directly at Fuchs, whose corpse lay slack-jawed beside him. The pulverized contents of the grenadier's skull spilled onto the muddy snow.

2

NIGHT FELL, AND THE SILENCE WAS PUNCTUATED BY DISTANT bursts of artillery. Now lying on his side, Matthias could see the flash of the heavy guns far beyond the woods. An unseen plane roared overhead and exploding flak lit the sky. The war continued on without him. He was a casualty far behind enemy lines and had been left for dead.

With difficulty, Matthias managed to draw a bandage from his tunic pocket and a morphine phial from a belt pouch. The opiate tempered the pain for a short time, but the burning soon returned to his limbs and chest. In desperation, the wounded soldier clutched the cloth bandage below his collarbone. He had no idea how many times he'd been hit, but he was certain that the chest wound would finish him. Each time he coughed, the rattling behind his ribcage grew louder. He remained huddled close to the ground. Matthias used the bodies around him for concealment only, for they no longer provided heat.

A light snow began to fall. The glow of the moon above illuminated the surrounding carnage.

Amidst the heavy silence, Matthias heard a low hiss. He assumed someone down the line was still alive. The sound grew louder, and he detected quick, purposeful footsteps from the pine forest beyond the road. He sunk against the ground again, fearing the Americans had come back to finish him off.

Matthias heard a deep voice issue a command in a language he didn't recognize. These were not soldiers, nor were they local civilians.

Matthias raised his head. A malformed human figure—almost naked in the clear, cold night—crouched beside the corpse of an MG42 gunner. It tore into the dead man's neck, burrowing deep into the flesh. Vulpine in its movements, it spat out bloody fragments of the panzergrenadier's tunic collar. Matthias recoiled in confusion as the thing exposed its face. The creature's chin was soaked in dark, dead blood. It bellowed another harsh command to its companion.

Despite his pain, Matthias was horrified. Nothing in the annals of war had prepared him for the sight unfolding before him.

Crouching low to the ground, the creature crept toward the remains of Oberleutnant Schnell. Matthias shut his eyes as a series of low sounds sent shudders across his flesh.

Anna! His eyes welled with tears at the memory of his wife. *Hilf mir!* The creatures from the woods slithered among the frozen corpses. They stopped to feed on a dead soldier just inches from where Matthias lay. Petrified, Matthias couldn't prevent his bladder from emptying. A dark stain spread across the crotch of his field-gray trousers.

The horrid sounds abruptly ceased. The pungent scent of his urine drew the attention of the filthy things scavenging in the darkness. Matthias' skin crawled as an emaciated shadow fell across him.

"Bitte! Ich bin noch am Leben!" Matthias gasped. *"Hilf mir!"* He clenched his teeth and squeezed his eyes shut. *"Schau mal weg! Mein Gott, nein! Schau sie nicht an!"*

The monster bent down and bellowed with ferocity. Its fetid breath was cold against the soldier's face. Its companion drew closer and a guttural roar sent waves of sickness from Matthias' stomach to his racing heart.

Matthias trembled as the creatures began to converse in a harsh, un-recognizable tongue.

"Čo je to?"

"Tento ešte žije. Čo by sme mali robiť s ním?"

Once again, they fell silent. The creature closest to him lowered its head to stare at Matthias with milky eyes. Its ears were pointed and misshapen. Dry scabs and swollen pustules marred the surface of its taut, leprous skin.

At last, the one towering above him spoke again.

"Dajte mu dar!"

A frigid hand covered Matthias' eyes and he felt broken teeth sink into his throat. The second creature's teeth pierced the sleeve of his overcoat and

8

the *feldbluse* underneath. Matthias screamed as the beasts tore into his flesh. They snarled in unison at the taste of his warm blood.

One placed its lips against his and regurgitated dead blood into his mouth. Matthias choked on the loathsome black ichor.

Suddenly, the assailants withdrew. The pallid hand fell away from Bartsch's eyes. One creature remained poised on slender haunches, holding a wiry appendage to its mouth. It mewled in fear and recoiled from something rumbling in the distance.

The glaring lights of an approaching vehicle caused the creatures to scatter into the nearby forest. Matthias was incapable of speech as he pushed himself to his knees.

He recognized the headlamps of an American Jeep turning at the intersection, as well as the groan of trucks in tow, changing gear. Before he could hide himself among the corpses, the Jeep passed him. Its occupants stared at the dark road ahead, unaware of the bodies strewn in the ditch.

Matthias fell to the ground and rested his head against Fuchs' imploded face. He waited until the distinct rumble of enemy traffic passed him in the dark. Shaking, he drew his fingers to his neck. He felt the damage the creature had done to his throat. The flesh surrounding the bite was numb to the touch.

The pain of the gunshot wounds ebbed away, but a newfound agony overwhelmed him. Matthias turned onto his stomach and pulled himself toward the same tree line where the creatures had disappeared. He dragged himself between the gnarled trees, grasping at tree roots and stones to traverse the snowdrifts and deadfall.

In time, he regained most of the feeling in his legs. After fumbling through the wet slush, Matthias rose on all fours and found the strength to scurry faster. With every agonizing movement, he expected his tormentors to lunge at him from the darkness.

Halfway into a clearing, his body seized. Matthias bit into his tongue. The rancid taste of dead blood filled his mouth again.

Somewhere beyond the forest, the familiar thump of an 88mm anti-aircraft gun again reminded Matthias that a war still raged around him.

He continued to crawl until he spotted an abandoned barn, torn to shreds by artillery bursts. As he crept towards the dilapidated structure, he could no longer hear the pulse of his heartbeat in his ears. His lungs ceased to draw breath. His veins had emptied, and his arteries had collapsed. Matthias tucked his body into a corner of the derelict barn, amidst crumbling stone, wood, and the brittle webs of long dead spiders.

The realization of his unnatural condition eclipsed all other thoughts, concerns, and fears—save for one.

Matthias Bartsch knew that he wasn't about to die.

He was already dead.

3

CORPORAL ERNIE RASMUSSEN CROUCHED IN A SHALLOW SLIT trench at the edge of the Belgian tree line. The soldier hadn't slept in two days. He pulled a wool issue blanket over his shoulders and turned up his field jacket collar to ward off the cold. Rasmussen was one of two sentries in the forward listening post. The rest of his rifle squad dozed in their well-concealed foxholes to the rear.

Black coffee and Benzedrine tablets from Doc Rutila had kept him on edge while he manned the dangerous position. His M1 rifle weighed heavy in his arms, so he cinched it tight against his shoulder and rested the forward stock on the cusp of the foxhole. Through the gun's iron sights, he scanned the horizon for movement.

Lieutenant Ellis—their platoon leader—had put him on LP/OP duty with explicit instructions to watch a dirt road about a hundred yards distant. Between the forest where the squad had dug in and the well-traveled trail, a barren field lay exposed. Light flurries eddied about, but the sky was cloudless. A bright moon hung above the shadowed pine forest. If the enemy materialized on the nearby road, he'd surely see them coming. A BC-611 handie-talkie lay atop the frozen soil beside him. On the off chance there was enemy contact, he was to radio platoon CP immediately and hold fire.

Earlier that day, as they'd been digging in, a procession of German Tiger II tanks had rumbled along the nearby road. Flanking the armored column were SS panzergrenadiers in oak leaf camouflage and white winter smocks. Stick grenades were shoved into their jackboots and utility belts. They moved on foot, ready to repel any Allies foolhardy enough to stage

11

an ambush. The battle-hardened SS troops were armed to a man with new automatic assault rifles. Battalion S-2 had warned Rasmussen's company about them.

He'd heard stories about the SS and how vicious they were—especially the 1st Panzer Division, which was rumored to be spearheading the assault. The SS were the most ruthless killers in Hitler's service, and had shown no quarter against the Russians on the Eastern Front. He knew another column of kraut armor could show up, make a turn to cross the open field, and wipe out his squad as they slept in their foxholes. Hell, they could do it before he had a chance to alert the CP.

A twig snapped to his left, and the corporal jerked his head toward the sound.

What the hell was that?

Rasmussen's heart began to race. He adjusted his helmet and surveyed the terrain with fearful eyes. There were only patches of moonlight to illuminate the forest. Shadows twisted across the snow as the wind howled through the trees.

Anything could be out in those woods.

Fuckin' wolves, for Chrissakes.

He glanced toward the handie-talkie, hoping he'd have enough time to contact Lieutenant Ellis if things went south.

What if he doesn't answer? What if the krauts are tuned in to the same radio frequency?

Rasmussen drew in a sharp breath as the sky lit up in the distance. The rumble of a rolling artillery barrage shook the snow from the pine branches above. He glanced over at Private Manzetti, who was fast asleep. A twinge of envy overcame the corporal. The young replacement was bundled in his issue blankets and had one gloved hand on his rifle's forward stock. In a few hours, the private was to provide watch relief until daybreak. Rasmussen, however, wasn't sure he'd be able to sleep even if he had the chance.

By the dim light of the moon, he noticed the safety on Manzetti's rifle was disengaged. He reached over and flipped the metal switch into the rifle's trigger guard. The last thing they needed was an accidental shooting in their ranks. If anything, it would draw the goddamn Nazis right to them.

Rasmussen flinched as an enemy artillery shell burst somewhere in the distance. He corrected the angle of his rifle so the sights lined up to a distant fencepost. With his eyes back on the road, he noticed a flicker of movement. He swallowed hard as an amorphous figure emerged from the drainage ditch and lurched forward. The corporal loosened his grip on his rifle and fumbled for the binoculars hanging around his neck.

After some adjustments, he could see the road and the fencepost, but the figure wasn't in his line of sight. Rasmussen let the binoculars drop as the figure stumbled through snowdrifts in the open field. He kicked Manzetti awake.

"Get on your gun," Rasmussen hissed at the bleary-eyed private. "We got company!"

Manzetti snapped to and slid against the front incline of the slit trench, his rifle at the ready. With a tangible threat in sight, Rasmussen was forced to regain his composure. He yanked on the antenna of the boxy radio and it crackled to life. He held the receiver to his ear and pressed the send button. "Corporal Rasmussen. Fox-Oboe-Peter-One. I got movement front and center. Over."

As he waited for the lieutenant to answer, the lone German soldier moved closer to the listening post.

"Convoy?" Ellis asked. "Over."

"No sir. Kraut infantryman. Over."

"Just one?" Ellis was incredulous. "Over."

Manzetti, now awake and alert, turned his attention to the approaching enemy soldier. Through the sights of his rifle, he watched the lone man stagger through fresh snowdrifts.

The wounded German had no weapon or helmet. His tattered greatcoat was dark with blood, and strands of hair hung against his sunken cheeks. The kraut's eyes were vacant and his lips were drawn together in a thin line. Manzetti glanced at the intruder's left sleeve. "No eagle on his arm. He's not SS. Just regular army. Want me to take him down, corporal?"

Rasmussen held up a gloved hand in the private's direction as he continued his conversation over the radio.

"Yes, sir. Just one man. No SS eagle on his sleeve and no weapon that I can see. Maybe a deserter. He's tore up pretty bad. Gonna need the doc up front. Over."

"You woke me for a prisoner capture?"

"Sorry, sir. It's just—"

13

"Listen here, corporal. Doc's back at the forward aid station. I'll get him on the horn. Meantime, you bring this guy in and check him for hidden ordnance, papers, whatever. You know the drill. Over."

"Wilco. Over."

"Maintain light and noise discipline, get him back to S-2, and don't bother me about this again. You're supposed to be watching for armor. Charlie Peter out."

With that, Ellis was gone. Static resounded through the receiver.

"Corporal?" Manzetti uttered with a weak voice.

Rasmussen dropped the radio.

From the edge of the forest, the enemy soldier glared directly at their foxhole. Despite the precautions Rasmussen had taken for cover and concealment, the German could discern their position. The corporal had captured prisoners before, and nearly all had jabbered on in their native tongue with hands held high. Some even pissed themselves when they realized they were under the gun.

This one was different. His arms were tensed at his sides. His fingers were curled into fists as if spoiling for a fight. There was something malicious about the lone German's empty stare. The would-be prisoner sneered as if surrender was the furthest thing from his mind.

In a flash, the corporal rose to his feet. The snow-dusted wool blanket fell from his shoulders. Rasmussen trained his rifle on the advancing enemy and bellowed the only warning he knew. *"Hände hoch!"*

But the German continued to forge a path toward them. He was only a few yards from the listening post where Rasmussen stood firm with his M1 at the ready. *"Hände hoch, you fuckin' kraut! Hände hoch!"*

Manzetti leapt to his feet and vaulted out of the foxhole, not sure what to do. Hirsch, a tech-5 light machine gunner, trudged up behind the LP. He was of German-Jewish descent and translated for the squad during prisoner captures. Hirsch waved his carbine at the private. "Manzetti, stand down! Let me talk to this—"

"Tell him to get on his fuckin' knees and put his hands on his head!" Rasmussen barked at Hirsch.

The translator stuttered for a moment. *"Auf...Auf die knie! Ja! Die knie! Hände auf den kopf!"*

Rasmussen wasn't surprised when the German didn't comply. The disheveled man stopped short of the corporal's rifle. He stood in defiance and swayed on unsteady legs.

Rasmussen and the German locked eyes. From somewhere beside them, Hirsch spoke up. *"Kannst du mich hören?"*

The German didn't answer.

"You can ease down, Rasmussen. I don't think he can hear anything."

"Oh, I think he can hear just fine." The corporal gestured with his gun barrel. "He just doesn't wanna do what we tell him."

The sound of double-buckle boots crunching on snow grew louder behind them. Doc Rutila passed through a patch of diffuse light. He was hunched over, one hand holding his helmet in place as he ran. His medic pouches, laden with bandages, morphine, and other tools of his trade, slapped against his legs.

Rutila stopped to catch his breath in the cold, then pushed his way between Manzetti and Hirsch. The veteran aid man assayed the strange visitor from head to toe. He narrowed his eyes for a double take. "This bastard's been hit six or seven times by small arms fire." Rutila stifled a cough. "Not only that, but it looks like a pack of wild dogs chewed on his throat. This guy oughta be dead. Hirsch, ask him for some identification."

"I think he's deaf," Hirsch replied. "Maybe a grenade went off and—"

"No." Rutila shook his head. "These are definitely gunshot wounds." He loosened the strap on his left pouch and dug inside for a Carlisle bandage. "See those hard leather boxes on his belt? He's a medic like me."

"That explains why he's still on his feet," Manzetti said. "Prolly shot himself up fulla morphine. Once that wears off, he's history."

When Doc Rutila reached out to take the German's radial pulse, the stranger grasped his wrist. He tilted his head to gaze at Rutila, who looked back at the German with curiosity and dread.

"Zimmerman," the injured man rasped.

"What'd he say?" Hirsch exchanged glances with Manzetti. Rasmussen didn't move.

The German lifted his pale eyes to glower at the translator. "Miller."

"What the—" A puzzled look crossed Manzetti's shadowed features. In desperation, he looked around at his compatriots.

"Luttrell." The German addressed Manzetti in a low growl. He had trouble pronouncing the name, but he spoke with conviction. "Fenton Luttrell. Poquoson. Virginia."

"*Suchst du diese Leute? Amerikaner?*" Hirsch managed. His tone was shaky, and he cinched his hands around his carbine.

"What's he sayin'?" Manzetti shouted. "What the fuck is wrong with this guy?"

"I don't...I mean..."

"Out with it, Hirsch!" Rasmussen snapped.

"He's either looking for these men or he thinks we're—"

"Grayson." The German lowered his head at the rifle barrel pointing at his chest. He spat out the name and locked eyes with Ernie Rasmussen.

"Hey!" Rutila exclaimed. "Hirsch, tell this idiot to let go of my—"

"Zimmerman!" The German howled as he jerked Doc Rutila's arm from its socket with a wet snap. Before any of the soldiers could react, the prisoner pulled the medic to his chest, and prevented Rasmussen from taking a clear shot. Dazed no more, the prisoner locked his arms around Rutila and sank his teeth into the aid man's neck. Bright red blood soaked the faces of the attacker and his victim. Rutila's scream echoed through the pines, and he kicked and thrashed as the assailant heaved him off the ground.

Rasmussen made no move, but Manzetti charged toward the writhing combatants, his finger on his rifle's trigger. "Holy Mary mother of God," Manzetti wailed. "Hirsch, tell him to get the hell off the doc! Tell him!" Despite his close proximity, Manzetti couldn't line up a clear shot.

With his teeth buried in the flesh of Rutila's neck, one of the German's arms slipped free. He flung the medic's helmet aside and dug his fingers into Rutila's scalp. The attacker twisted his victim's head halfway around and broke his neck.

Before the aid man's corpse hit the ground, the German lunged at Rasmussen and wrenched the rifle from his hands. Manzetti tried to shoot but his trigger wouldn't budge. He was too terrified to disengage the safety.

Hirsch put two .30 caliber pistol rounds into the intruder's left shoulder, but the bullets failed to stop his onslaught. Rearing back on his heels, the German swung Rasmussen's rifle by the barrel in Manzetti's direction. The rear stock smashed into the private's face with enough force to splinter into wooden shards. Manzetti's helmet flew off as his skull burst through his scalp. The private's teeth, blood, and brain matter covered Hirsch and sent him reeling.

"Luttrell!" The madman screamed as Manzetti's limp body fell against Hirsch. The machine gunner collapsed under the dead private's weight. He emptied his carbine's magazine into the treetops.

Rasmussen withdrew his bayonet from its scabbard and bum-rushed the German. He slid the short blade into the enemy's upper chest and wrenched the weapon from side to side. Rasmussen stared into the face of the attacker.

Glistening blood slicked the German's chin as he bared his teeth. His eyes had grown darker than the surrounding shadows. Blood spilled over the marauder's lips as he bellowed a single word.

"Grayson!"

The German swung the mangled rifle into Rasmussen's upper jaw. Roused by the sounds of close combat, the rest of the squad advanced in confusion through the trees, their rifles leveled toward the intruder. The corporal—who stood in the line of fire—was riddled with bullets meant for his attacker. He slumped forward and clutched at the tattered remains of the German's greatcoat.

Rasmussen fell face first into the blood-spattered snow. Hirsch screamed obscenities nearby. Prone and in agony, Ernie Rasmussen didn't think of home, or his mother, or his sweetheart back in the States. He knew he was about to die.

Before he blacked out, Rasmussen felt jagged teeth pierce his neck as the ruthless predator pinned him to the ground. He choked out a final, rattling breath as a probing tongue traced the gash in his throat.

4

THE FIRST RAYS OF DAWN CREPT THROUGH THE PINE FOREST. An artillery barrage to his rear woke Matthias Bartsch from his stupor. He glanced over his shoulder at an irregular row of Tiger IIs discharging rounds from the distant road. Waffen-SS infantrymen were charging an Allied fighting position to his far right. Muzzles flashed in the dusky air as a clash of arms commenced a half-kilometer down the line. They were too far away to notice him, but he knew the battle could change direction at any moment.

Matthias had no recollection of how he'd gotten from the abandoned barn onto the battlefield. He only remembered a vivid dream of executing his killers. The empty, gnawing hunger that had consumed him was sated.

Rifle and machine gun fire echoed through the woods. Grenades flashed and exploded in his peripheral vision. The far-off screams of the wounded and dying were drowned out by the Tigers firing in battery.

He glanced down at his lowboots, which were rust-red and smeared with human gore. In his hands, he clutched an American rifle bayonet. Its point had been dulled. The hilt was loose, and every inch of the blade was stained with blood. Matthias dropped the bayonet to inspect his hands.

The fresh remains of dismembered GIs were scattered at his feet. Severed arms clutched broken rifles. Ropy intestines and organs spilled from gutted carcasses. Olive drab uniforms had been shredded to scraps, and contorted bodies lay frozen in the snow.

Jetzt erinnere ich mich.

He wiped his hands on the rough wool of his coat and noticed the bullet holes that had turned his uniform into rags. Matthias jabbed his fingers through a prominent tear and probed the flesh beneath his tattered garments. There was no evidence that he'd ever been shot or stabbed. Frantic, he tore off his greatcoat, tunic, and undershirt, and ran his hands over his bare chest. The blood he'd taken in had somehow healed his wounds.

Ich tat es.

Above the treetops, the ominous sound of low-flying fighter-bombers converged on his position. He picked up his torn shirt and slipped it on. He would've taken the clothing from his victims, but their uniforms were in worse condition than his own. As Matthias dusted off his bloody tunic, a ray of winter sun hit his bare arm.

He felt a sharp pain rise from within. The smell of scorched flesh wafted to his nostrils as wisps of smoke roiled around his exposed skin. In confusion, he slipped on his tunic and coat, and the burning ebbed away.

Matthias spied something familiar on one of the dead soldier's jacket sleeves. The men he had killed wore the same division badge as the ones that shot him. He squatted down, tore a patch off the sleeve of a corpse, and shoved it in his pocket. The sound of approaching aircraft engines brought him back to his feet.

He gazed skyward as a formation of American P-51s dropped low. The fighter-bombers opened up on the Tigers and the SS men in the distance. The rosy clouds of dawn burned his eyes, and his face began to blister.

Das Sonnenlicht!

Matthias spun in a circle, desperate for a place to hide from the rising sun.

A reflexive instinct urged him to seek shelter at all costs. But with the turmoil behind him, he couldn't hide under a blanket in a hole in the ground.

Lauf!

Possessed by a newfound vitality, Matthias sprinted between the pines. He dodged low-lying branches and deadfall as if he could foresee any obstacles blocking his path. His senses were more acute, his gait was faster, and at that moment, he feared nothing but the rising sun. The lifeblood of twelve men coursed through his veins and gave him power and instinct beyond his wildest imaginings.

As he sped through the forest, he recalled the men he maimed and killed hours ago. None of them had been who they seemed. He'd only seen what he wanted to see—the faces of his killers. The blood he tasted was laced with anger, hatred, and fear. Each drop had been positively electric.

Matthias emerged from the forest onto a side road where a tank battle had occurred days before. As he felt the heat of daylight bearing down on him, the fledgling vampire dove into the back of an Opel *Blitz* truck. The thick canvas cover provided adequate protection from the sun's rays. Matthias closed the rear flap and settled into his makeshift hiding place.

Even in the darkness, he could see every detail around him with astounding clarity. Along the benches of the truck bed sat six dead panzergrenadiers, frozen into grotesque poses by the cold. Each had been executed with a pistol round to the head. One of the corpses was close to Matthias' size and build. He checked the dead man's tunic pockets for a paybook, and it was there. He read the owner's name and number on the document. Bit by bit, he undressed and replaced his uniform and identity. To the war and to the world, he was now Oberfeldwebel Erich Neutze.

With little fanfare, he tore the buttonhole ribbons from his old tunic and ripped the two pinback award badges from the breast pocket. For better or worse, he'd earned them and intended to keep them. As he held the trinkets in his bloodstained hand, he remembered Anna's picture.

Matthias tore through the pockets of his old uniform until he found a cigarette tin and the cardstock photograph. He held it with care by the edges so as not to mar its surface. Without looking, he slid his dead wife's picture into the cigarette tin and dropped the metal box into the pocket of his new greatcoat.

Matthias couldn't bring himself to look at her face. Not after what he had done. Instead, he busied himself by checking the remaining pockets before casting his old clothing aside. He recovered the American patch, a Skat deck, an extra bandage, and something smooth that snaked around his spindly fingers.

As he held the object up for inspection, Matthias was overcome with revulsion. Wrapped around his hand was Anna's pearl rosary. She'd given it to him before he was sent to the Eastern Front. The silver crucifix horrified the vampire, and he flung the rosary to the floor. For safe measure, he kicked it under one of the wooden benches.

Matthias sat on the floor of the abandoned truck in confusion. He couldn't reconcile the thrill of murder with the emptiness and dejection he suddenly felt. Those creatures that attacked him by the road hadn't killed him—they'd given him their own mysterious powers. Although this affliction restored him to life and imbued him with strength and the will to survive, the price of his continued existence would be incalculable.

Matthias closed his eyes and drifted into a discomfiting torpor. With the setting sun, he'd return to the roads and forests in search of prey. As he sank into a deeper sleep, a veil had been lifted within the recesses of his mind, indicating a clearer sense of purpose.

"Poquoson. Luttrell," he muttered to himself. "Fenton...Luttrell. Poquoson...Virginia..."

5

Occupied Germany, 1946

WHEN THE WAR ENDED IN 1945, MATTHIAS FOUND HIMSELF in the American sector after Germany was divided. He never returned to Darmstadt, but moved from town to town where he took on odd jobs and used different aliases, depending on whether he was in Stuttgart, Munich, or Frankfurt.

Now dressed in ragged civilian clothes, he carried only an army rucksack and a battered cello case. Matthias traveled on foot at night. There was little to differentiate him from the thousands of indigent war veterans wandering the occupied countryside. Yet unlike other transients living hand-to-mouth, he appeared clean-cut, youthful, and had a conspicuous need to request an invitation before entering a private residence. Matthias spent as much time as possible within earshot of the US Army troops policing his ravaged country, and proved to be a quick student of the English language.

American soldiers often stopped him to ask for papers. Once, a pair of irritable MPs made him open the cello case so they could examine its contents. Matthias stood aside, his powerful arms crossed as they inspected his precious musical instrument. Unaware that they were looking at a stolen 1712 Stradivarius worth several thousand dollars, the MPs closed the case and bid Matthias on his way.

He kept the division patch in his pocket, but none of the troops he found stationed in Bavaria, Hessen, or Württemberg wore the same insignia.

In Augsburg, he showed the patch to a high-ranking American officer who couldn't understand his broken English. Although Matthias received no information about the division in question, the cultured officer paid the vampire handsomely for an unaccompanied cello rendition of Offenbach's *Les Larmes de Jacqueline* for the amusement of his young French bride.

Matthias returned to the officer's lavish home later that evening and killed them both. The requested piece had been one of Anna's favorites. He let the couple bleed out slowly and watched with detached indifference as they died on the bedroom floor.

Wherever Matthias went, townspeople and peace officers alike were sometimes confounded by mysterious or unexplained disappearances. He was never a suspect in any crime, for displaced persons filtered in and out of towns and cities looking for work on a regular basis. He made sure to never stay in one place for too long.

Only once in his travels did Matthias meet another like himself. He spent a few weeks prowling the Frankfurt underground when he encountered his first undead counterpart. The vampire, who wore the remnants of an American soldier's uniform, was hiding in the city sewers where day and night held no meaning. He fed on rats, stray animals, and insects. As a consequence, the sewer-dweller had taken on the characteristics of something less than human. The feral vampire's eyes were pale and wept yellow pus. His teeth were broken and chalky. At first, Matthias had mistaken the fledgling for one of the monstrosities that had turned him during the war. It soon became clear that the pitiful creature was harmless. When he recognized that Matthias was a vampire like himself, he approached him with curiosity and wonder.

Before the creature could speak, Matthias pushed him against the arching brick wall and inspected his sleeve. The patch he wore matched the one in his pocket.

The soldier didn't speak a word of German, but Matthias was able to ask him in English where his division was stationed. His name was Arnold Price. He informed Matthias that his comrades were National Guardsmen and had already been sent home.

Price also told Matthias how he'd been turned. He said that monsters followed the armies to feed on the dead and dying. As far as Price knew, they'd come from the Eastern Front. The vampire then broke down and admitted he couldn't commit murder for survival. Over and over, he stated he wasn't a killer, and never could be. Thus, he had never tasted human blood.

Before Price could further explain himself, Matthias punched a fist into the weaker monster's chest and tore its heart from its splintered ribcage. Price stared at his attacker with a mix of shock and relief. His lips trembled and his mouth fell open. Matthias sneered and snapped Price's neck, granting the pathetic creature a quick and merciful release.

Once Matthias learned the men of the division were no longer in Germany, Cherbourg became his destination. At the seaport, Matthias booked passage on a tramp steamer to New York City. He registered under the ruse that he was a poor musician who'd sat out the war as a captive of the Soviets. Matthias was given what he asked for—a windowless room with a bunk and a chair so he could practice his cello. During the course of the voyage, no one complained when the mournful sounds of the vampire's instrument could be heard from the bowels of the cargo hold.

The ship docked at Manhattan with five unaccounted crewmembers. Within days, Matthias had blended into the teeming masses. He played his cello in the Bowery subway station for spare change. In a month, he'd acquired false paperwork to prove his American citizenship and a steady night job appraising musical instruments for a pawnbroker. Whenever asked about his past or what he did in the war, Matthias said that he was the son of immigrants fleeing the Nazis and was declared 4F due to a heart murmur.

There was no record in any archive of a German soldier named Matthias Bartsch executed during the Ardennes Offensive. The only evidence of his service to the Wehrmacht was in a cigarette tin at the bottom of his rucksack. Yet his dog-tag was still missing, so Matthias had ventured across the Atlantic to retrieve it.

6

Poquoson, Virginia. July 1957

AS THE MIDSUMMER SUN BEGAN TO SET OVERHEAD, TWO young boys trotted barefoot down a dirt path. Sandy clumps of soil clung to their waterlogged feet. The eldest boy stopped, balancing his fishing pole on his rawboned shoulder, and brushed away the sand from his left foot. What remained stuck to the hand he wiped on the short roots of his kid brother's flat-top haircut.

"Get bent, Bobby!" Junior landed a punch in the older boy's side. Bobby stumbled into the tall switchgrass hanging over the path.

"If you know what's good for ya, you'll quit bein' a damned goof." Bobby righted himself and the boys continued along the path. The plastic bobbers on their fishing poles swung as they crossed the uneven surface beneath them.

"Hey, Bobby," Junior piped up with enthusiasm in his voice. "When Pa gives us quarters to go to the flicks tomorrow, can we see *Curse of Frankenstein* again?"

"Like hell. You had to sleep with the light on for three days after you saw it last time, you little crybaby." Bobby delivered a glancing blow to Junior's shoulder.

Junior stuck out his lip in dejection. "It *was* scary." He raised his head and grinned. "But it was a good kinda scary. And it's in color, too, so it's worth more than some crummy black 'n' white western. C'mon, don't be such a wet rag about it."

"I dunno, Junior. We'll see." Bobby looked toward the sky in the west. The setting sun filtered through the thick weeds framing their footpath. He spoke in earnest. "We can watch it again if you promise you won't go on

25

about monsters anymore. They ain't real. There ain't no ghosts, or mummies, or space aliens. OK?"

Junior nodded in silence. As they meandered home after an unproductive afternoon of casting along the banks of Whitehouse Cove, the brothers remained quiet. Around them, a chorus of frogs grew louder as they passed through the marsh. The water lapping at the soggy ground beside the path was dark and brackish. Junior shuddered.

"You sure there ain't no monsters, Bobby? I mean, really sure?" Junior gripped the cork handle of his fishing rod as he surveyed the marsh. The last light of the summer sun fell below the horizon.

"Yeah. Except for the commies, there ain't no monsters. Now what'd I tell you a minute ago? You wanna see that flick again, you need to shut your face. And if we get in our seats tomorrow and you start bawlin' when you see the creature, we're gonna tear ass right outta there, got it?"

"Alright, Bobby. When Frankenstein wakes up, I won't get scared this time."

"Dammit! Frankenstein's the name of the doctor. 'Sides, I can prove that monster ain't real. There's an actor playing him. His name's Christopher Lee. He fought in the war just like Pa!"

Junior nodded, his feet sinking in the mud. His pegged jeans were sopping wet. "Bobby?"

"Yeah?"

"You think someone could actually bring a dead man back to life?"

"Heck no! Keep it up with the stupid questions and I'll knock your block off."

Junior looked up at his older brother with a pained expression. "I reckon we better high tail it home before Pa whips our asses."

"Aww, he's probably three sheets to the wind by now. You know how he gets on Friday night when Ma goes an' plays bridge. He won't even hear us come in if we're real quiet."

The brothers rounded a bend in the narrow trail. In the waxing moonlight, a well-dressed man stood in the middle of the footpath.

His imagination busy with the prospect of real monsters, Junior nearly dropped his fishing pole and his bait pail. The brothers stopped in their tracks as they assayed the man's long wool coat, his black fedora, and his neatly pressed suit.

The stranger's skin was pale, and he fixed his gaze on the brothers with a hint of malice. Beneath the man's blue eyes were high cheekbones and an angular jaw. His chest was wide and imposing, and he towered over the boys. Junior was mesmerized and fearful. Bobby wasn't so impressed.

"This here's private property, mister," Bobby lied. "My Pa's gonna shoot your ass if he finds you wanderin' around back here."

The man wasn't cowed by the ten-year-old boy's threat. Instead, he returned Bobby's sneer with an air of confidence that made the boy's shoulders sink in defeat.

"Is Fenton Luttrell your father?" The man spoke perfect English, but there was something foreign about the tone of his voice.

Junior stepped behind his brother. Bobby, now a bit uneasy, still replied with a hint of temerity in his voice. "Yeah, what of it?"

"I'm trying to find him. I'm a touch lost out here and was hoping you could show me to your house."

"Are you some kinda salesman? Because my Ma don't want another vacuum cleaner." Bobby's stance remained obstinate.

The stranger in the coat and fedora, who wasn't bothered by the oppressive summer heat or the undulating clouds of mosquitoes, tilted his head sideways and laughed. "I'm no salesman. I was in the war with your father. I told him I would be stopping by tonight."

Bobby's eyes narrowed. "What'd you say your name was again?" He drew his calloused foot through the dirt, as if making a line for the strange man to cross.

The stranger stood motionless, still blocking the footpath. Junior was now halfway behind his braver older brother. To the young boy's horror, the man's shoulders seemed to grow wider and more solid with every passing second. As he held his breath, Junior realized there were no sounds save for his own breathing and that of his brother. The croaking frogs had fallen silent, and the summer air was still and calm.

"I didn't," the man answered. "You can call me Bartsch. Your father and I were in Belgium together in 1944."

The older boy shook his head. "You look awful young compared to my Pa. How do I know you ain't tellin' stories about bein' in the war?"

"You don't. You just have to trust me. Now if you take me to see your father, I'm pretty sure he will remember me. All you have to do is take me to your home, and he will tell you he was expecting my visit."

The stranger peered into the wide eyes of the younger Luttrell boy. "There's nothing to be afraid of. Your father and I go way back. I was in town, so I gave him a call and he invited me over for a beer."

Junior nodded. Bobby shifted his fishing pole to his opposite shoulder. "Well, you seem to know my Pa alright, 'cause the only way he'd let any high-talkin' son of a bitch like you in our house is if he's got a few beers in him. Come on and we'll show you the way." Bobby motioned for the stranger to follow. "You're almost there, anyway. I'm surprised you didn't see the porch light through them trees. It's right behind you."

Bartsch spun on the heel of his spit-shined black shoe and regarded the dim light in the distance. "I see. Well, why don't we walk together? You can show me in and tell your Pa his army buddy is here to see him."

Bobby led the strange man down the path, while Junior cowered behind and kept his distance. "So were you there when my Pa took out that kraut machine gun nest at the Bulge?" Bobby glanced over at the tall man, who was treading the wet ground with little effort. "He's got a whole mess of kraut dog tags hanging on the wall by the bookshelf. My Ma told him he's got a screw loose, but she knows her place not to touch 'em. He won the Silver Star for killin' them Germans."

Junior could sense there was something sinister about the stranger's reaction. "I remember it like it was yesterday. You know, your father saved a lot of American lives that day."

They crossed the backyard toward the screen porch of the house. "So what'd you do in the Army?" Bobby asked.

"I was a medic. Not a hero like your Pa." Bartsch smiled as he ascended the stairs to the porch beside the Luttrell boys. Bobby held the door for the mysterious stranger. In the glow of the porch light, Bartsch looked paler than he had in the shadows. Bobby caught his glance again, and Bartsch nodded at the kitchen door.

Bobby, with Junior in tow, led the stranger into their home. The elder boy dropped his fishing pole in the corner. "Hey, Pa!" he shouted. "That army buddy of yours is here to see ya! He said his name was Bart! The medical fella!"

From a distant room, Fenton Luttrell responded in a gruff, disinterested tone. "Army buddy? Dammit, Bobby! Whoever the hell it is, tell 'em ta bring me another Blue Ribbon, would ya?"

Bobby walked over to the refrigerator and procured two beer bottles. He handed them to the stranger. When their palms touched, a chill shot up the boy's arm. Bobby Luttrell was unsure if the unwelcome sensation had come from the ice-cold bottles or the pallid skin of his father's friend.

"Go on down the hall to the den," Bobby stammered, shocked by the inexplicable cold. "Pa's in there watchin' the television."

The stranger departed, his leather soles rustling the shag carpet of the hallway. Bobby looked back at his kid brother. Junior was behind the edge of the kitchen counter, halfway out of sight. Bobby heard the door to the living room open and close.

Fenton Luttrell reclined in his worn chair, his feet propped on the ottoman. His elbow rested on the arm of the chair, which was spotted with cigarette burns. A ceramic German beer stein lolled in his fingers as his eyes remained riveted to the flickering picture tube. Alcohol and his job as a pipe-fitter at the shipyard had aged him harshly. With his close-cropped hair, hard-bitten features, and perpetual scowl, Luttrell looked much meaner than he had in the war.

Fenton heard the door close as he took another swig of cheap beer from his stein, a souvenir he picked up during occupation duty in 1945. Luttrell was suddenly aware that the room had grown colder. He felt the presence of someone glowering at him by the door. He didn't turn to look right away, as his senses were dulled by alcohol and fatigue. His attention was held by a poorly choreographed gunfight on television.

"Who'd my boy say you was again? A medic?" Luttrell slurred his sentences. "All the pill-pushers I knew were God-botherin' bastards."

He looked at the door, but the man in the suit was now standing a few feet from his chair. Fenton Luttrell jumped with a start. "Goddamn!" He found himself enraptured by the stranger's piercing eyes. "You look like a G-man or somethin'. My boy said you was in the army with me?"

Luttrell tried to focus as the man doffed his fedora. His hair was long and pomaded flat against his pale scalp. The sides were shaved razor-close.

Just like the krauts used to wear their hair.

The man towered over Luttrell with crossed arms.

"My boy says you're Bart? Bart what? Were you in Item Company? 'Cause I sure as shit don't remember you."

Ignoring the words of the drunken veteran in the chair, the well-dressed man walked to the wall where the German dog tags were hanging from a wooden peg. Next to the collection of aluminum disks was Fenton Luttrell's Silver Star. It was displayed, along with his Combat Infantryman Badge, in a framed presentation box against crushed velvet backing. The stranger ran his fingers over the dog tags as if looking for one in particular.

"Yeah. You remember the day I picked those up? I won my Silver Star that day."

Bartsch didn't answer. Instead, he perused the tags with a spidery hand.

"Hey, Doc. I'm talkin' to you!" Fenton Luttrell spied the two beer bottles the suited man was holding in his free hand. Suddenly, his throat was parched. "Hey, don't just stand there like the village idiot. Bring me one a' them beers!"

The man stood near the wall and continued to rifle through Luttrell's war trophies.

"Whose outfit was you in?" Luttrell narrowed his gaze. "I remember all the battalion aid men and you wasn't one of 'em."

Matthias Bartsch reached out his slender musician's fingers and tore one of the German dog tags off the wall. The frayed leather cord snapped as if made of sawdust. He turned to Fenton Luttrell and pitched the dog tag into the man's lap.

Luttrell didn't look at it.

"You son of a bitch! You come in my house and think you got the stones to..." Luttrell trailed off, his mouth set in a curious frown. "Who...who in the hell are you?"

Luttrell's jaw grew slack as his mind wandered back to a cold December day in 1944. His hands began to shake, his eyes grew wide, and his heart throbbed in his ears. Bile welled up in his throat as he struggled to swallow. Fenton Luttrell was overcome with terror.

"No." Luttrell shook his head. "It ain't possible. Not *you*." Sweat rolled down his forehead despite the chill that followed Matthias into the closed room. "How did—"

"How did I find you, or how did I survive?" Matthias interrupted.

"Both," Luttrell choked. He lost his grip on the beer stein, which hit the floor with a muffled thud.

"I heard one of your comrades give your name and hometown that day," Matthias explained, his accent no longer disguised. "After you shot me."

"I was—I mean, we were just followin'—"

"As to how I survived, let's just say I didn't." Matthias' eyes smoldered with hatred. Fenton Luttrell winced at the man's unbreakable stare, ignoring the din of the blaring television and the spilt beer on the carpet.

"Are you some kinda goddamn ghost?"

"I was number 1207. It's stamped on the tag in your lap." Matthias slowly parted his lips.

"But you ain't dead. I must've missed you."

"Believe me, you didn't miss that day. You even stopped to reload."

Luttrell struggled to stand. He held out a hand in protest, clenching his teeth. "And what of it? A couple days before we lined you up at them crossroads, a buncha you krauts killed about a hundred POWs. *Our* boys."

"Malmédy." Matthias nodded, his free hand clenched by his side. "An act perpetrated by Waffen-SS fire-eaters. I didn't even hear about that until the war ended."

Luttrell was on his feet, reeling. He pointed a calloused finger at Matthias. "You stay the hell away from me, you bastard! We were just doin' what the brass told us to do."

"I don't need a history lesson. I was on that roadside. Standing in front of your rifle."

Matthias reached into his coat pocket and withdrew an M1911A .45 pistol. He held it at arms' length and thumbed off the safety.

"I paid a visit to your former lieutenant a few months ago. Down in Alabama. A real tough guy. Didn't even put up a fight." Matthias gestured with the pistol barrel. "He wept like a baby as I ripped his throat out. And that was *before* I divested him of this sidearm. I certainly hope you will meet your end with the dignity befitting a recipient of the venerated Silver Star."

Luttrell was incensed. "I ain't got a lick of remorse for any one of you! If you aim to kill me with that pistol, then be done with it."

"Kill you with this? Not my intention at all," Matthias shrugged. He pitched the beer bottles onto the carpet next to his feet. "This is just to open you up. To get your blood flowing. Shooting's such an impersonal way to kill a man. You, of all people, should know that."

Fenton Luttrell ducked behind his chair, although it offered him no cover at all.

Matthias squeezed the trigger without mercy or compunction. The report from the .45 was deafening. The drunken man fell over his chair and sprawled on the floor. His trembling hands clutched his mangled innards.

31

Junior pounded his fists against the wooden door and cried out for his father.

Matthias descended on Fenton Luttrell and tore a large gash in his throat with his canines. He drank greedily from the struggling man's carotid artery as the door to the living room clattered open.

Junior stood at the door, his mouth agape as his father writhed in agony. Tears welled in the boy's eyes. He was frozen, his stomach clenched in knots as squirming tendrils of fear branched throughout his body.

He looked on in horror at the nightmarish spectacle before him. Time slowed to a crawl as blood rushed from his temples. He felt faint, and the room swam with pulsating shadows. Bobby was down the hall looking for the shotgun. His older brother's frantic demand to call the police rang hollow as Junior hadn't the strength or courage to obey him. Too frightened to cry out, he watched in mute terror as the black-clad stranger crouched over his father.

Matthias propped himself up, his bony white fingers spread against the faded carpet. His face was buried in the crook of Fenton Luttrell's neck. Strange convulsions rippled down the man's back. Junior realized the significance of the slow, rhythmic movements. The stranger was swallowing.

He's drinking Pa's blood. Like a vampire from the movies.

Junior could feel his legs beginning to give out beneath him. "Pa?" he managed.

The dying man fixed an anguished gaze on his son.

Matthias withdrew from Luttrell's throat. Blood pooled on the carpet. It stained the fabric of the overturned chair and parted into two dark streams at the base of the television.

In a singular motion, Matthias stood and turned to face the dead man's son.

The vampire glared at the boy, his stony features awash in bright red blood. The gore-soaked stranger's pomaded hair hung around his face. It glistened in the flickering light of the television.

Matthias picked up the aluminum dog tag from the blood-drenched carpet. He leapt onto the sill of the open window and slid the pistol under his coat. The bloodless corpse of Fenton Luttrell lay contorted on the carpet. Junior collapsed against the wall and blinked.

The strange man who murdered his father had disappeared without a trace.

Monsters are real.

From behind, Bobby's hand grasped his tiny shoulder. Only then did the boy scream.

7

Williamsport, Virginia. October 2014

LUSH WAVES OF SOUND POURED FROM THE SPEAKERS, SHAKING the doorframe and windows of the rattletrap sedan. Matthias Bartsch sped through the late shades of dusk. The mournful strains of Henryk Gorecki's 3rd Symphony enveloped his keen senses.

Matthias was preoccupied with his forgotten dreams of the conservatory and his career as a cellist—dreams that the war and his transformation had taken from him.

The sprawling symphony passed its first crescendo. The strings died away to herald somber, resonant piano chords and the plaintive lilt of a solo soprano. Yet the ghostly voice failed to soothe him.

He spun the car into an empty parking space and cut the engine. The music continued to play.

A familiar desire to feed welled up in his throat. Matthias ran his hands over his mouth but the hunger gnawed at him. He cleared his mind of the painful memories and smoothed his pomaded hair in the rear-view mirror. Once satisfied that he looked presentable, Matthias reached under his leather jacket to clip a plastic I.D. badge onto his orderly scrubs and eased the car door open.

Matthias left his unassuming car in the dark, empty lot of the nursing home. He walked towards the dim light of the side entrance and tightened his hands to mitigate the painful urge wracking his body. He willed the frenzy inside to remain still, so he could at least act human.

The beast within grew silent as he stepped into the heated confines of the staff entrance. Matthias approached the nurses' station to sign in for duty.

Amy, the twenty-something night nurse, had been infatuated with the mysterious German orderly since he first appeared at Serenity Springs two weeks earlier. She blushed and stood to greet him.

"Guten abend, Herr Bartsch," she said.

As Matthias scrawled his name on a clipboard, she hoped to capture his attention. "I thought maybe I should practice my German."

Indifferent to her flirtation, Matthias' expression didn't change, nor did he look at her. "What do you have for me tonight?"

"Uh, I think Anthony wants you on dinner cleanup, so you'll need to grab a cart and begin collecting trays. Mrs. Willis made a mess again."

Before Amy could judge his reaction, Matthias replaced the clipboard and walked away. He slipped into the locker room to deposit his leather jacket. Upon leaving the room, he took an empty tray cart and wheeled it down the scuffed hallway tiles.

From the open doors, he heard the groans and quiet sobbing of the demented elderly. Some writhed in their beds. Others whimpered beneath their blankets. In one room, a nurse's aide attempted to spoon-feed an insolent old man. He extended a liver-spotted hand wrapped in I.V. tubing and batted the spoon away. Matthias continued down the hall.

People died at places like Serenity Springs Elder Care every day. No one raised an eyebrow, and no one looked for patterns. Family members were notified with a scripted telephone call. The nurses, aides, and orderlies went about their business—the latter stopping only to help load the remains into a white van from a nearby funeral home. Death gave the orderlies a purpose to clean vacant rooms and sterilize bed sheets.

Such a degree of clinical apathy afforded Matthias many opportunities to sustain himself on the blood of the dying. The job at Serenity Springs was the most recent in a long line of similar positions. Matthias had worked night shifts at hospitals, clinics, and nursing homes across Eastern Virginia for years. He fed from patients in these institutions and moved on to other jobs before anyone noticed anything suspicious.

However, a more personal reason had prompted him to apply for the job at Serenity Springs. As he neared a door with a placard marked J. GRAYSON, the vampire felt the pangs of a familiar animosity. Matthias scotched the wheels on the cart and stood before the entrance. It remained closed. He extended a finger and traced the name on the small sign.

Matthias had been tracking James Grayson for months. Eventually, he discovered the decorated WWII veteran was a patient at this particular nursing home. Using false paperwork, Bartsch applied for an orderly's job with the express purpose of exacting his revenge.

Matthias rapped his knuckles against the door three times. "Mr. Grayson, may I come in?"

The door opened on squeaky hinges. "Yeah," a deep, lucid voice answered, inviting the vampire to enter the room.

"Food Services. I'm here to clean up your supper."

Another orderly, Karl, greeted him with a stack of soiled linens in his arms. "Hey! It's the new guy."

Matthias paused. "Where is Mr. Grayson?"

Karl yanked a rubber sheet from the mattress. "He passed away a couple hours ago. He didn't have no family either." Karl shoved the soiled sheets into a red bag lining a laundry cart. "They came in the meat wagon to pick him up an' that was that. Way I see it, it's a blessin' from the Lord when any of these old folks pass on."

Matthias recoiled at the maudlin religious sentiment.

The son of a bitch died before I could kill him.

None of them are left.

Matthias turned to leave the room. "Hey, whatever your name is!" Karl called after him. "There's a new lady a few doors down that you'll need to check on. Seems like they bring a new one in every time another soul makes its way to heaven. The Lord sure does work in mysterious ways."

The vampire ran his tongue along his canines.

"Jeremy already took her supper," Karl continued. "I reckon she needs cleaned up now. Check her I.V. 'cause she already pulled it out twice today. She was sundownin' right bad. This one's a fighter."

Matthias stepped out and pushed the empty food cart down the hallway. After passing a few vacant rooms, he stopped at the door the senior orderly had mentioned moments before.

There was no placard, but a dry erase board had been affixed to the door. One of the nurses had written WELCOME GRETL FLEISCHMANN! Around the cheerful text was a makeshift border of hand-drawn balloons and flowers. At the bottom of the board were numbers signifying the patient's medication schedule.

Matthias paused. A weak voice beyond the door prattled on as if chastising an unruly child. He could hear traces of an accent.

Prussian?

He knocked on the door. "Mrs. Fleischmann, Food Services. May I come in?"

He waited for the invitation. From behind the thick door, he could already smell her blood. It coursed through her decrepit body, driven by an enfeebled heart.

When Mrs. Fleischmann answered, he pushed the door open and inspected the layout of the room. It was barren and undecorated. A pile of cardboard boxes containing her personal effects were stacked next to a vinyl chair. He glanced at the frail figure on the bed.

The woman appeared to be in her late eighties. Her gaunt legs were bare below the hem of her hospital gown. She had kicked the covers away in a fit of rage, and her hospital tray lay overturned on the floor. Her arm was covered in angry welts from where she had removed her I.V. Fresh tubing ran to an insertion site on her bony wrist, which was secured with surgical tape. She raised a trembling hand to ward Matthias away.

"I don't want to eat now," she insisted in a raspy voice. "My own boy left me here! I have nothing! Nothing, you hear?"

Her accent was distinct, and Matthias felt the urge to address her in their native tongue. He glowered at the raised veins on her hand. The smell of blood was stronger.

Matthias approached the bed. "Mrs. Fleischmann, you must eat. If you don't eat, you will have to be intubated. Do you understand?"

He reached over her and straightened the blanket to cover her legs. "How would you like that? A feeding tube down your nose?"

Gretl took a shallow breath and prepared to lodge a protest. Matthias turned to look into her dark brown eyes. Along the creases of her face, tears had pooled and dried into an opaque crust. His gaze rendered her mute. She was suffering. Matthias could feel the despair emanating from the old woman as he touched the sagging skin of her arm.

"Now you must be good for me, Gretl. No more tearing out tubes." Matthias gestured to the saline bag suspended above her head, then the various smaller pouches containing her medications. "Don't you *want* to feel better?"

Mrs. Fleischmann's eyes darted over Matthias' features. Her drooping face, ravaged by age and disease, grew taut. "I know what you are," she whispered.

Matthias returned her baleful stare.

"What do you think I am?" He tightened his grasp on her left arm.

The elderly patient raised her hand and wagged a finger in his direction. "You may be fooling everyone else but I know."

"Mrs. Fleischmann, I need to check your I.V. Can you stay still while I..." Matthias trailed off as he looked down at the old woman's loose skin.

The clear I.V. tube framed a faded six-digit number tattooed lengthwise down her forearm. The ink was old and the numbers were nearly illegible. Matthias froze.

Gretl Fleischmann's right hand tugged at his shirt. His tarnished aluminum I.D. disk fell out of the wide collar, twisting on its chain. The woman grasped his dog tag in her right hand. "You come to take me with the others, yes?"

The thirst for blood was extinguished. He glanced at the withered countenance of the woman on the bed.

He recalled Darmstadt boys in their crisp *Hitler-Jugend* uniforms, throwing stones at the Jewish butcher's window on Elizabethstrasse. In his mind, he heard their mocking chants of defamation. *"Juden raus! Juden raus!"*

The population of Darmstadt had grown smaller as Matthias awaited his induction into the *Wehrmacht-Heer*. One morning, he noticed several empty seats in the conservatory, but no one said a word about the musicians taken to the segregated *Judenhäuser*. Then, while Matthias was riding an armored column toward Stalingrad, the Darmstadt Jews were taken to labor camps. Few bothered to ask what had become of them, but no answers were given to those who did.

Matthias placed Mrs. Fleischmann's left arm by her side. With her other hand, she continued to pull at his dog tag.

"I know what you are. I know why you are here. It is because I am not fit for working." Tears welled in her eyes.

"They say it is not painful." Her voice quavered. "The printer's wife said you will kill us quickly. Please! No more suffering now!" The old woman yanked on Matthias' neck chain, but her feeble, arthritic hand lost its grip and fell across her chest. "I am ready to die."

Matthias struggled to speak but felt nauseous and ashamed. He and every compliant German was responsible for placing Gretl Fleischmann in a squalid dormitory at Birkenau. There she was fed stale bread and potato soup, and was forced to labor for her own survival. As a young man, Matthias had been indifferent to the machinations of the Nazi party. Yet his silence had put men, women, and children into gas chambers. His blind obedience had filled mass graves.

Matthias grasped the woman's arm again.

"Es tut mir leid."

She pursed her thin lips, then spoke in a plain, demanding tone. "Do not apologize to me. Just follow your orders. I don't want to live like this anyhow. I lost everything. Do you know how that feels, *soldat?*"

"Yes. Yes, I do."

"Then you know why I wish to die." Mrs. Fleischmann placed her right hand over her beating heart. "End it."

Matthias drew her arm to his lips, but the hunger was no longer there. It had been replaced by something alien and incomprehensible. He didn't need the old woman to remind him. He knew exactly what he was.

A monster.

An abomination.

Matthias left the room with the cart in tow and made his way to the dispensary. As he approached the door, he noticed the security guard a few yards away at the nurse's station. The man in uniform leaned on the counter, his attention fixed on Amy.

The vampire paused to meld with the shadows. He waited until the guard was distracted before he slipped into the darkened pharmaceutical closet. Working his way along the shelves, he retrieved a vial of Propofol, two vials of potassium chloride, and two needles.

Matthias returned to Mrs. Fleischmann's room. He stood beside her bed and filled a needle with Propofol.

"You will sleep now, Gretl. And there will be no more pain."

He found a prominent vein in her arm and injected the anesthetic. The woman smiled as she licked her parched lips.

"I know what you are."

Her window of lucidity had closed.

Matthias knelt by the bed. He prepared a dose of potassium chloride strong enough to stop her heart. When he rose to administer the drug, Mrs.

Fleischmann no longer protested. She was fast asleep. Matthias jabbed her abscessed arm and injected the lethal dose. He discarded the needles in a container mounted on the wall and stuffed the empty vials into his carry bag. The vampire removed the pulse oximeter from her left index finger and disconnected the heart monitor from the wall.

No one is checking her vitals anyway.

Mrs. Fleischmann's chest rose and fell beneath the thin blanket. Her body began to seize as her heart went into cardiac arrest. Moments later, Gretl Fleischmann was dead. Matthias stepped over to her bedside and traced the numbers on her arm one last time.

He slipped through the door and returned to the locker room. After donning his leather jacket, he entered the hallway and stopped at the front desk. The security guard was gone. Amy glanced up and smiled when she saw Matthias.

"I apologize, but I am not feeling well. I don't think I'll be able to finish the rest of my shift. My tray cart is by the dispensary door."

Amy noticed that Matthias was trembling. Although he always appeared pale to her, he looked extremely ill.

"Please tell Anthony I'll return to work as soon as I can."

"Um, OK," she said. Amy rested her chin in her hands, unable to stop staring at the orderly. "I hope you feel better soon!"

Matthias started towards the door, stepped into the cold, and made his way across the parking lot. The autumn wind whipped around him. Beneath his shirt, he could feel the dog tag against his flesh.

As he crossed the damp asphalt, his emotions began to ebb away, and the primal bloodlust returned.

I can't afford to be careless.

I'm a murderer.

It had taken Matthias years to accept his strange and unnatural fate. However, now he faced a terrible certainty. Despite his predatory nature, long dead emotions—which did not serve who, or what, he was—had resurfaced.

If I can't control this, it will end me.

8

PROFESSOR EDISON RAYMER, A TRIM BLACK MAN IN HIS EARLY fifties, tempered his booming voice for a brief moment. From behind the lectern, the imposing educator overlooked the students seated in elevated rows before him. In his left hand, he thumbed a small remote control, and an overhead projector advanced to display an engraving of Vlad Tepes seated at the head of a long table. The vicious leader dined with apathy among the impaled corpses of his victims.

After adjusting his glasses, the professor resumed his lecture. "One of the more famous anecdotes concerning Vlad Tepes perfectly illustrates the mixture of fear and reverence that his subjects felt for him. Tepes was so confident that his people would never steal from him that he placed a gold cup in the central square of Târgoviste. He told the townspeople they could drink from the cup and use it freely, but warned that if anyone dared to steal it, they'd be impaled along with the rest of his enemies near the Brașov forest."

The professor paused for dramatic effect. "The cup remained on prominent display for several years."

As Dr. Raymer spoke, his students sat in silence. When they enrolled in Professor Raymer's North American Folklore course, they had done so with an awareness of the professor's difficult reputation. Last week, he lectured on mid-nineteenth century spirit mediums. This week he was discussing vampires. Although the students were perplexed by the tangential direction of his class, none dared to question the content of their professor's lectures.

Raymer advanced the slide to reveal an oil painting of a slender woman clad in a tightly-cinched corset and a ruffled lace collar. She bore a piercing yet dour expression.

"A little over a century later in Hungary, Erzsébet Bathory—known to most as the Blood Countess—was accused of murdering dozens of peasant girls. Some accounts suggest that her victims numbered into the hundreds, while other estimations are even higher. Bathory is considered to be the first and most ruthless female serial murderer to date."

Raymer gestured to the portrait. "This was a high-ranking noblewoman—notorious for her vanity—who allegedly drank and bathed in her victims' blood to preserve her waning youth. But before long, she grew careless," the professor noted. "In 1610, she was brought to trial. She was found guilty and imprisoned in Csejte Castle, where she died four years later."

A girl near the back of the lecture hall turned her notebook over and continued to record her professor's words onto a new sheet of paper. Raymer cleared his throat and continued.

"There is little to no evidence to suggest that Vlad Tepes or Elizabeth Bathory were genuine vampires." The professor halted to let his words take root. "The sheer number of contradictory historical accounts, legends, and anecdotal evidence makes it incredibly difficult to parse fact from fiction."

A wry smile tugged at Edison Raymer's lips. "But humor me for a moment." He stepped down from behind the podium. "How many of you believe in the existence of vampires?"

Raymer rarely solicited opinions from his class. Most of his pupils wrinkled their brows and stared at him in disbelief. Others exchanged wary glances of confusion and uncertainty. As if in a chess game, they awaited his finishing move.

"This is not a rhetorical question!" Raymer clasped his hands together. "Let me see a show of hands, please. How many of you believe in vampires?"

Not a single hand went up. The professor nodded in reflection.

"Skepticism is always healthy. It's a necessary counterpoint to blind faith, which is never commendable in any circumstance. As anthropologists, we are first and foremost scientists."

A few of his pupils muttered in agreement. Others began to wonder if the even-tempered, unshakable Edison Raymer had suddenly lost his mind.

"But skepticism can also make one vulnerable," he added. "To discount a world beyond our limited capacity for reasoning is to ignore the things that could undo the very fabric of existence. Lovecraft warned that 'some day the piecing together of dissociated knowledge will open up such terrifying vistas of reality, and of our frightful position therein, that we shall either go mad from the revelation or flee from the deadly light into the peace and safety of a new dark age.'" The professor never stopped to check his notes and recited the quotation from memory.

"As scientists and skeptics, Lovecraft's vision of cosmic horror undermines our most valued principles. To believe might seem naïve. But to deny is simply a prelude to madness."

Raymer's exhortations were lost on most of his students. The majority nodded out of sheer habit. Sean Tenerowicz glanced at Chloe Matheson, a fair-haired sophomore, and mouthed the words "what the fuck?"

Chloe shrugged and kept her eyes riveted to the stern instructor.

Although relishing the tension he'd crafted among his pupils, Raymer shifted the direction of the conversation to something more palatable.

"Let us rephrase the question. This time from a purely mythological perspective. What exactly is a vampire?"

No one answered. A student a few rows from the front of the room muffled a sneeze and shrank with embarrassment at her timing.

Finally, a junior with tousled hair and thick glasses raised his hand.

"Mr. Casella?"

"A vampire is a monster that feeds on blood to stay alive."

"OK," Raymer replied. He made no effort to hide his dissatisfaction with Casella's unimaginative response. "How about some more details? What else? Mr. Ackerman?"

"A product of *eastern European* folklore?"

"Indeed," the professor nodded, ignoring the pupil's implication. "But that's a rather limited perspective. There are vampire myths and accounts in practically every culture in the east as well as *the west*."

The classroom grew quiet once again.

"I'm not sure I can make this question any plainer," Raymer declared. "But let's break it down into component parts. What are some common characteristics of the vampire?"

Daniel Casella tried to regain the professor's favor and spoke up right away. "They always burn in sunlight."

Another student answered without raising her hand. "They have fangs."

Intimidated by their professor's impatience, the students spoke in quick succession.

"They're afraid of crucifixes!"

"And garlic!"

"They can't cross running water!"

"You kill 'em by driving a stake through their heart!"

"You get turned into one after you get bit on the neck."

The last point was refuted by several students.

"No, you gotta drink vampire blood to become one!"

"Yeah, it's not a disease. You're thinking of zombies."

"That's quite enough," Raymer interjected. The sudden wave of enthusiastic participation came to an abrupt end. "Miss Di'Anno, Mr. Caldwell. You're both correct. In most legends, the fiend must share its blood with its victim in order to make another vampire."

Raymer advanced the slide to show a black and white image of Bela Lugosi bent over Helen Chandler's bed. "But as I expected, your collective knowledge of the vampire doesn't extend too far past the writings of Bram Stoker and the liberal film adaptations of his novel. What Stoker didn't plagiarize from Sheridan Le Fanu, he pillaged from European folklore. The vampire that exists in our modern American consciousness is a product of the silver screen, diluted into a homogenous archetype over the course of several decades."

Another student spoke up from the fourth row. She cleared her throat while brushing a lock of dark hair behind her left ear. "But aren't there sickos out there who drink blood and stuff? You know, like those goth people or whatever they're called? Wouldn't you consider those people vampires? I mean, where's it say that a vampire has to be some kinda monster that comes back from the dead?"

Raymer's eyes glistened with visible satisfaction. "You raise an interesting point, Miss Vardaman. You're right. Vampires do not necessarily have to be dead. Some don't even suck blood. We've all met at least one individual who wears us out with their mere presence. These so-called psychic vampires feed on the energy of their victims. More specifically, the classic *femme fatale* of late nineteenth-century fiction and early *film noir* often preyed upon the finances of foolish bachelors. These fantasies represent yet another variation of the vampire myth."

Raymer returned to the podium and picked up the remote to advance the slideshow.

"Part of the enduring appeal of the vampire is its metaphorical flexibility. But it is the vampire of folklore, the vampire of myth and legend, the creature that by all rational estimations should not exist. *That* is the most fascinating aspect of this subject."

Raymer clasped his hands together with uncharacteristic enthusiasm.

"History is littered with tales of individuals, such as Tepes or Bathory, who were accused of vampirism. There was even a serial killer in Germany, Peter Kürten, who was nicknamed the Vampire of Dusseldorf. But here on our own soil, there are dozens of vampire legends exclusive to this country."

The professor took a deep breath and advanced the slide, predicting his students' reaction before the image materialized. A sepia daguerreotype of an end-stage tuberculosis patient replaced the film-still of Count Dracula. Groans of revulsion echoed through the lecture hall.

"Tuberculosis." Raymer's voice grew loud and commanding again. *"Consumption.* The process of being consumed. Devoured. Used up." He paused. "This disease, as we know, is a wasting disease, and is highly contagious. It was arguably the most dreaded illness of the nineteenth century, and the catalyst for a wave of vampire hysteria in New England that was on par with the Salem witch trials. Throughout the 1800s, whenever an outbreak of consumption flared up fears of vampirism were not far behind. These incidents drove otherwise sane people to commit ghoulish acts of exhumation and grave desecration.

"In 1854, the Ray family of Jewett City, Connecticut, was stricken with consumption and lost both of their sons. The survivors also succumbed to the illness. The Rays came to believe that their dead sons were rising from their graves to drink their blood. The family exhumed the boys' bodies and burned them in their coffins to stop the purported supernatural attacks."

After advancing the slide to a portrait of Henry David Thoreau, Raymer adjusted the lapel microphone clipped to his sweater vest and continued.

"The incidents involving the Ray family were by no means isolated events. Even Thoreau—a salt of the earth, no-nonsense skeptic—alluded to these events in his journal. And I quote, 'the savage in man is never quite eradicated. I have just read of a family in Vermont—who, several of its members having died of consumption, just burned the lungs and heart and liver of the last deceased, in order to prevent any more from having it.' End quote."

Raymer stopped to let the weight of the philosopher's words sink in. His next slide was a modern photograph of an unassuming archaeological dig in a dilapidated cemetery.

"There's no current estimation of how many so-called vampires were destroyed in their caskets during these outbreaks, but examples are still being uncovered in our modern age."

He nodded at the screen.

"This photograph was taken during the 1990s in Griswold, Connecticut, where a red-painted coffin was removed from a family burial plot. The interred, known only as JB, had been beheaded in his coffin, and his bones were deliberately rearranged. Archaeologists found rib fractures indicative of staking, while the coffin itself had been smashed."

Raymer tapped his fingers against the podium as the room fell silent once more. The transition into present day examples had arrested the attention of nearly all of his students. With the professor's unexpected pause, a few lifted their heads in anticipation for him to continue.

"Of course, in all cases, these corpse mutilations did nothing to stop the spread of tuberculosis. For this reason, the New England vampire panic is often dismissed by historians and anthropologists as a superstitious reaction to a worldly disease."

Raymer shifted his position at the lectern, and noticed a student in the front row sketching in the margins of his notebook. The professor stepped from behind the podium, his lips pressed together in an unforgiving scowl.

"So, can we attribute this savage behavior to archaic beliefs spread by uneducated farmers in a century where for many, the developments in science and technology were considered to be on par with witchcraft?" Raymer moved with purpose toward the sketcher in the first row. "Or, as usual, did history simply repeat itself?"

No one answered as Raymer advanced the slide to show two shirtless men, pale as ghosts, posing for the camera. The picture was grainy, as if it had been taken on an old Polaroid camera. The men had shaggy bangs and long sideburns. One had his lips on the wrist of the other, and the entire shot appeared to have been staged for shock value.

"On Long Island in the 1970s, a rash of so-called sexual vampirism arose around Sayville and Fire Island. Partners were sexually aroused by biting one another and sucking the blood from—"

"Fuckin' faggots!" the sketch artist interrupted in a deliberately loud whisper. The student returned to his handiwork with disdain. A coterie of upperclassmen in varsity letter jackets stifled laughter at the comment.

Raymer paused in front of Joshua Bailey, a stocky young man in a worn ball-cap and white fraternity shirt. The professor reached down and flipped his pupil's notebook over to a clean page. Bailey raised his head to level an indignant stare at the professor.

Raymer matched his student's defiant glance.

"Is there a problem, Mr. Bailey?"

Bailey shifted in his seat, but kept his eyes locked on his professor. An insolent smirk spread across his face, as if he'd been waiting for this opportunity for the better part of a semester.

"You know what?" Bailey began in a thick southern drawl. "Yeah...yeah, there is. And it's right there on the screen." A few of his cohorts nodded in agreement. "What's it gonna be, Ed? Last week you rambled on about séances, and now we're talkin' about vampire fags? Why are you wasting our time with this?" Bailey sized up the professor from head to toe. "I thought this was supposed to be an anthropology course, not a class on spook hunting."

Raymer peered over the wire rims of his spectacles at the upperclassman, who tapped his fingers on his small wrap-around desk. The middle-aged professor's eyes narrowed.

Bailey shrugged and looked to his peers for support. "I mean, you stand up there spouting these whacked-out theories and nobody calls you on your sh—"

"Get out of my class." Raymer pointed to the exit. "Now."

Bailey dropped his pen to the floor. His voice trembled as adrenaline rushed through his system. "Is this your way of answering my question?"

"I don't have to answer to you, Mr. Bailey," Raymer replied, folding his taut arms across his chest.

"You wanna answer to Dean Ritter, then?" Bailey stammered. "Wouldn't be the first time, from what I hear."

"What you've heard is of no importance to me, as you are no longer a student in this class." Raymer nodded toward the lecture hall doors, his tone even and undaunted. "Now quit wasting my time. I'd like to finish my lecture."

"What the fuck ever," Bailey muttered. He rose to his feet. The other students watched as he slung his book-bag over a broad shoulder and charged past the baleful eyes of Professor Raymer. Before leaving, Bailey tossed his notebook and textbook into a wastebasket near the heavy doors of the lecture hall.

The professor heard the student utter another offensive epithet before the door clicked home. He dismissed it with nonchalance and turned to face the class once again.

"As I was saying, the so-called sexual vampires of the Fire Island scene reached a state of arousal by the act of drinking one another's blood. While at the time this was considered a form of sexual deviance, psychiatrists have identified this behavior as a mental disorder called Renfield Syndrome. Since some of you seem to have read *Dracula* or more likely, you've seen the movies, I trust I don't have to explain who Renfield is or what he represents?"

Again, the professor paused to adjust his spectacles. He stepped forward to rest a foot on the bottom riser of the carpeted stairs. His dark eyes shifted from row to row.

"Patients suffering from Renfield Syndrome not only believe they need human blood to survive, but often attain sexual satisfaction or a psychosomatic sense of power from the consumption of blood, as well as other bodily fluids. Studies have shown that the disorder first manifests itself as auto-vampirism, which then graduates to the imbibing of animal blood before culminating in rituals involving consenting adults. Or—in much rarer cases—unwilling victims."

A few undergraduates shuffled papers and adjusted their seats. Raymer turned his back to the classroom and took his place behind the podium. He resumed his lecture with a commanding tone.

"I wanted to spend a few more minutes discussing the particulars of modern vampirism, but due to Mr. Bailey's unforeseen disruption, we'll have to pick up with this topic when we meet next week." He glanced at his wristwatch. "I believe we're almost out of time for tonight."

The tense atmosphere of the lecture hall dissolved as the students began to gather their belongings.

"Not so fast!" The professor raised his voice above the growing din. Most of his students ignored him as they unzipped their book bags and shoved their notebooks inside. Raymer glided back to his desk and opened a leather-bound folio. He removed a stack of papers marked heavily with red ink.

"These proposals are abysmal. The grammar, as usual, is atrocious. The topics themselves are unacceptable, which suggests that many of you need to start taking this class and its subjects much more seriously."

The professor's remarks only made his students more restless. They glared at him, impatient for dismissal.

"I expect these proposals to be revised by our next class meeting. Your topics must be approved by me before you begin your research and outlines for the final paper. In case you've forgotten, your annotated bibliographies are due in two weeks. If you don't have an acceptable topic, you're going to have a hell of a time compiling research."

With an indifferent nod, Raymer indicated that class had at last adjourned. His students rose in succession and began to shuffle toward the front of the room.

A line of upperclassmen passed by Raymer's desk. They formed a semicircle and began to pick through their papers. One by one, they snatched their proposals and stepped away, staring in disbelief at the lengthy comments marring the cover pages. A few pupils groaned. One student crumpled her paper in her hand and stormed through the lecture hall doors.

As the room emptied, Raymer noticed Jennifer Stroud descending the steps quietly. Straight blonde hair framed her delicate features and fell against her navy pea coat.

"Miss Stroud." Raymer acknowledged the junior as she took her proposal from the dwindling pile.

The young woman looked up and clutched her notebook to her chest. "Yeah?" she asked in an uneven tone.

"I'd like you to stop by and see me sometime tomorrow afternoon for a short paper conference. This is not a request. It's a requirement. If you expect to pass this course, you have some serious revising to do."

The undergraduate pursed her lips to lodge a protest, but said nothing.

"In choosing your subject, you decided to tread a well-worn path, which is wholly unchallenging and far beneath your abilities. I was hoping to see something better from you."

Jennifer inhaled sharply. As Raymer continued to chastise her, she stared at the unmarked dry erase board behind him.

"Instead, I'm going to have to labor through another overview of Native burial mounds in white folklore. I get a paper on this every semester. It's completely pedestrian."

"OK." She nodded. "I'll stop by tomorrow after my statistics class. I'll be there around four."

"Please understand, Miss Stroud. I usually hold my office hours before my classes on Tuesday and Thursday, so I will be making a special trip to campus just to meet with you. If you miss our appointment, it will be considered an unexcused absence."

"I understand, Dr. Raymer," the girl said timidly. She kept her eyes on him as she made her way to the doors.

"Very well. Goodnight, Miss Stroud."

Without responding, she disappeared into the darkened hallway. Raymer listened to her soft footfalls on the tiled floor outside his classroom. He powered down his laptop, collected the unclaimed papers to shove in his briefcase, and followed his students out into the October night.

9

T HE LATE AFTERNOON SUN STREAMED THROUGH THE HALF-
opened blinds, bathing the professor's office in a warm amber
glow. Edison Raymer had just finished writing a short email to
Jennifer Stroud, who hadn't turned up for her paper conference.
The correspondence was brusque and a bit heavy-handed, but he'd dealt
with time-wasters all week and had reached the proverbial end of his tether.

After minimizing the screen of the department-issued desktop, Raymer
rose to gather his belongings. Dust particles swirled through the quiet air
as he stepped into the hallway and turned to secure the lock of his office
door. He pocketed the jumble of keys and bent to gather his worn leather
briefcase. The professor cast one final glance at the placard centered on the
mahogany door—DR. EDISON RAYMER, PhD.—and spun on his heel
to make his way down the empty hall.

Most of the faculty had rushed through their afternoon lectures and had
already gone home for the day. The odds of bumping into a colleague and
enduring idle chit-chat were significantly diminished due to the impending
weekend. He relished Fridays in particular, for graduate-level seminars never
convened on this day of the week and professors were just as eager as their
students to depart Waverly Hall for the weekend.

As Raymer strode down the corridor and passed the faculty lounge, a
sharp voice rang out from the unlit room.

"Doctor Raymer?" Dean David Ritter emerged from the shadows, and
leaned against the frame of the rectangular archway. He was dressed, as

usual, in an ill-fitting pinstripe suit. The jacket strained to contain his middle-aged bulge. "Calling it a day?"

Raymer stopped and tightened his grip around the handle of his briefcase. "Just finishing up some last-minute grading," he responded. The professor took in the furrowed expression of the balding man in the doorway. "What brings you to the anthropology department?"

Ritter cleared his throat before he spoke, an earmark of his cigar habit. "Just tying up a few loose ends."

"I see." He felt the nagging suspicion that Ritter had much more to say.

"Anything special planned for the weekend?" the dean asked in a patronizing tone.

Edison Raymer shifted his briefcase from his left hand to his right, glanced at his watch, and then looked back at the dean. "No," the professor said. "As usual, I have some lecture notes to prepare and review."

"Ah," Ritter replied with a slow nod. "The life of a dedicated scholar. Not much of a weekend, is it, Ed?"

"I can't think of a better way to waste my time."

The two men lingered before one another in strained, heavy silence. When the dean broke the lull in their stilted conversation, Raymer was certain that the officious man was provoking him.

"That's something I've always admired about you. Your unwavering dedication. Your willingness to go above and beyond the usual protocol." The dean paused. "You know, it's precisely the kind of thing we like to see here at Williamsport."

"I'm sure it is," Raymer said.

The dean studied the professor's expressionless face.

"Well, listen," Ritter began. "Not to blindside you, Ed, but I spoke with Joshua Bailey earlier today."

"Oh?"

"Yeah. Bright kid. Shit-hot offensive end for the team, if you know what I mean."

The stout man had been a quarterback on the Williamsport College football team in his halcyon days. As a result, he often sided with the unruly athletes that disrupted classrooms across campus. After a pause, Ritter continued.

"Unfortunately, he's lodged a complaint against you. He says you threw him out of your class yesterday when he questioned the relevance of your lecture."

"Oh really?" Raymer withheld any further comments. He knew the dean would be more than happy to fill the silence.

"Yeah, and this is a direct quote from his lips to my ears. He was under the impression that he had registered for an anthropology course and was surprised to sit through numerous lectures on ghost busting. Does this ring a bell, Ed?"

"No, because 'spook hunting' was the exact phrase Mr. Bailey used," Raymer corrected. "And neither racist nor ethnic slurs are tolerated in my classroom."

"Of course not, Ed," Ritter replied, softening his tone. "Josh conveniently omitted that particular detail from our conversation."

"Well, if it comes down to my word against his, I have an entire auditorium of witnesses to corroborate that particular detail," Raymer noted with bitterness. "I'm sure at least half of them will tell you the truth."

The dean chuckled and unfolded his arms before taking a step toward Raymer. "Listen, Ed. I don't wanna bust your balls about this. But I think it'd be in everyone's best interest if Mr. Bailey withdraws from your class and—"

"Wait a minute," Raymer interjected. "If he gets a 'W,' he can just retake another class."

"Well, he certainly won't receive a refund from the Registrar. The deadline's already passed."

"Are you kidding me?" Raymer could no longer disguise his frustration. "None of these kids pay for their education themselves. They take out loans, find some state grant, or ask their parents to foot the bill. Especially undergrads."

"I'd say that's a rather unfair generalization to make, Dr. Raymer."

"It's a slap on the wrist, David. And I might as well tell you right now. I won't sign off on Bailey's withdrawal form."

"Suit yourself." The dean sighed. "We'll set up a formal meeting. I'm booked solid Monday, so I'll have to work it in on Tuesday afternoon. You know the procedure."

"Fine." Raymer's reply was short and clipped, and he made little effort to temper the scorn in his voice.

"Well, I guess I'll be seeing you between classes on Tuesday," Ritter replied, forcing an insincere smile. "Take care, Edison." The broad man turned to depart down the opposite end of the hall. "Enjoy your weekend."

Raymer opted not to dignify the dean with a response. He stormed down the corridor, past the empty classrooms, and through the heavy doors of Waverly Hall. The professor continued on his homebound walk across the leaf-strewn greensward, weaving between students on their way to the dining hall or early parties. When Raymer passed though the brick archway at the perimeter of the college grounds, he took a deep breath and stopped to clean his glasses.

That washed-up son of a bitch has the audacity to call me out for doing my goddamned job.

Raymer picked up his pace as he crossed the busy street and sped along the cracked sidewalk. Within minutes, he stood at the door to his townhouse, fumbling with his keys as he clutched a stack of junk mail under his arm.

Once inside, the professor dropped his keys and the pile of mail on a side table. He bent to set the briefcase at his feet and hung his coat on a rack by the door.

He made his way through the kitchen, slid the narrow bolt on a door leading to the basement, and hustled down the stairs. Aside from a small area where a pristine tool bench sat unused, the basement was set up like an *ad hoc* gymnasium. A sweat-stained towel was draped across the handlebar of a treadmill. From one of the joists along the ceiling, a jet-black heavy bag hung from four chains. It was evident from excessive wear that the professor frequently assailed the punching bag. An adjustable incline weight bench sat parallel to the cinderblock wall, which was lined with steel racks bearing several rows of dumbbells.

Raymer removed his wire-rim spectacles. He loosened his tie, then unbuttoned his dress shirt, folded it neatly, and set it on the workbench. His lean arms bristled with sinewy muscles. Raymer began loading forty-five pound plates onto the bar that spanned the incline press. When finished, he slipped onto the bench, adjusted his position, and pushed the bar off the rack. With brisk, fluid motions, the professor pressed and retracted the barbell. Raymer continued the set until his arms gave out. He slammed the bar onto the rack and sat up, hyperventilating.

The professor stood and stretched, then donned a pair of boxing gloves. He broke into a slow trot and squared off with the heavy bag. Raymer began

54

jabbing the cloth-filled sack, alternating between his stronger and weaker arm. The professor threw each punch with precision.

As he coordinated his breathing, Raymer let loose an alternating barrage of hooks, uppercuts, and snap punches. Dust billowed from the bag with each strike. He landed a cross punch that sent the bag into a spiral, recovered, then continued to assail his target. He pictured David Ritter—and Joshua Bailey—on the receiving end of every blow.

10

WITH HIS BACK ARCHED AND HIS EYES CLOSED, MATTHIAS drew the bow across the bridge of his cello. His left hand glided up and down the ebony fingerboard, and he swayed in time with the opening phrases of Fauré's C minor *Élégie*. The vampire played with slow, deliberate strokes, adding an exaggerated vibrato to lengthen the notes. Amidst the lulling despondence of the music, he savored the slight hiss of the rosin-glazed bow as it traversed the strings. He elbowed his way through the end of the melody's first cycle, which swung like a pendulum between two raw and elongated notes. Matthias sought in vain to imagine the proper piano accompaniment in his head, but to no avail.

This is all wrong.

He switched to the buoyant strains of Bach's G major prelude. It was a piece he'd performed in the Darmstadt Conservatory to the applause of a faceless crowd. It reminded him of his youth, before the *Wehrmacht* put him in uniform and sent him to the Front. The bow ricocheted on the heavy strings.

As he fingered the ascending and descending scales, he thought of Anna. The curve of her hip. Her soft, flowing hair. The way she playfully called him Matti. These thoughts had haunted him since his encounter with Gretl Fleischmann at the nursing home. As he played with rote accuracy, the airy lightness of the piece clashed against the darkening emotions within him.

Matthias loosened his grip on the bow and let his fingers rest across the strings. Strange and forgotten shades of his former humanity had awakened within him.

And he was terrified.

But rage returned to quash his fear. It shook every fiber of his being. Matthias discarded the Baroque acrobatics of Bach for the harsh dissonance of a starker composition. He struck the bow across the bridge and ripped the first half-dozen bars of Kodaly's B minor sonata from his belabored instrument. He clenched his teeth and sawed through the strings, his eyes ablaze with wild abandon.

He suddenly rose, lifting the priceless cello without effort. Matthias laid the Stradivarius gently on a filthy couch pitted with cigarette burns. A single incandescent bulb hung overhead, swinging with his movement. He paced across the small room and fought the urge to pick up his metal cigarette box from the table.

He passed the tin, and his keen vision traced its warped surface. Throughout the war, he'd kept the slender box in his lower tunic pocket. When he was in Russia, where medics were expected to fight like regular *soldaten,* his holstered P08 had rested atop the tin. The box was all he had left of those wasted years. Instead of fighting a senseless war, he could have been at the conservatory, or at home with his young wife.

Matthias flipped open the lid of the cigarette tin and removed his military awards one by one.

He had been given the Iron Cross Second Class for bravery under fire.

The *Allgemeines Sturmabzeichen* was granted to medics for participation in repeated combat assaults.

He'd received his jet-black wound badge for the Russian bullet he had taken in his throat.

A scrap of blood red ribbon had been threaded through a tarnished bronze medallion. The Order of the Frozen Flesh he'd earned for his *Ostfront* service in 1941.

These medals had been awarded for honor, courage, and sacrifice. Yet each of the badges was marred by the crooked swastika, a symbol of terror and oppression. Sadness welled up inside him as he thought of Gretl Fleischmann and her people.

You fought for a lie.

Matthias steeled himself as he filed through a stack of photographs from the cigarette tin. He paused to look over a glossy snapshot of Fritz Bauer, a young *schützen* who was cut in half by a Soviet machine gunner. Matthias turned the picture over. He didn't want to see the boy's placid face again.

At the bottom of the tin, the vampire dug out the photograph that he dropped in the mud the day he died. It was of Anna, sitting in their modest parlor with her legs crossed. Blonde tresses fell around her cheeks to rest upon her shoulders. He recalled the smooth print dress she was wearing in the picture. He had touched and embraced her in that dress many times.

Matthias ached at the sight of her face. His senses failed to reach back through the decades and fully restore the memory of his wife. Her essence was lost, and her touch was a vague and fading numbness.

They'd met at the conservatory, where she was a pianist. Under the direction of the *Kapellmeister,* they were first paired to rehearse Brahms' sonata in E minor. Behind the shiny grand piano, Anna tiptoed between the slow, snaking phrases of Matthias' cello. The young musicians chased each other's melodies. The dizzying scales of her playing burst into life as Matthias met her every rise and fall. His instrument had been slightly out of tune, yet he played on, convinced that his passion would compensate for any unintended dissonance.

His hand began to tremble as he held the picture. While he was courting Anna, his country was ravaging France, Denmark, and Norway. His induction into the service was fast approaching and his days as a musician were numbered.

His thoughts returned to the Darmstadt boys in their Hitler Youth uniforms and the Jewish butcher shop. He'd walked past the shattered windows and cursing children with his cello case at his side, ignoring the sordid scene.

I could have run them off.
I should have done something to stop them.
Anything.

Repulsed by his unpleasant recollections, Matthias began to file the photographs back into the tin.

The last picture atop the stack was a bit out of focus. Three medics huddled together and smiled for the camera. Matthias stood in the center towering over the others. Red cross brassards were wrapped around their left arms. Behind them, shadowed figures stood frozen in place—featureless and spectral. A bearded man in a black frock coat clung to the mesh of a locked gate.

His division had billeted in Warsaw before moving eastward, and out of curiosity, the *soldaten* had visited the Jewish ghetto. As he stared at the

58

photograph, Matthias realized that he didn't become a monster that night in 1944. Before his death, he was an apathetic man who served an evil cause. Every life he had saved in battle had only helped prolong the pernicious aims of the Third Reich. His legacy was a black mark on history, and his unnatural rebirth an even greater abomination.

The act of avenging his execution now seemed pointless. Matthias had wasted decades hunting down a handful of aging veterans—none of whom even bothered to fight him for their lives. It had been mere bloodsport, and he felt unsatisfied by revenge.

My enemies are dead and gone.

So what purpose do I have now? Survival?

This is no way to live.

The photograph of Anna, and the cello on the couch, was the only proof that Matthias Bartsch had ever possessed the capacity to love. He closed the tin, disgusted by what he'd done both in life and in death. His resolve—his very will to prolong his unnatural youth—was eroding piecemeal. But he had no power to stop it.

What I've become—what I am—is far worse than what I was.

I should have died in that war.

11

EDISON RAYMER REACHED FOR A BOTTLE OF WHISKEY ON his coffee table and poured a generous amount into an empty tumbler. He took a quick, hard swig of single malt and perused the documents scattered haphazardly across his leather couch. While he strained to read some notes he'd scribbled in one of the margins, he returned the bottle to the table's cluttered edge. In doing so, he almost toppled a stack of books piled up nearby.

The doorbell chimed in the hallway. Raymer collected his lecture notes and shoved them into a manila folder. Without thinking, he tossed it onto the coffee table before staggering into the hall. His oxfords squeaked on the hardwood floor.

"Door's open, Veronica." His deep voice boomed through the empty foyer.

He could discern Professor Veronica Upham's silhouette behind the frosted glass pane of his front door. The latch clicked and the diminutive woman, a few years his junior, let herself in. Her thick auburn hair was parted in the middle, but had become tousled from her walk in the night air. She was out of breath as she dropped her messenger bag by the door.

"Sorry I'm so late. You know how these departmental get-togethers go." The middle-aged divorcée removed her knitted gloves and shoved them into the pockets of her long coat.

"Not really." Raymer met her at the door and helped her remove her coat. "You know I try to avoid department functions at all cost."

"I know you do," Veronica said. "But it wasn't so bad this time." Although he didn't ask, she proceeded to tell him about the campus event.

"Just another colloquium. One of my students presented a paper on Eliot's *Middlemarch*. The department chair went all out. Had it catered. Heavy *hors d'oeuvres*. And when I say heavy, I mean full spread."

"We were supposed to have dinner tonight," he reminded her. "I ordered you linguini from Sal's. I went ahead and ate, and put yours in the fridge."

"Maybe I'll heat it up later." The English professor clutched her midsection. "Couldn't eat another bite right now."

"Suit yourself," Raymer said and led the way into his living room. "I'm in here." Veronica followed him as she attempted to fix her hair.

"Can I get you a drink?" he asked, rubbing his hands together in the dissipating cold.

Veronica spied the bottle on the dark wooden table. "I'll have what you're having."

Raymer smiled furtively. He poured a well-measured shot of Glen into a tumbler, and handed it to Veronica.

"Much obliged." She lifted the glass and took a sip of the warm amber liquor. Her eyes swept across a series of Simon Marsden prints adorning the living room walls. The dreary landscape photos had cost Edison a small fortune. "Like I always say, this place could use a woman's touch."

Raymer nodded with indifference as Veronica sat on the couch and crossed her legs. He stood nearby as she leaned forward, ever curious, and began to sort through his collection of books.

"So this is what you do when I'm not around on a Friday night?" She picked up a book and read the title aloud. *"The Terror That Comes In the Night: An Experience-Centered Study of Supernatural Assault Traditions.* Are your students giving you nightmares, Ed?"

Raymer didn't answer as she rifled through the pages. He leaned over a wingback chair and watched with detachment as Veronica held back a smirk. The margins of the book were blackened with meticulous personal notes.

Veronica set it aside and picked up another. *"Vampires, Burial, and Death: Folklore and Reality."* She craned her neck to read the next title. *"The Vampire: His Kith and Kin.* Montague Summers. Of course." She frowned, tossing the aged leather volume onto the couch and reached for a well-worn paperback of Don Augustin Calmet's *The Phantom World.* "Now I see why you wanted that Thoreau quote. So this is what you've been lecturing on this week?"

61

"More or less." Raymer shoved his hands into his trouser pockets. "You didn't seem so concerned when I was covering transcendental mediums. In fact, you—"

"Ed, I'm not here to play judge and jury. I'm just curious why you've got all these books everywhere."

"I'm not finished with them yet." He stepped over to the coffee table to rearrange the disordered books. As he leaned over and locked eyes with the English professor on the couch, she moved to change the subject.

"So one of my colleagues had some interesting things to say about you after the colloquium."

Raymer lifted his glass with a sigh. "What now?"

"Well, she was in your building today. You've met Dr. Pelletier, no?"

"I don't recall."

"Eighteenth-Century British Lit. Early thirties. You know, one of those social butterfly types." Veronica swirled the liquor around in her tumbler. "Anyway, our printer was on the fritz and she needed to make copies of a handout or something. So she went next door to Waverly Hall, where she overheard you and Ritter in the middle of an argument. While she was at the copier, you walked out. Then she saw Ritter heading for the men's room. Apparently, he said something like 'I've got that son of a bitch right where I want him.' What the hell did you—"

"Stop." Raymer drew in a breath. His features hardened. "Don't spread any more rumors. I'm sure the campus is gossiping away right now, and I don't need you adding fuel to the fire. As for what I did, that's—"

"Oh, just tell me what's going on!"

"Long story short, I dismissed a football player from my class last night." He paused to tighten his shoulders. "Permanently."

"For what?" Veronica narrowed her eyes as she took a sip of scotch.

"A pattern of insubordination and disruption that finally came to a head."

"Stop being vague, Ed. It's me."

"Well, apparently, Joshua Bailey thinks I'm teaching a course on 'spook hunting' rather than anthropology."

"He didn't say *that*, did he?"

"Oh yes he did," Raymer insisted. "The racial epithet came on the heels of a homophobic remark, which I didn't even bring up in my conversation with Ritter. I showed Bailey the door, he stormed out in a breathtaking display of petulance, and I went back to my lecture."

"Don't you think you overreacted a bit?" Veronica's eyes widened. "You've never been so thin-skinned about that kinda stuff."

"Now wait a minute. This kid—"

"Christ, Ed, after the way you handled that plagiarism incident last semester, you know Ritter and the Board are watching your every move. And that man has his head so far up the football program's ass that—"

"As an educator, I stand by my actions. And my defense in this matter is ironclad. Can we just drop this, please?"

"Not 'til you tell me what Ritter said to you in that hallway."

"He wants me to let Bailey withdraw, and I refused. We set up a meeting for Tuesday to make the dismissal official. That was all."

"Look." Veronica raised a hand towards her colleague. "I think Ritter's got something up his sleeve and your reputation—hell, maybe even your job—is on the chopping block. If I were you, I'd—"

"To be frank, I couldn't care less what Ritter has in store. I've had my fill of apathetic upperclassmen, dullards, and class clowns. Time-wasters! All of 'em!" He downed the contents of his glass and poured a double shot.

Veronica could tell he'd hit the bottle hard long before her arrival. "If you're still using your lectern to promote your personal obsessions, Ritter's gonna have your ass."

"Are you questioning my course syllabus, Dr. Upham?" Raymer chuckled in disbelief. "Again, I didn't hear any howls of protest last week when I told you I'd be covering spiritualism. Just because we're sleeping together doesn't give you *carte blanche* to cherry-pick my—"

"Is that what we're doing, Ed?" Veronica slammed her glass down on top of Raymer's books. "Sleeping together? Because it's been months since—"

"Let me finish." Raymer raised his voice. "When it comes to the occult, you have your own agenda."

"I could say the same thing about you and your obsession with vampires! Really, Ed."

"I've told you time and time again about my graduate work with Critchlow at Annandale. You heard the tapes from the Aston boy's case." Raymer sighed and shook his head. "But you weren't there. You didn't see what I saw."

Veronica glanced at a framed photograph hanging on the far wall. She'd seen it a hundred times. A young Edison Raymer stood beside Dr. Jerry Critchlow, a self-proclaimed vampirologist.

"I know, Edison," she said. "But Critchlow died a disgrace. I'll admit he was brilliant and he knew his subject well. But his Van Helsing complex derailed his entire career. No one took him seriously."

Before he could answer, she picked up the bottle and refilled her tumbler, splashing scotch onto the cover of the topmost book.

Raymer wasted no time mopping up the spill with a cocktail napkin. Veronica wasn't about to let up. "I mean, I just don't want you to end up like him," she said. "Despite your broad knowledge, you always find your way back to the subject of vampires and vampirism. Over and over again."

"Just like you and your Victorian parlor games with Peter and Janice. Let me remind you, I've sat in those circles with you, and never witnessed anything as convincing as the Aston case."

"Bullshit! You've seen and heard some extraordinary things at those sittings and you know it! We've experienced genuine paranormal phenomena and have proof there's at least *something* beyond death. But vampires? Seriously? You're wasting your time, Edison."

"Should I devote my time to the science of table rapping?" Raymer crumpled the wet napkin into a tight ball. "Channeling? Clairvoyance? Past-life regression? That's not what I'm after. Those kinds of phenomena can be traced back to some hidden region of the mind. Some shadowy corner of the brain we've yet to fully understand."

After a sip of whiskey, Veronica shifted her weight on the couch cushions. "Well, the same can be said for every alleged case of vampirism. It's basic abnormal psychology. Renfield Syndrome. TB epidemics. I know the history just as well as you do."

"Do you?" Raymer pitched the napkin into a nearby wastebasket.

"Of course," she replied. "Now granted, I didn't interview the Aston boy or his parents. I didn't spend time in the house where the events took place. But you were there. I get it. I'm not the enemy here, Ed, but you really should listen to yourself. You're defending what I'd call an untenable position, and you won't—"

"When I played those tapes for you, we had this same goddamn argument. You never took any of it seriously. And you can't deny that."

"What, Ed? What am I supposed to take seriously? I told you what I think. Jeffrey Aston had a very active imagination. At best, it was a case of poltergeist activity. Whether he was aware of it or not, that kid was responsible for everything."

"No," Raymer said. His features grew stolid as he spoke. "You're wrong. By the time we got involved, the occurrences were getting worse, and the boy was getting sicker. His parents were a mess. They'd taken him to every doctor in the area. Hematologists. Psychologists. They all said the same thing. There was no underlying cause for his condition. No disease like leukemia or any other rare blood disorder. He was tested for all of them and the tests came back negative."

"OK, so where exactly did all this happen again? The book never gave a specific location, did it?"

"Why does it matter?"

"Think about it." Veronica ran her fingers through her hair. "That kid's parents could've been shuffling him from one backwoods country doctor to another. Maybe he was misdiagnosed?"

"Repeatedly? Not possible. Although Jerry changed the names and locations in the book to protect the family, this occurred about forty miles from here, in the suburbs of Richmond. The Astons had access to the best medical care in the state."

"OK..." Veronica looked at the ceiling as Raymer filled another glass with scotch. The alcohol had relaxed him, and he was compelled to revisit the story.

"At first, Jeffrey wouldn't talk to us. They kept him upstairs. He was just a seven-year-old kid, but he was bedridden for weeks. They were keeping him alive on vitamins and applesauce. If he ate anything else, he'd throw it up. They had a specialist come in every other day to give him transfusions, as the boy was losing blood with no rational or logical explanation. Except for what he'd been saying all along."

Raymer stared ahead with a blank expression and wiped a bead of sweat from his brow.

"When Jeffrey finally agreed to talk, I hauled our equipment upstairs so Jerry could interview him. The kid looked like a living skeleton. His arms, neck, chest, and legs were covered with scars. Like he'd been bitten or cut open. But Maggie told us she'd never found a drop of blood on the sheets, and she changed them daily. I was dumbstruck, but Jerry managed to coax the whole story from him."

Dr. Upham reached for her drink. She was surprised by Raymer's unexpected candor.

"It was on the tapes, remember? Jeffrey told us that every night, he'd wake up and see a girl in a yellow dress standing at the foot of his bed. From his description, she was probably no more than twelve years old. He said he couldn't move or cry out to his parents who were asleep down the hall. She had some...some sort of *power* that kept him immobile. Then he said this girl would crawl onto his bed and bite him. She'd take a measure of blood, then lay there and watch him. If the boy attempted to speak, she'd slip her hand over his mouth and shake her head. Sometimes, after she drank his blood, she'd cradle him in her arms. She held him so tightly against her chest that the boy often struggled for breath."

Veronica's skin crawled as she imagined the scene her colleague described.

"Then, he'd blink and she'd be gone. Other times he'd fall asleep and wake with a start to find his bedroom empty. But Jeffrey claimed she appeared every night, without fail."

Raymer downed the rest of his drink as Veronica clutched her thighs. She took a deep breath as he continued.

"Of course, we set up equipment to record his room at night. But it knew we were there and didn't show up."

Raymer paced across the room to his bookshelf and spun around.

"At that point, the parents became desperate. They conferred with Jerry who told them he'd bring in a Roman Catholic priest to perform an exorcism. He had that kind of pull, as you know. So the Diocese sent Father McCallum. He was ex-military. Did two tours as an army chaplain in 'Nam. The last guy you'd ever picture as an exorcist. But he performed the rite with conviction. More than once. But the Aston boy just sat there like a stone. Afterwards, the priest told the parents to get the boy out of the house and as far away as possible."

"So they just left?" Veronica asked.

"Gone in an hour. They wrapped him in blankets and drove off without a word to either one of us. On the kitchen counter, they left a phone number. That was it. We decided to stay there overnight to take pictures for the case files and look around for anything suspicious we might've missed.

"I remember the sun was setting when I was looking around the master bedroom. Jerry was with the priest, and I could hear them chatting downstairs. But before I knew it, everything went quiet. Then there was a flicker of movement behind me. I couldn't pinpoint the source, but I felt like I was being watched. So I turned to look in the mirror above the Aston's dresser.

Behind me, in the far corner of the room, was a girl in a faded yellow dress. I didn't move or turn to face her. I just leveled the camera at the mirror."

Raymer resumed his pacing, then stopped in front of the fireplace. His hands were beginning to shake.

"I tried to take the photo but the film began to rewind. And I was paralyzed. There she was. Right there in the same room with me. The tension was palpable. I could sense the hatred this thing felt, and it was directed at Jerry and me for what we'd done. For the first time in my life, I knew real fear. I made the mistake of looking down at the camera, and when I glanced up—"

"She was gone," Veronica finished with a faraway voice.

"I ran downstairs and called the number the Astons had left. The boy's grandmother answered the phone and said they hadn't arrived yet. She assured me she'd have Oliver call me when they got there. I sat by that phone for hours until it finally rang. At first, he wouldn't let me talk to the boy. He said Jeffrey was sleeping. Eventually I wore him down and they woke him up. The first thing Jeffrey said to me was 'you saw my friend, didn't you?' Then the line went dead. Oliver must have hung up the phone."

Raymer paused and smoothed his graying beard. "The next afternoon, Oliver called back. He told us Jeffrey died early that morning at the grandparents' house. There was no service, and we never heard from the Astons again."

Veronica held up a hand before Raymer could continue. "OK. First of all, you never said *anything* about this figure in the mirror before. Why the hell not?"

"I wasn't entirely sure what I saw."

"And now you are? All these years later?" She frowned and straightened the hem of her skirt. "Look, Ed. Is it possible you just imagined it? You were obviously stressed out, keeping long hours, and—"

"Don't be absurd! You really should know better than to suggest I—"

"And you really should have mentioned this...this...this little *epilogue!*" Veronica took a deep breath to regain composure. "So what did Critchlow say about all this?"

"I never told him," he replied with a sour expression.

"What?" Veronica raised her hands in disbelief. "Don't you think that's a pretty significant omission? Jesus, Edison! It might've actually *helped* the credibility of Critchlow's study!"

"What the hell are you talking about?" Raymer stared her down. "First you suggest I was hallucinating, and now you're attacking me for withholding pertinent information? You're completely contradicting yourself!"

"No, I'm just trying to make sense of all this!"

"The reason I never told Critchlow is because I knew no one would believe what I saw. I had no proof! I didn't want to *jeopardize* the investigation. I thought the nature of the boy's trauma would speak for itself. But that obviously wasn't enough to convince people of the truth."

"For Christ's sake, Edison! Did it ever occur to you that you went into this case with preconceived notions? Or that you're misremembering things now so all the pieces fit?"

"What kind of fucking amateur do you take me for?"

"OK. Fine." Veronica leaned back and crossed her legs. "But there are still a few things that don't add up. Kids have imaginary friends. That's nothing new. Jeffrey was an only child, so—"

"I know that," Raymer replied. "But usually, they imagine children of their own age and gender. Yet Jeffrey was visited by a pre-pubescent girl. And most kids don't claim their imaginary playmates attack them and drink their blood!"

"Yeah but at the same time—"

"I saw that thing with my own eyes. You weren't there. You can't possibly understand what I saw, or what I *felt* in that room."

"Whatever you saw, or think you saw in that mirror, I'm telling you for the last time. That boy died from self-inflicted wounds."

"He was too young, Veronica!" Raymer pounded a fist against the mantelpiece. "Do you really think a seven-year-old would've been capable of cutting or *biting* himself like that? And where the hell did all the blood go?"

Veronica had no idea how to reply. She bit her lip and avoided Raymer's gaze.

"I know how Jeffrey Aston died," he insisted. "I saw his killer standing behind me in that mirror."

"That doesn't make any sense! He didn't even die in the house! So are you suggesting she followed him? That's not even consistent with vampire lore! They don't travel through fucking mirrors. They're not even supposed to cast a goddamn reflection!"

"Then how do you explain it?" Raymer folded his arms across his chest. "Go ahead. I know you're just dying to say it."

"Well, if we put aside the obvious, it could've been an intelligent haunting. The figure you saw has all the characteristics of a spirit, not a vampire. She appeared out of the corner of your eye and disappeared as soon as you saw her. But it's far more likely that the commotion in the house triggered some kind of psychical imprint or—"

"And there you have it." Raymer clapped his hands together. "Dr. Veronica Upham has come along and solved the case!"

"Or *the boy* made it all up and caused the disturbances himself. You know as well as I do that this incident can be attributed to—"

"Telekinesis," Raymer said. "Misdirected psychokinetic energy."

"Well? Why not? The wounds could've been psychosomatic and the girl could've been a projection. A way for him to focus his energy. And what he imagined was so strong that the energy left an impression, which would explain how you saw it." Veronica concluded and took a shallow breath. "Look, I never said he did it consciously or tried to deceive you and Critchlow. On the other hand, maybe there was something haunting the house, but—"

"Unbelievable," he muttered. "So I tell you it was a vampire, and you fight me at every turn. But if I said it was a ghost? Or that a new house with little to no history was haunted? Well, sure. Why not?"

"You asked me what I thought," she said. "So I told you."

"Why is it that you have no problem believing in ghosts and all the usual paranormal bullshit, yet you can't accept that vampires are out there? Give me one good reason." He clenched his teeth. "Just *one*."

"It's empirically impossible." She gestured to the coffee table. "You've read all these books! Your lectures on vampires always come back to the same point. The mere idea of a creature that lives by night, sucks blood, and has supernatural strength is the stuff of legends. Outdated superstitions now explained by modern science. Come on, Ed. This is an Occam's Razor moment if there ever was one! The simplest explanation? Vampirism is either a disease of the living or a peasant myth. That's all. There's no mystery about it."

"You're still avoiding the question, Veronica. Why would you defend the existence of ghosts with your dying breath, but insist vampires are a mere superstition?"

Veronica's heart sank.

He can't be serious. He just can't be.

"How about this?" she managed. "The moon. It reflects sunlight. As a scientist, you know that's why the moon glows, so to speak. Now most of your mythical vampires have an aversion to sunlight. That being said, why don't they burn in the moonlight?"

"I don't know," Raymer answered. "Because it's not *direct* sunlight? You, of all people, know that literary vampires subvert and contradict much of the folklore. Lord Ruthven, and by extension, Stoker's Dracula, could move about in a weakened state during the day. The moon restored Ruthven to life and gave Varney superhuman speed and strength."

"Well, clearly, you've paid more attention to the details of Victorian penny dreadfuls than my students have."

Raymer ignored Veronica's ill-timed attempt at levity. "I've always theorized that the weaknesses of the vampire are psychosomatic in nature. Individuals suffering from Renfield Syndrome or Porphyria might also be influenced by what they've read or seen in films. One of my former students recently proposed a similar theory in regard to exorcisms."

Veronica studied Edison Raymer's stony features. "Now you're talking like the man I know and care for deeply."

"Because I'm suddenly playing the skeptic when it comes to anything but spiritualism?" Raymer was still annoyed despite Veronica's efforts to defuse the tension. "I admit there's a lot about these creatures that I can't account for. Not yet, anyway."

Veronica hesitated before she replied. She spoke softly and gazed at the floor. "So this is why you're always down in the basement. And why you're so engrossed in these books and just going through the motions on campus." She raised her eyes with apprehension. "You plan to go...to go looking for them. To prove they're real."

Raymer pressed his lips together and turned to look out the window into the darkness beyond.

"Why not?"

Veronica's breath caught in her throat. She was at a loss for words. Intrusive thoughts crowded her mind as a disquieting hush fell between them.

He's so close to the edge now.

Worse than ever.

But I can't stand by and watch him self-destruct. He'll piss his life and career away over a silly obsession. Just like Critchlow. But right now, I gotta play by his rules.

Veronica spoke up. "Edison?"

"Yeah?" He nodded in her direction.

"Why don't you go get the tapes from the case and we can give 'em another listen? I promise I'll try to keep an open mind."

"Really?" Raymer asked. He was disarmed by his colleague's sudden change in temperament. "Are you sure?"

"Absolutely," Veronica replied, choosing her words with care. "Maybe you're right, maybe you're not. Only time will tell. But for now, maybe we should just start at the beginning."

12

A GRAY SEDAN LURKED IN THE TALL GRASS ALONG State Route 619, idling across the road from a dilapidated mobile home. The front door of the trailer was lit by a single lamp, and the driveway was littered with the rusty detritus of neglected automobiles. Matthias, behind the wheel of the car, watched another minute pass on the dashboard clock.

6:13 a.m.

The vampire had cased this remote trailer before and considered the possibility of acquiring it for himself. As on previous nights, Matthias' keen hearing distinguished the sound of a man and woman arguing. At approximately 6:30, the man would exit the trailer. He'd slam the rickety door in anger and leave for his meager job.

This morning, he won't make it out that fucking door.

With the headlights off, Matthias pulled his car into the driveway. Painted in a crude scrawl on the mailbox was the name STILES. He eased his sedan onto the unkempt lawn, between a battered pickup truck and the rusting hulk of an old muscle car. Quietly, he slipped on his worn leather jacket and emerged from the vehicle.

Matthias crept across the overgrown yard towards the trailer's front door. He could hear a commotion inside. Every spiteful word rang in his ears. Above the smell of burning pork, he could discern the enticing aroma of blood.

Matthias stood, adjusted his coat and approached the door. He pounded on the metal frame with three sharp raps. Inside, the quarrel ceased.

72

"Who the hell?" The man's angry voice resounded. "Dammit, Allie, did you call the staties on me again?"

After a short pause, the perplexed woman spoke in a hushed and anxious whisper. "I swear, Jack, I didn't call no cops!"

Matthias could sense the man approaching the door. "Who the *fuck* is outside my house? On *my* goddamn property?"

"Please, sir," Matthias spoke in a clear voice. "My car is broken down and I need to call a tow truck. It will only take a minute."

"Goddammit, ain't you got a cell phone or somethin'?"

"I can't get a signal out here. It's a dead zone. Please, just let me in to use your phone."

There was no answer. Matthias heard faint whispering and footsteps pacing the length of the mobile home. A minute passed before he heard the unmistakable sound of a 12-gauge shotgun being racked. "Hear that?" the voice from inside queried.

"Jack, stop it and just let him in. He needs help."

"Bullshit, Allie! Shut your fuckin' trap and finish cookin' my goddamn breakfast!"

"I can pay you." Matthias clenched his fists. "Fifty bucks. Cash. This is an emergency."

Stiles took a moment to consider the offer.

"Alright," he addressed Matthias again. "Any fuckin' around and I'll drop you. I wanna see the money first. Then you go straight to the phone, make your call, and get the fuck outta my house, got it?"

"Yes sir," Matthias answered.

The vampire ran his tongue across his incisors. He tightened his hands with anticipation. Stiles unlatched the door and began to pull it open. With blinding speed, Matthias elbowed his way into the mobile home and charged at the armed man. Although taken by surprise, Stiles was able to fire a single shot at Matthias. The tight cluster of double-ought buck hit the vampire in his chest.

Unfazed, Matthias pounced on the gunman. He knocked both the shotgun and a box of shells from Stiles' hands, then pinned his body to the floor. In one fluid motion, he snapped the man's neck.

"Jack! Oh, Christ!" Allie Stiles screamed and dropped a hot pan of scorched bacon to the floor.

Matthias sprung upward. He stood nearly a foot taller than Mrs. Stiles. He stepped towards her, his boots heavy upon the linoleum floor. She cowered against the sink, eyeing the shotgun by her husband's body. She looked to Matthias in desperation. Her bloodshot eyes welled with tears. "You killed him! Why? Why did you..."

Matthias didn't answer. He inched towards her, a low growl catching in his throat. Realizing that her only hope was to pass the intruder and grab the shotgun, Allie prepared to move.

She froze when she noticed that the invader's chest, peppered with buckshot, was bleeding. His shirt was torn to scraps, and glistened with dark blood. Despite the grievous wound, the vampire stood firm. There was no evidence he was in pain.

"Please...please d-don't! Please! For the love of Christ! Don't!"

Matthias halted. A wave of disgust swept through his body. Enraged by the woman's hysterical prayer, he yearned to tear her to pieces.

The vampire tempered his voice with an uncanny charm. "Allie, this will be so much easier if you come to me. Just let yourself be taken." His pale blue eyes held her captive.

She surveyed the murderer's angular jaw, his prominent cheekbones, and his slick blond hair. Allie was particularly enraptured by a thick lock that fell around his eyes just so.

Allie took a step forward. She felt an unfamiliar warmth rising within her, a consumptive desire she had never felt for Jack—or any man.

Matthias beckoned again. This time he pointed at the confines of the trailer around them. "I can make all *this* go away. Here...take my hand."

The woman staggered forward, her eyes locked on the strange and imposing man. She craved his strong embrace and hungered to feel his mouth on hers.

Suddenly, the trance was broken. She took a confused step backward, and her glistening eyes returned to the motionless form of her husband. "N-no," Allie stammered. "No! Get away from me! Get the hell away from me!"

"Dammit," Matthias cursed under his breath. With his teeth bared, he leapt forward.

Allie managed to scream, yet failed to shield her face from the attacker. She fell to the floor as the vampire clenched his hands around her wrists. He wrenched her arms from their sockets with two hollow *cracks*.

She opened her mouth to wail again as his teeth pierced the flesh of her slender neck. Tendons and arteries were ripped from her throat as blood flowed into her assailant's mouth. Before her vision went black, she saw him rise to his feet, wipe his mouth on a dishtowel, and turn towards the body of her husband.

Matthias knelt down and placed a firm hand on the man's wrist. The vampire's strike had left Stiles paralyzed and unresponsive, but his heart beat an irregular rhythm. Matthias bit down on the dying man's carotid artery. When the blood no longer came, Matthias staggered to his knees. He spat out a clotted measure of the viscous liquid. The blackening ichor splattered along the dead man's back.

"Fucking filth." Matthias stood over his quarry and felt the vital sustenance course through his dead heart. The cello was forgotten. His wife was a distant memory. He stood in the confines of the trailer's living room, reeling as the blood took effect. Dead nerves and sinew sparked to life as he fought the urge to tear the corpses into shreds of bone and flesh.

Matthias' rage was tempered by the rising of the sun outside. He could discern the first rays of dawn beyond the kitchen's grimy windowpanes.

He assessed the cramped interior of the trailer—now the scene of a double homicide. Yet Matthias knew the present scenario could easily be refashioned as a murder-suicide. To the police, it would seem an all-too-familiar story. Having endured years of shame, and physical abuse, Allie Stiles reached the point where she no longer loved her husband—or herself.

Matthias stooped and picked up the 12-gauge, and racked another shell. He leveled the barrel inches from the dead man and kicked the corpse onto its back. As the limp body of Jack Stiles rolled across the threadbare carpet, Matthias squeezed the trigger of the shotgun. The chest cavity exploded, splashing blood across the living room floor.

Shotgun in hand, he spun to face the remains of the dead woman. Matthias took a few steps in her direction and shoved the barrel of the shotgun into her mouth. He racked another shell. A second blinding flash lit the interior of the trailer as slick blood and shreds of tissue erupted from Allie's head. The gruesome mess splattered against the kitchenette wall.

Matthias leaned over the corpse and flipped the shotgun upside down. He positioned her hands around the weapon and angled the smoking barrel into her mouth. The corpse of Allie Stiles lay frozen as he stepped back to admire his handiwork.

At dusk, once he had slept and the shotgun wound had healed, Matthias would set the Stiles' trailer ablaze. He lamented the loss of another potential hiding place, but people would soon come looking. The police would find the scorched bodies in their present positions, but there would be no questions of blood loss or strange fingerprints.

He had done this before many times.

After turning off the greasy stove, Matthias pushed his way into the hall and tore open a closet door. One by one, he ripped out the shelves and tossed the towels into an adjoining room. The dim hallway grew brighter as the muted light of morning rose beyond the yellowed curtains. The blood-drunk vampire continued to hollow out the closet until it was gutted.

As Matthias stepped inside, he picked up two towels and closed the door behind him. He could feel the searing heat of daylight crawl across his ashen face and hands before the dark of the tight closet enveloped him. He shoved the towels along the gap between the door and the torn carpet to prevent any light from seeping into his hiding place.

The vampire stood against the wall and closed his eyes. He traced the sticky wound on his chest that would heal with sleep and crossed his arms. His legs stiffened, and he arched his back into an inhuman position.

†

Anna was at the piano in their modest home on Elizabethstrasse. She turned to face him, but he wasn't there.

He couldn't have been.

It was September 11th, and he was with his division fighting somewhere near Eifel.

He tried to touch her face. To smooth her flaxen hair. But he could only watch in silence.

The walls began to rumble around her. Sheet music slipped from the piano and drifted to the floor. In the hutch against the far wall, plates shook and fell forward.

Anna dropped her hands to clutch her belly—as if she could somehow protect the child inside from the oncoming firestorm. She glanced in horror at the rafters above. Air raid sirens began to wail as Anna struggled to stand. Her eyes were wide and imploring. In the distance, flak batteries opened fire.

The thunder of British planes in the night sky grew louder. Falling bombs spiraled towards the heart of Darmstadt.

"Matti?"

"Aussteigen!"

"Matti! Rette mich! Rette unsere kinder!"

"Heraus!"

There was a bright flash, and Anna disappeared in a whirlwind of splintered wood, shattered glass, and fractured blocks of cement. Above the explosions and the roaring flames, Anna continued to cry out to him.

"Matti!"

Had he been able, he would have wept.

"Matti! Halte mich!"

"Anna," he whispered. *"Es tut mir leid."*

"Matti..."

The vampire's mind went blank.

Outside, the sun crested high above the tree line. It gleamed on the slick tar patches, which covered the lonely state road. A large garden spider began to spin a web across the side-view mirror of Jack Stiles' pickup truck.

Inside the dark closet of the mobile home, the predator slumbered undetected—hidden from the scalding rays of the bright morning sun. As the day wore on, oblivion held Matthias Bartsch against its cold, lifeless breast.

13

"IT HAPPENS, EDISON." VERONICA CLUTCHED THE DUVET AROUND her naked body and placed a comforting hand on Raymer's bare back. "God knows we both had too much to drink last night and stayed up way too late."

Clad only in a pair of boxers, Edison Raymer sat on the edge of his bed and offered no reply. He dug a well-worn file underneath one of his fingernails and slid it from side to side.

Veronica flipped a lock of tangled hair away from her forehead and pushed it behind her ear. She began to massage Raymer's shoulder, but he immediately tensed up and shrugged her hand away.

"Look, Veronica. I've got a lot on my mind right now." He started to file a fingernail. "You actually slept last night while I stayed awake staring at the goddamn ceiling."

"If you're upset about last night I told you, it's—"

"Can we please drop it?"

"Fine." She pulled her hand away and wrapped the quilt around her body. "So what's on the agenda for today? I don't have to be anywhere until this evening."

Raymer held up a hand to inspect his nails in the morning light. He had filed them all into thin white arcs. "I have research to do."

"OK." Veronica frowned and leaned against the headboard. "Anything I can help you with?"

"No," he answered. "I just planned to do some reading. Then maybe work out later this afternoon."

"Is that my cue to go?"

Raymer shrugged and pitched the nail file onto his nightstand. "It's up to you. Don't you have papers to grade?"

"A few. But I thought you'd wanna get outta here for a while? You know, run some errands. Get some lunch, and then maybe go for a walk?"

"What gave you that impression?"

"Well, maybe you *should* get out of here a bit," she insisted. "Put those damned books aside for an afternoon and get some fresh air."

Raymer raised his head and sighed. "I feel another lecture coming on."

"No, I'm just looking out for you, that's all."

"Well, stop it. I've managed to survive on my own this many years. I can look out for myself."

"Goddammit, Edison!" She twisted the blanket in her pale hands. "What the hell's going on with you? You've never been like this. You wander around this empty house all the time when you're not teaching, and you're preoccupied with all this vampire shit. Your only meaningful contact with the outside world is through me, and that's not saying much."

"No, it really isn't."

Veronica pursed her lips at his remark. In frustration, she began to dig through the bedclothes. She fished her bra from under one of the pillows, slipped it over her shoulders, and clasped it around her chest. She spun her legs over the edge of the mattress and snatched her panties from the floor.

Raymer rose and turned to face her with crossed arms. "So I guess now you're gonna stomp out of here in a huff?"

"Clearly I'm not wanted."

"I never said that." Raymer shifted his weight. "But I'm not in the mood for a passive aggressive lovers' quarrel."

"You're never in the mood for *anything*." Veronica sprung out of bed and reached for her rumpled skirt. "Whatever, Edison. I tried. I won't even bother to ask you about tonight because I know exactly what you'll say."

"See?" Raymer pointed his finger. "Right there. Passive aggressive. This is the part where I'm supposed to ask you 'what's going on tonight?' And then you'll say—"

"Nevermind."

"And then you'll say—" He raised his voice to drown her out, but she spun to face him and cut him off.

"I was going to ask you to come to Janice and Peter's. Just to get the fuck out of this house. Even if you don't wanna join the circle, you can at least come along and feel superior to the rest of us." She slapped her hands against her thighs. "Why the hell not?"

"You're right about one thing." He nodded. "That's the last thing I want to do tonight."

"Like I said, I never should've bothered to ask." She pulled up her skirt and cinched it tight around her waist. "I just wish I knew when things started to fall apart between us. Because if it was something I did, I'd try like hell to fix it."

Raymer furrowed his brow as he watched her dress. "Well, now that you mention it, I wasn't the one who skipped out on our dinner plans last night to attend yet another colloquium. I made the effort and you decided impressing your colleagues was more important than—"

"You made the *effort?*" Veronica laughed as she slipped into her blouse. "You picked up take-out from a fucking Italian restaurant! You call that effort?"

"I'll be the first to admit I've been preoccupied with my work." Raymer leaned forward and began to straighten the sheets on his bed. "But I'm not the only one that takes our relationship for granted. You showed me where I rank last night. And your message was heard. Loud and—"

"Oh for fuck's sake, Edison!" Her hands began to tremble as she buttoned her blouse. "If I didn't care about you, I wouldn't be here. Look, this is ridiculous. I'm sorry I was late last night. It's not like I could skip out on the damn thing. She was my student, and I assigned the goddamn paper. I sort of had to be there, you know?"

Still avoiding eye contact with her, Raymer shoved the loose sheet under the mattress and pulled it taut to the head of the bed.

"It really doesn't matter," he muttered under his breath and bent to pick up the thick bedspread.

Now fully dressed, Veronica turned and watched him as he flung the comforter across the bed. With the edge of his hand, Raymer tucked the bedspread over a mound of doubled pillows. He cut in front of her and continued to straighten the duvet with a blank expression.

"I don't wanna fight with you, Edison." She bit her lip and slid her feet into a pair of flat-soled shoes. "I told you, I'm just worried about you. Maybe bringing out those tapes last night wasn't such a great idea."

Raymer didn't answer. He stormed past her and down the narrow hallway to the bathroom. After flipping on the light, he began to run the shower. He emerged a few seconds later and gave Veronica a searching look.

"I know what you're thinking, and I'll tell you again for the last time." He pointed at her. "I'm not obsessed. I just know I'm right. And if you quit nagging me and trust me, I'll prove it to you."

"But you *are* obsessed, Edison." She clasped her hands together and took a step forward. "Please. Just listen to yourself. If a panel of psychologists had been privy to our conversation last night, they'd probably have you committed."

"I thought I was speaking to a *friend!*" Raymer shouted above the running water. "Of all people, I thought you'd be the last one to judge me."

"I'm not judging you," she said as her eyes glistened with tears. "I just—"

"I think you're afraid. You're moving out of your comfort zone. Beyond the proverbial bell, book, and candle. And I don't think you can handle it."

"You're right!" Veronica nodded. "I *am* afraid. But I'm telling you. There's no such thing as..."

"You can't even say the word, can you?" Raymer glared at her as steam from the shower curled around his shoulders.

"Vampires, Edison." Veronica wiped her nose against the back of her hand. "There! You happy?"

"That's right, Veronica. *Vampires,*" Raymer replied. "That's all that concerns me right now. Vampires. The living dead. That's what I'll be researching, and that's what I'll be *searching* for! So if that disturbs or upsets you, you can go sit on Janice's couch with a glass of screw-top Chardonnay and try to guess which knee Peter's using to rattle the table."

"Edison, that is *not* fair. You barely—"

"I still have no idea what you and those people get out of your amateur séances. As for me, if you can't accept my preoccupations, then I don't know how many different ways I can tell you. Leave me be!"

Before she could reply, Raymer turned his back to her and disappeared behind the bathroom door. Veronica hung her head and stood motionless in the dark hallway. She felt as though her legs might give out from under her, so she leaned against the wall to steady herself. After a moment of bitter reflection, she took a deep breath and slowly descended the stairs.

14

MATTHIAS BARTSCH GRIPPED THE STEERING WHEEL AND glanced out the filmy driver's side window at a drunken college student. The young woman, clad in a sorority sweatshirt, staggered down the sidewalk. He slowed down to take in her dark hair, olive skin, and slender figure.

Not her.

She won't do at all.

The vampire maneuvered the gray sedan through the campus drives of Williamsport College, alert and attentive. Arvo Pärt's *Tabula Rasa* spun in the CD player. The lush string arrangement was distorted by the car's factory speakers. Matthias sighed and drew his fingers across his lips.

What you are doing is foolish. Something you can't afford to be in this day and age.

His car passed a trio of co-eds waiting at a crosswalk. Again, he studied the girls carefully.

No.

They're just not right.

Matthias braked to a stop and waved the students across. They didn't acknowledge him as they scurried past.

He pushed the car forward, his booted foot on the gas pedal, and rounded a curve. Matthias closed his eyes for a second and saw only Anna. The vampire shook his head at the recurring memory and focused on the hunt ahead of him.

On Saturday night, Matthias had torched the Stiles' trailer. He managed to flee the scene before the fire department and police arrived. Although twenty-four hours had passed, he still reeked of gasoline and acrid smoke. The stench lingered in his nostrils and reminded him of the day he died.

The blood from Jack and Allie Stiles had mended the gunshot wound in his chest. When he awoke Sunday evening, the hunger had returned. He drove into Williamsport to hunt again.

But this hunt would be like no other. And if it didn't pan out, he would repeat the process until he found the right one. It was only a matter of time until he did, and he would not falter.

As he turned right onto Mill Spring Road, he accelerated past the outer perimeter of the college.

If this doesn't go as planned, I can correct the problem.

The streetlamps illuminated a blacktop devoid of traffic and sidewalks free of pedestrians.

Correct the problem and try again.

A group of figures cut across a manicured soccer field in the distance. Through the closed window and over the music, he could hear laughter. Matthias felt a consummate envy for the living. The pampered college students in their dormitories along the road knew only comfort and privilege. True struggle was alien to their generation, and the bitter taste of loss was foreign to most of them.

He brought the sedan to a complete stop and turned right on red at a barren intersection. The Georgian brick buildings of the college disappeared in his rear-view mirror, but Matthias kept his eyes on the tree-lined sidewalks flanking his car. The bright lights and loud roar of a city bus drew his attention back to the road. As he passed the grimy vehicle, an elderly black man with a shock-white beard stared out the window at him. Matthias met his accusatory glance, but the rider never looked away. The man shifted his fedora away from his forehead, and his eyes followed Matthias' car as the bus lumbered away.

He knows.

Like Gretl.

He knows.

Matthias made a series of turns and the odd passenger was soon forgotten. He cruised by a middle-aged couple walking their dog and kept driving. The road widened, and he spied the lighted sign for St. Luke's Catholic

Church. The customizable lettering advertised a Knights of Columbus Sunday supper. In the shadows, a young woman with blonde hair stepped off the pavement and onto the stone walkway leading to the church. She clutched at her pea coat, and her scarf fluttered in the wind.

Her.

Matthias slowed the car to a crawl. He watched the girl traverse the path to the church entrance. He thumbed a switch and the passenger side window clattered down with a strained hum. Night air flooded into the cabin of the sedan, and Matthias watched as she struggled to open the heavy wooden doors to the vestibule.

Her.

A large cross rose into the dark sky above St. Luke's bell tower. The vampire looked away and began to steer the car forward. He noticed a Plexiglas bus shelter not far from the walkway. Matthias nodded as he surveyed the graffiti-tagged structure. The bench was empty and the garbage can had overflowed.

I want her.

The vampire noted the direction the girl had been walking. He turned the car around and drove until he found a side street. A long hedgerow ran parallel to the sidewalk, and Matthias smiled to himself. He spun the wheel and parked along the curb of the lonely residential drive, which ended in a *cul de sac* lit by a single streetlamp. Most of the homes appeared vacant. FOR SALE signs littered the overgrown lawns.

Matthias killed the ignition and sat in silence for a moment. He nodded a second time in affirmation. He pulled his keys from the ignition and opened the driver's side door. Before leaving his car behind, he opened the trunk and spread out a torn plastic sheet. As he ran his long fingers over a roll of silver duct tape tucked behind the wheel well, he was overcome with anticipation.

Her.

†

Jennifer Stroud descended the stairwell and navigated a maze of dark corridors until she emerged in the church sanctuary. She made her way toward the narthex and pressed her full weight against the heavy wooden doors to exit St. Luke's.

The door slammed behind her as she quickened her pace. She was running late for her applied chemistry study group. As Jennifer glanced up the stone path to the street, she glimpsed a tall, broad-shouldered man standing by the bus shelter. His features were pale, but sharp and handsome.

Oh, hell. He's pretending not to notice me.

She walked up the path and ignored the stranger at the bus stop. To avoid him altogether, she cut across the lawn until she reached the sidewalk. Jennifer maintained her brisk pace as her shoes clicked on the pavement.

I hate being out here after dark. I should've taken Amber's offer to pick me up on her way home from work.

She walked a bit further. Above the pulse pounding in her ears, she heard heavy footsteps falling in a steady rhythm. She remembered the man at the bus shelter.

He's following me.

Jennifer clenched her fists. She refused to glance over her shoulder.

Almost breathless in the cold air, she managed to shout a warning. "Whoever the hell you are back there, I've got pepper spray! So leave me alone!"

Her pursuer was undeterred, and the sound of his footsteps grew louder. She dropped a hand in her pocket to grip the canister of pepper spray. In that tense moment, curiosity got the better of her and she spun around.

The stranger from the bus stop was about fifteen yards behind her. His black motorcycle jacket and slick blond hair gleamed as he passed under a streetlamp. The stranger's penetrating gaze sent a shudder down Jennifer's spine.

She turned around and began to walk again, hoping she'd meet another pedestrian, or that a car might appear on the road to flag down. She knew she couldn't outpace the stranger. At once, Jennifer was terrified of the man closing the distance from behind, but a small part of her bristled with anger.

I won't be a victim.

Not to some sick bastard like this.

"I swear," she called out. "I'm gonna nail you, so just leave me alone!"

As she quickened her pace forward, she muttered a prayer under her breath. When Jennifer was a few feet from the curb of a gloomy, unlit side street, she glanced over her shoulder.

The man was gone.

She breathed a sigh of relief and turned to face the path ahead. There was nothing in her field of vision except the worn black leather of a motorcycle jacket.

Before she could cry out, the stranger overpowered her. His calloused hand covered her mouth and a strong arm wrapped around her neck. Pepper spray in hand, she flailed her arms and kicked her legs. The virulent mist from the canister fogged the air around them as her fingers tensed on the trigger. Although she fought with all her strength, she couldn't break the stranglehold.

Branches snapped and scratched her face as the attacker pulled her through the hedgerow and onto an overgrown lawn. Her chest heaved as she struggled to breathe. He laid her down in the tall grass behind the hedge, rested his angular jaw on her soft cheek, and whispered in her ear.

"Don't scream."

She could feel the inhuman chill of his flesh against her own.

"Anna."

Thrashing beneath his weight, Jennifer managed to strike her attacker in the jaw with the heel of her palm. The man didn't flinch. He pushed her head flat against the ground and pressed his cheek against hers a second time. The stranger spoke in a low whisper. "Just a moment of pain, and we'll be together."

Jennifer Stroud screamed in desperation and thrust her knee into her assailant's groin. Again, her struggle didn't faze him. He opened his mouth and drove his teeth into the flesh of her neck. She managed another scream before he clasped his hand over her mouth again.

A dog began to bark as the lawn and hedgerow was bathed in light. The owner of the house threw open his door and charged onto the porch with a baseball bat in hand. He was a squat black man with a shaved head and dark tattoos on his arms.

"Hey, get the fuck off her!"

The attacker pushed Jennifer's head back, and she could see the barefoot man in a T-shirt and boxers on the porch of the ramshackle house behind them. She whimpered for help, but her cries were silenced.

"Jesus Christ! Denise! Call 9-1-1!" The man leaned over the edge of the porch. "There's a fuckin' sicko out here attackin' some girl!"

Jennifer felt a warm dampness around the stranger's lips, and her head began to spin. The homeowner descended the porch steps and edged across the lawn.

The attack ended almost as quickly as it began. Matthias sprung to his feet with blood dripping from his chin. He leapt backward as the wide-eyed man reached the scene of the crime. He swung his bat at the stranger, recovered, and swung again, but missed his mark. Jennifer's assailant disengaged and bolted through the tall hedge.

"That's right, you peckerwood fuck! Run off like a goddamn coward! Come back an' I'll split your fuckin' skull!"

The homeowner's wife was on the porch now, pulling a terrycloth robe around her waist. "Cops're on their way, Joe! What the hell's goin' on out here?"

Joe fell to his knees. He slipped his shirt over his head, wadded it up, and pressed it against the wound on Jennifer's neck.

"Hey, girl! Help's on the way. Try an' stay awake!" A sharp tap on the cheek roused her.

"Wha..." Jennifer managed.

Along the street, porch lights flickered on and dogs began to bark. Somewhere in the distance, a car engine roared to life. Tires screeched as an unseen vehicle peeled onto the main street and sputtered away.

"My...my..." Jennifer could barely breathe, much less finish her sentence.

Other residents were gathering around Jennifer as Joe Wilkins kept pressure on her neck. A collection of unfamiliar faces loomed above her.

"Big guy... fixin' to rape her I think..."

"Didn't get very far. Did'ja hit 'im, Joe?"

"Nah...took a swing or two but he ran off."

"You get a good look at 'im?"

"Too dark out here. Like I said, some big-ass peckerwood in a leather jacket. We'll let the cops take care a' him!"

Jennifer Stroud's eyelids fluttered. Her body went slack as Joe's neighbors continued to swarm around her. In the distance, the sound of approaching sirens grew louder as Jennifer slipped out of consciousness.

15

MATTHIAS TORE OFF HIS BLOODY SHIRT AND SHOVED IT into a trash bag. Bare-chested, he paced across the carpet of his dingy apartment, muttering to himself.

"That was *stupid*," he whispered. Before he could restrain himself, he swung his powerful arm backward and punched a hole in the drywall. "Fucking *stupid*."

He jerked open the door to a small walk-in closet and pulled out a military surplus duffel bag. Inside was at least $10,000 in small bills, rolled, bound, and stacked. After he donned a clean shirt, Matthias pulled down the rest of his clothing from hangers. He stuffed shirts, trousers, and hospital scrubs into the duffel bag, then pitched it onto the couch.

What were you thinking out there?

That you could just drive around and choose some random girl from the college campus or city streets?

The vampire dumped a crate full of CD cases into the duffel bag, then zipped it up. The cheap stereo, the couch, and chairs—even the old black and white TV—belonged to the landlord, who lived two states away. They'd never met face to face, and Matthias had accepted the renter's agreement over the phone. The property owner only charged him $200 a month cash to stay there, and kept the rental off the books. Everything had been under the table to avoid taxes.

If someone put me in a lineup in front of that man, he wouldn't know me from Adam.

But the girl you left on that lawn would recognize you.

Once his belongings were in the car, there'd be no evidence he'd ever been on the premises. Without a bank account or credit cards, Matthias was a virtual ghost in the modern world. His cellphones were pre-paid. He always picked up his checks at work, and cashed them at a run-down convenience store. He gave false information on his work applications. But he knew this wasn't occupied Germany sixty-odd years ago. He couldn't just disappear from a town or a job without a trace.

I should have killed her, then killed the man with the baseball bat. I shouldn't have been out there in the first place.

What the hell was I thinking?

He slung the duffel bag onto his shoulder, picked up the trash bag, then made his way out to the parking lot.

You knew exactly what you were thinking, Bartsch.

The frustrations, the loneliness that never bothered you before. All those vivid dreams of Anna.

You want a companion. A woman to replace your wife.

He unlatched the trunk of his car, dropped the sack into the empty space, and flung the bag of refuse beside it. Before sunrise, he planned to dump it in the waters of a swamp out in the county.

You won't stop looking until you find someone like her.

Matthias left the trunk ajar as he returned to the apartment, still cursing under his breath.

"To hell with that. I have to lay low. Maybe even find somewhere and sleep until this passes over."

He yanked his cello case from its upright position and flipped open the lid. With great care, he placed the Stradivarius into the worn case, along with its bow. Matthias plucked each string on the cello before closing the case.

You fucked up before and always covered your tracks.

But this time, you left a victim alive. A victim you were about to turn. Someone called the police. There were witnesses.

Before leaving with his cello, Matthias donned his leather jacket and shoved his cigarette tin into a side pocket. He slipped out with the case and locked the door behind him.

You have the other apartment, registered under an alias. And you also have the cabin on Route 619.

But Matthias couldn't lay low. He was expected at work later that night. His paycheck from the week before was sitting in his locker. If he didn't show up for his shift at Serenity Springs, he'd only raise further suspicions.

Matthias dropped the apartment key to the pavement and kicked it under the welcome mat.

You haven't fucked up this badly in awhile. The world is very different now, and you won't be able to run from this.

But they haven't found you yet.

He opened the rear door of his car and slid the cello case into the back seat.

You can't change your appearance, but you can change how others see you. How you dress. How you conduct yourself in public.

Before opening the driver's side door, he reached to close the trunk.

Or you can leave town, but you'll also leave a trail for the authorities to follow.

Matthias slid into the front seat of his car and started the engine. The Arvo Pärt CD blared through the speakers, and he switched off the dashboard stereo. Within minutes, he was on the bypass and headed toward the city limits.

An hour before sunrise, a cold rain began to fall. He'd parked his car a mile off the road in a desolate part of the woods where no one was likely to come looking. Indifferent to the downpour, Matthias waded into a shallow swamp and shoved the garbage bag under a submerged log.

Once the bag with his bloody clothing had been ditched, he changed into his work scrubs and clutched a thick wool blanket under his arm.

The vampire crawled into a long, dry culvert. He pushed as far away from the entrance as he could, sat against the sloping concrete wall, and covered himself with the blanket.

When he closed his eyes, he saw Anna's face again, and ached for her.

You will do this again, Bartsch. The longing is too real. The compulsion is too great.

It took seventy years, but now you know. Existence is meaningless. Without her, you might as well walk into the sun and give up.

But that's not you.

Next time, you'll get it right.

For now, you have to plan.

Have patience.

Next time.

16

D ETECTIVE RUDY PETTIT REMOVED HIS IRISH TWEED HAT
to reveal a balding head and scant comb-over. He leaned against
the front reception desk of Williamsport General Hospital
and tapped two fingers on the flat surface. The detective was
short, pudgy, and pushing past sixty—with a bushy moustache, wandering
eyes, and a persistent cough. Beneath the folds of his beige overcoat, a
shoulder holster concealed a two-toned Glock 32. After dedicating more
than thirty years of his life to the Williamsport Police Department, Pettit
was expecting to retire within less than a month.

An older nurse, who'd been typing data into a computer, spun to face
him. She eyed the visible firearm under his coat. "Can I help you, sir?"

Without a word, he flipped open his wallet to reveal a silver badge and
dropped it on the counter. The nurse raised her brows. "Oh. You're here
about the Stroud girl?"

"Very perceptive," he replied.

The nurse hung her head to avoid the ill-mannered detective. "Well, I
guess you don't need a visitor badge, then." She slid a clipboard and pen over
the counter without standing up. "But you still have to sign in. Hospital
procedure."

Pettit gave a curt nod and scrawled his name on the visitor roster.

"Don't forget to put the arrival time," the nurse said.

"Believe it or not, I've done this before."

"If you say so. She's on the fourth floor. Room 437. You'll know it because there should be a cop sitting by the door. I can't guarantee she'll be awake. She went through surgery when they brought her in."

Detective Pettit dug into his coat pocket for a pen and a small notebook. He began to write as the nurse went on about how much blood the girl lost and how she had to have a skin graft. The entire time, he never looked up, nor did he acknowledge anything she said. He leaned forward, breathing heavily, until the nurse stopped talking. Pettit kept jotting notes until he saw fit to slide his pen through the spiral binding.

"Where can a guy get a cup of coffee 'round here?" He hacked into his sleeve.

The nurse eyed him with suspicion.

"Upper respiratory infection. Just gettin' over it." Pettit spoke with a slight southern drawl as he pointed to his throat.

"Then you'll need to wear a mask when you see her," the nurse warned. "It's hospital policy."

Pettit walked away without another word, mashed an elevator button, and stood with his arms crossed. When the doors clattered open, two orderlies attempted to maneuver an elderly woman in a wheelchair. Pettit muscled his way into the elevator car before they could make a move. One of the bulky orderlies glared at him, and he sneered back. "Well, you gettin' off here or you wanna go back upstairs?"

"Asshole," the orderly muttered.

Pettit watched them leave and jammed a thumb against the 'close door' button.

When he stepped out of the elevator, Pettit spent ten minutes searching for the vending machines. He retrieved his instant coffee and loitered at a small condiment cart. There, he dumped packets of artificial sweetener and powdered creamer into the overflowing cup. Pettit took a sip, shook his head at the poor quality of the hospital coffee, and meandered down the hallway toward 437.

The uniformed cop by the door was reading a newspaper, which he promptly folded and slid under his chair.

"Detective." He greeted his superior officer. "She's sleeping. I was just about to..."

"Cool it, kid, and get that paper back out." Pettit gestured to the floor.

The police officer did as he was told.

"Flip to the front page."

Pettit scanned the headlines. There was nothing about the crime he was there to investigate. Not yet. "Did you read the actual news, or did you skip straight to the sports scores?"

The policeman glanced up at the older man. "The actual news, if you want to call it that."

"Well, has this little incident made the paper yet?"

"No, it hasn't."

"It will soon enough." He pushed open the door and wandered into the Stroud girl's private room.

A nurse was changing Jennifer's I.V. drip. She looked up and put a finger to her lips. In defiance of her request, Pettit unleashed a barking cough. Jennifer Stroud's eyes opened, and she shifted on the hospital bed.

Pettit set his hat and coffee cup on a nearby tray, and held up his badge to the nurse. He nodded at the door. "I'm here to get her statement. In private."

"Look, officer, she's in no condition to—"

"Like hell." Pettit put his badge away and tapped his wristwatch. "Now I got other places to be, so you get on outta here and let me do my job."

"She's waking up from general anesthesia. You're not gonna get much outta her," the nurse proclaimed.

"We'll see."

"Fine." The nurse rolled her eyes and departed from the room, closing the door firmly behind her.

Detective Pettit took out his notebook and prodded Jennifer Stroud's arm. The young woman was still coming to, and he took note of the thick bandage wrapped around her neck. An oxygen tube snaked under her nostrils, and numerous I.V. bags hung from a pole beside her bed.

"Miss Stroud?" He waved his pen inches from her face.

Her eyelids fluttered open. "Who...who are you?"

"Detective Rudy Pettit, Williamsport P.D. I need to ask you a few questions about last night."

Jennifer raised a hand to brush a lock of hair from her eyes. She answered in a raspy voice. "I really don't wanna talk about it right now."

"I'm not givin' you an option. Now, for the record, you *are* Jennifer Stroud, twenty-one, from Wilmington, Delaware?"

"Yeah." She glanced past the detective and focused on the door. "Are my parents here yet?"

Pettit shook his head. "Just you and me. No one gets in to see you 'til we're done here. Your folks were notified, and I expect they're on their way. So..." He began to scribble on his notepad. "You left St. Luke's at what time last night?"

"I dunno." She slowly licked her parched lips. "I think...maybe... eight o'clock?"

Pettit took a sip of coffee and noted the time. "Anybody see you leave?"

Jennifer tried to sit up. Pettit made no move to help her. He tapped a foot on the tile floor as she adjusted her pillows. "I don't think so."

Pettit nodded. "And you were there to eat dinner?"

"No. To help out with serving. I don't understand what that has to do with—"

"You see the suspect *before* you went in the church?"

"No." The young girl closed her eyes and took a deliberate breath. "But... he was...he was standing at the bus stop on the sidewalk when I left."

"You sure it was the same guy?"

"Yeah." She nodded. Tears began to well in her eyes. Pettit's expression remained stoic as he waited for her to continue. "I tried to avoid eye contact or anything like that. I glanced at him once but didn't approach him."

"Can you give me a basic description, so I can get a BOL on this guy?"

"A what?"

"A BOL. Be On Lookout. You know, like an alert to all the patrol cars and officers on the street," the detective explained. "Now how 'bout that description?"

Jennifer shook her head. She grimaced and forced herself to remember the features of her attacker.

"Miss Stroud?"

"He was tall...maybe six-foot-two or three? Big shoulders. Light eyes. He was pale and had blond hair. A weird haircut, too. It was shaved on the sides but long on top. All slicked back. Like some kinda punk or skinhead or something."

"Clothes?"

"Black. His boots, jeans, and jacket were all black."

"Got it." Pettit looked up from his notes. He ignored the silent tears streaming down Jennifer's face. "So you started back towards campus and he followed you?"

"Uh-huh," she replied with a faraway gaze.

"And what happened next?"

Jennifer's lip began to tremble. "That's when he caught up with me. And he..." She trailed off and wiped her nose against her hospital gown.

"Come on, Miss Stroud." Pettit made little effort to disguise his impatience. "Don't flake out on me here. You're doin' just fine. I need you to try to remember what—"

"What if I don't want to remember?"

Pettit clenched his teeth at the girl's outburst. "That's not an option."

Jennifer stared at him through her tears. Her shoulders quaked as she failed to repress a wave of sobs. "You're treating me like *I'm* the criminal, when he's the one who attacked *me!*"

"Calm down, Miss Stroud," Pettit replied. "If I'm ever gonna catch this son of a bitch, I need information, and I need it fast. Now if you need a minute to collect yourself, that's fine. But I ain't got all day. When I get all the details from you, I'll be on my way."

"Un-fucking-believable," Jennifer muttered. She kept her eyes on Pettit and shook her head. Her initial anxiety gave way to feelings of disdain. Rudy Pettit remained unfazed.

Jennifer folded her arms across her chest. "So what else do you wanna know?" She winced with the sudden movement and lifted an unsteady hand to the wound on her throat.

"Did you do or say anything to provoke him?"

The girl grew incensed. "What are you going to ask me next? If I was wearing a mini-skirt? Like I was asking for it or something?"

"You got a mouth on you," Pettit remarked. "In this day an' age, that don't surprise me. So I'll ask you one more time. Did you do or *say* anything to provoke him?"

"I told him to back off and that I had pepper spray," she admitted.

"And he didn't stop?"

"No." Jennifer pursed her lips. "He didn't."

Pettit nodded and scratched a few lines into his notebook.

"But...but that's when things got weird," she added after a moment of reflection.

"Right," Pettit mumbled. "So let's cut to the chase. Seein' how this ends up with you on the ground bleeding from your neck, you're gonna have to be much more specific when you say *weird*."

"One minute he was behind me, then he was just... *gone.*"

"Did he duck into the hedges?"

"Let me finish," Jennifer insisted. "I turned back around and he was blocking my path. There's no way he could've gotten there without me knowing it. No way he—"

"Alright, Miss Stroud, I'm gonna need you to level with me now. Were you under the influence of any controlled substances at the time? Alcohol? Weed? Somethin' harder?"

"No!" Jennifer grasped the bed rails and cringed from the strain she'd put on her neck.

Pettit spoke as he wrote. "Tox screen."

"What?"

"Forensics is somewhere pickin' through your clothes. Lookin' for hair, fibers, and what-not. When they get done, I'm gonna have 'em test your blood for illicit substances."

"But I just told you—"

"I know what you told me. I just don't know if I believe it or not."

"But—"

"So when this guy *appeared* in front of you, he dragged you into the bushes?"

"Yeah. And he was strong. I got him in the face with pepper spray and it didn't stop him. I fought to get away, but he wouldn't let go. At first, he was trying to choke me..."

As Pettit wrote, he let out a long cough. Once he caught his breath, the detective acknowledged her. "Go on."

"Then he said something."

"What'd he say?"

"He told me not to scream. And he called me by some other name. Then he said—"

"What name?" Pettit stopped her.

"Anna." She nodded her head. "He called me Anna."

"You sure about that?" Pettit glanced up at her.

"I'll never forget it. He even pronounced it *ah-nuh,* like he was foreign or something."

"Is that when he got sexual with you?"

"What?"

"It's just between you and me, Miss Stroud."

"No. But he...he did say something else. And that's what made me scream."

96

"OK..." The detective paused.

"It wasn't perverted or anything. I mean, it was weird but it was also...sincere. Like he was trying to, I don't know, *console* me? Is that the right word?"

"You tell me, Miss Stroud," Pettit replied in a deadpan voice. "You can start by repeatin' what he said."

"He said there'd be a moment of pain, and then we'd be together. When I heard that, I screamed and he bit me." She gestured to the padded gauze around her neck.

"Is that when he tried to rape you?"

"Goddammit, no!" Jennifer shouted. "You're not listening to me! It wasn't like that. Not at all. It was...was something else. Something *worse.*"

"Worse?"

Jennifer fidgeted in the hospital bed and drew her arms close to her chest. She continued to stare past the detective at the whitewashed walls ahead.

Pettit narrowed his eyes. There was something about the girl's reaction that unsettled him.

"Look, Miss Stroud, I've investigated at least a hundred or more sexual assaults around that school. I've been on the force for thirty-odd years, and I've taken reports where perps have said odd things like this before. You know, playin' out some sick fantasy..."

"No, that wasn't it. He..."

"I mean, I get it," Pettit interrupted her. "You sure the bite wasn't accidental? You fought back, I assume? You sure he didn't just try to plant one on your neck in the heat of the moment and then—"

"Detective, listen to me." Jennifer's features grew stolid. The fear returned to her eyes. "Something was really off about this guy. The way he talked. The way he moved. It...it wasn't natural."

"What do you mean?"

Jennifer struggled to choose the right words. She pointed to her bandaged neck. "You saw what he did to me." Her voice sank to a low whisper. Tears streamed down her face. "I don't know how else to say it. He came off like...like a vampire. A *real* vampire."

"Aw, shit! And there it is," Detective Pettit tossed his pen on the bedside tray. He pointed a finger at Jennifer Stroud. "I knew it was comin'! But I sure as hell didn't think you'd believe it."

"I know what I saw. You asked me to tell you what happened and—"

"Listen, when the press crowd their way in here, you can't go tellin' them you got attacked by a goddamn vampire. I mean, everything this guy said and did sounds like a serial rapist. You know, casin' you out, followin' you, the physical abuse, and the attempt at sweet talk—"

"For the last time," Jennifer interrupted. "He never tried to rape me. He bit my neck and *drank my blood!* What part of that don't you understand?"

Pettit deposited his bulk into a bedside chair. He shook his head as the girl continued to argue her case.

"I'm telling you. This guy wasn't human. I don't even remember seeing him take a breath!"

He snatched the pen from the tray and began to write in his notebook. When he stopped writing, he rubbed his left eyebrow and looked up at the girl, who was watching his every move. Pettit made a half-hearted attempt to redirect the interrogation.

"So you're lyin' in the yard and eventually, the owner of the house comes out. Is that correct?"

"Yes."

"OK. So this guy, Joseph Wilkins, comes out on his porch with a baseball bat and runs the guy off. Then all the neighbors show up?"

"I guess so. I don't really remember."

"And now here we are," the detective muttered.

Pettit tapped his pen on the notebook for a few seconds, then reached up for his coffee. "So I gotta ask. Why vampires? You like those kinda movies?"

Jennifer shook her head. "I'm not making this up. I didn't ask for any of this!"

"Vampires..." Pettit repeated the word and sipped his cooling coffee. "Well, there's a rational explanation for all this. I've never dealt with anything like it, but there's a special breed of pervert that gets off on drinkin' human blood. Pretendin', for lack of a better word. I can't remember what the shrinks call it, but—"

"Renfield Syndrome." Jennifer cut him off.

Pettit glanced up at the girl with some surprise. "You know about this?"

"Yeah." Jennifer leaned back against her pillows. "In fact, we were discussing it in class on Thursday night."

"You a psych major?"

"No."

"Takin' a psych class for the credit requirements?"

"It was anthropology. And the professor was lecturing on vampires. It's a Tuesday-Thursday class and he'd been going on about them all week."

"I'm gonna go out on a limb here, Miss Stroud." Pettit reached up and scratched his head. "Do ya think maybe this is why you've got vampires on the brain? You're stressin' out over midterms or whatever and—"

"And I took a bite out of my own neck? Are you serious?"

"OK, so was the attacker someone from your class? Or your professor? What's the connection?"

"I don't know! I never saw this guy before."

Pettit sighed. "If I get a sketch artist in here this morning, could you give her a good idea what the perp looks like?"

"Absolutely." Jennifer crossed her arms. "I'll never forget that face."

"See, here's my concern." Pettit's pen still hovered over his notepad. "And this is just a hypothetical, but there could be more of these guys with this... this...what'd you call it?"

"Renfield Syndrome."

"Yeah, that. So I'm gonna need the name of this professor."

"Edison Raymer," she said without missing a beat. "But it wasn't him."

"He might know somethin', though." Pettit began to write. "Hell, he might even have an idea who attacked you last night. See, the State Mental Hospital over on the Peninsula brings in professors all the time as analysts an' advisors. Hell, even courtroom witnesses. So I wanna have a sit-down with this Raymer character."

"Well, he knows a lot about vampires. And he's a world-class creep himself. They call him Evil Ed around the dorms."

Pettit cracked a wry smile. "Safe to say y'all don't care for the man?"

"That's an understatement. He pulled me aside after class on Thursday about a paper I'm writing. Told me to come to his office Friday for a private conference. The whole thing freaked me out, so I didn't go. Then he sent me a bitchy e-mail that afternoon. I wouldn't be surprised if Raymer was leading some vampire cult, and that guy was one of his—"

"OK, Miss Stroud. I get the picture. I'm gonna ask you again to keep this *conjecture* outta the press. And trust me, once the word gets out, the local stations and newspapers'll be around to see you. Don't go tellin' anyone what you just said to me, 'cause it's unsubstantiated rumor, and that's probably all it'll ever be. You go tellin' those folks a vampire assaulted you, and we'll be beatin' the crackpots away with a stick down at the precinct."

"Well, you're in luck, Mr. Pettit." Jennifer sank into her pillows. "I don't really feel like talking about this anymore. I just wanna go back to sleep 'til my parents get here."

"You're gonna have to buck up and at least talk to the sketch artist. I'll make sure she's over here as soon as possible. Forensics is gonna want to talk to you as well. They may even need to do a physical examination of sorts."

"How many times do I gotta tell you I wasn't raped?" Jennifer glowered at the detective as he stood up to collect his things.

"You also told me you were attacked by a vampire. So, when forensics gets here, they'll wanna see those bruises on your wrists and forehead, and maybe take some snapshots of your neck with the bandage off." Rudy Pettit took on a grave countenance. "Now, dependin' on the results of that tox screen, I may be back to see you as well. And you know when we catch this guy, you might have to take the witness stand in his trial. I'm not about to sugarcoat it. You got a long, hard road ahead."

"But—" Jennifer Stroud sat upright in bed as Pettit shoved his notepad into his coat pocket.

He stopped at the door. "Yeah?"

"Are you going to talk to Professor Raymer about all this?"

"I reckon I'll talk to your dean first," Pettit said. "Ritter and I go way back. We played football together back in the day. I'd kinda like an unbiased opinion on this Raymer guy before I darken his doorstep." He paused to let his words sink in.

Jennifer nodded, and clutched herself tighter.

The detective donned his hat as he opened the heavy door. "You take care now, Miss Stroud." He did his best to fake sincerity. "Concentrate on gettin' better, cooperate with this investigation, and remember what I said about keepin' all this between you and me."

17

SHORTLY BEFORE LUNCHTIME, DEAN DAVID RITTER USHERED Detective Pettit into his stately office. Despite the massive teakwood desk and the nineteenth-century reproduction furnishings, the walls were covered in framed prints of a young David Ritter in his blue Williamsport jersey on the gridiron at Botetourt Field. Rudy gave the photos a once over, and his eyes wandered to a shelf laden with trophies and commemorative footballs.

"Shit, Dave." Rudy Pettit hung up his coat on a rack near the door and removed his hat. "You built quite a little shrine to yourself in here."

Ritter slapped Pettit on the back and the two old friends clasped hands. "Been a long time, Rudy. You haven't changed a bit."

"Now that's bullshit and you know it." Pettit was on his second cup of coffee, this one courtesy of the dean's administrative assistant. "We're both old, bald, and fat. You went off to college and I sat in the stands watching you, Frank, and Gary play college ball. Don't think for a second I didn't wanna be out there with ya."

Ritter leaned against his desk with a grin. "Never woulda thought otherwise. Have a seat."

"How's Phyllis?" The detective already had his notepad and ball-point pen in hand.

"Still a bitch. Spending every dime I make on interior decorators and custom landscaping." Ritter gripped the edge of the desk and stared at his friend. "So let's talk about why you're really here."

"Well, judgin' from the bags under your eyes, you were awake all night worryin' about this Jennifer Stroud thing and how it was gonna affect your administration." Rudy covered a cough, then took a sip of piping hot coffee. "Damn, that's good."

"Sumatra." Ritter nodded. "Full-bodied dark roast. Nothing but the best here."

"Just how much were you told about the crime?"

"The officer I spoke with—Alderson, I think—said Miss Stroud was on her way back from St. Luke's when she was sexually assaulted. The guy put her in the hospital, and would've done worse, but someone intervened. Then he ran off."

"There's a little more to it than that." Rudy sighed as he uncapped his pen. "I just came from the hospital. Took a statement from the Stroud girl. Now, believe it or not, the guy bit her on the goddamn neck. Then he said some strange shit to her. She's got it in her head the perp's some kinda vampire."

"That's absurd." Ritter, still nervous, managed a laugh. "Was she on drugs or something?"

"Don't know yet. I ordered a tox screen, but she's real creeped out, you know, and—"

"Let me cut to the chase, Pettit." Ritter moved to take a seat behind his desk. "About ten minutes before you showed up, I got off the phone with that girl's father. He was furious. Wanted to know how something like this could've happened to his daughter at my school, on my watch. Now, I tried to explain that she was off-campus and involved in a non-curricular activity. He just kept yelling."

"Christ." The detective rubbed his temples. "These kids ever do anything for themselves? They got no sense of responsibility. My old man woulda whipped my ass if I came home tellin' a story like that. These fuckin' parents lawyer up if little Johnny gets detention."

"I know, Rudy. I deal with this shit everyday." Ritter shifted in his desk chair. "Anyway, I need you to be blunt. I know this incident's gonna cast a pretty long shadow across this campus. So what can I do to minimize the damage?"

"I'll tell it to you straight." Pettit took another sip of coffee. "This time, I don't think you can do anything. Half that interview consisted of her goin' on about some freak professor here who's been lecturin' on vampires, callin' her aside for private chats in his office, and sendin' her nasty e-mails."

102

Ritter's breath caught in his throat. He folded his hands on his spotless desktop. "Is that so?"

"I wrote his name down. Somethin' nerdy. Hold on." Rudy flipped through his notebook. "I figured I'd come see you and find out if this guy's a fuck-up before I go an' see him myself."

Ritter's hands tightened, and his stomach knotted in anticipation.

"Got it. Anthropology department. Edison Raymer. That name ring a bell?"

Ritter's face blanched. "More like a goddamn fire alarm. That fucker's been a thorn in my side for some time now." The dean could hardly contain his excitement. "In fact, he and I are currently in the middle of a shitstorm because he mishandled a classroom incident involving another student. Josh Bailey. You know, Number 34 on the team? This bastard wants to flunk him. That happens and Bailey's GPA'll drop too low to play out the season."

"I know that kid. Talented son of a bitch. You lose him, you might as well kiss your winnin' streak goodbye."

"No shit. And all Bailey did was call him out on the content of his lectures...uh, more or less."

The detective nodded. "Now, we're gettin' a bit off subject, because I'm here about the Stroud girl."

"Right." Ritter drummed his fingers on his desk. "But you asked if he's been a problem for me, and to put it mildly–"

"He sounds like a piece of work, that's for sure." Pettit clutched a hand over his mouth and coughed once. He shook his head. "This whole vampire thing rubs me the wrong way, and the girl had some pretty unflattering things to say about this Raymer character." Pettit flipped a single page. "She says the students call him Evil Ed. So be honest. Put the campus politics aside and give me the straight dope. You think this guy might've had anything to do with this?"

"Frankly, I wouldn't put anything past Edison Raymer," Ritter answered with a stern expression.

"Well, she's got vampires on the brain, and I have a feelin' it's gonna be hittin' the press like shit against a ceilin' fan. Now all this might just be an odd coincidence, but I wanna talk to this Raymer guy. I'm gonna give him a description of the perp. See if any lightbulbs go off. Maybe there's somethin' to the Stroud girl's wild accusations, maybe not."

The two men sat in silence for a moment. Ritter's features sunk as he contemplated what the detective was implying. Ritter took a deep breath.

"So what can I do to run interference? There has to be something."

Pettit stood and loosened his necktie. "You can start by givin' me access to Edison Raymer's disciplinary records, his e-mail account, all that stuff. Now usually, I'd have to present a warrant, but right or wrong, Jennifer Stroud's about to plaster probable cause all over that guy's forehead, and by extension, your school here."

"Anything you need, buddy. It's all yours." Ritter began to breathe hard. "I just want to see this through."

"Now, he's not a suspect," Rudy warned. "I'd call him a person of interest. But when the press and the media get ahold of this, it's gonna get ugly." Pettit reached for his hat and coat. "I got other leads to pursue, so if you don't mind, just have all that information faxed to my number here."

Detective Pettit dug through his pocket and dropped a frayed business card on Ritter's desk. "What you do about this professor's your business, but if I were you, I'd deal with it quick and clean, no matter what I turn up. From my end, I'll do what I can to run some damage control."

"I can't thank you enough for coming to me first, Rudy." The dean rose to shake his old teammate's hand. "Hopefully, we can catch up under better circumstances soon."

18

"KATELYN, YOUR PAPER'S DEFINITELY SALVAGEABLE," Professor Upham reassured the student seated by her desk. "In your revision, however, I want you to think more about the Bishop's character. Do you think he was genuinely religious?"

The mousy girl shook her head. She clutched the strap of her backpack in one hand and the red-inked paper in the other. "Not really," Katelyn admitted. "No. He seemed more concerned with how nice his monument was gonna be than his reward in heaven."

"Right," Veronica replied. "And what evidence is there in the poem to prove that?"

"Well, it's a really long poem." Katelyn sighed in frustration "And Browning just goes on about all this random stuff."

"First of all, it's not Browning. It's the Bishop," Veronica corrected. "Browning's the author. He's the man behind the poem, pulling the strings. He's using the Bishop as a mouthpiece. That's how the dramatic monologue works. The reader is to decode the message that's hidden between the lines. So you're looking for clues to support the idea that the Bishop's religious convictions are flawed. He's a hypocrite. That's your thesis statement."

Katelyn nodded, yet only caught about a third of her professor's advice. She cleared her throat and hoped to regain her professor's confidence. "I mean, there's a lot of evidence. Like the part about the Lapish Lazoolee or whatever and the Madonna's breast. That's kinda blasphemous. And I guess that part about the Jew's head was pretty anti-Semitic."

"I'd say so. You're definitely on the right track, Katelyn." Veronica glanced at the clock on the wall. "Look, you'll be fine. You know what you're doing now, so I'll see you in class on Wednesday. Let's say your revision's due by Friday? That way you can try to relax and take your time with it." Veronica smiled and hoped to put the girl at ease.

Katelyn thanked her and skirted out of Veronica's office. The professor jostled her wireless mouse to activate her idle desktop. She maximized a browser window, hoping to find a new message from Edison.

Veronica hadn't heard from Raymer since she left his townhouse late Saturday morning. After their argument, she was too distraught for company and cancelled her plans with Janice and Peter. She had spent the rest of the afternoon cursing herself for how she reacted to Edison's preoccupation with the Aston case.

You just had to push him, didn't you?

The two professors had talked into the wee hours of Saturday morning. They reviewed the Aston tapes but continued to bicker over the details of the case. Like in the early days of their affair, she hoped their heated debate would lead to lovemaking. Yet the more she challenged Edison's view, the more he pulled away until he completely shut down and went to bed.

And that's when things really went to hell.

Veronica leaned back in her chair. As she chewed absent-mindedly on her pen, her thoughts returned to the Aston boy's case. The boy's confession was unsettling, but she was still convinced he was somehow responsible for the disturbances. There was no question that the Aston case offered extraordinary evidence of paranormal phenomena.

But vampires?

A knock on the doorframe roused Veronica from contemplation. She glanced up from her desk to see Mary Elizabeth Coffey, the first-year American Lit professor, standing in the doorway. Professor Coffey's face was pale and her expression grave. "Veronica. Did you see the news?"

"No?" she blinked in confusion. "I've been teaching all day. What's going on?"

The assistant professor lowered her voice. "You live out near St. Luke's, right?"

"Yeah. I can see the bell tower from my bedroom window. It's just a few blocks over. Why?"

"A student was walking home from St. Luke's last night and got attacked. Jennifer Stroud. It's all over campus."

"I heard some sirens last night, but didn't see anything on the news this morning. What exactly—"

"The police chief was just on TV a few minutes ago to declare a county-wide manhunt for the suspect." Mary gestured to Veronica's flat screen monitor. "Check your faculty account. Dean Ritter just issued a statement and a mandatory curfew for all resident students."

"What happened to her?"

"She was yanked into somebody's yard and the guy tried to rape her or something. Bit her on the neck. Fortunately, a neighbor came outside with a baseball bat and scared the bastard off. Channel 3 interviewed him before the chief came on. I don't—"

"She was bitten?" Veronica's eyes grew wide.

"Yep," the younger professor confirmed. "Pretty sure they said it was on her neck. Kinda like—"

"A vampire?" Veronica dropped her hands in her lap.

"I was tryin' not to think about it that way, but yeah."

Veronica fell silent. Sensing her colleague's discomfort, Professor Coffey attempted to ease the tension.

"Probably some Halloween prank. Still, it's a little weird."

"I don't know what to say," Veronica replied in a low voice. "I mean, I had Jennifer in a freshman survey course. But I don't remember her too well."

"I know, right?" Mary Elizabeth ran her fingers through her hair. "She's in the hospital and hasn't given a statement to the press. She probably won't, either."

Vampire. The word sent a shudder down her spine.

When Edison hears about this, it's all over.

He'll flip the fuck out.

Oh Jesus.

"Mary, what did...what did the guy look like," Veronica asked. "The suspect? Did they say?"

Professor Coffey could see the fear in Veronica's eyes.

"Um, they said he was tall. Blond hair." The younger woman strained to recall more details. "I don't know. The sketch is all over the news. Christ, I've been walking to work every day. I'm afraid to go home tonight with this psycho on the loose. Would you mind if I catch a ride with you?"

Veronica rose from her desk on unsteady legs as Mary Elizabeth continued to prattle on. "I live over in off-campus housing. It's on your way. I really don't feel safe and...hey, are you listening?"

"What?"

"Can you drive me home?" The assistant professor looked wounded.

"Oh, yeah, sure. I have a class at three, so meet me in the faculty lounge at four-thirty."

"Thanks," she replied. "I'll see you then."

As Professor Coffey wandered away, Veronica picked up the phone and called Edison's extension. There was no answer from his office. She tried his cell, but it went directly to voicemail.

"Hey, Ed. It's me," she spoke into the receiver. "I'm sorry about Saturday, but I need you to call me as soon as possible. I'm dead serious. As soon as you get this message. We need to talk. God, I hope you don't delete this. Uh, I should be home by five o'clock. I know you don't watch the news, but you may want to...look, just call me, OK?"

19

EDISON RAYMER LEANED AGAINST THE SLEEK EXTERIOR OF his jet-black SUV. With a sense of foreboding, he looked over the decrepit exterior of the rotting split-level house.

He'd already spent the better part of the day driving around Richmond. His first stop was an occult bookstore called Luther's Inkwell in the Fan District. As he was checking out, he asked the store owner for the address of a metalworker who could provide four silver ingots. The owner was nonplussed, but wrote down the address for Tredegar Metallurgy. When asked what sort of ritual he was planning with so much silver, the professor didn't offer an explanation.

After walking out with an armload of used hardbacks, Raymer ate lunch at a Greek restaurant on Broad Street. He then drove to the metalworker's shop using his onboard GPS for guidance. There, he exchanged a large sum of cash for the foot-long silver cylinders—each about the diameter of a silver dollar.

On his way home, he took a remote exit off I-295 and drove a mile to visit an abandoned suburb called Dutch Gap Trace. The neighborhood was in shambles. Most of the modest middle-class homes, built in the early 1980s, had been boarded up and left long ago. The winding streets had led Raymer to the end of a *cul de sac,* where he parked and spent a few minutes behind the wheel to gather his wits.

The Aston house was the only derelict home in the suburb surrounded by a perimeter fence. A rusted metal sign which read NO TRESSPASSING hung from the chain links. Beyond the waist-high grass inside the fence, the clapboard structure rose toward the sky. On first glance, there was nothing imposing or terrifying about the place. It looked like every other house in the old neighborhood.

But the place had acquired a reputation over the years.

The tall fence and padlocked gate hadn't kept the local delinquents out. Along the perimeter, there were holes big enough for a man to slide through. The exterior of the house had been tagged by graffiti artists. Most had been content to scrawl their names or aliases, but there were quite a few inverted crosses and pentagrams. Most of the windows had been smashed, and beer bottles glistened among clumps of switchgrass in the afternoon sun.

A slight breeze rustled the dead leaves in the gutter. Raymer stepped over the curb to approach the fence. He straightened his necktie and smoothed his argyle sweater. The well-dressed man dug a hand into his trouser pocket as a strong gust of wind blew along the empty street. Leaves and old newspaper scraps eddied around him as he pried open the cut in the fence and slipped into the Aston's yard.

As he strolled towards the crumbling brick porch, he wondered if the Astons ever sent for their belongings. Raymer stopped when he reached the curving walkway to the porch steps. He recalled the day Oliver Aston carried his son down the driveway in a mad dash. The boy's mother was already waiting in the station wagon.

He followed the overgrown path to the house. As he mounted the front steps, Raymer braced himself for a confrontation with any squatters or truant teenagers that might be lurking inside. He pressed his ear to the door, but heard neither voices nor movement within. The professor stretched out a gloved hand and tried the tarnished handle of the front door. As he expected, it was locked.

With a vacant glance to the street behind him, Raymer lowered his shoulder and rammed the front door. The door splintered, but did not yield. On his second attempt, the professor kicked in the door with all his might. A cloud of dust eddied upward after the door crashed to the floor. Raymer cautiously stepped into the foyer of the deserted house.

As his eyes adjusted to the darker atmosphere within, Raymer was assailed with the acrid stench of urine and stale beer. The air itself was heavy and musty, and debris was scattered everywhere. Edison surveyed the scene as memories of Jeffrey Aston—and the elusive vampire who haunted him—returned in full force.

You saw my friend, didn't you?

Jeffrey's trembling voice on the telephone replayed in his mind. As frightened as the boy was, Raymer also detected a feeling of relief. As if the boy finally had confirmation through what Raymer saw.

He probably did think this thing was his friend at first. She took advantage of him. Used her appearance to charm him or coax him. That's how she got into their house.

Raymer balled his hands into tight fists. A chill ran down his spine, accompanied by a rush of adrenaline. He was captivated by a single thought—one that simultaneously thrilled and terrified him.

What if she's still here?

But Raymer could sense that he was alone in the house. His pulse slowed to its normal pace and his tense muscles relaxed. With a slow and deliberate step, he began to walk from one room to the next.

The Astons hadn't sent for their furniture. Everything that had been there in '86 was still in the house. The living room couch had been cut to shreds, the remaining pictures on the walls were smashed, and the television's screen was shattered. As Raymer walked along the first floor, he recalled specific moments of the field study.

The dining room table had at least fifty names carved onto its surface, and was covered in cigarette butts. Yet Edison remembered sitting there across from Maggie Aston with a microphone in hand as she wept about her son dying upstairs.

In the kitchen, Raymer pressed a flat palm on the exact spot where Oliver had left the phone number. The same one Raymer called after seeing the figure in the mirror. Using the wall for balance, he kicked his way through the trash left in the front hall and stood at the bottom of the staircase.

The risers disappeared into a dark hallway above. A sinking feeling overcame him as he ascended the stairs.

In the long hallway on the second floor, he stopped to peer into Jeffrey Aston's room. The hospital bed they'd rented for him in his final days had never been returned. The mattress was bare and stained. An I.V. pole lay overturned on the floor. Raymer prowled around the room with the light from a single, shattered window to guide his footsteps.

Right here.

He shifted his position to stand with his knees pressed against the bed's footboard.

This is where she stood every night. Waiting for him to open his eyes so he'd know what she was doing to him.

Trepidation gave way to outrage. At that moment, Edison Raymer wanted to confront the monster that killed Jeffrey Aston and stake it to the hardwood floor. He yearned to watch her burn to ashes as the sunlight poured through the dusty, cracked windowpanes.

He left the boy's room and traversed the hall to the master bedroom. Raymer stood before the mirror where he'd seen the vampire.

"Show yourself," he whispered. "I know you're still out there. And I know what you fear."

Raymer traced the mirror's frame with his stare. Along the top, some clever teenager had carved the admonition SAY BLOODY MARY x 3. As if in a dream, he slowly reached out and drew a hand across the dusty reflective surface.

A swath of the mirror now clean, he could see the broken bedframe behind him, and the dark corner where the girl in the yellow dress lurked many years ago. Raymer stood transfixed, as if the vampire might appear at any moment.

The vibration of his cell phone in his pocket roused him from his trance. He made no move to see who it was.

He dropped his hands to his sides and slumped his shoulders. Without a hint of ceremony, Raymer left the house, crossed the yard, and slipped through the rift in the fence.

The drive home was a blur. He forgot about Richmond, the books he'd bought, and his expensive lunch. Even the silver rods—which he planned to grind into stakes—had faded from his memory. Although he was behind the wheel of his SUV on the busy interstate, part of him still stood at that mirror.

Waiting.

Instinct propelled Raymer along the narrow streets of Williamsport. Eventually, he pulled into his driveway as the sun set in the west. The resolute professor staggered out of his vehicle, ignored the mail in the letterbox, and fumbled for his house key. In a daze, he managed to unlock the front door of his townhome.

Maybe you followed me here and I'll see you tonight?

In the foyer, Raymer brushed by the side table. There were six messages on his phone, but he pressed the delete button twice and the counter reset to zero. He stopped to look up his own staircase at the waiting shadows.

Consider this your invitation.

I'm going to kill you. Maybe not tonight, or tomorrow night. But I will find you. And when I do, I'll drive a silver stake through your ribcage and pierce your fucking heart.

Any hints of fear were gone. Edison Raymer felt nothing but anger. It had remained with him like an unwelcome visitor since he stood at the foot of Jeffrey Aston's bed.

Riser by riser, he made his way up the stairs and was enveloped by the dark hallway. When he entered his bedroom, Raymer kicked off his shoes and sat on the edge of the mattress. He leaned forward to stare into a mirror, which he had recently repositioned to emulate the arrangement of furniture in the Aston's master bedroom.

I'm waiting.

20

ANTHONY FOWLER, THE NIGHT MANAGER OF SERENITY Springs Elder Care, placed his elbows on the messy desk and leaned forward. "This behavior is highly irregular for you, Mr. Bartsch." He rubbed his temples and tried to avoid the piercing gaze of the orderly sitting across from him. "So, I need to know exactly what happened back there in Mr. Hodges' room."

"The patient was in violation of the lights-out rule again. He had his television on at a disruptive volume." Matthias leaned against the backrest. "I went in and simply turned it off, prompting his fit. When I—"

"Let's stick to procedure, shall we?" Fowler interrupted. "We refer to our guests as residents. I need that to become second nature to you. Anyway, you entered his room shortly after ten?"

"Yes."

"And let me guess, he was watching his Monday night football game?"

"I didn't pay attention to what was on the screen. I just turned off his TV."

"Don't you Europeans call soccer football?" Fowler laughed at his own remark.

"I'm an American citizen, sir." Matthias corrected him with a cold stare.

"Sorry." Fowler took a quick sip of lukewarm coffee. "Please continue."

"When I turned off the TV, he pointed his finger at me and started to shout. He claimed he had seen me on the television. I tried to calm him down and explain the rules."

"Wait, why did he say you were on the television?"

"I don't know. Perhaps when I turned it off, he saw my reflection and got mixed up. Mr. Hodges' dementia has been getting worse."

"In the future, I want you to simply let Mr. Hodges watch his television. Close his door if the other residents complain."

"Why is he exempt from the lights-out rule?"

Anthony leaned forward and spoke in a hushed tone. "His son has given us a considerable amount of money in donations, and continues to do so. Yes, the rules should apply to everyone, but the last thing I want to do is anger Mr. Hodges' son. We need every cent we can get. You understand?"

"I believe I do." Matthias glared back in disgust.

"Now, another matter. One of the residents complained about you earlier tonight. He said you were a little rough and impatient with him. Is there something going on I need to know about?"

"I haven't been feeling well." Matthias pointed across Fowler's desk at an open file. "You should have a record that I went home early on Thursday night." Matthias retracted his hand to brace his chin. He tapped his prominent cheekbone. "Amy signed me out."

Matthias repressed a shudder as he remembered what had happened in Mr. Hodges' room. He thought it best not to mention that, instead of football, the dementia patient had the channel on the ten o'clock news. He saw a police sketch on TV, along with information about a regional manhunt for a possible serial rapist. It was clear that the girl Matthias attacked had been questioned, and now a crude representation of his face and distinctive haircut was all over the local channels. Probably the internet as well. And it would certainly be on the front page of the local paper in the morning.

Matthias shook off his concerns and returned his attention to his boss.

"Yeah." Fowler looked over his notes. "That's all here. But I stressed this during indoc and I'll reiterate it again. If you're feeling sick, you must stay home until you get better. We can't afford to risk some sort of viral outbreak among the residents, you know."

Fowler sighed.

"You're a good worker. Hell, you do most of the heavy lifting around here without bitching and moaning like the other orderlies your age. I've never had to write you up for an infraction before, so I think I'll let this pass with a warning. I suggest you go home and don't come back until a doctor gives you the all-clear."

Matthias remained stony and unmoved. The manager continued in monotone.

"Anyway, you haven't accrued much sick leave, but we can advance you a few days. Just go home and sleep it off. Take a few days." Fowler closed the folder.

Matthias stood and yanked the chair back. He stopped at the door. "If you don't mind me asking, what happened to Jared Parker tonight?"

Fowler glanced up. "Oh, that." He sighed and clasped his hands around his coffee mug. "We had to let him go."

"May I ask why?"

"Hell," Fowler conceded. "I'm sure the rumors are already flying, anyway."

Matthias nodded as his supervisor continued.

"We inventoried all scheduled substances in the dispensary this morning. Without going into detail, there was a slight discrepancy. A couple hours ago, we started checking outgoing bags and lockers." Fowler stood and braced himself on his desk. "We found narcotics in Parker's backpack. He'd left it in the lunchroom during the search." Fowler removed his horn-rimmed glasses and shook his head. "I guess he thought we wouldn't look there. Of course, the kid is saying he was framed. This kinda thing's happened before. I even had a pharmacist a few years back who had a Dilaudid habit. Caught him skimming. Glad we nipped that one in the bud."

Fowler paused as Matthias continued to glare at him.

"Now I have to make a report to the DEA and fill out more goddamn paperwork..." he trailed off. "Anyway, Parker must've been doing this for a while. We didn't recover the Propofol he took, and I have no idea what he'd want with two vials of potassium chloride."

"Maybe he was looking to kill off a rival dealer," Matthias suggested.

Before Anthony Fowler could speak, the vampire stepped into the hallway and closed the door behind him. Reeling, he braced himself against the wall.

What have I done?

21

THE SIXTY-FOUR YEAR-OLD MAN RECLINED ON HIS COUCH with a cold beer in hand. He flipped through channels on his widescreen TV with a universal remote.

"Ain't nothin' good to watch this time of night," he said aloud to no one. He often walked around the house talking to himself, as his wife had passed away from breast cancer years ago.

The man's mind wandered back to the prospect of retirement from the shipyard. How the next three months as a shop foreman seemed to stretch out before him. His gaze wandered to the mantelpiece of his fireplace.

Two triangular flags sat side by side in presentation boxes. The first had been presented to his mother after his father's death for distinguished service in World War II. The second had also been presented to his mother at the Suffolk Cemetery in honor of his brother, a Marine who'd been killed somewhere in the wreckage of Hue City during the Tet Offensive. They'd buried an empty casket that day as there were no remains to send home after the landmine exploded. His brother's faded picture—a striking young man in dress blues and a white cap—sat on the mantel next to the flag.

Mounted above the fireplace were the man's own decorations. He'd been an army combat photographer in Vietnam, and was in basic at Fort Benning when his mother called to report his brother's death.

The man flipped through the channels one last time.

If I don't find nothin' this time around, I'm off to bed.

He stopped on Channel 10, just as the late night news was beginning. The aging man rose and wandered into the kitchen, where he dug through the refrigerator for an ice cold beer.

From the adjoining room, he heard the strains of the evening crime report.

When he returned to the couch, he snatched up the remote and adjusted the volume. "...police in Williamsport have been searching for any leads concerning the attempted rape and abduction of a twenty-one year-old college student. A county-wide manhunt was issued earlier today and has been extended to all adjoining municipalities in the Tidewater area."

The man reached for his beer and grasped the bottle by the neck. He took a drink as the reporter continued.

"Police have released a composite sketch of the suspect from last night's brutal sexual assault. If you have any information pertaining to the case, or have seen the suspect-at-large, please call the Williamsport Crime Line."

When he saw the sketch, the man dropped the beer bottle onto the carpet at his feet. The reporter moved on to report a double homicide in Hampton, but the man's pulse rushed in his ears and his hands began to shake. He removed a pen and a crossword puzzle book, and on the back cover, he jotted down the number while it remained fresh in his memory.

He hit the mute button on the remote and reached for the telephone. The veteran checked the number as he punched it in, placed the receiver to his ear, and waited for the operator to pick up.

"Williamsport Police Department Crime Line. Sergeant Falkner speaking. How can I help you?"

"I, uh...have some information. About a crime in your area." The man could barely contain himself. His heart raced, and his bladder felt slack.

"And which case is this in relation to?"

"The girl. The college student," he added, swallowing hard before he spoke again. "I've seen the suspect before, but I'm afraid you ain't gonna believe me if I tell you when."

There was a pause on the other end of the line. The policeman sounded as though he was reading from an instruction book. "Sir, please remain calm. Before I take down any information pertaining to the suspect, can I please have your first and last name? If, for your personal safety, you wish to remain anonymous we can—"

"No need for that bullshit. Name's Luttrell. Fenton Luttrell, Jr."

22

A T HALF-PAST EIGHT O'CLOCK TUESDAY MORNING, EDISON Raymer's phone began to ring. The professor had prepared a Spartan breakfast of plain, unbuttered toast and two scrambled egg whites. He had just glanced at the front page of the Williamsport Herald when he rose to pick up the slim-line telephone.

"Edison? Dean Ritter. I'd like to see you in my office as soon as possible."

"I was under the impression we were meeting this afternoon," Raymer responded. "Can it wait?"

"This is a matter of some urgency," the dean insisted.

"OK." Raymer glanced at his unfinished breakfast. "I'll be there in fifteen minutes."

He hung up the phone before Ritter could reply. Raymer folded the morning paper in half, then scraped his eggs into the garbage disposal. Without delay, he retrieved his cap, coat, and gloves from the hall closet. After dressing for the windy autumn morning, the professor left his house on foot.

He walked across the narrow street and down the sidewalk toward the edge of campus. Within a matter of minutes, he entered the administrative offices of Williamsport College. The receptionist at the front desk looked up at him with a slight grin.

"Can I help you?" She broke eye contact with the professor to arrange a stack of departmental printouts.

"I'm here to see Dean Ritter."

"Oh yes." The middle-aged woman nodded. "He's expecting you."

Raymer opened the ornate wooden door to the dean's office to find David Ritter standing beside his meticulously organized desk. As Raymer nodded to the dean, he removed his cap and gloves. "You wanted to see me?" He took a free hand to unwrap his scarf.

"Please, Ed. Have a seat." Ritter held out an open palm. The dean closed the door and returned to his desk.

Raymer sat down on the couch. With a steady gaze and a flat tone, he broke the silence. "So, regarding Mr. Bailey's withdrawal request, I thought I made it clear on Friday—"

"I've already handled that matter." Ritter pressed his lips together in a smug expression. "Mr. Bailey will be allowed to withdraw from your course. His punishment for his insensitive remark is the loss of three credit hours. I feel that's severe enough." With both hands, the dean rubbed his balding head. "This meeting has nothing to do with Joshua Bailey."

"If that's the case..." Raymer trailed off and twisted his gloves in anticipation. "What's this all about, David?"

Dean Ritter adjusted the chair behind his teakwood desk. "I'd like to hear what *you* think it's about, Edison."

"Frankly, sir, I have no clue."

Ritter placed his elbows on his desk and folded his hands beneath his chin. "Christ, have you been hiding under a rock the past twenty-four hours?"

"Pardon me?" Raymer scowled. "I don't follow."

"Surely you're aware that one of your students was sexually assaulted on Sunday night."

"What? No. Who was it?"

"Jennifer Stroud."

Raymer took a deep, cleansing breath. "I'm sorry to hear about Miss Stroud. I was out of town yesterday. I just sat down to read the morning paper when you called. I don't watch the evening news. Or any television for that matter. So—"

"Your whereabouts yesterday are none of my concern," Ritter interrupted. "But it couldn't hurt for you to start preparing an alibi."

"And what exactly is that supposed to mean?"

"It's not my place to divulge the details. I'll leave that to the police." Ritter sneered.

"The police?" Raymer furrowed his brow.

"Yesterday morning, I received a visit from the detective who took the Stroud girl's official statement. Let's just say your name came up in the course of our conversation."

"Dammit, David. In what context? I'm tired of playing guessing games with you!"

"You know, I'd have written it off if you weren't somehow at the center of it all." Ritter tilted his chair. "I don't know how else to put this, but Jennifer Stroud was bitten on the neck during her attack. She was convinced that the, uh, rapist or whatever, was drinking her blood. When asked where she got that idea, she mentioned something quite similar to Mr. Bailey's claim. Namely, that you've been lecturing on vampires and vampirism in your anthropology class."

"So?" Raymer tightened his grip on his leather gloves. "If you review my syllabus, the subject of vampires is clearly outlined as part of the curriculum for my American folklore course."

"I'm not finished, Ed." Ritter clenched his jaw. "After speaking to Detective Pettit—who I assume will be paying you a visit in the very near future—several alarming facts were brought to my attention. As I said, the Stroud girl referred to you in the official statement. Her remarks were very unflattering. She told the investigator that you've taken her aside and requested private meetings with her—"

"Now wait just a goddamn minute!" Raymer snapped. "I offered to come in on *my time* to hold a paper conference with her so I could help her revise her research proposal. A meeting she decided wasn't worth attending. So if she's—"

"First of all, Edison, it's not *your* time. It's the department's time. You're required by the university to hold regular office hours throughout the week. Which brings me to my next point. Stroud also told the police you reacted in a very tactless manner when she didn't show up for this conference. She said that you sent her a rather unprofessional e-mail, which she interpreted as a threat."

"That's ludicrous. I've never threatened a student."

"You and I both know that *that's* not true." Ritter laughed and leveled his gaze at the professor. "Anyway, I had the head of information services pull the e-mail from the exchange server. Two minutes later, I read it over myself. You know damned well what you wrote was tactless, not to mention arrogant."

"Where's the e-mail now?"

"It's been turned over to the Williamsport Police Department, along with a record of your prior infractions. I gave them every single complaint brought against you by students *and* faculty. Let me just say it was a very thick file."

"You know," Raymer said. "I can explain how this entire incident, as it were, could be easily misconstrued by—"

"I didn't ask for an explanation. That ship has sailed. It's my duty to minimize any and all negative attention to this institution, and that's a job I take seriously. Now, all prior issues aside, we have an assault victim that's mentioned your name to the police, along with some mumbo-jumbo about vampires. Nonsense she heard in *your* class." He picked up a piece of paper, slid on a pair of reading glasses, and scanned over the printout. "Along with vampires, your students have been subjected to lectures on spiritualism, demonic possession, hauntings, witches..." he paused for a moment to catch his breath. "Haitian Voodoo, Native American peyote rituals, and shamanic curses. I presume they were tested on all this idiocy?"

"Of course. Again, it's on the syllabus, which your administration approved."

"Dr. Raymer, I don't think you understand my point. So let me make myself crystal clear." The dean peered over the rims of his reading glasses. "You're now a person of interest in a police investigation which has the entire campus on lockdown. This school—and, by extension, my administration—is now under the proverbial microscope. And it's all thanks to some pervert and your horror-movie bullshit, Edison!"

"This is absurd," Raymer shot back. "A student gets attacked, and because she has an axe to grind with me due to *her* poor performance in my class, I'm now a suspect?"

"I never said that," Ritter corrected. "You're a person of interest."

"It doesn't matter. You've spearheaded a witch-hunt against me for personal reasons, and, by some irony of fate, Jennifer Stroud's statement gave you the ammunition you needed to rake me over the coals." Raymer sneered at his boss. "Of course, I wouldn't expect anything less from you."

"I don't know what's more despicable here," Ritter said. "That you continue to circumvent the rules and regulations as a professor at my school? Or that you've brainwashed this girl and refuse to take any responsibility for your actions whatsoever?"

"If I were to seek legal counsel on this matter, you wouldn't be sitting there with that smug expression on your face."

"I don't give a good goddamn! Let's face it, Edison. You're through. Enrollment for your classes has been on a steady decline. I've had students in my office practically once a week, begging to be withdrawn or reassigned to another professor. And after that incident with the McCoy girl, you know full well why you haven't been assigned any graduate seminars."

"What in hell are you talking about, Ritter?" Raymer was taken aback by the dean's unexpected reference to his former graduate assistant.

"You know *exactly* what I'm talking about! Sending that girl off to the lion's den to interview some—"

"She was perfectly capable of handling herself. For Christ's sake, David, it was her idea!"

"It was irresponsible and you know it! This is a liberal arts college. This isn't fucking Quantico!"

"I won't apologize for my role in Miss McCoy's research. If I hadn't pushed her, she wouldn't have recognized her potential. And I'm proud to say she's gone on to distinguish herself as a respectable scholar and already has a few publications under her belt."

"Well, that's more than I can say for you, Edison. You haven't produced a memorable article in years. All your past accomplishments have been marred by scandal and derision. Your arrogance has not only turned the student body against you, but the entire faculty as well. You have been repeatedly disrespectful and dismissive to myself and the board of directors."

"Are you done, Mister Ritter? Because frankly, I don't think that you, or the police, or Jennifer Stroud, or Josh Bailey has anything remotely resembling a case against me. In fact, if you were to get off your lazy ass and audit one of my lectures, you'd see that I do my job with expertise and acumen. And with a level of *professionalism* that others in my department sorely lack."

"Right." The dean laughed, pleased that he had finally struck a nerve in the obstinate man sitting before him. "You can go on feeling superior. Feeling persecuted. Feeling like you're a martyr for your own misguided convictions or whatever other delusions of grandeur you've built up around yourself. But I've already filed a request to have your tenure revoked. Professor Donaldson will be taking over your classes for the rest of the semester, and from here on out, you'll be suspended with pay until a formal hearing occurs in mid-November."

Raymer sat in silence. He was no longer stunned by Ritter's proclamations. He was completely resigned to his fate.

"In all my years, I've never seen such impertinence or arrogance in an educator," the dean remarked. "And for someone who claims to be so smart and superior to everyone else, you sure did fuck up this time, Ed."

From across the desk, Ritter leveled a finger at Raymer.

"You don't deserve to be a college professor. With a record like this, I doubt you'll ever find an institution that's foolish or desperate enough to hire you. Hopefully, for the sake of future students, you'll never work in academia again. And there's nothing else to it."

The dean rose from his chair and walked toward his office door. He could barely contain his elation.

"Now, to take a cue from your own method of dealing with confrontation and differences of opinion, I'd ask you to kindly gather your things and get out of my office."

Raymer slid his gloves over his hands, wrapped his scarf around his neck in a loose coil, and propped his ivy cap on his head. Before walking out the door, he turned to face the dean. He glared at the man over the rims of his spectacles.

"You can expect to be hearing from my lawyer before the close of the week." Raymer spoke in a collected and even tone.

"I look forward to it." Ritter withstood the challenge and gestured one last time toward his office door.

Edison Raymer left the administration building without further incident. He darted across the campus greensward, indifferent to the churning winds that tore at his scarf. He crossed the busy street and bounded onto the opposite sidewalk. With a decisive step, he walked home, his eyes fixed forward and his head held high.

23

ETECTIVE PETTIT LEANED AGAINST AN UNMARKED
police cruiser, shifted his aching feet, and drained the last
drop of coffee from a Styrofoam cup. With the brim of his
hat cocked over his eyes, he stole a quick glance to his right
and tossed the empty cup into the boxwood hedge across the sidewalk.
The wind picked up and carried the empty vessel into the yard beyond. It
tumbled across the grass, which was shorn flat.

"Hey!" A voice called out from his left. "That's my yard!"

Pettit turned as a well-dressed, slender black man approached him at
an effortless clip.

"Sorry 'bout that, pal." The detective began to dig through his coat
pocket as he looked the stranger in the eyes. "You Edison Raymer?"

"I am." Raymer slowed his pace and stopped a few feet from the plain-
clothes investigator. "And you must be the detective that just got me fired."

"Not sure I can take all the credit for that." Pettit held up his badge.
"Rudy Pettit. Williamsport P.D. Here to see you about—"

"Jennifer Stroud." Raymer finished his sentence as he fished his keychain
from his trousers. "I was expecting you. Come on in," the professor beckoned.
"And, if you don't mind, would you gather your litter from my front lawn?"

Pettit froze, still holding out his silver badge, and shook his head in
disbelief. Raymer was already bounding up the walkway as the detective
forced himself to move. He followed and made a short detour to pick up
the cup. As Pettit bent down, he watched the man unlock his front door.

"So Ritter just shit-canned you?"

"About twenty minutes ago," Raymer answered. "Technically, my tenure was revoked and I've been suspended with pay. I won't get shit-canned, as you so eloquently put it, until I sit before the board of directors in November."

"Tough break." Pettit held a hand against his back as he stood upright and winced in pain. "But like I said, not the reason for my visit."

"Ritter told me I was a person of interest," Raymer mentioned as he held the door open for the aging detective. Pettit slipped past him into the foyer. "Can you translate that from police jargon into the Queen's English?"

"It boils down to someone involved in a criminal investigation who hasn't been accused of or charged with a crime." Pettit and Raymer squared off in the foyer. Both men doffed their hats.

"So is this the moment where you ask me what I was doing Sunday night?" Raymer's breath caught in his throat for a second. "That is when this incident with Miss Stroud occurred?"

"I figured you heard all the gory details by now. If not from the news, then from Dave Ritter."

"No, he stuck to the subject of my inevitable termination." Raymer unwound his scarf and draped it over the hook on his coat rack. "Go ahead and have a seat in the living room." He reached out and took the crumpled coffee cup from Pettit's hand. "And I'll throw this in the rubbish bin for you."

As Raymer darted into the kitchen, Pettit squinted at the framed Marsden prints adorning the living room walls. "It's funny," he called out. "You ain't comin' across like a man who just got axed from a well-payin' job."

Raymer appeared in the wide entryway between the foyer and the den. "Maybe it hasn't sunk in yet. However, I'm not in the least surprised by what happened this morning. It was a long time coming."

"Wow." Pettit moved towards a crowded bookshelf and read over some of the titles. "You really are into this vampire stuff, Edison. Mind if I call you that? Edison?"

"Fine by me."

"Well, listen here, Ed." Pettit ran his finger down the spine of a book that caught his interest. "Yesterday I had a flurry of questions lined up to ask, you know, about the crime and Jennifer Stroud's statement? But I slept on it last night and realized that girl was probably talkin' out her ass. I figure she got all bent outta shape over some academic shit between the two of you, and she decided to drag you down with some pervert we can't manage to find."

126

Before Raymer could speak, the detective continued.

"We're lookin' for a foreign guy, white, mid-to-late twenties. Blond hair, blue eyes. So I can't help but feel that standin' here talkin' to you is pretty much a waste of time, no?"

Raymer removed his spectacles to polish the lenses on the hem of his sweater. "Well, that's one way to put it."

"Look." Pettit waved his hands. "I wasn't tryin' to come off as racist or nothin', I just meant you don't fit the description of the suspect."

"I get it." Raymer narrowed his gaze. "So why are you here then?"

"Good question, 'cause I should be out lookin' for this guy before the trail goes cold. I mean, we ran his info through our database of sex offenders. Came back with nothin'." Pettit gazed at one of the black and white photographs on the wall. "There was this one case a few years back. Some kids disappeared in the woods along the river. Case is closed now 'cause we couldn't find the sick fuck who took 'em. I don't wanna see that happen here again. With that in mind, I thought there might be some credence to somethin' the Stroud girl said in her statement. So that's where you come in."

"How can I help?"

"She says she got attacked by a real vampire. Even claimed the guy basically *teleported* around her. You believe that shit?"

"Vampires are a myth," Raymer lied. "Now granted, there are some individuals out there who *think* they are vampires."

"Yeah, she brought up somethin' called Renfield Syndrome? Said she heard the term in your class. So I thought maybe you'd done some consulting work at the State Mental Hospital or somethin' and could help me narrow some shit down."

"I'm not a psychologist, Detective Pettit." Raymer slid his glasses back on and adjusted the frames. "Although I was once involved in a rather unique field investigation."

"But you know the particulars of this disease, right? At least enough to rule it out?"

"I've read an exhaustive amount on the subject, yes."

Pettit dug through his pockets. He pulled out a small collection of photos and handed them to Raymer.

"Now these pics were taken by our forensics team. That's Jennifer Stroud's neck wound. If you look close, you can see the teeth marks."

Raymer flipped through each of the gruesome photographs.

"They had to take skin from her inner thigh to fix what had been torn off and chewed up. Pretty nasty shit, eh?"

"One could say that." Raymer returned the photos to the detective. "So what do you want to know?"

"What you just saw there, is that a common M.O. for these so-called real-life vampires?"

"No." Raymer's answer was curt and emphatic. "The majority of individuals afflicted with Renfield Syndrome limit themselves to auto-vampirism or cutting. Most are content with just drinking their own blood. And like a potential serial killer testing the waters, some occasionally move on to animals. But I can count on two hands the number of documented cases where sufferers attacked a person and did damage like you just showed me."

"You serious?" Pettit raised a brow. "So I can rule that out?"

"Look." Raymer crossed his arms. "In this day and age, an individual with this rare illness can usually find a willing partner. There are websites, chatrooms, even clubs dedicated to this sort of thing. These people usually participate in consensual bloodletting, which has its risks, but it's less messy and probably more fulfilling sexually."

"Right." Pettit eyed the professor with suspicion. "Now you mentioned clubs. You mean like a nightclub? Like that place with all those freaks down by the docks?"

"Possibly." Raymer shrugged. "But these kind of people don't want attention. They rarely wander from their own underground circles. Furthermore, they're not going to wear outlandish make-up or clothing because they prefer to blend in with regular folks like you and me. From what little I've heard about that club you mentioned, I don't think that's a place these people would go."

"Fair enough," Pettit replied. "Now you don't think we're looking at some one-in-a-million kinda scenario, do you? I mean, you said these people *usually* have consensual partners. And they *usually* don't attack or kill people. But what if—"

"Well, detective, there are always variables..."

"OK, so are we lookin' at some kinda gang or cult? Should I be expecting to see more of this shit in the future?"

"No," Raymer said. "I don't think you've got anything to worry about. In fact, I'm not entirely convinced that there's anything particularly vampiric about this crime in the first place."

"An' why's that?"

"In my opinion, Miss Stroud was attacked by a sex offender. A very *inefficient* one at that."

"How you figure?"

"Well, think about it." Raymer clasped his hands behind his back. "I'll bet this was the first time this guy ever attempted anything like this. In his mind, it was all foreplay. Maybe he never meant to cause this kind of damage? When he bit her neck, she fought back or simply jerked her head, and the result was a life-threatening avulsion. That's my impression."

"Well, you *are* the expert here." Pettit raised a curious brow.

"Most people don't seem to appreciate my expertise, or so I've found," Raymer admitted. "However, I am curious about one thing. What prompted the attacker to stop?"

"Oh." Pettit took a second to collect his thoughts. "Some guy came outta his house with a baseball bat an' ran him off."

"Did anyone else get a good look at him?"

"No one but Jennifer Stroud. She provided the sketch that we've been circulating through the local media."

Raymer leaned back on his heels for a moment. "I haven't seen it."

"It's in today's paper." Pettit gave Raymer an odd look. "You ain't seen it yet? We put it out to four local stations yesterday afternoon."

"Yesterday I was up in Richmond until dusk, and I generally avoid television altogether." Raymer leaned forward again. "As for the morning paper, I was sitting down to read it when I got called on the carpet about an hour ago."

Pettit nodded. "Alright, so in your expert opinion, I ain't gonna have to arm my beat cops with crosses and holy water, am I?"

"You're not dealing with a vampire. Real or otherwise." Raymer forced a smile. "For example, Miss Stroud's assailant didn't turn into a bat and fly away from the scene of the crime. I'm sure he got in a vehicle and drove off. Did anybody get a make, model, or license plate number?"

"Shit, if they had, we'd have him in lockup by now." Pettit shifted his weight. "Nobody saw nothin', though the homeowner and other witnesses heard a car door slam and tires peelin' outta there. That tall hedgerow around the yard blocked their view of the street, I guess."

"And Jennifer Stroud couldn't tell you anything else when you took her statement? Did the man say anything to her, perhaps?"

"Well yeah, there was one thing." Pettit hesitated. "But as I'm sure you know, Professor Raymer, I'm not really at liberty to discuss the particulars of this case."

"I assure you, Detective Pettit. Anything you tell me will remain purely confidential. You have my word."

"Aw, hell!" Pettit sighed and scratched his head. He began to thumb through his notebook. "The guy called her someone else's name. He called her Anne...or Annie? No. Wait. Here it is. *Anna.* That was it. The Stroud girl said that's how she could tell he was some kinda foreigner, 'cause of the way he pronounced it."

"I see," Raymer noted. "That *is* odd. So maybe this man was laboring under some kind of psychotic delusion? In any case, the chances of Jennifer's attacker being a victim of Renfield Syndrome are very unlikely. Did she say anything else?"

"Well, like I said before. She was all traumatized and got pretty defensive. But I've seen that a thousand times in these assault cases." Pettit straightened his posture. "To be on the safe side, I had forensics run a tox screen on her after she brought up the vampire thing, and there were small traces of alcohol in her bloodstream."

"Unreliable testimony, maybe?" Raymer tensed his shoulders and let his hands drop to his sides.

"Could be." Pettit shrugged. "I suppose time will tell. Well listen, Ed, I've taken up enough of your time. I best be on my way."

"Not a problem, detective." Raymer braced himself against a bookshelf. "I hope I was helpful. And I hope you find this guy."

"Thanks, me too. In the meantime, I should prolly take your name and number. Just in case we need any more information from you down the road a-ways."

Raymer withdrew a card from his wallet, and flipped it over to the blank side. "Can I borrow your pen?"

Pettit slid out his ball-point and gave it to Raymer, who jotted down his contact information on the back of the card. "Ignore the stuff on the front." He pointed at the Williamsport College logo. "As of now, it's null and void."

"I suppose so." Pettit donned his hat. "But a smart guy like you? I'm sure you'll be back to work in no time."

Raymer ignored the detective's comment as Pettit flung open the front door.

"Take care, Edison."

"You as well."

In a matter of minutes, Pettit was in his cruiser, lurching back and forth as he tried to exit the parallel parking spot. Raymer watched through the kitchen window until the detective managed to free his vehicle and drive away.

As if nothing had happened since breakfast, Edison Raymer took his seat at the kitchen table and opened the Williamsport Herald. On the front page was the crude composite sketch of Jennifer Stroud's attacker.

He poked the drawing with his index finger.

"Finally."

24

ABOUT AN HOUR AFTER DETECTIVE PETTIT'S DEPARTURE, Veronica Upham barged into Edison Raymer's foyer. Her eyes were swollen from crying as she threw her arms around the professor. "It's all over campus." She hugged him tightly.

Raymer stood still, unsure of how to respond to the woman and her outpouring of emotion.

She leaned back and pressed her palms against his chest. "So what're you gonna do, Ed?"

"Nothing right now. But sometime next week I'm going to tender my resignation. I'm not going to let Ritter have the satisfaction of calling me before the Board in November."

"Wait, what? You're just gonna let them..." She trailed off as fresh tears formed in her eyes. "Aren't you going to fight this?"

"No, Veronica. I'm not."

Raymer led her into the living room and stood by his liquor cabinet. "Can I fix you a drink?"

"Don't you care about any of this, Edison? Ritter's gonna win!"

"First of all, you need to get ahold of yourself. I don't need another migraine. *Especially* after this past weekend."

Veronica grasped a bottle of scotch by the neck and palmed a tumbler. She uncorked the bottle, slammed the tumbler down on a side table, and filled the glass with single malt whiskey. "This is your life, Edison Raymer! Your goddamn livelihood."

"What makes you think academia was, is, or ever will be my life's work?"

132

"You've been a professor for twenty-five years!"

"And I've hated every goddamn minute of it." Raymer crossed his arms and glared at her.

Veronica rolled her eyes. "Can you just let your guard down for one minute? Can you ever show some...some humility? You fucked up, Ed. They fucked you. Whatever. It's OK to be angry. It's OK to be worried about—"

"I'm not angry. Nor am I worried," Raymer answered. "David Ritter did me an immense favor today. He freed me from my obligations to that insipid institution. I'm done wasting my time. No more politics, no more compromises, and no more ass-kissing."

"Yeah, and no more money." Veronica drained the glass of whiskey. She winced as the alcohol burned her throat. "You've lost your mind, and all I can do is sit here and watch you crash and burn. You'll be lucky to get part-time work as an adjunct at a community college with the charges Ritter's levied against you."

"Veronica, enough already. Pour yourself another drink and have a seat."

"Don't patronize me, Edison." She wanted to cry again, but fought back the tears. "I came over here to talk some sense into you. To light a fire under your ass and get you to fight this suspension. But you just stand there like a goddamn statue and tell me how your profession isn't your life's work."

"Let me put it into terms that might be familiar to you. My profession's been nothing but an albatross around my neck." Raymer's eyes gleamed in the late afternoon light. "My life's work has yet to happen. But now, it looks as if I might get a chance to pick up where I left off in 1986."

"Oh, for Christ's sake, Edison. Don't even say it! Please tell me you're joking."

"The joke's over, Veronica. And after twenty-five years of playing court jester for a bunch of pretentious imbeciles and students that grow more dim-witted each semester, I finally have a course to follow. A purpose."

"As someone who obviously cares for you more than you care for yourself, I think you owe me an explanation. I understand where the bitterness is coming from, and if I could stop teaching and just read and write and...and travel, don't you think I would? But this is the real world."

Raymer left the room and walked into the foyer.

"So now you're just gonna walk away? I ask you to stop being vague and you just shut down. Goddammit, I've put up with this long enough, and if you don't come back and tell me exactly what you're going on about, I swear you and I are finished. You hear me? I've reached my breaking point with you!"

When Raymer returned to the parlor, he held up the front page of the newspaper, which he'd folded in half. He punctuated his words with fury as he pointed to the police sketch. "Right. There."

"What? I don't—"

"Of course you don't understand. When have you ever had to test the courage of your convictions, Veronica? You profess these grandiose occult beliefs, but in the end, you're a tourist. You've never had to face something so evil and so unclean that the very foundation of your reality falls to pieces. Nor have you ever had to pick up those pieces and muster enough courage to fight back."

"I don't know what to say to you. I just don't."

"Why is it so hard for you? This is all fun and games when you down a few glasses of Merlot, don your grandmother's lace and pearls, and start scribbling inane messages from some wandering spirit! What the hell do you think you're tapping into?"

"But I—"

"I'll tell you. *You* are not tapping into anything. You're just bored, Veronica. You play the role of eccentric Victorian professor flawlessly, with your Browning quotes, your tea-leaves, and Tarot cards. But you're an amateur. A fake. And a bore."

She stood with her mouth open in shock.

"The only reason I've tolerated you this long is because deep down, I know you want to believe."

"Believe in what, Edison?"

"Listen to me now, because I'm only going to tell you this once. If you won't stand *with* me, you stand *against* me."

"You're starting to fucking scare me."

Raymer pressed his finger to the police sketch again. "It's my belief that this so-called *man* is, in fact, a vampire. I can't make it any plainer. Even for you. I think we can track it down. I think we can trace it back to its hiding place. And I think we can kill it."

Veronica was mortified by the frenzied conviction of her colleague. She studied him in disbelief, half-blinded by her tears.

"Say something!" Raymer roared. Veronica flinched as he took a threatening step toward her. His shadow loomed tall and menacing across the hardwood floor.

"I...I don't know what you want me to say."

"I want you to say what you think."

"I think...I think..." Veronica stopped herself before she would regret her words. She knew that a far less direct approach was required of her.

"If vampires are real, I think you're foolish to want to kill them." She raised her eyes and tried to look at him. Her words and voice seemed foreign to her, as if these moments in Edison Raymer's living room were the remnants of some bizarre dream. "What makes you think you even can kill them? You are, of course, a stubborn son of a bitch. But if there is such a thing as vampires, and even if only half of the myths and legends concerning them are true, how are you going to be any match for *them?*"

"They have their weaknesses," Raymer replied. "Quite a few, actually."

"OK." She nodded thoughtfully. "But how many of 'em are out there? Why haven't they made themselves known?"

"The reason we're having this conversation, Veronica, is that a few of them *have* made themselves known. Don't you see? That's the point!"

"But think about it, Ed," she cautioned. "If they do exist, do you understand what this could mean? Can you imagine the impact this would have on society? On theology? *History?* Shouldn't we *study* them? Try to understand them?"

"I already understand them." Raymer balled his hands into tight fists. "And there's nothing more to study. There's only predator and prey, and it's my intention to turn the tables. With the execution of that singular pursuit, my life's work will be fulfilled."

"Jesus Christ," Veronica muttered.

"So..." Raymer nodded at Veronica's half-empty glass of whiskey, "I want you to finish your drink and then I want you to go home. I don't want a repeat of Friday night. Take some time and sleep on it. Come back tomorrow with a clear head, and be ready to tell me where you stand."

"Edison, I don't need to sleep on anything. All I want is for you to—"

"All I *want* is some peace and quiet," Raymer cut her off. "Now, you came barging in here, uninvited, and after the day I just had, I'd like to be alone. Can you understand that?"

"That's all you're ever gonna be, Edison," Veronica warned him. "Alone."

"So be it," he replied and pointed to the foyer. "Now get your coat."

25

THE PAPER SHREDDER WAS GRINDING SO LOUDLY THAT DE-
tective Rudy Pettit didn't notice Sergeant Falkner enter his office.
The uniformed policeman leaned over the cluttered desk and slapped
a sticky note on Pettit's computer monitor. The detective jumped
with a start, and flipped the switch on the industrial-strength shredder.

"Christ on a crutch! Didn't your mama teach you how to knock, sergeant?"

"I did, sir." Falkner, a tow-headed twenty-something, blushed in earnest.
"That thing was so loud and you were so busy, that—"

"What's this shit?" Pettit snatched the note from his flat-screen monitor
and skimmed it over. "Who's Amy Harvey?"

"Sir, you're probably aware I work the Crime Line from eleven to seven
on weeknights."

"Yeah, what of it?" Pettit picked up a folder and rifled through it. He
pored over the yellowed pages paper-clipped inside. Tim Falkner didn't
answer as he clasped his hands behind his back and stood at attention.

"Sergeant, you see that calendar on the wall?"

"Yes, sir."

"In three weeks, my retirement begins and I can finally say fuck you to
Chief D'Amato and all you goons." He reached up and stroked his balding
head. "Until then, I've gotta get rid of thirty years of reports that I've already
entered into this goddamn computer. So unless you have something to say
about this note you brought me, then get walkin'. Comprende?"

"Well, detective." Falkner's cheeks grew redder. "The calls have been
pouring in since we showed the suspect's composite on the Monday night

news. E-mails, too. But there were two callers in particular that I think you might be interested in. Amy Harvey's one of 'em."

Pettit glanced up from the file. "Alright, have a seat, kid. What'd this Harvey woman say?"

"She's a nurse over at Serenity Springs. You know, the eldercare place. She recognized the suspect. Now, most of the calls I've gotten have either been vague, or been lunatics pretending to be the guy. None of 'em gave a name. She did, and I wrote it under her number there."

Pettit craned his neck to read the note. He struggled with the pronunciation. "Matthias Bartsch?"

"Yeah. He's been working there as a part-time orderly for a little under a month. Night shift. And, like the internal BOL says, he's a tall blond foreign guy with an odd haircut."

"Sounds like our boy. She give an age range?"

"I didn't ask."

"Now, sergeant," Pettit began. He leaned over the stack of folders to get a clearer view of Falkner. "I gave you a specific set of instructions. Next time you get a legit caller, you need to ask them everything, you hear?"

"Yes, sir. But—"

"What, you got somethin' else on this guy?" Pettit picked up his coffee mug and blew on the piping hot liquid. "I mean, he sounds like our suspect."

Falkner nodded. "Ms. Harvey said that every night this Matthias guy's been on the wards, one of the old folks died. Nothing remarkable. No evidence of foul play. They just passed away quietly."

"Prolly just coincidence. I mean, people go in there and never come out. Ain't that the idea?" Pettit closed the file on his desk and placed it with the others. "Anyway, it sounds legit to me, so I'll send a black-and-white over to scope the place out. Get some presence there to give things a look-see. He might even be dumb enough to show up for work, right?"

"Well, there are some other pieces to this puzzle that just don't add up." Falkner clasped his hands together. "I called the manager over there and asked for Bartsch's info."

Pettit nodded. "Good show, kid."

"Not really," Falkner said. "The address, social, and phone number they had on file for this guy were all bogus. No luck with bank or payroll records, credit cards, cell phone records. Nothin'. You'd think a guy bein' careful enough to hide his identity wouldn't try to assault a woman on her way—"

137

"I'll talk to Frank McCain. See if he can cover the nursing home for a couple days."

"Uh, sir," Falkner piped up in a timid voice. "McCain's working that trailer fire. You know, the murder-suicide case? Wouldn't it be better if you just went over there yourself?"

"Don't come into my office and tell me how to do my job, kid." Rudy Pettit shook his head, then took a sip of coffee. "Now, you said there's two callers I need to look into. Tell me 'bout the second one."

"Well, sir, you're gonna hear all about that one straight from the horse's mouth. The guy's sitting downstairs in the lobby with a sleeping bag under his arm. Said he drove over here from Poquoson. Made a point to tell everyone that he used up all his personal leave from his job at some shipyard, and that he was gonna camp out on the street by the station house until we let him up to see someone of importance. Those were his exact words, more or less."

"The guy sounds like a goddamn nut job. Kick him the fuck out. If he sets up camp, cite him for loitering."

"Listen, detective," Falkner pled. "You gotta talk to this guy. He's called the Crime Line seventeen times. He won't leave us alone. This character's not gonna let a citation stop him. He claims over and over that he has crucial information about the suspect. But he won't share any of it over the phone."

"Of course not." Pettit exhaled and drummed his fingers against the edge of his desk. "What the hell. Send him up. I'll be done with him in less than five minutes. You can count on that."

After Pettit waved the desk sergeant away, he flipped open another folder full of old notes and began to pull the staples so they'd go through the shredder. He didn't bother to take out his pen or notebook. Instead, Rudy Pettit glanced at the wall calendar and the X's he had marked off. As his mind wandered to thoughts of selling his home, divorcing his wife, buying a fishing boat, and heading for the Florida Keys, a loud knock resounded on the doorframe.

"Come in," Pettit managed. "Take a seat, please."

When he snapped to, a wiry man about his own age with a full head of shock-white hair sat down in the chair across from his desk. He was wearing a denim jacket, black jeans, and cowboy boots. The man studied Pettit with a suspicious and cantankerous glare.

"So I hear you been crank-callin' my Crime Line," Pettit said. "Let me tell ya a few things about—"

"Don't you people ever stand up and shake a man's hand anymore? Show a little civility, for chrissakes!"

Pettit leaned back in his chair. "Well, pardon me! Did I catch your name?"

"No, 'cause I didn't give it to you, did I?" The man glowered with disdain. "The name's Fenton Luttrell, Jr. Most people call me Junior, but since I don't know you, it's Mr. Luttrell."

"OK, Mr. Luttrell." Pettit took another sip of coffee. "I've done nothin' all week but chase down dead leads about this case. So pardon me for not gettin' up." He held out his hand. "Now, go ahead and tell me what you know about this suspect. And don't forget all the top secret information you couldn't tell the desk sergeant on the Crime Line."

Luttrell raised his voice. "The son of a bitch you're lookin' for killed my father. Killed him while I stood and watched." Luttrell's eyes grew wild. "And you wanna know the worst part, officer? I couldn't do a damned thing to stop him."

Pettit leaned across his messy desk. "You live in Poquoson? That's outta my jurisdiction. Did you file a police report on the guy?"

"Oh, yeah." Luttrell nodded. "The cops came. They dusted for prints and took photographs. The whole nine yards."

Pettit raised a brow. "If that's true, we'd have his prints on file, and they'd turn up in our database from the crime scenes." Pettit's words were met with a disapproving glance from Junior Luttrell. "Jesus Christ, did ya get the guy's name at least? And what was his beef with your father?"

"He said his name was Bart or something. Sounded like he was from overseas. As for what he had against my Pa, I got no idea. Fella just walked into our house, pulled out a Colt .45 pistol, and shot him point-blank."

"You said you couldn't stop him. Did he injure you?"

"He never laid a finger on me," Luttrell replied.

"Then why in the blue fuck didn't you try to stop him?"

Luttrell gripped the armrests of the chair as his face flushed. "Let me ask you somethin'..." He paused to read the nameplate on the cluttered desk. "...Detective Pettit! If you was seven years old and some guy muscled his way into your house, shot your Pa, then dropped to his hands and knees and sucked out every last drop of his blood right there in front of you, what would *you* have done about it?"

Rudy Pettit was taken aback. "Hold on there, chief. Did you say..." He pressed his fingers against his temples, which had already begun to throb. "You...I mean...*when* did this happen?"

"1957."

The detective slipped his right hand over his mouth and began to scratch his chin. He exhaled heavily through his fingers. All the while, he fought to maintain his composure.

"Now, I know how it sounds," Luttrell continued. "And judgin' by that look on your face I reckon you're thinkin' I should be up at the state mental hospital for tellin' a story like this. But I swear to Christ it's the truth."

Pettit shook his head, then looked down at the frayed notebook pages on his desk.

"Look here," Junior added. "I never forgot that man's face. When that picture showed up on the tube the other night, I thought I was seein' a ghost. But that ain't no ghost. It's somethin' worse."

Pettit had reached his breaking point. "Mr. Luttrell, I don't know what kinda shit you're tryin' to pull here this mornin'. But I can tell you one thing, an' it's the gods' honest truth. I don't appreciate you comin' in here and wastin' my time with this cock-and-bull story. It's an insult to me, the department, and the victim of this assault. Now, get your ass up from that chair and see yourself out!"

Luttrell slammed a fist down on the desk. He stood and hunched forward, so the two men were face-to-face. "Listen here, Pettit," he snarled. "This ain't how you're supposed to treat a Vietnam veteran!"

"I don't give a rat's ass if you impaled Ho Chi Minh on the end of your granddaddy's bayonet. Crazy is crazy. An' I don't fuckin' discriminate."

"If you think I'm lyin' 'bout this you can go fuck yourself! Call the police over at Poquoson and have 'em look back through their records!"

Pettit was unmoved. "If you're threatenin' me, Mr. Luttrell, not only are you way outta line, you're about two steps away from lockup."

Luttrell sank back into the chair. His eyes brimmed with spiteful tears. "I've spent my whole life waitin' for someone to catch that son of a bitch. So I ain't leavin' here 'til you bastards call those Keystone Cops out my way and start swappin' stories. Got it?"

"Alright." Pettit was flabbergasted. "I've heard just about every line of bullshit under the sun in my thirty years on the force. And cases like this bring out nut-jobs in droves. But there's somethin' about your story that strikes me as odd." The detective cradled his coffee cup. "You said the man's name was Bart?"

"Mister, you got your head screwed on backwards if you think *that's* odd when I just told you the man drank my father's blood!"

"Yeah, maybe," Pettit said. "But I got another tip that I'm lookin' into, so I'm gonna ask you a simple question. D'you think, if you can remember back to 1957—"

"I ain't senile, detective."

"Let me finish, dammit. If you can recall, do you think he could have said his name was Bartsch, and not Bart?"

"He coulda said that," Junior confirmed. "Why you askin'? You know somethin' 'bout him?"

"We got a lead," Pettit said coldly. "But I'm not at liberty to say from who. Now I'll ask you again. Could he have said Bartsch, and not Bart? B-A-R-T-S-C-H?"

"I guess so." Junior shrugged and made a mental note of the spelling. "Couldn't half understand the bastard due to that weird accent of his, even though he spoke real good English. Better than most around here anyway." Luttrell stared at the filing cabinets behind the detective. "He said he was in the Battle of the Bulge with my Pa the day he won his Silver Star. But when he got to talkin' to my Pa, he acted like he had been fightin' for the wrong side, if ya catch my drift. Like he was some pissed-off kraut who wanted some get-back for what my father did in '44. So yeah," Luttrell nodded. "Bartsch it is. Sounds about right to me."

Rudy Pettit paused and took a moment to gather his thoughts. Luttrell sat on the edge of the chair, waiting for the detective's reaction. Pettit stifled a cough, then cleared his throat. "If I was to ask your opinion about Bartsch, what's the first thing that comes to mind if ya had to describe him?"

"A goddamn vampire! And like I suspected all my life, he's still around here somewhere!"

Pettit pushed his chair back and tore open his desk drawer. As he began to dig for something, Luttrell continued.

"You gotta understand, I been scared shitless he'd find me my whole life. Hell, if you'd believe it, I re-upped twice in 'Nam 'cause I felt safer *in country* than in my own hometown!"

141

His features livid, Pettit removed Edison Raymer's card from the drawer, leaned forward as far as his flabby gut would allow, and slammed the card on the edge of the desk in front of Junior Luttrell.

"And that's the last straw. I'm sick of all this vampire bullshit!" Pettit gestured to the card. "Pick up that card, Luttrell."

Rendered mute by the detective's outburst, Junior did as he was told.

"This Raymer guy's a certified vampire expert. I'm just a dumb-shit police detective looking for a pervert. You wanna talk about vampires, you call that guy. Not me." Pettit wheezed for a moment. "In fact, if you ever call the Crime Line again, or show your face at this station house, you're gonna be charged with filin' a false police report. It'll be a class six felony charge, too. The last thing I'll do before I retire at the end of the month is make sure the desk sergeants know who you are. So don't even think about comin' back here in a few weeks and tryin' this shit again."

Pettit bolted out of his chair to point at the door. "Now get the fuck outta my office!"

Fenton Luttrell, Jr. rose to his feet and walked to the door. When he reached the threshold, he turned Raymer's business card over in his hands once, and spun around on a heel. "So you ain't gonna call Poquoson and get the story from them?"

"Go!" Pettit kicked the paper shredder, then pushed the files off his desk. The folders hit the floor, scattering papers and photographs under his feet. "Get out!"

Luttrell stepped into the hallway, and stormed toward the elevators. Rudy Pettit's heart pounded in his chest. He sat down in his chair, breathing heavy, and fought to regain some semblance of composure. The enraged detective pulled out a handkerchief and mopped up some of the coffee he'd spilled. As he flipped the damp cloth over in his hands, he turned his attention to the evergreen tree outside his office window.

"What the fuck did that guy have to gain by coming in here with a story like that?"

In his mind, the detective replayed the entire conversation. He decided to place a call to Poquoson. After a brief conversation with the department's secretary and a short time on hold, he confirmed that a Fenton Luttrell *had* been murdered in the mid-summer of 1957.

"Pretty grim stuff," the secretary said.

Pettit requested the case report, a scan of the fingerprints, and an itemized list of the evidence found at the crime scene. The secretary confirmed that the files would arrive by fax within the hour.

In the meantime, the detective stayed busy. He requested a copy of Amy Harvey's statement from the desk sergeant and read over the report several times. The nurse's story seemed rock-solid.

After an interminable wait—which involved two additional cups of coffee and numerous trips to the men's room down the hall—Pettit's fax machine squealed to life.

Rudy skimmed the pages one by one as they emerged in the printout tray. When the transmission ceased, he sorted through the case files of Fenton Luttrell's murder in July of 1957.

It was just as Junior had described. Fenton Luttrell, Sr. had been shot in the stomach with a .45 caliber bullet. The coroner had determined that Luttrell's death was the result of the gunshot wound, but was also careful to document a series of violent lacerations on the victim's throat. The man's larynx had been torn out and the coroner noted an unusual amount of blood loss. The report suggested that the wounds in the victim's throat occurred posthumously after the family dog attacked the corpse. The gunshot, on the other hand, was attributed to an unknown assailant who persuaded the Luttrell boys to let him into the house so he could rob it. The details Junior and his older brother provided back in 1957 matched Amy Harvey's description of Matthias Bartsch to the letter.

Rudy Pettit paused for a moment. Once again, his heart began to race. "The old bastard was tellin' the truth," he muttered aloud.

The detective looked at the papers on his desk, then glanced at the wall calendar. He thought of Jennifer Stroud and the reputation of Dean David Ritter. He envisioned the inevitable shitstorm that would occur if the press got word of what he had just discovered. Paperwork. Press conferences. Nosy reporters. Exclusive interviews. Expert testimony by Professor Edison Raymer.

Bela Lugosi, live at eleven.

Without further hesitation, the detective began to feed the Luttrell files into the electric paper shredder. By the time he left for lunch, Rudy Pettit had convinced himself that Fenton Lutrell, Jr. had never visited his office.

26

RAYMER HAD ALREADY GONE SIX ROUNDS WITH THE PUNCH-ing bag in his basement when the doorbell rang upstairs. He jammed a boxing glove under his bare armpit and wrenched it off. Before he removed the other, he thumbed the pause button on his stopwatch.

Once he dropped the gloves on the floor, he moved to the foot of the basement stairs. "Door's open, Veronica!" he bellowed in a near-breathless voice. "I'll be up in a second!"

The front door slammed shut with enough force to rattle the inner walls of the townhouse.

She must've come here to give me a piece of her mind.

Well, it's best she bails out now before things jump off.

I don't need any distractions.

Raymer donned a tight-fitting tank top and mounted the stairs. He made his way through the kitchen, and sensed something wasn't quite right. In the foyer, a man wearing black jeans over snakeskin cowboy boots leaned against the wall. The stranger doffed his coat as Raymer entered the foyer.

"Who the hell are you and what are you doing in my house?"

"Look here. I'm only half-deaf, but I swore I heard somebody say to come on in," the man replied. "The goddamn door was unlocked. Even in a high-class neighborhood like this, it ain't a good habit to—"

"You'd better tell me who you are, because right now, you're an intruder in the wrong house." Raymer raised his fists. The professor's muscular arms tensed up, and he was ready to start throwing punches again.

144

The white-haired man held up a familiar card. "Put'cher damn fists down. I ain't here to rob the place. You *are* Edison Raymer, right?"

"Where'd you get that card?" Raymer narrowed his eyes. "That looks like the one I gave to a detective yesterday."

"You'd be right on that count. Man's name was Petty or Pettit, I think. Goddamn son of a bitch ran me off and told me to come see you."

"About what?"

"Vampires. One in particular." The sixty-something man was spry and lean. He thrust out a hand as a gesture of good faith. Raymer eased up and gave him a firm handshake. "Fenton Luttrell, Jr. Pleased to make your acquaintance."

"Dr. Edison Raymer," the professor replied with a wary tone. "Is this Detective Pettit's idea of a joke?"

"Fuck that imbecile. I tried to give him info on the bastard who attacked that girl. He didn't believe what I told him, so he ran me off."

Raymer crossed his arms, still ready to make a defensive move if necessary. "What exactly did you tell him?"

"That the so-called man he's lookin' for is a stone-cold killer."

"So why'd he send you to me? I still don't follow."

"Would you believe me if I told you that suspect of theirs ain't a man at all? He may've been once, but he ain't no more. He killed my father when I was a boy. In 1957."

A slight smile tugged at Raymer's lips. "I believe you'd better come in, have a seat, and tell me everything you know."

The two men sat opposite one another in the professor's living room. As Fenton Luttrell, Jr. recounted the details of his father's murder, Raymer listened with rapt attention. When the older man finished, he stood up and gave Luttrell the once-over.

"Now before you start shootin' all kinda holes in my story, I swear on all that's holy that what I just told you is the truth."

"You'll get no argument from me." Raymer nodded once. "The evidence speaks for itself. When he met you and your brother on the path, he was already manipulating you."

"Whaddya mean?"

"He led you to the house for a reason. According to the legends, a vampire cannot enter one's home unless invited. So he coerced the two of you to let him in."

"I'll be damned." Junior shook his head. "You mean to tell me that if we'd just run him off, my Pa wouldn't—"

"You can't be blamed for your actions. There was no way you could've done anything different."

"Well, my brother stood up to him." Luttrell squirmed in the leather chair. "I was the one cowerin' the whole time."

"And yet your brother still let him in, no?"

"Yeah." Junior stared at the wall. His voice was wistful. "Yeah, he did."

"So when you saw him next, you just heard a gunshot. He was on top of your father, tearing into his neck?"

"That's what I saw. And like I told that detective, I never forgot that fucker's face. Not even after—"

The front door swung open and closed with a *bang*. Veronica Upham charged into the foyer, glanced around, and locked eyes with Raymer. She shook her head as she pushed her way into the living room. "I guess I must be a glutton for punishment, especially after the way you treated me yesterday. So I made my decision and..."

She trailed off as she noticed the stranger in the parlor. He stood and smoothed out his dusty black jeans. Veronica turned her attention back to her colleague. "Can I speak with you in private?" Her hazel eyes twitched back and forth as she awaited his answer.

"Veronica Upham, this is Fenton Luttrell, Jr." He held an open palm in the man's direction.

She turned to face him, and cocked her head. In a cordial tone, she addressed Raymer's guest. "It's a pleasure to meet you, Mr. Luttrell."

"You can call me Junior."

"OK. If you don't mind, Junior, I need to speak to Dr. Raymer in the kitchen." She enunciated every word, as if speaking to a child.

"Fine with me." Junior shrugged, then looked at Raymer. "I'll just wait right here 'til y'all come back."

Edison turned to face Veronica. "That won't be necessary, Mr. Luttrell. In fact, I think Dr. Upham needs to hear everything you have to say before she makes her...*decision.*"

"Goddamn you, Edison."

Veronica made for the liquor cabinet, and Raymer grasped her arm gently. "Lay off the alcohol. I want you clear-headed when you hear this man's story."

She flung herself onto the couch, folded her arms, and glowered at Raymer. "So what's this all about?"

"Mr. Luttrell—"

"Please, it's Junior. Mr. Luttrell was my father."

Raymer adjusted his glasses. "OK, Junior, let me catch you up to speed on a quarrel Dr. Upham and I have been having for quite some time now. She says that vampires don't exist. I, of course, took up a contrary position based on personal experience and extensive study."

Veronica leaned to one side and flipped a lock of auburn hair out of her eyes. "Junior, your new acquaintance here is certain that vampires are not only real, but that they walk among us. And I'm certain he's out of his fucking mind."

"Wait a minute." Junior raised a hand. "If you bet this man money on the matter, you better pay him now. I don't believe vampires exist, ma'am. I *know* they do."

"Oh, this is just great!" Veronica clasped her hands in her lap. "The lunatics have multiplied."

"You think I'm crazy? I've heard that all my life. But I saw what I saw. And it's haunted me since 1957."

"Edison, can you explain what this man is doing here?"

"Junior Luttrell was referred to me by Detective Rudy Pettit of the Williamsport Police Department. It seems they're not interested in entertaining the very likely possibility that Jennifer Stroud's attacker was a vampire." Before Veronica could interject, he cut her off. "Not a lunatic with Renfield Syndrome, but a German soldier who died in Belgium circa 1944 and has somehow returned."

"Just listen to yourselves." Veronica gnashed her teeth and looked up at the ceiling. "Fucking *Nazi* vampires? You're both—"

"Insane?" Junior finished her sentence. "Dr. Upham, I was seven years old when I first saw that...that *thing*. His name is Bartsch. Somethin' like that. He tricked my brother and me into invitin' him into our house. Bastard came to take revenge on my father for something that musta happened between 'em in the war. When he was still a man, I guess. At first, he shot my Pa. Point blank. Right in the stomach. But then he bit into his neck and drained him dry. All I could do was stand and watch."

Veronica lowered her head. She was surprised by the degree of conviction in Luttrell's voice. She felt a twinge of guilt for prejudging him, but wasn't convinced his story was true.

"Ever since then—hell, even when I was sleepin' in a foxhole on patrol in Vietnam—I saw that dead thing's face," Luttrell continued. "Christ, I still see him in my dreams sometimes. Even if I tried not to think about him. And then, on Monday night, I saw that face on the television."

"What, you mean the police sketch?" Veronica's attention shifted back to Edison. His expression hadn't changed the entire time.

"That's right, ma'am. I knew then and there it was the same fucker that killed my Pa."

"Ed, do you believe him?" she asked. "Do you honestly believe this story has anything to do with what happened to Jennifer Stroud?"

"Every word. The evidence is too clear to be refuted. The vampire's appearance, his accent, his mannerisms, even the method of attack corresponds with the information I've gleaned about the assault on Sunday night."

Veronica could only shake her head in disbelief. "Is there even an iota of doubt or skepticism left in you, Dr. Raymer? Do you still even think of yourself as a scientist? Because, frankly, I don't see a—"

"You do understand that when I hunt this vampire and bring him down—"

"We!" Junior interrupted. "You ain't goin' out to kill that son of a bitch without me. I swear to Christ I wanna see that fucker burn!"

"OK, when *we* hunt this vampire, I plan to take several precautions. We'll adhere to scientific methodology whenever possible, and we'll document everything for posterity."

"Hell, I can't wait to put a few rounds in that bastard!" Junior exclaimed.

"I'm sorry, you're planning on shooting him?" Veronica eyed the excitable man with bemusement.

"Fuck yeah! Aren't you supposed to take these things down with silver bullets? I've got a reloadin' setup in my basement and can make some in varyin' calibers."

"Are you two planning to kill a vampire or a werewolf?" Veronica rolled her eyes. "I hate to say it but I think you're both batshit crazy. I've never—"

"Silver represents the chastity of Artemis, the Moon Goddess. As the moon holds power over the vampire, so does silver," Raymer noted. "Come on, Veronica, you know this. Nothing silver will kill a vampire, but it should stun or paralyze it. A silver stake to the heart, for example, binds the vampire to the ground beneath it. Likewise, bullets cast of—"

"Can you even *make* bullets out of silver?"

"Sure you can," Junior said. "Though it has a higher melting point than lead and it's gonna have inferior ballistic properties, 'cause silver's a harder metal than lead. Hell, it's denser than steel. I can just fill the hollows of a few JHP rounds with melted silver, and we're all set."

"So, *Junior*, where did you get your degree in chemistry?" Veronica asked.

"I've been workin' at the goddamn shipyard since I came home from 'Nam. This is all basic shop knowledge. Only a fool would pay money or sit in class for four years to figure out somethin' as simple as metalwork."

"Touché, Mr. Luttrell." Veronica sunk into the couch cushion behind her. "I guess I stand corrected. What do you think, Edison?"

"I think you're acting petulant and derisive."

"No," Veronica corrected. "I'm acting as the sole voice of reason in this room right now. You two have known one another for what, an hour at best? And you're already plotting to take down a *vampire*? You're both gonna end up spending the rest of your lives in prison for murder."

"I wouldn't consider the elimination of such a creature murder."

"Tell that to the goddamn judge!" Veronica shouted. "But go ahead. Humor me. How *do* you plan on killing it?"

"Decapitation or fire," Raymer replied without hesitation. "Although there are other less direct methods."

"Yeah, well, last time I checked, decapitation and fire would kill just about anybody."

"Well, exposure to *sunlight* should not only kill it, but also provide evidence of the vampire's abnormal biology. In fact, if properly recorded and documented it could be—"

"Oh, for Christ's sake!" Veronica interrupted. "How the hell do you even plan on finding the damned thing? You gonna break into the local cemetery and start digging up a bunch of coffins?"

"No," Raymer said. "I've posted a map on the wall in my basement. A map of Williamsport and the surrounding area. So far, there's only one thumbtack to denote the location where Jennifer Stroud was assaulted. But it's a start. As we uncover more information, I should be able to chart a pattern in its movements. From what I know, there's nothing random about the way a predator—natural or supernatural—hunts its prey."

"Hold on, now." Junior leaned forward and knotted his fingers. "Trackin' the fucker like that's gonna take forever and a day. Now I told you, that detective had a name. He even spelled it out. Bartsch. B-A-R-T-S-C-H. Said he was followin' up on another tip."

"Did he give you any other details?" Raymer spun to face the older man in the highback chair.

"Nah." Junior shook his head. "Conversation went south after that. But he must know somethin' else. Maybe we oughta pay him another visit?"

"No, I don't think so," Raymer advised. "I think Detective Pettit's been about as forthcoming as he's going to be."

"Well, if they ain't gonna do anything about this, it don't look like we got much choice. I say we man up and go out there. Find him and—"

"Mr. Luttrell," Raymer said. "You really should leave the logistics of planning to me."

"I can't do that. See, you academic types love to talk, but you never act. If we wait too long, then—"

"Then what?" Raymer challenged him. "You've sat by and let this monster run amok since 1957. You know full well what it is. Did you ever try to get out there and hunt it yourself?"

"Well, I don't suppose—"

"Then we need to be careful and methodical with our planning and execution here. This vampire slipped up and gave us a starting point. And, under the right circumstances, I think I can prompt it to make the same mistake again."

"Really?" Veronica stole a glimpse at the liquor cabinet. "All you've got is a thumbtack on a map, the scant information that's been released to the press, and an admittedly coincidental story from 1957 as witnessed by a seven-year-old boy." She caught herself and addressed the older man across the room. "No offense, Junior."

"None taken. I don't expect you to believe me. My own mother didn't at first. Your friend Edison here's the first man to take my word at face value."

"My friend Edison's become an obsessive and deranged zealot. And your story's given him the final push he needed to plunge over the edge."

"Veronica, there's much more at work here. If he really is what I believe him to be, I think catching him might save a few, if not many lives." Raymer relaxed his arms and took a deep breath. "Now, I agree we need to take stock of things and do some leg-work. We know the police aren't going to pursue the lead Junior's given them. So it's up to us. And I think we can do it, as long as the right variables are in place."

Against Raymer's instructions, Veronica rose and crossed the living room to stand before the liquor cabinet. As she ran a finger along a row of whiskey bottles, she spoke. "I'm not committing to anything right now, but let's say I were to join you two in your little vampire hunting romp." She shook her head as she uncorked a familiar bottle of single-malt scotch and poured herself a generous glass. "If only to keep you two from doing anything stupid and to ensure you don't ram a stake into some small-time sex offender's heart."

"I don't plan to act in such a rash manner," Raymer said.

"Hear me out, Edison. If we do this, we're gonna need all the facts we can gather before we attempt to confront this individual. Even *if* Junior's story checks out. We can't just go charging out of here with stakes and holy water and wander around town based on one incident alone. We need to know for sure that this is—"

"What the fuck do we need to know?" Junior cried out. "We got a name! Now we get out there and find him as soon as possible and kill the son of a bitch. It ain't rocket science!"

"Would both of you just shut up for a minute!" Raymer bellowed. He faced Junior. "As much as I hate to admit it, Veronica's right. Finding and catching this thing's not gonna be so simple. If what you're saying is true, he's blended into society for *seventy* years." Raymer stressed his words with a stern glance at Junior. "But, we do have at least one thing going for us here. This vampire almost got caught. For some reason, he got careless. I think I have a good idea why, and we might be able to use it to our advantage."

Veronica knocked back the glass, swallowed a fair bit of scotch, and smacked her lips. "I'm all ears, Edison."

"When I talked to Detective Pettit, he mentioned something about the attacker calling Jennifer by another woman's name. He called her Anna, and pronounced it like a German would. Now there are a couple possibilities here. One, this vampire is becoming unraveled after all these years. Or he's hunting women that remind him of someone from his past. A wife or lover, perhaps? If that's the case, he would've singled out Jennifer Stroud based on her appearance. There may have been something about the way she looked or carried herself that reminded him of this woman."

"You may be onto somethin', Doc," Junior piped up.

"Or my initial assessment of batshit crazy may still be a valid diagnosis." Veronica took another drink. "So how does this help us?"

"It's simple. If he's looking to create *another* vampire, then odds are he might try it again. I mean, we don't know if he's aware of how much heat he's brought down on himself. He could be out again tonight, cruising for another tall blonde in her early twenties. If so, we could possibly bait a trap for him."

"I've heard enough wacky shit this afternoon to last more than one lifetime. But this?" Veronica shook her head. "This is possibly the most irresponsible thing I've ever heard. Who the fuck are you gonna use as *bait*? What, are you gonna ask me to wear a blonde wig and dress like the Stroud girl? If that's the measure of your brilliant plan, then you can forget it."

"Not you." Raymer scratched his chin. "If you plan to assist in the hunt, I need you behind the lens of a video camera. Besides, I'm sorry to say you don't fit the profile. You're too old."

Veronica pursed her lips as Junior repressed a chuckle. "Thanks for that. So what are you planning to do? Call Jennifer Stroud and ask her to stand out on the street while we film the whole thing?"

"Not exactly."

"Who in their right mind would ever agree to something like this?"

Junior shifted in his seat, and let out a long sigh. He was growing impatient with the pair of bickering professors.

Raymer raised his left hand to pacify Luttrell and to prevent any further outbursts from Veronica.

"When Ritter was chewing me out yesterday, he brought up Laura McCoy. You remember her, don't you?"

"Wasn't she..." Veronica struggled to place the name.

"She was my graduate assistant. Went to Sussex One State Prison to profile that serial killer before his execution."

"Jesus Christ. *That* graduate assistant?" Veronica suddenly remembered the scandal surrounding McCoy's M.A. Thesis. "You wanna open that can of worms again?"

"Actually, we're on perfectly cordial terms. She's working on her Ph.D. at the Annandale Institute. Studying parapsychology and criminology, or so she said when I last heard from her."

"So you wanna ask her to do this? To be bait?" Veronica asked. "After all the shit you put her through for her thesis? All the fallout when Ritter got wind of it?"

"First of all, Ritter isn't a part of this anymore," Raymer reminded her. "And the whole thing about interviewing Desmond Barker was Laura's idea. She insisted on it. And rather than persuade her to pursue a more mundane research topic, I accepted her proposal."

"Did you even try to persuade her?" Veronica folded her arms and leveled an accusatory stare at her colleague.

"She was gonna do it regardless, so there was no point trying to stop her. The girl has guts, and I'm positive she still does. She didn't think twice about confronting Barker. Furthermore, she has more than a passing interest in the occult. Her dissertation is on exorcisms and the role of—"

"Sounds good to me, Doc!" Junior clapped his hands to speed up the conversation. "Let's get her down here!"

Veronica was far less eager to admit Laura McCoy into the picture. "You're not seriously going to get her involved in this, are you?"

"Do you have any better ideas?"

"Well, yeah, we could drop this whole goddamn thing and come back to reality!"

Raymer ignored her and reached into his pocket for his cell phone. "Look, I can call her right now. Annandale's only a four hour drive away. Like most grad students, she'll probably be grateful for the distraction, and I'm sure she'll welcome the challenge. In any event, the most important thing here is that—"

"She looks like Jennifer Stroud." Veronica finished his sentence, and then finished her drink. The English professor set her glass down and refilled it to the brim. "Well, you're probably right about one thing. Laura McCoy will jump at the chance to be a part of this lunacy. If you're not careful, though, she'll start shooting that mouth off and your vampire will take off in the opposite direction. Shit, he'll head for the airport and hop the next red-eye back to Berlin."

Junior broke his bemused silence. "For the love of Christ, will you two quit gabbin' and make the goddamn phone call? That thing might live forever, but we ain't got that luxury. Let's get this show on the road!"

"Alright Junior," Raymer said. "Here's the first thing you can do. In my basement I have four foot-long silver rods. Do you have any way to grind them into sharp stakes?"

"Of course," he replied. "I can get a lathe operator to do it over at the shipyard. All I gotta do is slip him a Jackson bill an' he won't say a word."

Raymer reached into his pocket, withdrew his wallet, and passed Junior a fifty-dollar bill. "Those silver rods cost me a small fortune. Give him this much instead and have him collect all the shavings. You can use them to make your bullets. Can you do this tomorrow afternoon? And be back here at my place before sundown?"

Junior slipped the fifty in his pocket. "Sure thing."

"Good," Raymer confirmed. "You should bring several changes of clothes, work gloves, firearms, and ammunition. You're welcome to stay here with me as long as necessary."

"I appreciate that, Doc." Junior nodded with approval. "Hopefully I won't be imposin' too long, if ya catch my drift."

Veronica stumbled over to a chair and brought the whiskey glass to her lips. "So what do you want me to do?"

"When you sober up, I want you to get re-acquainted with my digital video camera. You'll record and document everything we do. That's all I'm asking of you at this point."

Raymer stepped back to address both of his visitors. "Before we get started, there's one ironclad rule I'm laying down right here, right now."

"What's that?" Veronica asked in a slurred voice.

"No cops. Period."

Junior stood and straightened his trousers. "No problems here, Dr. Raymer." Luttrell cast a weary eye on Veronica and then glanced back to Raymer.

"Did you hear me, Veronica? No police. Can you handle that?"

"Sure." The inebriated professor shrugged her shoulders. "I'm not about to march down to the nearest station and tell 'em I'm an accessory to murder."

"I'm holding both of you to it. Junior, if you follow me to the basement, I'll get you the silver rods."

The older man nodded. As they moved towards the foyer, Veronica called out to Raymer. "Besides roping the McCoy girl into this hare-brained scheme of yours, what're *you* planning to do?"

"Some important research. And then I need to acquire a few additional things. Don't worry about it."

The two men disappeared, leaving Veronica to contemplate what was turning out to be the strangest afternoon of her life.

You can't walk away now. If you do, Ed'll be right. What did he say you were? An amateur? A fake? Oh yeah, and a bore.

Veronica downed the last of the scotch.

But you're not pulling him back from the precipice this time. Not with his new partner-in-crime. No, Veronica, you're not about to rescue him from the abyss.

You're jumping in with him.

27

AFTER JUNIOR LUTTRELL LEFT WITH THE SILVER RODS AND a promise to be back in twenty-four hours, Raymer peered into his living room from the foyer. In the short span of five minutes, Veronica had fallen asleep on the leather couch. Her head lolled against the back cushion as her limp fingers clutched an empty glass. Alcohol and her persistent quarrelling had worn her out.

Raymer sat down at the kitchen table and paged through the contacts on his cell phone. When he reached Laura McCoy's number, he pressed SEND. Laura picked up after two rings.

"Professor Raymer, I presume."

"You must have caller ID."

"You're in my contact list, you Luddite," the twenty-seven year-old doctoral candidate replied. "I haven't heard from you in ages."

"I've been busy," Raymer said.

"How's the Anthro department now that I'm not there to piss everyone off?"

"Funny you should say that. I've done a fair job of rattling a few cages in your absence." He moved to change the conversation. "Do you have a few minutes to talk?"

"Sure. I'm sitting on the Metro and will be for the next thirty minutes. What's new and exciting in the world of Edison Raymer?"

The professor took a deep breath and exhaled. "Well, I'm about to embark on what you might call a very groundbreaking and potentially dangerous field study. And as far as I'm aware, nothing like this has ever been attempted in the world of academia."

"I see you haven't lost your flair for high drama," Laura quipped. "You have my attention, Dr. Raymer. So what exactly does this *potentially dangerous field study* involve?"

"To put it bluntly, affairs of a supernatural nature."

"I see." There was a pause on the other end of the line. "Judging by your earnest tone, I'm gonna guess it's something along the lines of your fabled Aston case? You gonna go back and try to catch the one that got away?"

"It's much more involved than that." Raymer crossed his legs and leaned forward. "But I'm glad that you remember the case."

"How could I forget it?"

Raymer quickly changed the subject. "So how's the dissertation coming along?"

"If that's your way of asking if I'm available, the answer is yes. I've got nothing but time on my hands. Besides, I need a break from all this exorcism business. The power of Christ can be exhausting." There was a pause on the other end, and the steady clicking of the subway train speeding on to the next destination filled the silence. "So you gonna spill the details about this field study or what?"

"Well, let's start with a caveat," Raymer said. "I'm freelancing this study, as I'll be resigning from the faculty down here in a matter of days."

"Whoa! That bad, huh?" Laura expressed genuine surprise at Raymer's confession. "Was it Ritter or the students that pushed you over the edge?"

"Both," Raymer answered. "But we can talk about that later. As for the study itself, some would say it's become a bit of an obsession for me."

"Why don't you just come out and tell me you're resuming your work on vampirism, Dr. Raymer?" Laura's tone was flippant. "When you weren't playing the role of hard-ass professor, that's all you ever talked about while I worked with you."

"This is different."

"How so?"

"Well, we're actually going to be tracking and hunting this alleged vampire. In fact—"

"Wait a minute. Who's *we*?"

"Dr. Upham from the English department and a gentleman named Fenton Luttrell, Jr., who had an encounter with the vampire several years ago."

"No departmental funding and a motley crew of non-anthropologists. Hell, Raymer, you fuckin' *need* me to come down there. Now when you say vampire, I assume you're using the term in the theoretical sense?"

"Literal."

Laura McCoy cleared her throat. "And just how literal are we talking here?"

"All the evidence that I've gathered suggests that we're dealing with something altogether extraordinary," Raymer explained. "The suspect in question doesn't appear to be some subcultural fetishist, nor does he exhibit the signs of Renfield Syndrome. Quite frankly, Miss McCoy, I'm convinced he's the real deal."

The quick-witted graduate student was finally at a loss for words. After a short pause, she spoke. "The *real deal,* huh? Christ. OK. Well, I sure as hell didn't expect you to have a midlife crisis of *this* caliber."

"It's not a midlife crisis." Raymer assured. "You know as well as anyone that I've been waiting for an opportunity like this for a very, *very* long time."

"Understood." Laura exhaled heavily into the phone before she continued. "Can you give me some background on the case then?"

Raymer stood and pressed his free hand against the tabletop. "Sunday night, an undergraduate was assaulted, and the attacker was driven off by a witness. The police are treating it like a botched rape attempt, but the perpetrator didn't attempt to rape her. He bit her neck and tore her throat open."

"Jesus!"

"So I spoke with a detective, and flipped the script on him. Got as much information out of the guy as I could. Fast-forward to this afternoon, when I got a visit from Mr. Luttrell. After interrogating the girl, the Williamsport P.D. put out a composite sketch, and this man recognized the girl's assailant. In fact, he told me this suspect killed his father."

"OK, that's fucked up. But I get the sense there's more. So what aren't you telling me?"

"Junior Luttrell insists that the same man who attacked the student killed his father...in 1957."

"Wait a minute? What?"

"According to Luttrell, the killer hasn't aged since he first encountered him when he was a seven-year-old boy. He claims the vampire's a German soldier killed by his father in World War II. Luttrell says he's certain that it's the same man in the composite sketch sent out by the police."

"What's your gut feeling on all this?" Laura probed. "You think this *Junior* character's for real?"

"I wouldn't be wasting your time if I had any doubts."

"So..." Laura drew out a long breath. "What do you need me for?"

Raymer's tone grew clipped and curt. "Before I say another word, I want to be abundantly clear about the danger you would be facing and—"

"I'm a big girl. I can handle it," Laura interrupted. "Just spit it out."

"I think he's beginning to hunt young women who fit the description of someone from his past."

"So you need bait, in other words." Laura was blunt, and spoke as if she could read his mind.

"Still interested?" Raymer rapped his knuckles on the table as he awaited the girl's response. "Come on, Laura. You've never been one to shy away from an adventure."

"Stop trying to coerce me!" Laura scolded her mentor. "You sound like a total creep when you start pullin' that shit. Anyway, I'll do it on one condition."

"And what condition is that?"

"If he whisks me away and makes me his vampire bride, you have to promise not to interrupt our wedding."

Raymer smirked despite himself. "So you're not freaked out by this idea?"

"Are you kidding? Of course I am! But I'm also bored shitless up here. Besides, I know you. Everything has to meet or exceed your standard of scientific rigor, so clearly, you've thought this through. Strict adherence to the truth, Miss McCoy!"

"I'm glad my lessons weren't lost on you." Raymer switched the phone to his left ear. "How much time can you spare?"

"A few days. About a week at this point," Laura replied. "I'll have to bring my laptop and work a little while I'm down there, though. Shouldn't be too much of an interference."

"That's fine," Raymer said. "Are you still going to the pistol range on a regular basis?"

"Not as much as I'd like to," Laura admitted. "But I got a concealed carry permit last year. Sort of an insurance policy for a dumb blonde who rides public transit everywhere in Northern Virginia."

"Good. We'll provide a firearm for you, as I wouldn't expect you to—"

"All I need is a ride to Williamsport. I'm totally in."

"Would you prefer a rental car or train tickets?"

"Train." She didn't hesitate. "I'm too irresponsible for a rental car."

"Then I'll buy your train ticket online. When can you be ready to leave?"

"Shit. Give me a chance to juggle my schedule a bit and I can leave early tomorrow."

"Check your e-mail in about an hour. I'm gonna book your round trip for one week. So Thursday to Thursday. That work for you?"

"I'll see you tomorrow. Sharpen up a stake for me."

"Miss McCoy, you need to take this as seriously as you took your Master's thesis." Raymer warned her. "You may be walking into the wolf's lair."

"Again, your flair for the dramatic never ceases to amaze, Doctor. I'll see you soon, and thanks for thinking of me."

The line went dead in Raymer's hand. He placed it on the kitchen table and snuck out through the living room so as not to rouse Veronica. Once in his study, he shut the door with a quiet *click* and logged onto his laptop.

After he booked the train ticket and e-mailed the confirmation number to Laura, he opened a browser to consult his favorite search engine. Raymer paused for a moment, then typed ANNA BARTSCH into the box. He watched the cursor blink before he hit the enter key. Immediately, he was bombarded with personal information about people sharing the same name on various social media sites. He narrowed the parameters by adding GERMANY 1944.

The screen filled with numerous links to sites located in Germany. Raymer began to scan through the results, but since his understanding of German was mediocre at best, he was unable to make heads or tails of the websites.

At the top of the screen, in a menu of hyperlinks, he noticed a TRANS-LATE button.

Most of the translated links came back in broken English, but the first link on the page appeared to be an obituary for an Anna Bartsch of Darmstadt. He clicked the link and was redirected to an electronic newspaper archive in German. There was a black and white photograph of a young woman with soft features, vibrant eyes, and upswept blonde hair.

Raymer opened a second widow and typed GERMAN TO ENGLISH TRANSLATOR. The professor opened the first link, then copied and pasted the text of the obituary into the left box of the translator.

The English translation came back fragmented and nonsensical in places, but he was surprised to find most of it legible. The young woman had been a piano teacher, and was killed in a night bombing raid. He scanned the second paragraph and read a sentence fragment aloud.

"Anna is survived by her husband, Matthias, a decorated soldier..."

He sat back in his chair, picked up a pen, and jotted down the name Matthias Bartsch on the wrinkled surface of his ink blotter. Intrigued, Edison Raymer leaned over his keyboard and clicked the back button on the browser. He typed MATTHIAS BARTSCH GERMANY 1944 and hit enter. There were three conclusive matches to the name, and a number of matches with Germany and 1944 omitted. He clicked on the links, but each of them was another dead end.

With a sigh, he began the tedious process of clicking each link with two of the four search terms missing. Halfway down the page, he gave up, and was about to power down when something compelled him to open the IMAGES tab. Various pictures cluttered the screen, and he scrolled down the page with his mouse.

A black and white photograph caught his eye, so he opened the link. The picture began to load, and he noticed a British flag icon at the top of the page next to a German tricolor of the same size.

He jerked his mouse and clicked to the English version of the page. The text header at the top of the crude web page read DARMSTADT CONSERVATORY, 1940. The picture displayed men in suits and women in white dresses, standing in rows holding musical instruments. A group off to the side was empty-handed.

His pulse began to race as he noticed a woman in the front row that looked familiar. Her hair was neatly coiffed, and he read her name at the bottom. ANNA LANDFERMANN, PIANIST. He scanned the names with anticipation, and pressed a finger against the screen to mark his place.

When he reached the names for the third row string section, his breath caught in his throat and he blinked twice to clear his eyes.

MATTHIAS BARTSCH, CELLIST.

Raymer's entire body trembled as he scanned the photograph for the man fourth from the left. The well-dressed musician was tall and broad-shouldered, and balanced his instrument with one hand on the fingerboard. His heart rate soared when he saw the cellist's face. The hair, eyes, and features matched the police sketch he'd seen in the paper. Raymer double-checked the name with the man in the photograph. They were identical.

"Veronica!" he shouted. "Wake up and get in here!"

It's him. Matthias Bartsch.

Veronica didn't respond to his call, so he bolted out of his chair and paced into the living room. Raymer shook the sleeping woman. As if in slow motion, Veronica stirred awake.

"Edison? What the hell?"

"I need you to collect yourself and get up. Right now."

"Leave me alone." Her voice was slurred. She squinted and swatted him away. "I feel sick an' jus' wanna sleep."

"Because you drank half a fifth of Scotch." Raymer grasped her forearms and pulled her to stand. "Now follow me and try not to knock anything over."

Raymer bounded into his study while she staggered along behind him. Veronica rubbed her temples and coughed. "What're we doin' now?"

"Look at this picture." He pointed to the laptop screen, his finger on Matthias' cello. "What do you see?"

"I dunno." Veronica shrugged. "A swing band? Maybe a classical orchestra? Wait a minute...Darmstadt Conservatory? 1940?" She exchanged glances with Raymer. "You woke me up for this bullshit? I don't get it."

"Because you're still fucking drunk," he snapped. "Hold on, if you can manage to remain standing for another minute."

"Y'know what, Edison? You're bein' a complete jerk right now. I mean you always were a pompous ass but you're really—"

"Shut up," he said. While she struggled to chastise him, he opened a second window to the Williamsport Herald's website and found the police sketch of Jennifer Stroud's attacker online. Raymer rearranged the windows, and zoomed in on the conservatory picture. Both images were now side by side. "Do you see it now?"

"It's...oh my God, Edison!" She held a hand over her lips and balled her fingers into a fist. Raymer could tell she was fighting nausea. "It's the same—"

"Do you remember what Luttrell said the man's name was?"

"Bartsch. Something like that, right?"

Raymer shrunk the photo and pointed at the names of the third row musicians.

Veronica furrowed her brow as she read them in a whisper. "Matthias Bartsch? Is that the same—"

Edison pointed at the fourth man in the row.

"Oh, Christ." Her chest began to heave. "This...this can't be real. It's a coincidence." She wrapped her arms beneath her breasts. "It's impossible."

"That's him." Raymer peered at her over the rims of his glasses. "That's our vampire."

"Did you show this to Junior?" Veronica suddenly sobered up. "If not, you have to call him now and get him back over here to see this."

"It can wait 'til tomorrow."

"Have you called Laura?" Veronica pressed the heel of her palm against her throbbing temple.

"She'll be here tomorrow afternoon."

Raymer left the images on the computer screen and helped Veronica back to the couch.

"We're gonna do this, aren't we?" She asked. "I mean, we're *really* gonna do this?"

Raymer held a finger to his lips and nodded. Veronica laid across the couch and he tossed a blanket over her. "Am I dreaming?" she asked.

Raymer slipped her shoes off. "Get some sleep and we'll talk about it later. If I'm gone when you wake up, I suggest you make some toast. Drink some water. A lot of it."

"Gone?" Veronica squinted at Raymer from her prone position. "You're gonna leave me alone after what you just showed me?"

"You were fine by yourself when you didn't believe a word I said. I'm sure you'll continue to be safe and sound regardless of what you now know to be true."

"You're an asshole," she muttered, and covered her eyes.

Raymer smiled. "As I said before you passed out in a drunken stupor, I have things to do. Important things before we begin our hunt. This is gonna move much faster than I ever imagined."

28

AS HE CLUTCHED A CROWBAR BETWEEN THE FOLDS OF HIS long black coat, Raymer stepped into the narthex of St. Luke's Catholic Church. A deathlike silence hung in the air, and he smelled faint traces of incense as he stole into the nave. The altar stood at the terminus of the central aisle atop a raised dais. The wall behind the altar was adorned with a gruesome painting of the Deposition from the Cross. The corpse of Jesus was being taken down from the instrument of torture and placed before his fainting mother.

Raymer averted his eyes and sped toward a marble stoup, which held a gallon or more of holy water. He glanced around the church and noticed an older woman kneeling in a pew near the altar. With caution, he leaned the crowbar against a nearby pillar and procured a wadded sack from his coat pocket. Inside were five thick glass flasks.

The professor placed them along the thick rim of the holy water font and uncorked the first flask. The sound was louder than he had anticipated, and the praying woman cast a scornful eye in his direction. He hid the flask from sight and dipped his fingers into the font. As she turned back to her devotions, Raymer made the sign of the cross and submerged the open flask in the water once again.

He was more careful when opening the remaining flasks, and in a few minutes he had accomplished the first of two tasks that drew him to the church. The second required him to be alone in the vast sanctuary.

One by one, he returned the flasks to the sack and shoved it into his coat pocket. He slid the crowbar beneath his coat and moved down the main aisle. He ducked into a row of pews and knelt on a padded footboard. Raymer pretended to pray as the woman glared at him a second time. When she turned around and pressed her forehead against her locked hands, the professor surveyed the altar. He noticed a door set into the left wall.

The sacristy. You need to get in there. Everything you need will be in that room.

It'll be locked.

Bide your time.

Wait.

Raymer pictured several boxes of communion wafers arranged in neat rows. They weren't sanctified, but they'd have to do. The formal consecration occurred during the ritual of Holy Communion.

The so-called Transubstantiation.

The woman near the altar began to gather her belongings, so Raymer ducked his head in mock prayer. He maintained his position until she left the church. The professor waited until he heard the front door's latch close. He rose and moved toward the altar, aware that if the front door was open, the parish priest was lurking somewhere in the building.

Raymer passed the altar and approached the unassuming wooden door of the sacristy. He turned the brass knob, but as suspected, it was locked. He slipped the crowbar from beneath his coat and wedged the notched end between the antique lock and the doorframe.

One chance to get this. Get in there, find the host, and get out. Run, if you have to.

Without further delay, he pushed on the pry bar like a fulcrum. The wood splintered as the door burst open. The loud clap of the breaking lock resounded along the hollows of the apse and into the vaulted hall of the nave. Raymer cursed under his breath and fumbled for a light switch. When he entered the small room, crowded with brass flowerpots and hanging vestments, he noticed a long table. Atop the table was a stack of square boxes.

Raymer held the crowbar under one arm and opened a box. Inside were communion wafers, wrapped in plastic. He pulled the sack out of his coat pocket and shoveled all the wafer boxes he could into the burlap bag. With the crowbar in one hand and the sack in the other, the professor slipped through the door and switched off the light behind him.

As he spun around to make his retreat, Raymer heard a door slam somewhere deep in the rear halls of the building.

The distinct noise was followed by the *click-clack* of leather-soled shoes on the hard tiles of a distant corridor. His heart pounding in his chest, Raymer darted for the aisle. He picked up his pace and aimed for the double doors leading to the street. As he was halfway to the narthex, a door burst open from behind and a voice called out.

"Hey!"

Raymer kept running. He knew it was the parish priest. The man's voice, however, was hesitant and timid. "Hey! Wait! Come back! Please!"

Raymer pushed his way through the narthex doors and into the night. In a matter of minutes, he was far enough away from St. Luke's to slow his pace. He caught his breath and crossed the empty street, careful to avoid a small crowd of undergrads on their way to a local coffee house.

Fortunately for Edison Raymer, none of the students recognized him. He turned into a narrow parking lot and pitched the bag into the back seat of his SUV, then stowed the crowbar under the driver's seat.

For the first time in years, he felt exhilaration and triumph. His plan was coming together, and soon he would be leading the hunt.

29

A THICK BLACK CIGARETTE SMOLDERED BETWEEN LAURA McCoy's fingers as she leaned against an iron railing. Her train to Williamsport had arrived early, so she hailed a cab and arrived at Raymer's townhouse around ten o'clock. The professor wasn't there, so she hid her overnight bag behind a bush and went off to the 3rd Street deli for an early lunch. After eating, she wandered around town for a while, and then returned to find Raymer's black SUV sitting in his driveway.

With her overnight bag and her backpack piled at her feet, Laura lounged on his front stoop. She was already on her second clove, and she knew Raymer wouldn't let her smoke inside. She wasn't about to be social until she had some nicotine in her system.

The cold October breeze didn't bother her. She had grown up in Illinois, where a bad Virginia winter was akin to early fall. Long blonde hair fell around her face and deep blue eyes. Laura clutched her great-grandfather's moth-eaten Ike jacket around her upper chest—a relic from World War II. Underneath, she wore a faded black shirt adorned with the iconic cover art from Joy Division's *Unknown Pleasures*. She sported a pair of combat boots, and her long legs were lost in black cargo pants.

As she took a drag on her cigarette, Laura saw a flicker of movement in the nearby kitchen window. Edison Raymer parted the curtains and tapped the windowpane. She shot back her best 'what-the-fuck' expression, shrugged, and held up her cigarette. The professor shook his head and disappeared from the window. Seconds later, Laura heard the tumblers of the front door lock turn over.

Raymer stuck his head and shoulders out into the cold.

"Still abusing tobacco, I see? How long have you been standing out here in the cold?"

Laura's full lips parted into a slight grin. "Well, it's good to see you again too, Edison."

"Put that damned thing out and come inside before you catch pneumonia," Raymer demanded. "With your smoker's lungs, recovery from an acute respiratory infection is probably not—"

"Nice ride you picked up there." Laura diverted his attention to the SUV. In the distance, she could see her reflection in the tinted windows and custom chrome rims. "How many times has Williamsport's finest pulled you over hoping to catch some Central American drug lord behind the wheel? Come to think of it, you do kinda look like that guy from *Breaking Bad*."

"Is that some mindless action movie?"

"Still living under a rock, I see."

Raymer ignored Laura's comment. "The key to avoiding hassles is not to draw attention—"

"Yeah, right." Laura dragged out the words with sarcasm in her voice, again pointing at the SUV. "You've never gone out of your way to avoid confrontation." She took a final drag, smashed the *kretek* against the railing, and flicked it into the street.

"Disgusting habit," Raymer muttered as he flung the door open. "I always thought such compulsive behavior was beneath you."

"Well, beggars can't be choosers when it comes to willing vampire bait." Laura hefted her bags only to step over the threshold and dump them in the professor's foyer. She narrowed her gaze and gave Edison a once-over. "You been lifting, Ed? Jesus fuck, your arms look huge!"

"Yes." He pushed his wire-rim spectacles up the bridge of his nose. He was unmoved by Laura's off-handed compliment. Having known the girl for several years, he knew that she masked her anxieties behind sharp-witted banter. "I've been training for a couple years now."

Laura stepped into Raymer's spacious living room.

"I love what you've done with the place," she commented with a mix of sincerity and critique. "Looks like a veritable museum of black metal album covers in here."

"Black metal?" Raymer asked with a bemused grin. "For someone with your level of intellect, your aesthetic tastes also remain a puzzle."

"Hey." She smirked. "Ya gotta turn it off sometimes and have some fun. Besides, you'd be surprised by what some of those bands write about."

"Talk to Dr. Upham about that. She was apparently a lot like you when she was in college."

"And where *is* the lovely and enchanting Veronica Upham?"

"She's teaching class." Raymer stepped into the kitchen and bade Laura to follow. "She'll be over after her seminar." He pulled out a chair and Laura sat down at the kitchen table.

"So what's her role in this vampire thing?" Laura kept her eyes on Raymer's stony features as he poured himself a cup of coffee from a percolator.

"She'll be filming what we do. Until last night, she tried to convince me that our pursuit of this creature was a mistake." Raymer paused. "Would you like a cup of coffee? Maybe some lunch? I could heat up—"

"I've already eaten, but a cup of sugar and cream with a splash of coffee sounds delightful." Laura glanced around the kitchen. "You really need to get some new furniture in here."

"Have you been formally diagnosed with ADHD yet, Miss McCoy?"

"You're funny." She leaned over the table as he approached with two coffee mugs in hand. "You, more than anyone, should know how amused I am by bright and shiny objects. No surprises."

Raymer slid her coffee across the surface. She glanced into the cup and frowned. "Not enough cream."

"You're a guest in my house, and like you said, beggars can't be choosers."

"OK," Laura said. "So what exactly are we gonna be doing and when do we start? I've only got a week, remember?"

"Did you tell anyone where you were going? Give any specifics?" Raymer seemed perturbed. "I need to know as soon as possible, because—"

"I told a colleague I was going out of town. That was it. Cancelled a few shifts at my part-time job with the same damned excuse. So spill it. What's going on?"

"I told you the backstory when we spoke on the phone. And if you checked your e-mail on the train, I wrote a more detailed version of everything so you'd show up fully briefed."

"Fully briefed?" Laura ventured a sip of coffee, which burned the tip of her tongue. "Sounds like you've lined me up for a suicide mission."

"Not at all. I'll be in control of the situation at all times." Raymer averted his eyes and surveyed the plain black liquid in his own mug. "But I want you to be aware of what we might be facing out there tonight."

"So we're moving that quickly?" Laura asked with an uncertain gleam in her eye.

Raymer nodded as he leaned back in his chair. "Here's my plan. Right now, we're testing the waters, so to speak. There are four of us now, including you and me. The layman is Junior Luttrell, as I mentioned earlier. He's the loose cannon of the bunch. The only one of us whose behavior I can't predict. But I think he knows his place in this endeavor, and so far, he's been cooperative, if not a tad enthusiastic."

"OK, and Veronica's gonna provide the shaky cam footage when we market this whole thing as an indie horror flick?"

Raymer wasn't amused. "I'll be directing everything from behind the scenes. But it is imperative when we set up that the vampire only sees *you*."

"Speaking of my role in all this, you really haven't told me what I need to do."

Raymer spun his coffee cup with an absent look in his eyes. "You'll sit at a bus stop and do your best job of acting uncomfortable by yourself in the dark."

"What if other people show up while I'm there? Or, more likely, a bus stops to pick me up before a vampire does?"

"First of all, I selected the location and observed it for a few hours last night. Not a single rider or bus showed up for over three hours. I called the transit authority for a schedule. Due to budget cuts, I was told no buses run this route after seven o'clock on weeknights."

"Sounds like you're on top of this," Laura said. "What about cops?"

"Not much we can do about that. So if an officer harasses you, cooperate and be accommodating. Then get up and leave. You'll go walk to where we parked, wait ten minutes, and return to the bus shelter."

"OK." Laura nodded. "So we'll be on the same street where this guy attacked the undergrad?"

"Yes. Do you remember where St. Luke's is?"

"Do I strike you as someone who spent six years at Williamsport frequenting local churches?"

"Never mind." Raymer was growing impatient with Laura's propensity for sarcasm. "It's on a two lane road a few blocks from Dr. Upham's house.

About a ten minute walk from the campus greensward. That thoroughfare gets heavy traffic during the day, but nothing significant at night."

"Got it." Laura blew on her steaming coffee again. "So I'll be armed?"

"Mr. Luttrell will be providing you with a firearm. For obvious reasons, you'll keep it concealed. From me, you'll be getting two weapons of a different sort."

"I'm intrigued." Laura rested her elbows on the table and propped her chin on her open palms. "Can you show me?"

Raymer stood and left the kitchen. When he returned, he set a thick glass vial of water and a velvet drawstring bag on the table before her.

"Is that holy water?"

"Yes." The professor took his seat. "Open the bag."

Laura looked inside and dropped two fingers. She withdrew a pinch of fine powder. "What's this?"

"Communion wafers ground to dust. If the vampire attacks you, you can blow it in his face. It should subdue him. According to one source from my library, it'll also render him night-blind."

"I never heard that one before."

"Well, consider this a part of the study. We can document its efficacy, and either confirm or debunk the source."

"Damn. You're serious about this, aren't you?" Laura eyed her mentor as she closed the bag. "You think this guy *really* is a vampire?"

"Yes," Raymer responded, "I do."

"So what am I gonna need the gun for? Will a gun even work?"

"Luttrell is loading silver-tipped bullets today, in addition to having stakes made from the same metal. You're aware of the alchemical properties that make silver abhorrent to vampires, no?"

"Of course. Lunar power. Purity. All that shit." Laura finally took a sip of her oversweet coffee. "It's the best kept secret in vampire lore. You know, pawning off silver as a means to dispatch werewolves in pop culture."

Raymer flashed a rare smile. "It took five minutes to explain that to Veronica yesterday."

"Explain what?" An indignant voice resounded from the foyer. After she kicked the front door shut, Dr. Upham moved to stand in the kitchen entranceway.

"Veronica." Raymer acknowledged her in surprise. "We didn't hear you come in. I thought you were teaching this—"

"I cancelled. Called in sick. After what we found online yesterday, I haven't been able to concentrate on much else."

Laura rose and approached the English professor with an extended hand. "Good to see you again after—"

Veronica pulled the lapels of Laura's Ike jacket apart and shook her head. "Joy Division? Were you even alive in 1979?"

Laura scowled and crossed her arms. "Were you alive when Tennyson wrote *Idylls of the King*? Or when Rossetti published *Goblin Market*?"

"I'm just surprised," Veronica countered. "I didn't think the whole goth thing was very fashionable these days."

"Well, I guess I'm a fossil of a different kind." She gave the middle-aged professor an accusatory once-over.

"I can see you're still a very *clever* young lady." Veronica forced a smile and extended her hand. "Truce?"

"Sure," Laura said. "Whatever."

Raymer cleared his throat before the two women resumed bickering. "In the spirit of professional camaraderie, I need both of you to put aside your petty differences. Besides, as we discussed, Veronica, I think it would be best if Miss McCoy stayed at your place while she's in town."

"Is that a good idea?" Veronica furrowed her brow. She glanced at Laura. "No offense, I mean, you're more than welcome. But, Ed, don't you think we should all stick together?"

"I get it." Laura intervened, hoping to alleviate the tension. "Dr. Raymer is afraid I'll run off with his collection of Marsden prints. And you're afraid I'll ransack your Duran Duran albums. I can assure you, I have no interest in either."

"How about we focus on the tasks at hand?" Raymer raised his voice as he would to regain control over a rowdy classroom. "We may get results immediately, or in a couple of days. If things escalate, we'll hold out here. All four of us. Until then, during any periods of down time, I think it's best that someone be in the area where the attack occurred on Sunday."

"I guess so." Veronica shrugged with a far off voice. Her mind was clearly elsewhere.

"You have nothing to worry about. As I'm sure you know, a vampire can't enter your home without an invitation. So you'll be fine."

"I still can't believe I'm doing this," Veronica mumbled.

Raymer pointed at Professor Upham, "If you have doubts, you better deal with them now, because I need everyone on point tonight at that bus stop. We need to be ready for anything."

"Look." Laura attempted to console Veronica. "All you gotta do is hold the camera steady. I'm the goddamn bait, remember?"

"I get it." Veronica nodded and forced a bitter smile. "I guess I'm intruding on the esteemed professor and his wide-eyed protégé. I'll be in the living room if you need me."

Raymer didn't bother to follow or appease Veronica's bid for attention. He stayed at the table, cradled his coffee mug, and shook his head in frustration.

Laura leaned over the table to speak in a whisper. "How the hell did you convince her to take part in this?"

"At this point, I'm not sure she's convinced of anything. Though she acted like it yesterday." Raymer took a sip of coffee. "But you wouldn't believe the arm-twisting I had to do before she saw—"

The professor was cut short by a sharp knock from the front of the townhouse. He rose and sped into the foyer to answer the door.

Junior stood on the welcome mat with a black tactical bag over his shoulder. Raymer glanced at his wristwatch. "We weren't expecting you until closer to four."

"Yeah, well I got shit done early." He muscled his way into Raymer's front hall and made a beeline for the living room. Junior draped the bag across the cushion of a wingback chair and began rummaging through its contents. Laura entered from the kitchen as Raymer followed behind. With her arms folded, Veronica glowered at everyone from her customary position on the couch.

After the necessary introductions were made, Junior retrieved the four sharpened rods from his bag and handed them to Raymer.

"He added some knurling at the top, so you can grip 'em better." Junior watched Edison inspect the tradesman's handiwork. "Didn't take him but an hour to do all four. Said if you had more, he'd be happy to do 'em at the same cost."

Raymer held a stake up at eye level and nodded in approval. "What about the bullets?"

"I went ahead and made my own tips. Now Miss Laura, you ever handle a firearm?"

Laura dug her concealed carry permit from her pocket. Junior squinted. "I've got just the gun for you." He handed her a snub-nose .38 as Veronica stood and began to pace around the living room.

"I can give you an ankle holster for that. Then you just untuck those pants on that leg and strap it around your boot."

"Sounds good." She indexed her finger to demonstrate trigger discipline. Luttrell smiled as he watched her take a professional stance and aim the short-barreled revolver. No one noticed Raymer steal into the foyer with the stakes in hand.

"My concealed carry weapon's a Glock 43 chambered for .380, so I'm not concerned about the recoil." Laura eyed the bag with a curious brow. "You got anything semi-auto in there?"

"To avoid feed problems, I only made the silver rounds for my revolvers. So you'll have to get used to that. Don't look like it'll be a problem for ya." Luttrell removed a chromed .44 Magnum revolver. "This is gonna be our heavy artillery if I gotta draw down on the bastard."

Veronica paused to take in the size of Luttrell's handgun, and then turned to the foyer entrance. "Jesus Christ, Edison!"

The others looked up as well.

Professor Raymer clutched a steel-headed hammer with a short handle. Slung over his shoulder—in direct contrast with his white dress shirt and black necktie—was a leather bandolier he'd crafted in his basement. Three of the stakes had been pushed through loops and secured tightly. The fourth stake he carried in his left hand. An ornate crucifix was jammed into his waist belt.

"Holy shit!" Laura laughed. "I guess you're ready to go, Dr. Van Helsing?"

Veronica was more disturbed by Edison's appearance. "If someone catches a glimpse of you out on the street like that, they're not calling the cops. They'll call the state hospital!"

Raymer gestured at Veronica with the hammer, which he wielded with little effort. "All I have to do is throw a coat on and no one will see a thing."

Laura pointed the .38 towards the floor. "Um...there's still the matter of that big-ass hammer. You plan to carry that thing around like Thor and *Mjölnir?*"

"Is that a problem?" Raymer surveyed the stunned faces of the would-be vampire hunters. "You'll thank me for it if that thing overruns us."

Junior raised his .44 Mag. "Not if I get him first!"

"Listen, gentlemen." Laura dug through Junior's bag to find the ankle holster and strap. "You mind telling your decoy here how the rest of you are gonna be watching my back?"

Raymer leaned the hammer against the doorframe and slid the fourth stake into his bandolier. "It's simple. The area behind the bus stop is just like the place where our vampire dragged his prey Sunday night. There's a tall hedgerow to conceal the three of us. I cased the entire area and can say with certainty that the yard and house behind the bus stop is actually abandoned."

Junior kept his attention on Raymer as he fit the ankle strap around Laura's boot.

"The three of us will be out of sight. If Matthias Bartsch approaches, you can face him down yourself, lure him to us, or just run into the hedges. Junior and I will take it from there."

"Doc?" Junior piped up. "How did'ya get a first name for this guy? He never told me his name was Matthias. Just Bartsch."

Veronica pressed her fingertips against her temples. "My God, Ed! You need to show him the picture!"

Raymer nodded. "Wait here."

He sprinted to his study as Junior wrinkled his forehead in confusion. He glanced at Veronica first. When his eyes wandered to Laura, she shrugged. "He sent me an e-mail. Said he found a picture of the vampire when he was still human."

"Son of a bitch didn't tell me!" Junior turned the heavy handgun over in his grip as Edison closed the study door behind him.

Raymer approached the older man with a sheet of glossy printer paper in his hand. "Take a look at this."

Luttrell set the Magnum down and donned a pair of reading glasses from his shirt pocket. Raymer handed him the enlarged photograph.

"Third row, fourth over."

Junior froze. With a trembling hand, he covered his mouth. "That's him!" He almost choked on his words. "That's the motherfucker right there!"

Raymer took the photo as Junior eased his slender form into the chair. The older man dug through his pocket for a pill case, and dropped two red tablets into his palm.

"No drugs, Luttrell. I need you sharp and—"

"It's a goddamn beta blocker," Junior interrupted. "You 'bout gave me palpitations with that picture."

"So that's definitely the man you saw in '57?"

He nodded once at Veronica as he dry-swallowed the Acebutolol capsules. "That's him. I swear to fuck I'm tellin' the truth."

"Well, the man who killed your father was indeed a German soldier," Raymer said. "He was also a concert cellist. And his name is Matthias Bartsch."

"I also told you that thing ain't a man!" Junior blanched. "It's a dead-alive monster. A fuckin' animal."

"Semantics aside, you've just corroborated the identity of our vampire."

Raymer handed the picture to Laura, and pointed at the angular-featured man with long fingers wrapped around the neck of his cello. A lump rose in her throat.

"Miss McCoy," the professor said. "Meet Matthias Bartsch."

30

DRESSED IN HOSPITAL SCRUBS AND HIS BLACK MOTORCYCLE jacket, Matthias drove through the night with the car stereo at full volume. He had set Offenbach's *Les Larmes de Jacqueline* to repeat in the CD deck.

Anna's favorite. I must have played it for her a hundred times. Then, one day, the Kapellmeister forbade the music of Jewish composers in the halls of the Conservatory.

Matthias was returning to work after a short leave of absence. Despite his intuition to skip town, he knew he had to maintain appearances at Serenity Springs or risk drawing further attention to himself. As he passed beneath hazy streetlamps, he tried to clear his mind and keep his eyes on the street ahead.

But his thoughts inevitably returned to his wife.

"Liebst du mich, Matti?" Anna's legs were crossed as she sat on the piano bench, her fingers entwined around a lock of golden hair. Her expression was playful yet demure. She caressed her thigh. The silk of her dress was smooth to her touch and maddening to his.

"Ich liebe dich."

Matthias passed the scene of his recent crime. Yellow tape was hung between two telephone poles and stretched across the sidewalk. It fluttered and twisted in the autumn wind. No one—police or otherwise—prowled the area where he had tried to turn the young woman a few nights before.

When that girl met me with those eyes—full of vigor and passion and fear—I felt alive again. Like I was bringing her close to me. I could've made her anew and loved her forever.

But everything went wrong. I was too eager.

Too careless.

He took his eyes from the road ahead to look into the dark woods to his immediate left. The intrusive thoughts of his wife made him feel unfocused and anxious.

One particular memory haunted him, as if it had just occurred moments before.

Anna admired his uniform as he stood on the railway platform. Other soldiers moved around the couple as if they didn't exist. His wife's fingers touched the patch on his right sleeve—a golden snake coiled around a straight rod. "Du wirst viele Leben retten!"

He could never forget her forgiving smile. Why she had chosen him when she could've had any man in Darmstadt remained a mystery.

Anna reached up and adjusted his mütze. She tilted her head and looked on him with pride.

"Mein tapferer Matti! Ein sanitäter!"

The couple inched forward with their arms tightly entwined. His heart broke with every step as his jackboots crossed the platform. She released him a mere step from the train that would take him eastward. "Wirst du auf mich warten?"

"Ich bin deine Frau. Ich werde ewig warten!"

I'll wait forever.

Matthias turned onto Benjamin Harrison Boulevard. His reverie was interrupted as he rounded a corner and approached the entrance to Serenity Springs Elder Care. In the front parking lot, two idling police cruisers lurked side-by-side amidst the other cars. The taillights of the black and white vehicles cast an eerie red glow across the leaf-strewn lawn of the nursing home.

The bright aura on the grass became the reflection of crimson signal flares. They lit the night sky above the smoking ruins of Stalingrad. Russian rifles flashed and popped from dark windows as he crawled through dugouts, his P08 in one hand and a bandage in the other. An officer's whistle resounded, and the incessant chatter of machine guns, both German and Russian, began. One by one, weary *soldaten* emerged from hiding and charged into the crossfire. In mere seconds, voices began to cry *'sani'* between the burned-out buildings. But Matthias found himself seated behind the wheel of his car. He had left the battlefield behind long ago.

The same panic he once felt as a living man who charged headlong into enemy gunfire now rose in him again. It was a sick, choking feeling of utter dread.

They know.

Instead of slowing to turn into the parking lot, Matthias continued past the nursing home, his eyes fixed on the road ahead.

They know. But what do they know? My identity? Is that why they are here? Or is it just because of the drugs I stole from the dispensary?

The calm façade that masked his icy demeanor eroded again. Matthias thrust his fists into the steering wheel, and the car swerved precariously. After he straightened the trajectory of the sedan, Matthias pressed on the brakes and pulled onto a side street. Eventually, he would drive back into downtown Williamsport.

The vampire had to feed. He had grown weak. And the suspicions he entertained after his meeting with the supervisor on Monday night were confirmed. He could never go back to the nursing home, and circumstances were worse than he had feared.

31

A BLACK SUV, FOLLOWED BY AN OLD VOLVO STATION WAGON, pulled into the unused parking lot between two empty buildings. Raymer, Laura, and Junior piled out of the SUV as Veronica emerged from the driver's seat of her wagon. Raymer unlocked the rear hatch and grabbed Junior's black bag. Laura hauled her overnight bag and her backpack to Veronica's car and tossed them into the back seat.

"Hey, Doc?" Junior asked. "You sure we should be parkin' here? Nobody's gonna come sniffin' around here, right?"

"I used this lot last night. It's perfectly safe." Raymer straightened his tie, and then slipped the bandolier of stakes over his shoulder. He positioned it carefully and picked up his hammer.

"Camera's rolling." Veronica confirmed after fussing with the expensive device for several minutes.

"Good," Raymer responded. "Now follow me."

Junior picked up the black bag and stooped under its weight. Veronica continued to film the others as Raymer waved them on. They followed one another in a broken diagonal line towards the opposite sidewalk. Veronica raised the camera to capture a shot of the church tower in the distance. Out of breath, she nonetheless attempted to play narrator. "That's St. Luke's bell tower. Jennifer Stroud was attacked while moving along this sidewalk in the same direction we're traveling."

They were a few yards from the bus stop when a pair of headlights appeared in the distance. "Everyone but Laura, break right!" Raymer waved a hand toward the tall hedges. "Right, I said!"

Laura slid onto the metal bench in the bus shelter. She was surrounded by three Plexiglas walls, which met to form angles at thin metal posts. The lean-to was held together under a sloping roof where a lone florescent light sputtered. Laura shifted herself into a comfortable position. The car passed without slowing and continued down the street.

Behind her, she could discern the others moving through the tall grass. Raymer's deep voice, as usual, gave directions. In a matter of minutes, the only sound Laura could hear was the wind and distant traffic. On the frigid metal bench, she pulled her Ike jacket against the cold. As Raymer had instructed, she made no move to look behind her or draw attention to the others beyond the hedgerow.

This is gonna be the longest night of my goddamn life.

Laura wrapped her arms around herself and watched a car pass by in the direction of campus. For the first time since Raymer had called her with his outlandish tale of vampirism, she began to feel apprehensive.

The wind rattled the small structure. Decayed leaves eddied in the nearby gutter. An eerie whistling assailed her ears as the wind passed over the bus shelter. It rose in intensity to mimic a human scream.

Laura drew her legs up to her chest to make herself as small as she was capable. She shuddered at the prospect of what could happen to her if Edison Raymer was right.

Come on, McCoy. Those three are behind you. That old shitkicker Junior's packing enough heat to blow just about anything apart. Fucking .44 Magnum. Shit, that thing's gonna rattle every window in the neighborhood. You got backup just a few feet away.

She remembered what Edison said about the guns being a last resort. That went against everything she'd learned from a few regulars at her Northern Virginia shooting range. If Matthias Bartsch even appeared across the street, she'd have the .38 ready and would drop the son of a bitch before he came near her.

Self-defense, motherfucker. We can ask questions later.

It was easy to lose track of time as car after car passed at decreasing intervals. This time of night—back in the warmth of her apartment after a long day at the library—Laura was usually famished. But sitting alone in the cold, she felt sick to her stomach.

The way Luttrell reacted to that old picture.

Now that was fucked up. There's no question something beyond the ordinary is going on here.

Besides, Raymer wouldn't do something this drastic and dangerous without careful consideration.

Would he?

Laura shifted her weight on the bench and crossed her legs. Through the hard leather of her boot, she could feel the cylinder of the snub-nose .38.

That's bullshit and you know it. Ever since you met that man, he's been obsessed with vampires. He's still looking for any opportunity to avenge the death of that Aston boy, and clear the record on Jerry Critchlow.

Another gust of wind picked up and stung her watering eyes. She shook off the discomfort and resumed her thoughts of Raymer's disgraced mentor.

That fucker's an un-person up at Annandale. His papers are gone from the stacks, and his published works can't be found anywhere on campus. If Raymer knew how tarnished Critchlow's reputation really was, he'd be livid.

All because of his obsession with vampires.

"Fucking vampires," she muttered aloud to herself.

What the fuck am I even doing here?

A mass of leaves blew across the empty street, and her attention returned to the landscape around her. To her right, a pair of headlights caught her attention. The rumble of a powerful subwoofer accompanied the bright halogen beams. A maroon four-door sedan rattled forward but began to slow down just before the bus stop. Laura could hear the laughter of teenage boys over bass-heavy hip-hop.

Goddamn stereo probably cost more than the car.

As the car lumbered past her, one of the boys inside shouted, "Do it!"

The command inspired another round of boisterous laughter. The passenger in the back seat stuck his head out the window and yelled, "How much for a hand job?"

"Why don't you go fuck yourselves?" Laura responded with her middle finger raised high. The car and its drunken occupants peeled off into the distance.

Well, at least some things haven't changed around here.

Before long the heavy stillness returned. It was as if the crude disturbance had never occurred, and Laura's mind began to wander again.

So Junior's doing this to avenge his father, who probably beat him with his belt every night before bedtime.

Raymer's out here to prove the existence of vampires and get credit for what his mentor could never do.

And I guess Veronica's here 'cause she's fucking Raymer.

So really. What are you doing here, Laura?

She reached into her jacket pocket to retrieve her clove cigarettes. After fumbling with her lighter, she pulled off her glove and lit the *kretek* with an exposed hand. The glove slipped from her lap and fell to the ground.

"Goddammit." She bent down to grab it, brushing off bits of clinging gravel and dead leaves.

You're avoiding the question, doll face.

Laura exhaled the spicy smoke past her lips. She watched as her breath hung in the air and dissipated into a series of tumbling swirls.

I don't fucking know. The thrill of the hunt?

She began to wonder just how long her unexpected vacation with Raymer and his fearless vampire killers was going to last.

Fuck this noise. The plan's half-assed anyway. If that bastard's been undead for seventy years, he's smart enough to know he fucked up, and probably won't try to nab anyone around here again. At least not for a while, if he's even still in this city.

Laura shoved her hands in her trouser pockets and fought off a sudden wave of nausea. She rubbed her eyes as a car approached to her right. Laura tensed up as she noticed brake lights reflecting on the pavement behind its rear bumper.

If it's those fucking kids again...

No, wait. Is that a cop?

The car got closer and then slowed to a crawl. In the glare of the headlights, Laura held up a hand and narrowed her eyes. A burst of adrenaline kicked in.

Alright, McCoy. Prepare your best "good evening, ociffer" and be ready.

But it wasn't a police car, just an old sedan. It was too dark to tell, but it looked to be gunmetal gray. She was certain that it wasn't the car full of teenagers that passed her earlier. The lone driver was a mere shadow behind the wheel. A mournful flood of classical music vibrated the car's windows.

This creep's checking me out. I know it.

Laura suddenly felt the urge to get up and run. Inscrutable feelings of fear washed over her, as if some entity or presence had passed through her subconscious mind. She sat bolt upright and stifled a scream.

The car sped away.

Thinking on her feet, Laura read the plate numbers out loud in a clear voice. She hoped that the external microphone on Raymer's high-dollar camera picked up what she said.

The gray sedan disappeared from view and she leaned back, perplexed and uneasy about what had just happened.

Fucking hell.

Something was...inside me.

I've never felt anything like that before.

Laura remained awake and alert as more cars passed by without slowing.

That was him. It had to be.

She shuddered at the thought that he might be turning around on some side street to make his way back to her.

Fuck that. He could sneak up on the others from behind somehow and get them one by one. If this thing is really what Raymer thinks it is, how the fuck are we gonna stop it? We'd be no match for him!

Laura swallowed hard, and managed to subdue her mounting panic. Her cigarette had burned down and she flicked a long ash to the pavement. As she reached to light another one, the silence and the cold began to lull her back into a false sense of comfort. Before long, and after nearly half-an-hour without another unusual incident, she closed her eyes and concentrated on the slow rhythms of her breathing.

A car horn roused Laura from a shallow sleep. As she opened her eyes and shivered, a police cruiser idled before the bus shelter. The passenger side window slid down and a Latina police officer with jet-black hair cinched into a severe bun called out.

"Ma'am. You can't sleep here."

A flashlight beam passed across Laura's face, and she recoiled from the bright light.

"You been drinking tonight?"

"No, officer," Laura managed.

"Well, if you're waiting for a bus, they close this route at seven every weeknight. You need a ride back to campus?"

"I'm not a student." Laura rose on unsteady legs and hunched her shoulders. She thrust her hands deeper into her pockets. "But thanks for the offer."

"So what're you doing on that bench?"

"Just waiting on a friend to pick me up." Laura assured the policewoman. "I just got a text from her a few minutes ago. She's on her way."

"You need to be careful out here, OK?"

"I will, officer." Laura withdrew a hand to wave. The policewoman retracted the window and drove away.

If the cops showed up, Raymer said to go back to the parking lot and wait ten minutes, then come back.

Still playing her role, Laura shuffled down the sidewalk, stopping every now and then to stretch or stifle a yawn. By the time she crossed the street she was wide-awake.

The young woman slid along the brick wall of an abandoned building to stop and sit on the hood of Veronica Upham's car. Before she could glance at her watch, three figures emerged from the shadows. Raymer led the others, and they had all of their gear.

"I swear I didn't mean to fall asleep, Edison. It just—"

"Not your fault." Raymer looked disappointed. "I didn't expect immediate results, even though I hoped we'd get lucky."

Veronica rubbed a hand through her wind-tousled hair. "We ended up shooting a few hours of footage. It's just after one o'clock."

"The car." Laura shoved her numb hands into her pockets. "Did you get the car that slowed down on film? I called out the plate numbers."

"Oh, yeah," Raymer said. "We got all of that. At first, we were suspicious, but it never came back."

"Did you see the driver through that night-vision thingy?" Laura asked.

"No. Just a shadow. We got the plate number, though." Veronica kicked at a loose clump of asphalt. "It sounded like he was blasting classical music." She glanced around at the others. "Did any of you recognize it?"

"Shit." Junior shifted the heavy bag. "If it ain't Haggard, Willie, or Cash, I'd never pick it out."

"Yeah, but how many people drive around blaring that kinda stuff?" Veronica insisted. "It had to be him."

"Well, we got the license plate," Junior noted. "That's about as solid a lead as I can figure."

"And how are we going to run those numbers?" Raymer asked. He lifted the rear hatch of his SUV. "Any of you a computer hacker in your spare time?"

"We can call the goddamn DMV." Junior spat on the pavement. "It's better than nothin'."

"But they're not going to tell us anything. Mark my words. On our own, we have no means of running the plates. No cops, remember?" Raymer turned back to Laura. "Did the police take your name?"

"No," she answered. "She was in a hurry. She thought I was a student and told me to be careful. I played it just like you told me and took off after she left."

"Goddamn cops," Junior swore under his breath as he pitched his tactical bag into the SUV.

"Yeah." Raymer shook his head. "Your encounter with the police changes things. I'd call it a setback, but not a deal-breaker." He slammed the hatch closed. "Trust me. This hunt is far from over."

"Edison!" Laura raised her voice. "They're right about that gray car. I think it was him. Something weird happened when that car slowed. It was like some, I don't know, manifestation passed through me. I'm not sure—"

"If you're right—and I'll review the footage when I get home—he was sniffing around our trap. Scoping things out. This is exactly what I expected he would do the first night." Raymer rubbed his hands together to ward off the cold. "Perhaps tomorrow night, he'll make his move, and we'll be ready."

"Fuck." Laura glanced down at her boots. "I don't think I can sit out here another night, freezing my ass off. And if I fall asleep again, and that creep decides to act, then—"

"We'll discuss things tomorrow." Raymer nodded at the station wagon. "In the meantime, Laura, go on home with Veronica. We'll regroup tomorrow morning with clear heads."

Veronica gave the camera to Edison as Laura slipped into the passenger seat of the Volvo. After a brief exchange, Veronica got in, rubbed her hands together, and put her key in the ignition. Raymer took off with Junior in the black SUV, sending a hail of gravel at them in his wake.

Laura fumbled with her seatbelt, then rested her head against the window. "You OK, kid?"

"I'll live." Laura exhaled to fog up the window. She drew a stick figure in the condensation.

Veronica eased the station wagon forward and swung out onto the street.

They passed the bus shelter. Laura fumbled with the heat vents, then stretched her hands forward to absorb the hot air.

This hunt is far from over, she mused.

In the back corner of the uneven parking lot, a car engine rumbled to life. High-beams flickered on. A gray sedan rolled towards the street and peeled out after the Volvo. It kept enough distance to avoid detection while the deafening strains of Offenbach shook the loose windows once again.

32

THE CLOCK ON PROFESSOR UPHAM'S LIVING ROOM WALL READ 4:37, but Laura was unable to sleep. She thrashed on the couch cushions and tugged the thick blanket around her shoulders. Her thoughts raced in opposing directions. Laura didn't know if she was excited or let down by the failure of their hunt. Additionally, her academic obligations nagged at her. She hadn't checked her e-mail since the train ride, and had at least thirty pages of notes to condense and revise for her dissertation.

Her sleep cycle had been thrown off by the previous morning's train trip and the times she dozed off at the bus shelter. Laura sat up and let the blanket fall away.

She was still wearing her cargo pants and Joy Division shirt, and hadn't bothered to take off her boots. Laura strained to lift a leg. In the moonlit living room of Veronica's two-story house, she could see the outline of Junior Luttrell's pistol in its ankle holster. She swung her legs off the sofa to place her booted feet on the floor, then hunched forward.

Laura's empty stomach was in knots. The nausea she experienced earlier was replaced by hunger. As she rose from her makeshift bed, she was overcome with feelings of dizziness. Alone on the first floor of a strange house, the young woman inched her way around the long coffee table. She stretched out her arms as her eyes adjusted to the darkness.

She found her Ike jacket draped over an easy chair and slipped it on. Her backpack—which contained her laptop and a heavy stack of notes—rested in the seat of the chair.

I need to get some work done. But I'm sure Raymer'll be calling bright and early with five or six new half-assed ideas.

With a sigh, she hefted her backpack by a single strap and flung it over her shoulder.

And I really don't wanna be around when Veronica Upham rolls outta bed and forces herself to be all congenial.

Laura wandered into the kitchen, hoping to brew a large pot of coffee and find something in the refrigerator she could heat up for an early breakfast. Then she could spend a couple hours poring over her notes. Maybe she could try to pound out a few more pages of her thesis. But all the preparation seemed like a herculean effort.

Fuck this. What's the name of that all-night diner two blocks away? Something corny, like the Dew Drop Inn. Upham here's a total granola. Fucking wheat grass, organic soymilk, and all that shit. Don't even need to open the fridge to figure that out.

I need some bacon, eggs, and coffee. Then maybe I can get some shit done before the day's festivities begin.

Laura found a notepad and pen in a cabinet drawer. She penned a quick note for Veronica about where she was going, and added her cell number so the English professor wouldn't worry when she woke up. Laura left her note in a conspicuous location on the counter, and then headed for the front door.

Even though she was accustomed to cold weather, the morning air took her breath away when she stepped outside. Laura pulled the door closed behind her, slipped her other arm through the backpack's remaining strap, and set off toward the sidewalk. In the glow of the sodium vapor lamps along the quiet drive, she stopped to orient herself.

She recalled cutting through this neighborhood on her bike as an undergrad to get to the main drag with all the fast food joints. Somewhere at the end of the *cul de sac* was a bike path that would cut ten minutes off her walk. Laura squinted in the dim light and could see a yellow pole marking the entrance to the paved trail. As she set off in the direction of the wooded path, a nagging voice inside her head posed an obvious question.

What if you run into this guy when you cut through those woods?

In defiance of all things rational, Laura spoke aloud as she neared the dark entrance to the copse of trees. "He's getting five rounds from a snubnose .38 in his goddamn chest, that's what."

189

Her breath billowed in the frigid air of the early morning, and a smile tugged at her lips. The weight of the revolver strapped around her boot was a deceptive comfort.

I rode my bike up this path at least a hundred times in the dark back in the day, and never once ran into any creeps or psychos lurking in the trees. Besides, I'll be damned if I'm gonna let this crazy fuck intimidate me.

Once she passed the entrance and rounded a corner, she noticed a row of colonial-style streetlamps astride the long measure of the path. The lamps were crafted from black wrought iron, and hadn't been there when she used the trail as an undergrad. The lights were reassuring, so she bounded forward with a quickened step, her mind on a hot breakfast and all the coffee she could drink.

The strange sensation she was being watched didn't hit her right away. But the eerie feeling crept over her as she neared a wooden footbridge, which spanned a deep gulley. A slight breeze blew around her, and Laura heard the dry rustle of dead leaves scrape across the pavement. The chunky heels of her boots thumped along the graded path. Withered tree branches snapped and creaked against the moonlit sky above. She realized that, despite her best efforts at personal protection, she was alone in the woods and quite vulnerable.

Laura's eyes swept every amorphous tree trunk and low-lying branch crowding the path as it veered toward the footbridge. Her heart began to race, so she closed her eyes and took a deep breath as she stumbled forward.

When her eyes fluttered open again, he was there.

In the time it took to blink, Matthias Bartsch had moved to block her. Laura had heard nothing, nor had she seen him detach from the shadows along the path. It made no sense to her rational mind, which was now overcome with a panicked survival instinct. The menacing figure had appeared out of nowhere and stood a few feet ahead of her.

Laura ducked and reached down for the gun in the ankle holster. Before she could raise her trouser leg, the vampire charged and tackled her to the ground. She landed on her back. Although her pack broke her fall, the laptop inside snapped upon impact with the pavement. Laura's head hit the asphalt, and before she could cry out, Matthias slapped a cold hand over her mouth. She felt something sticky and unyielding cover her lips as he withdrew his hand. A strip of duct tape kept her mouth firmly shut.

Laura took a swing at the vampire, but Matthias dodged her half-hearted attempt to fight back. He tightened his strong hands around her arms and flipped her on to her belly. He tore off her backpack and tossed it into the ravine, where it splashed into a shallow creek.

With a knee pressed against her, Matthias drew her arms behind her back and clasped them together at the wrists. From beneath her gag, she bellowed, but the vampire didn't react to her muffled protests.

Matthias bound her arms together with more duct tape, which he tore from a thick roll. He secured her kicking legs in the same fashion. The vampire had subdued, bound, and gagged Laura in less than a minute's time. Without effort, he flung her over his shoulder and carried her off the path. Her head lolled and smacked into his chest a few times before he dropped her in the leaves and pressed her head against the ground.

The vampire flipped her over and straddled her. Luttrell's revolver was in his hand. With a flick of his wrist, he popped open the cylinder and silver bullets rained down from the chambers. The gun was shoved into his belt as he leaned over to stare into her eyes. His gaze was at once terrifying and soothing. For a moment, she was hypnotized. But the vampire's stony features sank into a sneer, and he lunged at her bare neck.

The duct tape over her mouth stifled her screams as she felt his teeth scrape across her flesh and break the skin of her throat. A chill ran through her body as she felt his tongue enter the wound in her neck. Despite the inexplicable communion of pleasure and pain, Laura thrashed in protest. She fought to break the mental and physical control the monster had over her. Yet she soon found herself unable to move or resist. Laura McCoy could only stare into the dark sky beyond the treetops as her body seized with one last fibrillation. Her mind remained lucid and aware of each conflicting sensation—the continued pressure against her neck, the damp ground beneath her pinned arms, and the sucking sounds as the vampire drained her blood into his mouth.

Before her vision faded, the vampire tore away her gag. Laura didn't scream. Her will was gone as the attacker pressed his lips to hers. As the vampire's cold, dead blood filled her mouth, she felt no pain. No sadness. No pity or rage. There was only the alien sensation of his blood as it began to swell her arteries and rush through her veins. Laura's heart spasmed once before its pulsations ceased altogether.

Then, she saw as he saw.

Heard as he heard.

His memories flooded her mind. She was overcome with feelings of anguish and a vast, aching loneliness. Yet these impressions were soon eclipsed by a sense of power. Brute force and unmitigated cruelty. Murderous rage tempered by cold, calculated precision.

Scenes from a childhood she never lived, and lush phrases from beautiful music she'd never heard assaulted her senses. The sounds became images, and the visions shivered across her flesh. The figure of a young fair-haired woman smiled and stretched forth a trembling hand. She felt the urge to pursue her, to comfort her, but the woman's face twisted into a grotesque expression of agony. She was suddenly bombarded by the sound of gunfire. Shrapnel rained down upon her and threatened to bury her where she lay. She crawled through dirt, filth, and blood as the screams of the wounded and dying resounded on all sides.

"Sanitäter!" Laura cried out in her delirium. The vampire's thick black blood spilled over her white lips. She coughed as her eyes fluttered open. Her gaze, however, was hollow and lifeless.

Laura lay motionless as the vampire cradled her and stroked her hair. Sleep threatened to overtake her, and she surrendered to the soothing darkness.

33

THE EARLY MORNING SUNLIGHT GLEAMED THROUGH THE bedroom curtains. Veronica Upham stirred in her four-poster bed. She had been awake for some time as her mind replayed the events of the previous night. After careful thought, Veronica realized that she'd probably have to lay in the cold, wet grass for a few more nights before Raymer gave up the chase. She just wanted things to go back to the way they were before everything started to fall apart.

Maybe once Laura hops the train back to Northern Virginia, Edison will call this whole thing off. Maybe he'll even reconsider his resignation? And that irascible Luttrell character will go back to Poquoson.

Her thoughts turned to Laura, asleep on the couch downstairs. It was an odd feeling to share her home with someone else, even for a few days. Edison never once spent the night in her lonely house. The place had felt empty and lifeless since Tom had moved out years ago. Her mind ran over their last verbal confrontation, when he had blamed his infidelity on Veronica's inability to bear children. They'd both wanted a family, but Tom refused to adopt. Once their uncontested divorce was finalized, he took up with one of his graduate students, and was now the proud father of two young daughters.

Veronica got out of bed and slipped into a thick gray robe. She fetched an empty teacup from her bedside table and headed down the narrow staircase. She was planning to wake Laura and cook her a hearty breakfast, but when Veronica stepped into the living room, she was surprised to find an empty couch.

What the hell?

The English professor noted Laura's carry bag on the chair where she'd dropped her things, but her coat and backpack were gone.

Maybe she got fed up with Edison's bullshit and left?

Not without her overnight bag.

Veronica hurried to the kitchen and sighed with relief when she found Laura's note. She snatched the cordless phone from its wall charger and dialed the young woman's cell number. After four rings, Laura's curt voicemail greeting began to play.

"Dammit!"

God knows when she could've taken off for that diner.

Veronica slapped the phone against her open palm.

I'll give it five minutes and try her again. If she's run off to do what-the-fuck-ever, Ed's gonna flip his shit.

She tore open the refrigerator door and ducked inside for an orange juice carton. "I can hear that son of a bitch right now." She began to impersonate Edison Raymer as she poured a glass of orange juice. "Veronica, you were supposed to be watching her and blah blah blah..."

As she leaned against the kitchen countertop and drained the glass, she pictured Ed's stern gaze from behind his wire-rim glasses.

Those goddamn glasses. Always peering through them with that smug look in his eyes.

Veronica tried Laura's cell again, and this time, she left a long rambling message. As she spoke, she dug through a drawer for the phone book, and looked up the number for the restaurant.

A harried waitress picked up the phone as Veronica paced from the dining room back to the kitchen. She gave the woman on the other end a precise physical description of Laura and what she was probably wearing.

"Ain't no one come in here this mornin' lookin' like that," the waitress replied. Her voice was hoarse from years of smoking. Before Veronica could ask any additional questions, the waitress hung up.

The English professor began to panic. She called Raymer without wasting another moment.

"Good morning, Veronica." By the tone of his voice, she knew he already had a new plan of action. "Can you two be over here by eight o'clock? I've got some ideas—"

"Edison, Laura's gone."

When he didn't answer, Veronica attempted to fill the awkward silence on the other end of the line.

"I mean, she left a note that said she was going up to get breakfast on the main drag. I tried calling her twice and then it went straight to voicemail. So I called the diner and they said no one came in that matched Laura's—"

"Veronica, calm down," Edison said. "She probably just went to a different restaurant. Did you leave a message for her to call you back?"

"Yeah, but—"

"Then give her thirty minutes. If she doesn't call, try her again."

"Edison, listen to me. Something's not right about this. I think—"

"I said calm down. I don't know what kind of conclusions you're jumping to here, but—"

"I'm gonna go out and look for her."

"And waste the morning? Damn it, Veronica, we've got a lot to get done today. This isn't what I had in mind when I spoke of conducting fieldwork. We're up and ready to get started over here."

"You do what you want, Ed. But I'm going out there. I'll try to retrace her steps."

"Alright, keep your cell phone on and wait for her call. She's very conscientious and wouldn't ignore your concern if you left a voicemail. That much I know about Laura."

"Well, if she's so goddamned conscientious, where the fuck did she go?"

"Look." Raymer sighed through the phone. "I'm not happy about it either. This was incredibly irresponsible, not to mention stupid of her. But I'm sure we'll hear from her soon."

"You better fucking hope so!" Veronica's voice had become shrill. "Because if something happened to her, it's gonna be *your* goddamn fault!"

"Well, I left her in your care." Raymer cleared his throat. "Is there *anything* I can trust you with?"

"Now wait a minute, Edison. You're the one that—"

"For Christ's sake, Veronica! Just be patient. Junior and I will be over in ten minutes. I guess we can do some of our research from your place today."

"Fine. Whatever. Just let yourself in if I'm not here. There's a bike path the kids from school use as a shortcut. I'm gonna start there."

"OK," Raymer said. "We'll be there when you get back. And if she's decided to go wandering, it doesn't matter. Just as long as she's back sometime this afternoon. Technically, we don't need her until tonight."

"Well, *technically* she could be hurt or...or worse."

When there was no reply—condescending or otherwise—Veronica realized Raymer had already hung up on her. With a frustrated groan, she slammed the phone down and darted upstairs.

In a matter of minutes, she was dressed in jeans, a sweater, and a pair of running shoes. Before she left, she penned a quick note for Laura and taped it to the front door in case she returned.

The morning chill was compounded by gusty winds, which hinted that a bad winter was ahead. She cut across the street and made her way to the end of the *cul de sac*. Even in the early morning light, the trees surrounding the bike path entrance cast stark shadows on the sequestered trail. As she turned onto the pavement, a winded jogger passed her. The young woman wore a blue WILLIAMSPORT CROSS COUNTRY sweatshirt. Veronica slowed her pace to watch the undergrad disappear around the corner through the dense forest. She could hear the tread of the jogger's shoes on fallen leaves scattered along the path.

Veronica rounded the bend and was surprised to see one of her former students sitting on a park bench. It was Erin Hayes from her Brit Lit survey course last spring. The young woman wore a heavy coat and had her nose buried in a copy of Charles Brockden Brown's *Wieland*.

"Dr. Upham!" the undergraduate shouted. "Hey, what're you doing out here?"

Veronica tried to pull her thoughts together. "Oh, I live back on Copperstone Drive."

The English major nodded and gave the professor a concerned glance. "Everything OK?"

"Well, I'm looking for a friend," Veronica managed. "Have you been out here long?"

"Not really," Erin replied. "Maybe half an hour? I thought I'd get a start on my reading assignment for Professor Coffey's American Lit class."

"You see a woman pass by here? She's wearing an old army jacket and has long blonde hair. Kinda tall?"

"Nobody's come by looking like that." Erin shook her head. "That's your friend?"

"Yeah. I gotta go. I'm sure I'll see you around campus." Veronica wandered away as Erin returned to her book.

As she walked along the path, Veronica glanced back and forth into the trees lining the way. Foot traffic had picked up, and a few more joggers passed her. One nearly ran into her as her eyes wandered aimlessly.

"On your left!" The jogger nudged Veronica aside to avoid a collision. She was halfway across a wooden footbridge, and the rail broke her fall. She rested a moment as her eyes traced the clear stream below. Beer cans and food wrappers littered the banks of the rocky wash. As she leaned further over the railing, she noticed something familiar, yet completely out of place. She squinted, but the amorphous object lay half submerged in the shallow creek.

Veronica spun around and walked to the end of the footbridge. Using tree roots for balance, she worked her way down the sloping ravine. Briars and tall reeds whipped at her face and stuck her through the wool sweater. When she emerged from the stinging wet brambles, her heart dropped into her stomach. Laura's laptop bag was floating in the creek before her.

She picked up a fallen branch and dragged the half-sunken object onto the muddy bank. When she threw open the zipper, water spilled out, along with splintered fragments of plastic.

Oh fuck. No. Please. This can't be fucking happening.

Veronica removed the damaged laptop. It was completely smashed, as if it'd been dropped on concrete. Water gushed from the ruined device. Laura's handwritten notes were waterlogged and illegible. Her heart pounded in her chest as she shoved everything back into the bag and hauled it up the riverbank.

Her climb out of the ravine became a frantic scramble. As she reached the edge of flat ground, the winded professor yanked herself up by a sapling. When she took her hand off the withered leaves, her palm was red with blood. On her knees, she realized the dew-soaked leaves had been displaced. Some sort of struggle had occurred.

As she inspected her hand again, the morning sun glinted off a single silver bullet. The cartridge hadn't been fired. Now frantic, Veronica stumbled to her feet and called Raymer.

"Hey," he answered. "We're at your place. You find our missing hunter?"

"Edison, I'm gonna apologize for ever doubting you about any of this. I was wrong..." her voice trailed off. "So fucking wrong."

"What are you talking about?"

"Bartsch," she answered. "He's got Laura."

"How?" Edison raised his voice. "Where in the hell are you and how do you know?"

"I'm on the bike path at the end of the street. By the footbridge. He got her. Threw her laptop bag in the creek. And...and..."

"Spit it out, Veronica!" he snapped.

"There's blood everywhere."

34

"I'LL SAY IT AGAIN, AND FOR THE LAST TIME." VERONICA PRESSED a fist against the windowpane as she watched the setting sun. "The only thing we can do now is drop all this shit and go to the police. That's the only way."

"Fuck that!" Junior rose from Veronica's couch. Five silver bullets were lined up in a row before him on the professor's coffee table. "We all agreed. No cops! I, for one, am a man of my word, and I stick to what—"

"Stop it!" Raymer leaned on the mantelpiece. "First of all, what the hell are we gonna tell the police? That we're a group of vampire hunters? That one of us went missing after we pissed off the local bloodsucker? You think Rudy Pettit will believe that?" Raymer shrugged and regained his composure. "If we go to the cops with this story, we're fucked. They didn't believe Junior, and they sure as hell aren't going to listen to us now. So, as it stands, we've done nothing but argue all day. Instead of agreeing on a solid course of action going forward, hours have been lost rehashing the same tired and confused bullshit!"

Veronica leaned against the windowsill and shook her head. "Edison, everything's changed. We have a missing person on our hands!"

"She made a conscious decision to play a part in our hunt. What she did this morning by going out on her own? That was stupid, and it wasn't part of the plan. But what's done is done. She's gone and we need to move on. Change our *modus operandi*."

"That's it?" Veronica turned and locked her hands on her hips. "That's

199

all you have to say about this? Laura's fucking *missing*, Edison! Who knows what that psycho fuck is doing to her! Or...or what he's already done to her!"

Before Raymer could respond, Junior beat him to the punch. "That's all the more reason we need to act now and act fast. If y'all wanna get that girl back, we gotta find this fucker *now*. It's the only way."

Veronica ignored Junior, determined to push her stubborn colleague over the edge.

"Just admit it, Edison. Matthias Bartsch is smarter than you." Breathless, she pointed an accusatory finger at Raymer. "Go on and say it. He bested you. And God knows which one of us he's gonna grab next!"

"I won't admit to something that isn't true!" Raymer shot back, his eyes ablaze behind his spectacles. "What happened here was a series of bad decisions on *your* part! *And* Laura's. The plan was for you two to stick together, not split up for any—"

"Goddammit, Edison!" Veronica was hysterical. "This vampire we're supposed to be hunting isn't playing by your timetable!" She took a deep breath. "I think at this point, it's pretty safe to say that *he's* hunting *us!*"

Raymer crossed his arms and remained taciturn.

Veronica looked at Junior. "See, the big bad vampire slayer over there's got nothing at all. *Nothing.* He can't even admit he fucked up. And now we're in shit up to our necks with no way—"

"Veronica, sit down and shut the fuck up." Raymer removed his glasses and stroked the bridge of his nose. "The hunt continues. We don't stop until this creature is staked to the ground. We're still going to prove vampires exist by destroying this one. That part doesn't change." Raymer paced across Veronica's living room. "What we need to do is some detective work, because—"

"Listen here!" Junior waved a finger at the professor. "I didn't team up with you eggheads to fuck around. All these plans and theories are a goddamn joke. We can still get out there, pound the pavement, and—"

"And what?" Raymer countered. "What do we have to go on at this point but a name and a gray car? You called the DMV yourself and they refused to tell you anything." Raymer slapped his hands together. *"Boom!* Dead end. Drop that one from our search parameters. So this is the course of action I propose."

"Did you just man up and admit you've got nothing here?" Veronica laughed as she cradled her head, hoping to fend off an impending migraine.

"Because it sounds like the unsinkable Edison Raymer's springing leaks like the fucking Titanic."

"If you'd let me finish, I was about to tell you my plan."

"Don't let me stop you!" Veronica held out a hand.

"You were right about one thing. Bartsch has been one step ahead of us. So we need to re-align the so-called timetables."

"For fuck's sake, would you say somethin' that don't come off like a heapin' pile of horseshit, Raymer?" Junior knocked the neat row of bullets over like dominoes. They rattled on the surface of the coffee table. One clattered to the floor.

"You want me to dumb it down for you two?" The professor eyed the others with contempt. "If we want to catch a vampire, we need to start thinking like one. This creature hasn't survived for seven decades by being careless. What he did Sunday night was probably the first time he's fucked up in years. What time is it now?"

Veronica looked up at the clock. "Half-past five."

"Alright, turn on the TV." He picked up a remote control from a side table and tossed it into Veronica's lap. "Channel 13 starts their evening news at five, right? And they repeat the same stories every half hour until the national news comes on."

Veronica turned on the television and switched to the channel he suggested. Junior leaned back into the couch cushions with an impatient sigh.

"Now hear me out. We need to pay attention to the news. Even if nothing comes up." He pursed his lips and took a breath through his nose. "One of us should get online and start looking up local missing persons cases. Make note of anything weird. This guy's gone to great lengths to cover his tracks, but these days, everything is online somewhere. Individually, certain facts amount to nothing. But if we piece them all together, we may be able to uncover something about his hunting patterns."

Raymer stopped to let his words sink in. The newscasters chattered on TV about a gang-related shooting in Suffolk. "If you killed someone, how would you dispose of the body?"

"I don't know." Junior shrugged and shook his head. "Bury it?"

"No." Raymer clutched his chin. "If you drained the blood from a new victim every night, and the cops found those bodies, it'd be all over the news. No, he's either burning them, or he has some underwater dump site in one of the swamps along the James River."

201

"Makes sense." Junior nodded. "You know I got a police scanner a few years back that I've been meanin' to mount in my truck, but never got around to it. I can head back home and get it?"

"Good idea," Raymer said. "But not now. We're at war with an unseen enemy. We don't divide our ranks from sundown to sunrise. That rule is now ironclad."

Veronica drove her fingernails into the upholstery of her living room chair. "So we're gonna wait for a news report? Spy on the cops' radio chatter? This is fucking ridiculous!"

"As I insinuated, there may be clues that will point us in the right direction. We just need to narrow down the information. We could even go back to Poquoson's library and check the microfilm. See if Bartsch killed anyone else besides Junior's father. We have to do the leg work. Otherwise, we'll be pissing in the wind."

"No," Veronica said with malice. "We won't. Because he's gonna pick us off one by—"

"Hold on! Hold on!" Junior held up his hand and leaned toward the television. The others glanced up as the police sketch of Matthias Bartsch flashed across the screen. Veronica fumbled for the remote and turned up the volume.

"As the manhunt for an alleged rapist in Williamsport continues, authorities have released additional information on the suspect. While police have yet to release the name of the perpetrator in question, Channel 13 has now learned that the suspect worked as a night orderly at Serenity Springs Elder Care in Williamsport."

The picture onscreen changed to show external location shots of the nursing home, filmed at sunset for dramatic effect.

"While police have been pursuing new leads since Wednesday, the suspect remains at large. If you have any information regarding this case, you're urged to call the Williamsport Crime Line at..."

Raymer shot out of his chair to block the television. "See that!" The look on his face was one of vindication. "We have a lead right there!"

"So what?" Veronica asked. "Are we supposed to go traipsing down there and just ask for information on an employee named Matthias Bartsch? First of all, why would they tell us anything they haven't already told the police? And second, how do we even know he uses that name—"

"Ain't you been payin' attention?" Junior interrupted. "I told y'all when I was down at the station talkin' to that shitheel detective, he said *Bartsch*. He told me he had a tip, but wouldn't tell me where he got it. Now I'll bet you my pension he heard that name from someone who worked with that son of a bitch."

Raymer sat in silence, his mind obviously at work. As the other's waited for a response, the newscasters began reporting on another crime in Williamsport. A trailer on Route 619 had gone up in flames over the weekend with the inhabitants inside. The police were ruling it a murder-suicide based on the position of the bodies.

Raymer looked up at the screen, and blinked once. He gestured to Veronica, who glanced at the televised remains of the scorched mobile home.

"Puzzle pieces," she whispered.

Raymer stood up, straightened his necktie, and smoothed a hand over his graying beard. "Tonight, we do nothing. We stay here and lick our wounds."

Luttrell raised a hand in protest, but Raymer cut him off. "Junior, tomorrow you'll go back to Poquoson in the morning and get that police scanner. You might wanna melt down the family silverware and make some more ammunition for your little arsenal in that bag."

"Well, at least I'll be doin' somethin' instead of arguin' with a buncha uppity professors," he mumbled.

"Veronica, I'll compile a list of search terms for you to run through on your laptop. Try to think like him. How would you hunt so as not to draw attention to yourself? Who would you hunt? Where would you go to find victims?"

"OK." She nodded. "I guess I'd rather be doing research than freezing my ass off like last night."

"By sundown, we'll all meet back at my place. We probably won't have all the information we need, but, goddammit, we'll have more than we've got now."

"So what're you gonna do, Ed?" Veronica asked.

"I'm getting up early and heading down to Serenity Springs Elder Care. I'll introduce myself as a private investigator working for the Stroud family."

"And what makes you think you can just go in there and get confidential information that's already been handed over to the cops?"

"It's simple." Raymer cracked his knuckles. "When the occasion calls for it, I can be very persuasive."

35

RACKED WITH AGONY, LAURA McCOY GRIPPED THE mattress and twisted the bloodstained linens around her fingers. Her body contorted and she kicked her feet in a blind, feverish rage. Within her peripheral view, Matthias Bartsch was spreading plastic sheeting around the edge of the bed. He stopped to crouch by her side, then pressed the corners of the tarp around the bed frame. Laura groaned and tore at the bedding. Finally, he rose to look her over.

She was still dressed in her cargo pants and t-shirt, but her jacket and boots had been removed. The vampire extended a hand to rouse her.

"Laura."

Her eyelids twitched as she heard her name. She grasped his wrist in a futile attempt to pull him closer. His arms slack, the elder vampire stood firm beside his fledgling.

"Wake up." The tone of his voice remained cold as he jerked his arm away. Laura's limp hand dropped to the mattress.

"You!" Laura recoiled once she recognized the man before her. "Where am I?" Her voice was hoarse and sounded unfamiliar to her ears.

"It doesn't matter. No one will find you here."

"I don't understand." She shook her head. "You attacked me...I mean... what the fuck is going on?"

"*You* came looking for *me*. You and three others."

Still disoriented, Laura rose into a sitting position. She felt Matthias place his hand on her back.

"Don't touch me!" she shouted, flinging his hand away from her.

"Do you have any idea how foolish that was?" He shook his head. "That is why I came for you. I assumed you *wanted* to be found."

"The girl." Laura reflected. "The first one. She wasn't hunting you. Why did—"

"She was a mistake," the vampire admitted. "You, however, were not."

"That's a lie, you fucking psycho! You thought both of us were someone else! Anna, or—"

"Is that what the others told you?"

"How do you know about them?"

"Laura, I've been doing this for seventy years." Matthias crossed his arms. "Until now, no one has been *stupid* enough to do what you people did."

"So what am I doing here?" Laura pressed him. "Why did you spare me?"

Matthias placed a firm hand on her shoulder. An odd smile tugged at his lips. "You actually think I spared you?"

She was nonplussed. "I don't understand. You let me live. Even after I tried to...to pull a gun...that means—"

"What does it mean?" Matthias guided Laura's hand to the hollow of her chest. "You and your friends think you know what I am. So I can only assume you know what I am capable of." He placed her fingers between her breasts. "So tell me. What is missing? What is no longer there?"

Laura's eyes darted around the dimly lit confines of the room. She noticed a window where the uneven wall met the irregular ceiling. Every pane of glass was hidden behind thick cardboard. The edges of each frame were lined with heavy duct tape. Not a single ray of natural light could enter the room.

"Pay attention, Laura! Feel. With your hand."

"My heart." Her eyes grew wide. "I can't feel it beating. I can't...you... *what did you do to me?*"

Matthias turned and clasped his hands behind his back. Her panicked voice echoed through the apartment. "You chose to play the sacrificial lamb for those cowards. So what do you think I did?"

Hunger wrenched at Laura's gullet. It welled up from her bowels and threatened to render her mute. Yet with it came a sudden flood of anger and revulsion.

"You...you made me...like you? You motherfucking bastard! You turned me into a...a fucking monster!"

205

"There is no point in playing a victim, Laura. It doesn't suit you." He shook his head. "You can be much more than that."

Laura was dumbfounded. Thoughts and memories came in disconnected fragments. She could not fully distinguish her senses as one seemed to overlap with another. The insatiable hunger was the only constant. The only words she could find were accusatory, which risked angering her captor.

"You did this to me!" She tried to weep, but the tears wouldn't come. "Why?"

"I think you know why." Matthias lingered beside the bed, poised with the stillness of a statue. "You are a strong woman, but this is one fight you cannot win. Now, to live as I do, you have to feed."

"And what if I don't wanna *live* like you?"

"The pain you are feeling now will get worse, and you will rot away on that filthy mattress," Matthias remarked without emotion.

Laura tried to rise from the bed, but Matthias held her back. "You are too weak. Be still and it will pass. At least for a while."

She fell back into the bed and curled into a fetal position. Her teeth chattered and her body trembled. "It fucking burns! You...d-d-don't understand!"

Matthias fought the urge to look away from the suffering woman. His sharp features tightened.

"Of course I understand, Laura. I've had decades of hunger, but I had no one to see me through it." The vampire brushed a damp lock of hair from her eyes. "I will help you. But you need to trust me. Control the hunger, Laura. Master it. That's the only way you will survive. Who knows?" he paused with a shrug. "You might come to enjoy the gift I've given you."

"Fuck you!"

The vampire turned and took several quick strides to the door. "I'll be back shortly. In the meantime—"

"No, wait a minute!" Laura sat up and winced as pain shot through her chest. "Where're you going? You can't just leave me here!"

"If you want the agony to stop, you don't have a choice. You have to trust me now. I'm acting in your best interest."

Before slipping out the door, Matthias issued a warning. "Don't waste time looking for your cell phone. Or a way out. I'm the only one that can help you at this point."

Laura moaned and raised her eyes to look for Matthias, but he had already departed. A latch turned as the vampire secured the heavy steel door.

The craving gave way to nausea, and Laura turned on her side. She leaned her upper body over the bed and retched, but there was nothing inside her. She rolled forward and fell to the floor, then crawled across the plastic drop cloth. As she placed her hands on the crumpled plastic, she could feel dissolution occurring as her skin and the material pressed together. Laura could no longer feel the sheeting as a singular object. Beneath her fingertips, a billion molecules hummed and collided unnervingly.

Laura staggered to her feet. The room spun and pulsed with moving shadows. She braced a hand against the wall and was able to steady herself.

The material world as she knew it seemed to disintegrate around her. Laura walked until she reached the far wall by the locked door. She looked to her left, and the small room opened into a short hallway.

Laura moved forward until she stumbled into a piece of furniture blocking her way. The obstruction took her by surprise as time dilated around her. For a moment, she felt lucid again, and recalled the bittersweet taste of Matthias' blood in her mouth.

She concentrated on the room around her, which had ceased to oscillate. She noticed an ornate cello on a stand in the corner. The long bow rested against it.

Laura approached the instrument. She crouched on weakened legs and traced the spruce and maple body with her fingers. She touched each string, and could feel aftershocks of Matthias' passionate bowing and fretting. In her mind, Laura could hear the sounds he had coaxed from the strings. Notes of dissonance warred with beautiful melodies. Her captor's enduring pain and his most passionate memories seemed to emanate from the instrument's hollow body.

He loves this instrument as a father loves a first-born son.

Laura rose and glanced around the sparsely furnished room. All of the barricaded windows were close to the ceiling, suggesting that the room was underground or in a basement apartment. There were no lights save for a pair of dim wall fixtures. However, even in the low light, she could see everything in bold relief.

Laura noticed a tin box on a side table by itself. An inexplicable longing to open it and view its contents led her across the room.

She advanced towards the table, using the edge for balance, and opened the rusty cigarette tin. Laura removed Matthias' medals and awards from atop a stack of photographs. As she picked up a shiny black badge, a throbbing sensation passed through her throat and she felt her balance giving way.

This can't be real. It just can't.

Laura placed the Wound Badge on the table, and began to flip through the stack of photographs. One caught her attention. The snapshot was very old with a dull matte finish. It was a studio portrait of Matthias in uniform, but he only looked a few years younger. He wore high boots, a neatly pressed tunic with a breast eagle and dark collar, along with a field cap cocked to one side. He looked uncomfortable in uniform, and his expression was severe.

Before she flipped to the next picture, she noticed a white armband with a red cross on Matthias' left arm, along with an indiscernible black patch. Laura turned the picture over and a date was scrawled on the back. 1941. She looked at the photograph again. She was certain that it was him.

Raymer was right. He was a soldier. A German soldier in World War II. And he was also a cellist. The evidence is right here. It's all true.

She attempted to process all she had learned. The more she struggled to understand, the more difficult it became to comprehend the unquestionable truth.

He's a vampire.

He was killed in the war and somehow came back. He lived as a young man for years, watching those around him grow old and die.

Just as I will.

Laura almost screamed as her conscience thundered in her head. She rushed to put the photographs back in order, when a picture of a blonde woman in a light flower-print dress caught her eye.

She removed it from the pile. When compared to Laura, the woman was fuller figured and her hair was several inches longer than her own. But Laura could see a distinct resemblance between herself and the woman in the photograph.

She traced the sharp lines of the background, which faded into soft, blurred edges. On the back of the photo was an inscription:

ANNA BARTSCH

MATTI— ICH LIEBE DICH!

He thinks I'm his wife.

Laura cast a despairing gaze around the room.

But he called me by my own name?

Laura put everything back into the tin. In the process, she discovered another photograph of Matthias clad in battle gear. The German leaned against the scorched hulk of a Sherman tank. His helmet was painted white and adorned with red crosses. Beneath black leather suspenders and a belt with boxy attachments was a short white apron bearing another large cross.

He was some kind of doctor. Trained to save lives.

Now he takes them.

Laura piled the medals atop the celluloid photos. She pushed away from the table and clutched her stomach as the hunger returned. In time, she clawed her way back to the single bedroom. Sickness washed over her, and she needed to lie down. She eased her body onto the edge of the mattress and fell into a restless sleep.

36

AURA WAS JARRED AWAKE WHEN THE DOOR BURST OPEN violently. Matthias led a filthy middle-aged man across the threshold of the apartment. The vagrant was dressed in torn clothing with an old army jacket and a toque to ward off the cold. He reeked of soil, urine, and cheap wine.

"What the fuck you doin', man? Get'cher hands off my goddamn neck." The transient slapped a calloused palm at Matthias, who closed and locked the door. "You said you had..."

"Liquor?" Matthias finished. "Of course I do."

"Naw, you said you was gonna give me scratch for a bus ticket. So I can go back to Cleveland."

The man struggled to keep his balance, but Matthias held him upright. As his fetid breath quickened, the drunkard eyed Laura on the bed.

"Who's the broad? Your dime? Can I git a turn wit' her?" The bum grinned, flashing broken and missing teeth. "I'll bet she can suck a mean dick, right?"

Instead of acknowledging his crude remark, Matthias placed a hand atop the man's frayed toque and twisted his head like a corkscrew. A wet *crack* echoed through the room. The transient gasped and struggled for breath. Matthias backed away and let his victim slip to the floor.

Laura fell to her knees and crept across the plastic sheeting. Her hungry eyes fixed on the derelict's unshaven neck. She slid her buckling wrists forward, dragging her knees along the faded frieze carpet.

"Stop!" Matthias held out a hand. "Let me take care of this."

He walked into the hallway as Laura tore at her shirt. She felt nothing but the hunger, which she could no longer restrain. Beneath the pungent odor of the man's body and his soiled clothing, Laura could discern the scent of blood.

She gnashed her teeth and dug her fingers into her palms. Her blue eyes shimmered with a lurid gleam. Laura heard a kitchen drawer glide open, followed by a series of sharp metallic rattles as Matthias rummaged through the silverware. He returned to the bedroom with a knife in hand.

Laura rocked back and forth beside the vagrant's motionless body. Matthias held her back with one strong arm and jabbed the serrated blade into the vagrant's throat. The man's jaw dropped slack as blood began to pour onto the sheet.

Matthias nudged Laura forward, and she lowered her face to the man's bleeding neck. She closed her lips around the wound and drank, pressing her palms against the drop cloth. As the transient's blood filled her mouth, her fingers curled and her eyes tightened. She moaned and arched her back as she swallowed the dying man's blood. The hot blood circulated throughout her tingling limbs and nourished her famished body.

In time, the blood had ceased to flow. The vagrant's face was sunken and sallow. She leaned back on her haunches, her placid face smeared with her victim's blood. Her hunger had been temporarily sated, but it would compel her to feed again.

Her eyes swept the room, which seemed to pulsate with kaleidoscopic vigor. She glanced at the pale face of Matthias. His blue eyes were cold and unyielding. Her lip began to tremble as feelings of self-loathing and guilt uncoiled within her. Laura roared and beat the floor with her fists. She began to sob, yet still no tears fell from her eyes.

"What have you done to me?" Laura lifted her anguished gaze to the vampire looming above her. She covered her face with her hands, but thrust them against her lap when they left fresh streaks of blood on her cheeks and brow.

Matthias turned his back and paced across the room.

"Look what you made me do!" Laura threw her head back as the veins and muscles stiffened in her neck. A feral growl erupted from her throat. "You made me a killer!"

Matthias turned to witness a frightful transformation in Laura's features. He took a tentative step toward her.

"Stay away from me, you bastard fuck!"

"Laura, calm down. There's nothing that can be done. It's too late for—"

"The others will look for me, you know." Laura cut him off. Her voice was flat and inexpressive.

"It's too late for them to help you," Matthias insisted. "You are what you are. There is no going back."

"It doesn't matter. You're not gonna get away with this. They'll come for me. They won't stop looking!"

"Then they will die."

"The cops!" Laura's voice betrayed desperation. "They'll be looking for the man you just brought in here."

"Do you really believe that?" he replied. "Do you think this is the first time I've killed one of *his* kind? No one cares about these people. He was ignored in life and is already forgotten."

Laura stared at him. "It's only a matter of time before you fuck up again."

"So is that what it is?" The vampire chuckled. "You think I'm reckless because I let that girl go, don't you?"

She looked away from him, her eyes returning to the dead transient on the plastic sheeting. "Fuck you. You're a deranged killer and I hope my people—"

"I *am* a killer," Matthias admitted. He pointed to the corpse on the plastic sheet. "How about you? Do you take no responsibility for that man's death?"

"No!"

"Do you really believe that, Laura?"

"You brought him to me and dropped him at my feet. I had no part in his death. *You* broke his neck. *You* stabbed him. I merely..." She stopped herself, incapable of acknowledging her complicity aloud.

"Stop trying to convince yourself that you are innocent," Matthias warned. "Things have changed for you. You are no longer the person you once were. Accept it, or you will perish."

"But I can't live like this!"

"You have to feed. Do you think I plan to keep bringing you victims?" Matthias furrowed his brow. "If you don't let go of the past, there will be no future for you."

"Future?" Laura narrowed her eyes. "I'm fucking dead! You made me a monster! I have no future!"

Laura turned in disgust and rose to her feet. Her own words sounded absurd to her. She was surprised by the newfound control she had gained over her body. The dizziness was gone and her vision was clear. She stormed into an adjoining bathroom, and began to wash the blood from her hands.

Matthias followed. "You think I made you a monster?"

She ignored him and continued to scrub her fingers. The diluted blood swirled in the basin, and she remained focused on ridding the blood from her hands.

"I freed you," Matthias continued. "Now you never have to feel guilt or shame. You never have to consider the feelings of those beneath you, or regret any decision you make. You only have to answer to yourself." He paused to add one final caveat. "For now, however, you will answer to me."

Laura met his gaze in the foggy mirror and spun to face him. "Everything you just said. It's bullshit. You still cling to your past. That's why you keep that fucking box. And the only reason you did this to me is so you could replace *Anna* or whatever the hell her name is. Because you wanted a fucking companion to share your miserable existence. Not because—"

Matthias lunged at her and forced her hips against the sink. His face was just inches from hers. She felt him grasp a handful of her hair. The elder vampire jerked her forward, and forced Laura to confront herself in the mirror. He put his lips to her ear. "You will not speak of her that way! Ever!"

He pushed her closer to the glass. She studied her bloodstained face and the ashen pallor of her skin. Laura was arrested by her transformation. Her pupils had shrunk to mere slivers, but the irises had acquired a semi-violet cast. Her blonde hair had lost some of its luster, yet seemed thicker at the roots. Her lips were still red with the transient's blood.

"In case you were wondering, we *can* see our reflections in a mirror."

Laura spun and struck him across his face. "You didn't have to do this! What gives you the right to choose my fate?"

She raised her hand to deliver another blow, but he caught her wrist and held it fast. Laura tried to disengage herself from his grip, but Matthias forced her to relent to his superior strength. *"You* chose to hunt me," he reminded her. "You chose to follow the others. This is the result of your hubris. And I assure you, I won't be so *gracious* to your friends."

"Who the fuck are you to make that choice?" she repeated. "Besides, you didn't do this to punish me. You did this for *yourself!*"

"You don't know what you're talking about."

"Look at me!" Laura wiped the blood from her mouth. "Do I carry myself like her? Do I sound like her? Is it my hair? My eyes? The curve of my hips? What is it about *me* that reminds you so much of your precious Anna?"

Matthias pulled her to him. "You think I asked for this? I wanted to die in that war. Once she was dead and gone, I had nothing to live for. But I became what I am and I found a way to survive. So will you."

Laura retaliated with another blow to his chin. "You were no victim, either," she snapped. "You served an evil cause before you became this...*this thing!* You were a fucking Nazi!"

"Nazi?" Matthias released her, and pushed her against the sink. "Every able-bodied man was forced to serve. I wasn't given a choice. All I wanted to do was play music, and I ended up a soldier on the wrong side of history."

"Spare me. Every fucking German said that shit when the war was over." Laura grew bolder, and his presence no longer frightened her. She leveled her eyes to study his reaction. "So why don't you regale me with another story from your past? Tell me about her."

Matthias turned away. "Anna was a concert pianist. She was pregnant with our child when the Allies bombed Darmstadt. She and the baby were killed when our home was destroyed. I was at the front when I received news of her death. In a matter of months, soldiers from your country shot me down in a mass execution. I came here to hunt them."

Laura hesitated, allowing his words to sink in before she spoke again. "So then what happened?"

"Vengeance did not fill the emptiness," he stated. "And if one day you try to destroy me, it won't satisfy you either."

"I'm not so sure of that." Laura shook her head.

"Trust me. The sense of satisfaction is fleeting. When your enemy lies defeated before you, there is no rush of victory. Time simply marches on. The world around you changes, but you? You remain fixed. Stagnant. Dead."

Laura shoved past Matthias, who remained in the washroom. She stormed down the hallway toward his cello and tore the heavy instrument from its stand. With both hands wrapped around the polished neck, she swung the instrument with all her strength and smashed it against the concrete wall. The cello made a discordant sound as the strings snapped and sprung from the tuning pegs. The finely lacquered wood of the Stradivarius cracked and splintered. Before she could let go of the broken fingerboard, she felt an iron grip close around the back of her neck.

214

Matthias thrust her into the wall. She slid to the floor amidst the debris and flung herself over, leaning half-reclined against the wall. A proud smile twisted across her lips.

"You're wrong about revenge," she said, beaming with satisfaction. "That felt even better than I thought it would. I know you loved that thing as much as the memory of your dead wife!"

Matthias reached down to the floor and retrieved the bow. He placed it in her left hand as she struggled to stand.

"Here. Break the bow and your petulant act will be complete." There was no discernible emotion on his face. "But nothing has changed. You haven't hurt me, and you are still dead, Laura. Your life as you knew it is over. You will never see your friends. You will never see your family. Each of them will grow old and die while you remain the same."

"Fuck you."

"See?" Matthias noted. "It's already fading. Consider this a valuable lesson, which will serve you well as you adjust to your new circumstances."

She stood to face him, and he gestured to the bow she held in her hand.

"Break it. Enjoy your moment of triumph while it lasts."

She sneered and snapped the bow in half.

"Good. Now on to more practical matters." Matthias pointed to the corpse down the hall. "You always finish what you've started. You never leave your prey alive. You spare no witnesses. You leave no evidence for the police to find. You completely annihilate everything you seek to destroy, or *you* will be destroyed."

Laura sank to the floor and drew her legs to her chest. She sat amidst the shattered remains of the cello. Just as he promised, the spiteful feelings dissolved. In their place, she felt shame for her defiant outburst, along with the first inklings of curiosity and wonder. She glanced up at Matthias, but couldn't find the appropriate words.

"Immortality has a price." He offered his hand to help her to her feet. "So when the hunger rises in you again, you will kill. Just as I kill. Just as any predator in the wild is conditioned to subdue and kill its prey. That is what we are. You will master the hunt, just as you will learn to sublimate the lust for blood that spurs you on."

Laura hung her head. She was unsure how to respond to him. The confusion and guilt lingered, but curiosity was becoming paramount.

215

"I will teach you." Matthias lifted her chin. His gaze was stern yet sincere as he peered into her eyes. "Despite the curse that accompanies this gift we've been given, you will see before long there are many advantages to it as well."

37

WHEN HE STEPPED FROM HIS SUV AND STRAIGHTENED the wrinkles of his long coat, Edison Raymer certainly looked the part of a private investigator. He was dressed in black from head to toe, save for a white button-down shirt. The professor dropped his spectacles into his coat pocket and donned a pair of sunglasses. As dawn broke to the east, Raymer strode with purpose across the blacktop to the front entrance of the Eldercare facility.

A black and white police cruiser was parked across one of the handicapped spots. It was no surprise when the officer opened the window and hung an arm out.

"Sir?" The cop stifled a cough as the cold air flooded into his cruiser. "Hey, sir. You here from Norfolk? The Bureau?"

"No, officer." Raymer stopped and smoothed out the creases of his trouser legs. "Just here to visit my father. He expects me to dress up for the occasion."

"Shit, you could pass for FBI lookin' like that. Sorry to bother you."

Before the cop could close the window, Raymer held up a hand to stop him. "If you don't mind me asking, what are you doing here?"

"You haven't heard the news? Some guy who works here tried to rape a college girl on Sunday night."

"That was almost a week ago," Raymer noted. "I take it he's still at large?"

"Yeah, it don't look like he's comin' back to work. Hell, the detective on the case thinks the bastard's prolly in Mexico by now. I know you're concerned about your father and all, but this guy didn't do anything here

217

that we know of. Just some run-of-the-mill sicko who tried to get his rocks off on—"

"Thanks, officer." Raymer nodded and scraped a heel against the adjacent wheelchair ramp. "I won't take up any more of your time."

The cop shut the window and waved Raymer on. The heels of his leather-soled shoes clicked on the pavement as the main entrance doors slid open. He passed through and walked straight to the front desk. An exhausted young nurse with AMY on her nametag looked up at him from a dog-eared romance novel.

"Sir, visiting hours don't begin until ten o'clock."

"I'm here to speak with a supervisor." He dug into his pocket, pulled out a black eel-skin wallet, and flashed his Williamsport Faculty I.D. with his thumb strategically positioned over the college logo. Before Amy could inspect it, he shoved his wallet back into his coat. "I'm a private investigator hired by the Stroud family, and I'm here to get some basic information from the night manager on an employee named Matthias Bartsch."

"Oh...oh, yeah. I was the one who called the police and reported him when they put the sketch on TV." Amy's eyes widened. "I'll check and see if Mr. Fowler's still in his office." She picked up the phone. "Hold on a minute."

Raymer picked up a brochure and flipped through it as Amy Harvey pressed a speed dial button on the phone.

"Mr. Fowler? There's a gentleman up front who wants to see you."

The nurse paused, and Raymer slid his sunglasses down to the tip of his nose to watch her.

"No," she glanced up at Raymer with a half-smile. "He says he's a private investigator."

Raymer carefully removed his sunglasses and replaced them with his wire-rim spectacles.

"OK...I'll send him back."

Amy hung up the receiver and pointed down the hall to her left. "See that water fountain down there?"

Raymer nodded. "Yes, ma'am."

"Mr. Fowler's office door is right next to it. He's our night manager. He spoke with the police about the investigation."

"Thank you." Raymer nodded in return. "You've been most helpful."

He hurried toward the manager's door and gave three sharp knocks. A voice inside called out for him to enter. Raymer stepped into the office of the balding, nondescript supervisor. As he expected, Anthony Fowler had packed his briefcase and was preparing to leave. The timing couldn't have been better.

Fowler eyed the door and extended a hand. "Please have a seat, uh... what's your name?"

"Raymer. Private Investigator." He reached for his wallet again, and hoped that he could pass off his bogus I.D. a second time.

The night manager, who seemed pressed for time, shook his head. "Nah. I don't need to see your badge or anything if you showed it to the nurse. In fact, I'm kinda in a hurry here."

"This'll only take a few minutes." Raymer sighed as he withdrew his hand from his coat. "I'm here on behalf of the Stroud family."

"Who?" Anthony squinted as he gripped the briefcase handle and yawned. "Excuse me. It's been a long night."

"Not a problem, Mr. Fowler." Raymer leaned back in the chair. "Jennifer Stroud was the girl who was attacked by your employee. She was a student at Williamsport College. Her parents haven't been exactly thrilled with the way the local police have been handling her case."

"I can understand that." Anthony shook his head. "The detective who interviewed me was in and outta here in five minutes. I think his name was Pettit."

"Yes, sir. The Strouds feel that Rudy Pettit isn't taking the attempted rape of their daughter seriously. I've interviewed two other individuals who told me a similar story about that particular detective's flippant attitude and abrasive manner. "

"Between you and me, if that guy'd been one of my staff, I'd have kicked him out on his ass myself." Anthony glanced around the room nervously, as if he had just crossed the line with his personal commentary. "Hey, uh... none of this is going on record or anything, is it?"

"No, sir. I just wanted to ask you a few questions about Mr. Bartsch." Raymer eyed Anthony's sweaty brow. "I need a couple pieces of information, and then I'll be out of your hair."

"You're not a very observant P.I.," Anthony ran his fingers over his balding head. "I don't have much hair to speak of." Anthony Fowler laughed in spite of himself.

Raymer did his best not to show contempt as he took in a deep breath. "So, you were Matthias Bartsch's immediate supervisor?"

"Correct. And really, there was no indication whatsoever that he was some sorta...*deviant*. He came to work on time and did his job without complaining. Very formal. You could tell he was military at some point."

"Do you have his last known address and phone number?"

"Well, I've got what he put down on his application. His background check came up clean when he started. Again, no criminal record at all. I was just as surprised to discover he was the suspect as—"

"If it's all the same to you, Mr. Fowler, can I get a printout of that information?"

"Well, I already gave it to the cops—"

"Who aren't doing a very good job of finding Mr. Bartsch. Which is why *I'm* here."

Anthony sighed and set his briefcase down beside his desk. He threw himself into his chair and logged onto his computer. After a few mouse clicks, he pulled up a file and printed it out. Raymer leaned over and snatched it from the printer. After a cursory glance, he folded up the contact information and shoved it in his coat pocket. "Let me ask you something else. You said there was nothing odd about Matthias Bartsch. Did anything out of sorts occur while he was working here?"

"Like what?" Anthony's tone grew defensive. "Am I gonna need a lawyer when they catch this guy?"

"The Strouds don't plan to press charges on any third parties connected to him, such as employers or landlords. You can rest easy on that count. Now, back to my question—"

"Well, there was one incident, and something else that I can't substantiate but raised a red flag with me. Probably just a coincidence, but I tried to tell Detective Pettit about it anyway. He was halfway out the door before I could finish."

"Really?" Raymer's eyebrows furrowed. "Let's start with the incident."

"Well, while Matthias was working here, someone raided the dispensary. We caught that individual. It was some punk kid I'd brought on just to run bed linens back and forth to the laundry. The problem was we weren't able to account for some other drugs, and he denied taking those."

"Well, he was probably lying," Raymer said.

"I just...I can't imagine why a junkie would steal two vials of potassium chloride. That's some potent shit. I mean, they use that to execute death row inmates in this state."

"Perhaps I'm missing the point, but what does this have to do with Matthias Bartsch?" Raymer asked.

"Nothing I can prove, *per se*. It's just a hunch." Anthony sighed. "Are you gonna need anything else from my computer? I really gotta lock this down and get home. My kids have soccer practice, and I told my wife I'd—"

"I don't need anything else. But I'm curious about that hunch you just mentioned."

"Yeah." The supervisor nodded and glanced at his wristwatch. "See, Matthias only worked here a couple weeks. He came down with some respiratory infection I think, so he didn't work for a few days. With the whole thing about missing potassium chloride and all, at first I wondered if one of my employees—maybe even Matthias—could've used that drug on...I don't know, like...on the street. When I heard about that college girl I was kinda freaked out."

Raymer shifted in the chair. "Where are you going with this, Mr. Fowler?"

"Well, I thought about it a little more and figured maybe that was a bit of a stretch. But then I looked over the death records here, and I noticed a pattern. Like I said, it's probably just coincidence, because this is a hospice. No one who checks in gets better, if you know what I mean. We deal with death all the time, and it's usually pretty cut and dry. But the records show that every night Matthias was present for his shift, someone on the ward passed away."

Edison Raymer rubbed his hand over his mouth and nodded. For a moment, his mind wandered. "So you think this Bartsch character was killing your patients? Why? What for?"

"It sounds so ridiculous to hear someone else say it. But I'd be lying if the thought hadn't crossed my mind. Since he's been gone, we've only had one death during the night shift."

"Did you share this information with the police?"

"And have that joker Pettit sit there and laugh in my face? No way. I can't substantiate anything. It's just a silly hunch. I mean, you've heard about people so evil that they drain the life force from others, haven't you?"

"Well..." Raymer pressed his fingers against his temples.

"Maybe he was one of those types? I saw something about it on that paranormal investigation show. A psychic vampire, I think they're called? I don't know. He's German, so perhaps his grandfather was a Nazi and he inherited some sorta genetic drive to kill—"

"Mr. Fowler, if I were you, I'd keep that to myself and never mention it again."

"Sound advice that I'll surely follow." He wiped the sweat from his brow. "I probably sound crazy. That's what this job'll do to a guy." He glanced at his watch again, and moved to stand. "Is there anything else I can help you with, Mr. Raymer?"

"No, sir. You've been a great help. I'm sure the Strouds will be quite pleased if the information you gave me leads to the arrest of Matthias Bartsch."

"It was my pleasure." Anthony eyed the door.

Raymer stood and bid the supervisor farewell. Before leaving the building, he swapped his spectacles for his sunglasses. As he crossed the parking lot to his SUV, he kept his head down. The policeman in the cruiser was reading the newspaper, and didn't look up as Raymer stole a glimpse in his direction.

Raymer got behind the wheel of his SUV and buckled his seatbelt. He took out the folded sheet of paper and punched the address into his onboard GPS system.

No wonder the clever son of a bitch never left a trail.

The professor drove out of the parking lot as the GPS prompted him to turn right onto Benjamin Harrison Boulevard.

He took this job to feed on the dying. I'll bet he's been working nursing homes and hospices for years. The vampire gets his nightly blood, and the morgue writes off every victim as dead from some terminal illness. Easy feeding.

Veronica was right. This is one clever son of a bitch.

38

OUTSIDE EDISON RAYMER'S TOWNHOUSE, THE STREETLAMPS flickered to life as Veronica sat on the living room floor. She was surrounded by stacks of printed newspaper articles. All had been organized in some haphazard manner known only to her. In the basement, Junior Luttrell pounded away on the silver stakes with an engraver's kit. She'd been surprised to find out that Luttrell was quite artistic. They shared a lively discussion at lunch about his experiences as a combat photographer in Vietnam, and how he'd taken up woodcarving and engraving as a hobby to deal with the post-war stresses of civilian life. She immediately put him to work on Edison's silver stakes.

Luttrell's police scanner warbled behind her. Before Junior began hammering again, Veronica heard Raymer's SUV cruise to a halt in the driveway. Raymer bounded through the front door and into the foyer. He appeared in the entranceway to cast a baleful stare at the mess covering his living room floor.

Veronica looked up at him. "It's about time you got back. Where the fuck were you and why didn't you answer your phone?" She noticed that Raymer hadn't stopped to remove his coat. "Surely you didn't spend the whole day at that old folk's home?"

"No." Raymer seemed more animated than usual, until the irregular hammering began again in the basement. "Where's Luttrell and what's he doing?"

"I put him to work, and I think you'll be quite pleased with the results." She picked up a silver stake from beside her leg and held it out for Raymer.

223

"What the hell has he been doing to those, Veronica?" Raymer negotiated a path around the printouts to grab the sharp stake. His eyes were wide as he read the Latin inscription in precise gothic lettering above the knurled grip. *"Ex umbra in lucem."* He shook his head in disbelief. "From darkness into light."

Raymer looked down at the floor as the metallic pounding continued. "Junior did this? He knows Latin?"

"No," Veronica said as Raymer continued to turn the stake over in his hand. "It was in one of your vampire books. Turns out he had some kind of engraving machine in his truck. He was getting antsy, so I gave him the book and told him to go to town. I had to think of something to keep him busy."

Veronica flipped through yet another stack of papers. "So you plan on telling me where the hell you were all day?"

"I interviewed Bartsch's former manager. He gave me his last known address, so I checked it out."

"Wait, what?" Veronica raised her voice. "You went alone? What the hell were you thinking? You could have gotten yourself killed! I thought we agreed—"

"It wasn't like that." Raymer sat in one of the matching wingback chairs, still holding the stake. "Besides, I had holy water and the bag of communion wafers with me. It was a shitty basement apartment in the worst neighborhood imaginable. The cops had already been there, as there was yellow crime scene tape across the door."

The professor's eyes grew wide as he recounted the thrill of his discovery.

"One reason he's never been caught became quite evident to me today. He's been living completely off the grid. One bedroom apartments. Probably pays for everything in cash and uses disposable cell phones. I saw the—"

"So you broke into the apartment!" She threw her hands up in frustration. "And you tampered with a crime scene. What the hell's wrong with you?"

"I sat there for hours until the coast was clear. And, yeah, I broke down the door. It was a furnished apartment. Practically a flophouse. But Bartsch had covered every window with heavy cardboard and electrical tape. He locked the place down so tight that no speck of light could get in. This proves the aversion to sunlight myth, and means—"

"It means you're a goddamn lunatic, Edison. What if someone saw you?"

"Believe me, I made sure that didn't happen."

"Well," Veronica asked with a newfound sense of intrigue. "What else did you find in there?"

"Nothing at all, save for a rather conspicuous bloodstain on the carpet. It looked like he'd done everything imaginable to clean it, though. But you know what happens if you let blood sit too long on an absorbent surface."

"No, Edison, I don't. And most normal people don't know about that kinda shit, either."

"Alright, there's more," Raymer said, ignoring her remark. "The night manager at Serenity Springs told me something about our vampire he claimed he didn't tell the cops."

Raymer stopped to admire the stake again as Veronica sat up straight. "Well, go on!"

"So you're paying attention now? Good." Raymer laid the stake across his legs with care. "First of all, he said that Bartsch only worked there for a couple weeks. However, he claimed that every night he was scheduled, a patient on the wards died. Now, Bartsch hasn't been back since Sunday night. He knows the cops are looking for him."

"So what are you getting at?"

"With that information, we know how the son of a bitch has been feeding without drawing attention to himself. So after I checked out the apartment, I called every nursing home in the Tidewater area I could look up. About half of them confirmed that a German guy worked there for a few weeks as an orderly, then quit. This so-called "German" had other aliases. Neutze. Fuchs. Schnell. Landfermann. That last one was Anna Bartsch's maiden name. It was in the Conservatory picture, remember?"

"Edison—"

"He's been feeding on the nearly dead all over this part of Virginia for years. That's how he managed to avoid capture. I hate to admit it, but you were right. This vampire's one smart–"

"Edison, look at this." Veronica struggled to her feet and handed him a printed article from the Williamsport Herald's online archive. "I don't think he's been restricting his activities to the infirmed and elderly."

Raymer flipped through the paper-clipped article. He read the title aloud after skimming the text. "Shelter notes a decrease in local homeless population?"

"Like you said yesterday, Ed. *Puzzle pieces*. I've spent the day putting them together. That thing's been out there hunting. Picking off people that no one knows or cares about. And consider this statistic I uncovered. This year alone, there's been more instances of arson and car theft in this county than anywhere else in the state with a comparable population."

As Edison returned the article, she continued. "Nothing I've found today is conclusive in and of itself. And if you take any one piece of information at face value, it's meaningless. A dead end. And all of it might still be coincidental."

"Veronica, don't be so hasty." Edison stood up, laid the stake aside, and in a rare display of affection, took her free hand in his. "There are no dead ends. We're building a case here." He squeezed her hand. "An irrefutable case. Before long, we're going to find him."

"And what about Laura?" Veronica asked with apprehension. Although she was worried sick about the girl, she had deliberately avoided the topic since he returned home. "Do you think she's still with him? That she's still alive?"

"I suspect we'll find her too." Raymer paused, as if searching for the right words. "However, I'd say the chances of her still being alive are slim to none."

Veronica glared at her partner, searching for some indication that he felt something for his former student. His response confirmed her worst suspicions. She slipped her hand from his and turned back to the stack of newspapers on the floor.

"Did you and Junior eat yet?" Edison called out as he walked toward the kitchen. "I'd be happy to prepare something or we can order in again."

39

LAURA SLOUCHED IN THE PASSENGER SEAT OF MATTHIAS'
gray sedan. The past twenty-four hours had been a blur. If she
hadn't known better, she would have assumed it had all been a
terrible dream. She felt guilty when she thought of the homeless
man at Matthias' apartment, but other thoughts weighed more heavily on
her mind.

Laura recognized that she had no choice but to adapt to her circumstances. Her conscience was the only obstacle in her way. She was grateful
that the sequence of events had unfolded so quickly, because there had been
no time for reflection or analysis.

As she and Matthias sped in silence through the back roads of Virginia,
she let her thoughts run wild. Her initial fears were exchanged for cautious
feelings of exhilaration and empowerment. Laura couldn't help but wonder
what lay ahead.

She mourned little for the life she was leaving behind. Long estranged
from any living relatives, she had lived a scholar's life of isolation and seclu-
sion. She'd grown to detest the pretentious trappings of academia and felt
no kinship with society at large. The routines of ordinary life bored her. The
dreams of her few friends and acquaintances smacked of compromise and left
her unfulfilled. Romance was as elusive to Laura as it was predictable and
disappointing. She was too selfish to raise a child. The idea of motherhood
filled her with resentment and feelings of entrapment.

What had always inspired her was the promise of something beyond
everyday existence. Despite his condescending demeanor and irrefutable

sense of superiority, it was Edison Raymer that drew her to the field of parapsychology. If such a learned man could believe in something more, then why couldn't she?

Nonetheless, Laura was too smart to allow herself the security of spiritual consolation. Faith was the inevitable result of absolute despair. Those that couldn't face the abyss found hope in the convenient promise of the light. The threat of so final a darkness was too cruel and too much for most people to bear.

However, Laura's thoughts began to change after her abduction and unexpected transformation. She had entered the beyond. The veil was lifted, and a small portion of the great mystery was revealed. Death could be cheated. She and Matthias were indisputable proof of that. As it turns out, it was the darkness—not the promise of light or life—that provided answers.

Ironically, Laura's allegiance to Edison Raymer and her role in his personal crusade had been a matter of pure circumstance. To put it simply, she was bored and could think of nothing better to do with herself. The dissertation work had become tedious, so she would've welcomed any distraction, regardless of how absurd it may have seemed.

Her thoughts lingered on the subject of her former mentor. The discovery of Matthias Bartsch had clearly pushed Raymer over the edge. Without his pursuit of the occult, he had nothing. Yet despite his arrogance and fanaticism—hell, as a direct result of his stubborn obsessions—the cunning bastard actually managed to stumble upon the truth.

But Edison Raymer is no fucking hero, Laura reminded herself.

He only seeks to vindicate himself. He had no problem risking the life of his one and only protégé, and couldn't care less about what happens to Luttrell, or even Veronica Upham. Furthermore, he's too stubborn to admit that there are powers beyond his control. His only recourse is to destroy those powers, revealing himself to be a zealot of the most despicable and pathetic kind.

Laura was suddenly shaken from her reverie. The headlights of an oncoming car blinded her. The discomfort was temporary, and it took a moment to orient herself. Matthias' voice brought her back to the present moment.

"It's beginning to sink in now, isn't it?"

"Yeah." She cleared her throat. "I guess it is."

"I can't remember much of my first few nights." His German accent seemed more prominent to her after such a long interval of silence. "But I think that you are adjusting to it all rather well."

"I don't have much of a choice, do I?" She watched the moon hanging high above the trees. It appeared brighter than she recalled. The tree limbs seemed sharper, even against the dark horizon.

"Laura, the sooner you let go of this animosity and accept—"

"I didn't mean it like that." She broke her gaze from the window and turned to face him. "I meant that I know I have to accept this. There's no point fighting it."

Matthias offered no response and maintained his focus on the road. The shadow from a passing lamppost swept across his face. Laura could sense that he was pleased, and for the first time, the vampire's features had relaxed. The ever-present scowl that defined him had softened. There was a noble and handsome quality to his face, and suddenly Laura felt ashamed for what she had done to his cello.

After another mile, Matthias slowed the car and pulled onto the berm of the road.

"Why are we stopping?" Laura asked. As she looked out the window to gauge their surroundings, she could see nothing but row after row of trees on both sides of the road.

From behind the wheel of the idling car, Matthias handed an FNP 45-Tactical handgun to Laura. It was all polymer and steel—much heavier than her compact Glock. She noticed the boxy extension attached to its threaded barrel. "That some kinda silencer?"

"A dry suppressor," Matthias corrected. "It's impossible to mask the sound of a large caliber handgun, but we are stopping in a place where no one will hear us for miles."

Laura aimed the bulky combat pistol and indexed the trigger. "Must've cost you a small fortune."

"That pistol?" Matthias paused to reflect. "It cost the owner his life. That is all."

Matthias placed his palm against the slide and forced Laura to lower the .45 caliber handgun. "It's loaded with fifteen jacketed hollow point rounds. So even if you miss the first, second, and third time—"

"I know my way around guns." Laura raised the pistol to line up the sights. "I just don't understand why I need it."

"To cover our tracks. After you kill tonight, we have to dump the body." Matthias leaned over the seat and nudged the pistol. "If the body is ever found, the police will think they've just stumbled on another victim of gun violence. Something common to this region. There's a shooting every day in Hampton Roads, or up in Richmond."

Laura's heart sank when Matthias confirmed they'd come to the woods to kill. She knew it was inevitable, but everything was happening so fast now. Her apprehension gave way to excitement, for the vampire's words quickened the strange yearning to feed.

Pretty soon you'll be just as cold as he is.

With each kill, you'll lose another part of yourself.

Another part of your humanity.

And then you'll feel nothing.

Matthias nudged her shoulder. "Are you listening?"

Laura nodded as she inspected the handgun again. She ran her thumb along the decocker, then the slide release.

"If the body is found, it may prompt a short article on the back page of the morning paper. But if there appears to be nothing more to the story, it won't make the evening news."

"I understand." She hesitated. "I'm just scared. This is still a lot to take in, and now I'm about to become an accomplice to another murder."

"You can't think of it like that. It is—"

"I know, I know. Spare me the bit about predators and prey. I get it. But at the end of the day it's the same bullshit that serial killers use to justify their crimes. And, in a sense, that's exactly what we are."

Matthias gripped the steering wheel but said nothing. Laura eventually broke the silence.

"All the other stuff," she said. "The way I *feel*. The things I can see and hear. Even the way the fucking moon looks through those trees. The *power*. It's...amazing! But..." Laura bit her lip and stared down at the handgun.

"But you can't accept that you have to kill to survive." Matthias finished for her. "The scope of your morality has changed, Laura. You are now subject to different laws. If you don't kill, you won't survive. That's it." He reflected for a moment, and then answered with a variation on her own earlier words. "I guess you *do* have a choice. But in the end, I think you'd prefer only one outcome."

"You've got this all figured out, don't you?" Laura snapped. "Don't you ever feel remorse? Or disgust? Or...or guilt? Do you feel anything at all?"

"I feel many things," Matthias admitted. "And if you do well tonight, I promise I'll tell you all about them. I'll tell you anything you want to know. But now, you are still weak, and you need to feed."

"I need to feed!" She echoed his words with sarcasm. "Is it always gonna be this melodramatic?"

Matthias was caught off guard by her candor. "You're the first person I've spoken to at any great length in decades. I apologize if I've overlooked any subtleties in your language. I am not a native speaker. I have tried to adapt. But I guess there aren't many common words for what we are, or phrases for what we do."

"I'm sorry. I guess that's just something else I have to get used to." To prevent any further embarrassment, she moved to change the subject. "So are we just gonna sit here and wait for someone to come along? We've been driving out here for almost an hour and haven't seen many cars. Seems like this road's never used."

"That is why we are here."

"Then how are we supposed to find a...a..."

"Victim?" Matthias raised an eyebrow. "Get out of the car."

He cut the engine and stepped into the cold air. Laura opened the passenger side door and glared at him over the roof of the sedan.

"Well?" her voice was impatient. "Am I supposed to use my demonic charms to lure our *prey?*"

"No." He slid a cell phone across the roof. She caught it with her free hand. He eyed her with a small degree of suspicion and then nodded. "A simple phone call will suffice."

As Matthias walked to open the trunk, Laura followed behind him, holding up the phone. "I could totally call the police, you know."

"You could." The vampire shrugged. He leaned forward on the trunk to meet her gaze. "But then I'd have to kill you, and I suspect I'd begin to feel some of that remorse you mentioned. So don't do it. You've got a lot more to gain by seeing this through."

Laura smirked and looked down to avoid the vampire's eyes. "So who am I supposed to call?"

"A tow truck."

"What?"

"I programmed the number for a local towing service into the contact list while you slept today."

"OK…"

Matthias opened the trunk, and Laura looked inside. There was a tire iron, a roll of duct tape, a folded plastic sheet, and a pile of license plates from various states. Most of them bore expired registration stickers. Some had none at all. Matthias removed two Pennsylvania license plates with matching numbers. There were magnets affixed to the rear side of each.

"So what should I say?"

"Just tell them your car has stalled. Make up a name and give them a location."

"I don't know where I am."

"Route 619. About eight miles from town." Matthias held up one of the Pennsylvania plates. "Now, if they ask for plate numbers, this is what you say. Or, you stall the dispatcher. Act hysterical. Use your feminine wiles. You are more than capable."

Laura ignored his comment. She felt another queasy pang of excitement. The hunger had returned and suddenly, she could recall the salt taste of the transient's blood. She wanted more. All other thoughts or concerns were incidental.

With care, she laid the 45-Tactical atop the car and paced along the narrow shoulder of the country road. She opened the phone and stared at the illuminated screen. There was only one number in the contact list. She would say her name was Emily and that her car started to make a funny noise, so she pulled off the road. Now she was stuck.

No, wait. Say your name's Amanda. That's better.

This is totally fucked up.

But it's also kinda fun.

Laura was about to dial the number when a thought came to her. "What if they trace the call?"

"It's a TracFone," Matthias called out from the rear of the car. He had already removed the Virginia license plate and was replacing it with the one from Pennsylvania. "We'll dispose of it after you make the call."

Damn, he does think of everything.

Before long, Laura was speaking to the dispatcher. Matthias swapped the front license plate, which was also attached to the bumper with magnets. He returned to the rear of the car and tossed the Virginia plates into the trunk.

"Twenty minutes," Laura said. She handed him the cell phone. Matthias dropped the slim device to the asphalt and crushed it under the heel of his thick motorcycle boot.

"Just curious," Laura asked. "You got any more of those? In case we need one?"

"Plenty." He took the plastic sheeting, the tire iron, and a folded jack into his arms. "Now close the trunk, get the pistol, and follow me to the front of the car."

Laura obeyed the vampire as he spread the plastic sheeting on the ground. Matthias rested the jack on one corner of the sheet, and the tire iron on the other. The plastic still undulated gently in the autumn wind.

"So we're gonna wrap the body up," Laura observed. She put a free hand on her hip as she cradled the heavy pistol. "Makes sense. But how the hell do you plan on getting rid of the tow truck? That's pretty fucking conspicuous."

Matthias propped the hood open. "I thought I'd leave that to you."

"Wait? What? I don't know what to do!"

"You better start brainstorming," Matthias advised.

"But—"

"The dispatcher usually notes the location of the disabled vehicle, so you'll have to act quickly. When the driver approaches, get him to the front of the car and take the shot."

"So you want me to shoot him?"

"That's what the gun is for." Matthias shook his head.

"Don't be a dick!"

"Then use common sense!"

"This is anything but fucking common!"

"So what are you going to do about the tow truck?"

"I don't fucking know!"

"Laura." Matthias grasped her arm. "You need to start paying attention. Always study your surroundings. What did we cross about a quarter-mile in that direction?" He nodded to the east.

"A long bridge. Over some kind of lake."

"Remember the abandoned boat launch?" Matthias tightened his grip around Laura's wool jacket. "The water back there is deep enough to sink the truck. Keep your eyes open for details like that."

"Well, I can't *drive* a tow truck."

"I can. So you will watch and learn. Now concentrate on the kill. If you're going to learn to hunt properly, you've got to control the hunger in there." Matthias pointed a finger to her silent heart.

"I still don't think I can do this to some random guy. It's cold-blooded murder. What did he ever do to me?"

"This is growing tiresome." Matthias sighed. "Think about it this way. You and your friends didn't seem to have any qualms about killing *me*."

"Wait a minute!" Laura cried. "That's not fair! It's not the same."

"Isn't it?"

"Fuck you!"

"So we're back to that again." Matthias glared at the impetuous young woman. "You better learn and you better learn fast."

"Fine!" she shouted and turned her back to him. She began pacing along the berm of the road again.

He's right and you know it.

Quit being a bitch. He's all you've got.

"Hey!" Laura began rifling through her jacket pockets. "I got a question."

"Yeah?"

"Can I still smoke?"

"Sure." Matthias shrugged. "You won't die from cancer or emphysema if that's what you are worried about."

"Good," she replied. Only a few clove cigarettes remained in the crumpled box.

Better make 'em last. You probably can't make a run to the smoke shop before the next homicide.

Laura flicked her lighter. After struggling to suck in enough air, she managed to light the tip of the cigarette. She inhaled the smoke and began to cough. Matthias looked on with uncharacteristic amusement and pity.

"Guess I forgot how to breathe!"

"You don't need to anymore, so you will have to retrain your body to comply."

"Well, I always knew smoking was a psychological thing anyway." She looked over the cigarette between her pale fingers. "Whatever. It'll pass the time."

Shortly after she finished her second clove, a pair of slow moving headlights approached in the distance. Matthias stepped back into the tall grass. "I'll be in the woods watching you. Don't let things get out of hand, Laura."

"Wait! Stay here!" she called out. She felt dizzy and ill-prepared for the conflict ahead. "What the fuck am I supposed to do?"

"Let your instincts guide you. The hunger will take over." Matthias turned and wandered into the tree line before the truck came into full view behind the car.

Oh fuck.

Here we go.

40

WITH A TREMBLING HAND, LAURA SHOVED HALF THE pistol into the tight waistband of her cargo pants. The short Ike jacket concealed the rest of it. The tow truck stopped, and she heard the hiss of air brakes and the large engine idling. Laura continued to pace alongside the car.

An obese man with a bald head and a graying goatee stepped out of the tow truck. In the moonlight, she could see his grease-stained coverall. His embroidered nametag read SMITTY in cursive letters. He approached the car with a flashlight in hand.

"Evenin', Miss."

"Hi," she stuttered. "Thanks for, uh, thanks for coming so quickly."

"So you wanna tell me what happened here?"

For a moment, the fledgling vampire froze. She could only stare at the heavy-set man before her. She could see the tiny drops of perspiration beading along his jowls. The acrid stench of his body odor almost caused her to wretch.

Don't just fucking stand there, McCoy.

Do something!

Without a word, Laura withdrew the pistol from beneath her jacket. She took aim at the tow truck driver's head.

"Hey now, I don't want any trouble!" Smitty called out. "I ain't got no money, just a few—"

Laura closed her eyes and squeezed her finger, but the trigger wouldn't pull. When a second, then a third squeeze of the trigger failed, she lowered the gun in confusion and defeat. The gun was cocked and locked, and she fumbled in a panic for the external safety.

Smitty's initial look of shock had lapsed into desperation. "What the fuck are you doin'?" he yelled and stumbled backwards.

Laura charged forward. As she converged on the bewildered truck driver, he raised a hand in protest. Her successful pull of the trigger resounded with a muted *thump*. The metallic sound rang in her hypersensitive ears.

The fat man fell to the asphalt clutching his chest. There was no blood, as she'd missed him altogether. As luck would have it, Smitty was in cardiac arrest.

Matthias appeared behind her instantly. He pushed Laura against the car and grabbed her by the lapels of her coat. His German accent was thick and heavy in the heat of the moment. "You were supposed to wait until he was on the plastic!"

Matthias released her and approached the man a few feet away. His flashlight had rolled under the car, and Smitty clutched his chest, his eyes wide with fear.

"Help..." Smitty begged as he tore at his coverall. His skin was turning pale as his heart seized and failed him. Matthias took one of the dying man's legs and pulled him around to the front of the parked vehicle. He rolled Smitty onto the plastic sheeting, all the while ignoring his persistent wheezing and gasps for assistance.

"Get over here!" Matthias ordered. "And give me the gun!"

Laura obeyed. She handed the pistol to Matthias, who stood over the writhing man. He put a heavy boot on the victim's belly. "Stay still, and I'll help you," he lied.

Matthias leveled the pistol and shot the recumbent man in the throat. Smitty removed his hands from his chest and clenched them around his neck. His eyes twitched from side to side. Blood began to seep through his fingers.

Laura fell to her knees. She pried the truck driver's hands from his throat and bent forward. The fledgling vampire probed the gash with her tongue. As she placed her lips over the wound, the blood filled her mouth almost faster than she was capable of swallowing. Yet a new instinct took hold, and Laura found herself in tune with the gradually diminishing rhythm of her victim's death.

Matthias crouched beside the man's calf. He fired another round into Smitty's lower leg. Blood and gore sprayed onto his black trousers and the bumper of the car behind him.

As the material around the wound darkened in the moonlight, Matthias wrenched the man's leg toward his mouth. The vampires drained as much blood as they could from Smitty's body. Matthias looked up and wiped a smear of blood from his chin. Laura locked eyes with her sire.

"It's OK," he nodded to her. "We have what we need."

Matthias lifted the man's leg to retrieve the mushroomed hollow point from the sheeted pavement below. The vampire pocketed the round and stepped over the corpse. Laura tilted her head toward him. His expression was grim in the bright lights of the idling tow truck. She glanced down at the motionless body in front of her.

With his blood in her veins, the craving had subsided. But Laura felt no remorse for what she had done. There was no sudden outpouring of sorrow for the loss of human life. She was simply indifferent to the dead man's fate.

Matthias thrust a dirty handkerchief into her hands. "Wipe the blood from your hands."

As she avoided his eyes, Laura took the cloth. "Thanks, Matti." She provoked him without thinking twice.

"Choose your words carefully." Matthias removed the makeshift weights from the plastic sheet.

"Or what?"

"Or..." He trailed off as he wrapped the large man's body and placed the heavy jack along the seam of the shroud. "I might start calling you Anna."

He picked up the tire iron and walked around the car to retrieve the roll of duct tape. "We need to act quickly now."

Laura made no move to assist him. She crouched on her haunches and watched Matthias wrap the body. She struggled to think with clarity.

Matthias pitched the heavy corpse into the bed of the tow truck. He wiped his hands along his bloodstained pants and addressed Laura. "The keys are in the car. You will follow me to the boat slip, but not until you've walked around the vehicle and picked up any evidence we were here."

"Such as?"

"Shell casings from all those shots you fired." Matthias mounted a step into the tow truck cab and braced himself with the doorframe. "Once you've done that, put all the tools in the trunk and the pistol in the backseat.

238

Find a place up the road to turn around and meet me at the dock down by the bridge."

"I thought you were gonna teach me how to drive that tow truck?" She gave Matthias a scornful look.

"Not tonight. You needed to feed, and you needed to kill. You did both."

"Yeah, but I fucked up and—"

"No." Matthias shook his head. "You did well. Now, hurry up. Do as I say and follow me."

Matthias ducked into the cab, slammed the door, and released the brakes. The truck lumbered forward onto the pavement. Laura crouched beside the car and did as she was told. As she crawled on her hands and knees, picking up brass shells, Matthias roared past her on his way to the lake.

After pocketing the shells, she picked up the jack and pitched it into the trunk. She went back to fetch the tire iron, along with the thinning roll of duct tape. She made one last scan of the area surrounding the car and then slammed the lid shut. Before slipping behind the wheel to follow Matthias, she laid the .45 on the back seat.

In five minutes' time, she caught up to him. He had already lashed the corpse to the tow cable and was submerging the truck into the lake's murky waters. The headlights and motor were off. The vampire aided the truck's descent, and as he stood in chest-high water to watch the vehicle sink out of sight, Laura stepped out of the car.

"I suppose that legend about vampires not being able to cross water is bullshit?"

"Of course," he shouted back as he plowed his way up the concrete boat ramp. "But it's running water in the ancient stories. This lake is stagnant. Either way, that rule does not apply to us."

As Matthias approached her, she leaned over the open car door. "So what rules do apply to us?"

"You avoid the sun. That is the most important thing you need to remember. That along with drinking living blood to sustain yourself." Matthias stopped short of her. "Go collect the license plates from the trunk."

"Why?"

"Because we're ditching this car."

"And then what?"

"We pass through the woods to a safe-house," he replied. "There's a cabin up the road."

"Are you sure? What if we don't make it back before sunrise?"

"The clock in the car." Matthias nodded as he wrung the filthy water from his shirt between two strong hands. "What time is it?"

Laura ducked her head inside. "It's almost two in the morning."

"We have plenty of time," Matthias said.

She fetched the plates from the trunk. As she bent down to remove the Pennsylvania tag from the rear, Matthias stopped her.

"Leave it. We can't use that one again." He retrieved the handgun and removed the silencer from the threaded black barrel.

"So this is what you do on a so-called hunt?" Laura asked. "You drive along until you find some loser wandering around drunk, or trap a tow truck driver, and pull him into the car? You prey on the weak and unwitting?"

"If I were to trap a married woman with three children at home, or a professor from that college, what do you think would happen?"

Laura pressed her lips together for a moment. She felt compelled to remind the vampire of his weakness. "Well, you got pretty damn close to finding out a few nights ago."

"I told you," Matthias replied. "That was a mistake."

"I don't understand." Laura gestured to him. "Just look at you. You have power and strength beyond a normal man. How the hell did she manage to get away?"

"I was distracted," he admitted and cast his eyes downward. "I wasn't thinking straight. I never should have gone anywhere near that campus."

"Obviously." Laura folded her arms to appear angry. "So under normal circumstances, do you just break into a house, kill whoever's inside, and burn the place down?"

"I've done that." He slid the silencer into his pocket and gestured for her to drop the license plates. "Many times. But you have to be clever in order to gain permission to enter."

"Permission?" Laura squatted down to set the license plates in a neat stack. "Really? That whole invitation thing is true?"

"I'm afraid so," he replied.

"So we have all this strength and power. But we can't just walk into somebody's house? That's pretty fucking lame."

Matthias ejected the magazine from the pistol. It fell into his waiting hand. "I didn't make the rules. I just know what I've learned from experience. If we are not invited, we cannot enter a private home."

"What happens if we do?"

"We just can't go in." Matthias shrugged. He counted the remaining rounds in the magazine. "Now, the invitation doesn't have to be entirely sincere. It can be, and usually is, coerced. But the invitation must be extended."

"Can it be revoked?" Laura rose and dusted dry grass and dead leaves from her cargo pants.

"No. With all the various myths and legends, there's a bit of fiction, some conjecture, and a measure of truth." Matthias locked the magazine home, chambered a round, and engaged the safety.

"I guess we can't turn into bats or wolves either?"

"If we could, don't you think that would've been the first thing I showed you?" He shoved the pistol under his belt.

"Was that your attempt at humor?"

"Maybe." A wry smirk momentarily transformed the vampire's hardened features, but soon disappeared. He gestured to the car beside them. "Kill those headlights, and then release the parking brake."

"I know how to do it," Laura insisted. "I just thought you'd handle the car, since you already sank the truck, and—"

"You need to get your hands dirty, Laura. Both literally and figuratively." He crossed his arms and watched her with narrowed eyes. "Don't forget to shift the gear into neutral."

Laura dug her boot heels into the grass and pushed the car towards the incline, guiding the front tires with one hand on the wheel.

"Do we even have to kill people at all? Couldn't we just drink animal blood to survive?"

"No." Matthias' answer was clipped and decisive. "Since I was turned, I've only directly encountered three others like us. Two of them fed off the blood of the dead, and the other survived on rodents. All three were deformed, and I think that was the cause. There's no way to cheat this. To maintain our appearance and blend in with humans, we need their blood."

"Does the blood have to be healthy? I mean, what about diseases?" Laura reflected a moment. "Or drug users? Does their blood affect us negatively?"

"Not as far as I can tell," Matthias replied. "But I can tell you from experience that we can feed on the sick. As long as they're still alive, we are immune to any diseases, medication, or toxins in their blood."

"OK. So what about crosses? Holy water?" Laura thumbed the button to open the power window, then slammed the door and stepped away.

241

"Repulsive to me, and probably will be to you."

"I don't believe in God."

"Doesn't matter. As a Catholic in life, I did." Matthias rubbed his jaw. "The vampires that turned me were Slavic. I'll wager at one point they were believers in the Orthodox tradition. I think you inherit your aversions from the one that makes you. So my weaknesses are yours. And theirs are mine. I'm sure it goes back centuries. All the way to the beginning."

"So if a Jew or a Muslim had turned you, you're implying that—"

"Don't overthink it. Just know that Christian symbols and silver can weaken us." Matthias waved a hand at Laura, who had waded into the brackish water with the sinking car. "Push one more time so the tires clear the edge of the ramp."

Laura strained to maneuver the car. "Why are you so much stronger than me?"

"You have to keep feeding. At least until the blood restores you to full strength. It's like a prescription drug. It takes a few doses to reach its full effect." Matthias nodded in approval. "So many questions now."

"I've got a practical one." Laura fought to stand on the slick underwater slope. "What the fuck are we gonna do about a car?"

"There's one at the cabin, which isn't far away. Tomorrow night, we will hunt again. Then we clean out the last apartment. I think it's best we move on from here as soon as possible."

"There's still one other problem," Laura noted.

"Which is?" Matthias extended a hand to help her out of the water.

"Edison Raymer."

Matthias seemed puzzled by the unfamiliar name.

"My former professor," she clarified. "He won't stop until he finds you and kills you. Believe it or not, his whole life has revolved around some half-baked crusade to prove that vampires exist."

"Why?"

"It's a long story. Just trust me. You have no idea how driven he is."

"What about the other two?" Matthias asked. "I could sense them from the road. There was a woman and an older man, right?"

"Veronica's of no consequence," Laura remarked. "She's just an English professor. One of Raymer's groupies. The other guy..." Laura paused and eyed the vampire with scrutiny. "Well, that's another interesting story. His name's Fenton Luttrell, Jr. That name ring a bell?"

"Luttrell?" Matthias' eyes narrowed.

"Yep. He claims you killed his father back in 1957."

"Son of a bitch," he mused. "You sure that's his name?"

"Positive. So I guess Jennifer Stroud wasn't the first time you fucked up, was it?"

Matthias ignored Laura's comment and stroked his jaw. "He was just a kid. There were two young boys if I'm not mistaken."

"So?"

"So I suppose I have my limits."

"Bullshit! You probably left him alive on purpose. So he'd be traumatized the whole rest of his life. And now it's come back to bite you in the ass."

"Why should I feel threatened by these people?"

"Raymer's driven. He'll come after you. And now he's got a new sidekick to egg him on. Once they find out about me, they'll probably try to kill me too."

"Then I guess we need to deal with them."

"And do what?" Laura scoffed. "Raymer may be an asshole, but he's a tenured professor. Well, at least he was," she corrected herself. "Anyway, these are high profile people. We can't just kill 'em. And besides, I mean, fuck, I *knew* them, and—"

"No remorse, Laura. Our enemies—"

"Oh no!" She raised an accusatory finger. "Stop right there. Don't start lecturing me about cleaning up our messes. You're the one who left Junior Luttrell alive. Not to mention the girl from the college. You broke your own rules. And if we go after them, we're gonna be in a world of shit."

"So we won't pursue them," Matthias glared at Laura. "And no matter how *driven* they are, we will make sure they never find us."

41

EARLY SUNDAY MORNING, VERONICA UPHAM AWOKE WITH a start. The morning light beyond Edison's bedroom curtains was beginning to creep in. It was too early to tell if the day would bring rain or if only the room itself was overcast. Raymer had already risen and left a pile of rumpled sheets in his wake. He was likely downstairs planning his next scheme.

I'm so goddamn tired.

Veronica yawned and swung her feet over the side of the bed. Her joints ached and her neck felt stiff. After their argument the previous weekend, she hadn't dared bring up the subject of intimacy. In fact, she was surprised he hadn't prepared another place for her to sleep. This prompted Veronica to hope that after discovering the leads about Bartsch from the nursing home, Raymer's mood might have lightened enough that *he* would've initiated sex. But as he had done many times before, he showed no sign of interest in her, and answered her first tentative caress by turning on his side and slipping into a steady sleep.

I really could've used the distraction.

The least you could do after all this insanity is fuck me.

The frustrated English professor rose and let her thin satin nightgown slip to the floor. Careful to avoid the reflection of her nude body in Raymer's oversized mirror, she snatched his terrycloth robe from the back of the bedroom door, slipped it over her shoulders, and tied it around her slender waist.

As she flipped her hair out from under the collar of the housecoat, she caught a glimpse of her cell phone on the nightstand beside the bed. With a sigh, she darted across the room and snatched the phone from the table. Veronica dropped the thin device in the front pocket of the robe and dashed into the hallway.

"Edison?" she called out over the railing. She listened for a response but could only hear Junior's muffled snores from the guest room.

Veronica retreated into the close confines of the bathroom and turned on the shower. By the dim glow of a plastic nightlight, Veronica sat on the closed lid of the toilet and ran her fingers through her disheveled hair.

There's no point doing it. You know she'll never answer. She's already dead. And if she's not dead, she will be soon.

Or she's already like him.

Veronica clutched the cell phone and thumbed through the contacts in search of Laura McCoy's number. The bathroom began to fog from the humidity of the shower. A steady stream of hot water splashed against the porcelain tile.

What if Edison hears you? If you're going to do this you need to make it quick.

Before he comes up here.

She tapped her finger against the highlighted name and put the phone to her ear. After three rings, Veronica took a sharp breath when she heard Laura's voice. Her heart sank once she realized it was only her voicemail greeting.

"Hey, you've reached Laura. If you're not a telemarketer, lawyer, or poseur, leave a message."

"Laura?"

This is hopeless, Veronica.

"Laura. Hi, it's me. Veronica Upham." She clutched the thick fabric of the robe. "I'm...I'm not sure if you're getting any of our messages, or if maybe you've got your phone turned off. We found your laptop bag in the creek and there was, uh, I'm not even sure...I'm not sure you're even still with us..."

As the steam wafted through the claustrophobic bathroom, Veronica Upham began to cry.

"I'm so sorry this happened to you. I know we didn't know each other well. And I gave you so much shit 'cause Edison was so excited to see you again. I felt threatened but..."

Veronica choked back more tears and wiped her nose on her sleeve.

"Listen, I'm sorry. If you get this message, please call us back. Call *me* back!"

245

She took another deep breath but her voice continued to tremble.

"I won't tell Edison. I promise. I just need to know. I need to know if you're OK. If you're playing some kinda trick on him, it's OK. I'll play too. He's such a fucking asshole, Laura."

Veronica began to sob hysterically into the phone.

"Look, he doesn't care if you're alive or dead. He's obsessed. He's got us running around all over the fucking city. But he's not looking for you. He wants Bartsch." She spat the name into the phone. "He's looking for *him* and not you. And if this guy is what he seems to be, Ed's gonna get himself and the rest of us killed."

It suddenly dawned on Veronica that perhaps Matthias was screening Laura's calls.

"And Bartsch? Matthias Bartsch? If *you* can hear this message, we know who you are! We know *what* you are! But if you...if you let Laura go, I'll f-figure something out. We can tell Raymer that you..."

Veronica jumped and cried out when three loud raps shook the bathroom door. The phone slipped from her hand and clattered to the floor.

"Goddammit, woman!" Junior's voice was rough and phlegmatic. "You drownin' in there or somethin'?"

"Just a minute!" she called out. Her pulse raced as her heart pounded in her chest. "Lady problems!"

"Never mind," Junior replied. "I don't need a full report!"

Veronica bent over and grabbed the phone. The call had been disconnected.

Goddammit!

She frantically thumbed through the call history and tapped Laura's contact information to redial. There were no rings as the call immediately switched to voice mail.

"Hey, you've reached Laura..."

"Fuck!" Veronica slapped the phone against her thigh. She bent forward, clutched the hand towel bar, and fought back tears. After another minute, she couldn't bear the stifling atmosphere of the bathroom. She cut the hot water back and tore off the robe. Veronica stepped into the shower and wept. She was certain that she'd never see Laura McCoy alive again.

42

"ARE YOU READY?" MATTHIAS BARTSCH CRANKED THE ENGINE of their latest stolen car. He pulled the old white sedan back onto the empty bypass.

"I guess so." Laura sat in the passenger seat and tapped the suppressed barrel of the FNP 45-Tactical against her open palm. In the trunk she could hear the shovels and pickaxe they'd packed earlier rattling with the dilapidated car's transmission.

Matthias gripped the steering wheel as the speedometer hit sixty-five. "Is that apprehension I hear?"

"Resignation." Laura sighed and hefted the weapon. "This is just too much gun for me."

"You'll do fine once you get the feel for it." He glanced at the heavy pistol as she laid it across her thighs. "Now remember, the initial trigger pull on that gun is the hardest. Don't overcompensate if you have to take a second shot."

"I understand the theory. The practice is a different story." Laura drummed her fingers on the armrest, then adjusted her wool Ike jacket. "So where are we going?"

"To the interstate." Matthias hunched over the wheel and brushed the dust off the inside windshield. "With that in mind, you should be thinking about *how* you want to hunt this evening."

"We could pull over and I'll play the damsel-in-distress again. Like we did last night?"

"We'll be on a major highway. Probably not the best idea with all those big rigs passing us on their way to Richmond." Matthias shook his head. "Think of something else. Something you haven't done. When you repeat the method and means of execution one too many times, you get complacent. That will get you caught."

Laura pressed two fingers against her temple. "What about finding a town or something a few miles out from the bypass? Somewhere you've never been before?"

"I like that better." Matthias pushed down on the gas pedal as the sedan charged down an exit ramp and merged onto the highway. Despite his prediction of steady traffic, there were few oncoming cars or trucks on the road. "So what will we do when we find this town of yours?"

"I don't know yet. I need to think."

"Yes, you do. Eventually, it will become second nature."

"But you've put us in a situation where hunting is not ideal. We're out in the open, and like you said, on a traveled highway. I'm not sure—"

"Look to your right, Laura."

The headlights of the car shone on a distant figure. One arm was raised high, and a frame backpack hung from the hitchhiker's shoulders. As they got closer, it became apparent that the drifter had been on the road for a while. He had a full beard and long tangled hair. His flannel coat and torn jeans had seen better days. The sole of one shoe had been repaired with duct tape.

"Too easy?" Matthias asked.

"Pull over and pick him up." Laura slid the heavy pistol between her seat and the passenger door. It rested upside down and out of sight, so she could drop a hand and bring it to bear with little effort.

"You sure this is what you want to do?" Matthias began to slow down.

"Do it," she said.

"You will take him down? No fumbling with the gun? No missing this time?"

"Yeah, we'll pull off the interstate on some remote exit ramp and handle everything out of sight."

"You sure you're ready?"

"Yes, for fuck's sake! You *want* me to second-guess myself? Pull the fuck over!"

"Fine." Matthias hit the turn signal as he passed the hitcher, and swung onto the shoulder. He braked to a halt in the gravel and released the power locks on the doors. The hitchhiker ran to catch up to the slowing car, his backpack shifting up and down with every footfall. When he reached the sedan, he tapped on the driver's side door.

Matthias thumbed the window open. He said nothing as the unshaven wanderer leaned in to catch a blast of warm air from the heat vents. "Hey, y'all goin' to Richmond?"

Laura nodded and pointed to the back seat. "Yeah, hop in. Door's unlocked."

The hitchhiker was in his mid-thirties and reeked of body odor. Prison tattoos snaked up his sinewy neck. Even while trying to be congenial, the hitcher had a sour look on his face. He tore open the rear door and pitched his frame pack onto the seat behind Laura. He ducked in and closed the door behind him.

"Thanks for pickin' me up. It's fuckin' freezing out there."

"No problem." Laura glanced over her shoulder as the drifter settled in the back seat.

Matthias pulled back onto the highway as a semi roared past them in the left lane.

"Y'all mind if I burn one?" He held up a battered pack of cigarettes and a lighter. "Wind was too bad outside to light up. I'm about two minutes away from a full-blown nic-fit. Yo, I'll even crack open the window back here so's not to fume up your ride."

Laura looked at Matthias and shrugged. "Sure. Why not? You got a name?"

"Jason." He slipped a cigarette between his lips. "Jason Halleck." With a flick of the lighter, he ignited his cigarette and took a deep drag. "I'm from down in Carolina. Tryin' to get my ass to Richmond to see my girl." He held his cigarette between two fingers and gestured at Matthias. "So... you two together?"

Matthias and Laura exchanged a knowing glance. "In a way," Laura said.

"I didn't mean to get up in your shit." He grinned to flash a few gaps where teeth had been. "Just figured I'd ask. You know, bein' pleasant company and all." Jason pointed at the driver's headrest. "Your boy always this quiet?"

"Yeah," Laura replied as she glanced over her shoulder again. "We've been having communication problems lately."

"Aw, man. Y'all gotta talk shit out." Jason took another drag on his noxious cigarette. "Fuck, when I was in the joint the first time around,

Lee Ann came to visit every other day." The hitchhiker inhaled deeply and pitched the half-smoked cigarette out the cracked window.

"So what'd you go to prison for?" Laura asked.

"This." Jason wrenched a cheap 9mm handgun from under his flannel coat and held the scratched barrel inches from Laura's face. He tapped Matthias on the side of his head. The vampire behind the steering wheel eyed the robber in the back seat via the rear-view mirror.

"Whoa there!" Laura held up a hand. "You can take your finger off the trigger. We'll do what you want."

"Tell your boy there to run his pockets. I want cash and credit cards. Fuckin' PIN numbers, too. And if you got money on you, I want yours, too."

Jason glanced out the back window. "What you got in that trunk rattlin' around?"

"The usual stuff. A jack and a tire iron." Laura began to search her pockets with one hand. Matthias took out his wallet from his motorcycle jacket and held it up by his head. Not once did he take his eyes off the road.

The robber snatched it and thumbed through its contents. "Holy shit! You always carry this much cash?"

Matthias didn't answer.

"Y'all motherfuckers dealin'?" He gestured toward the front of the car. "What you got in the glove box? Crystal? X? Weed?"

Matthias drifted onto an exit ramp and sped up the incline. He stopped and turned right onto a lonely country road.

"Hey! Motherfucker! I said you were drivin' my ass to Richmond. What part o' that passed through your thick skull, Frankenstein?" He jabbed Matthias with the gun barrel, but received no reply.

Laura took off her seatbelt and put one hand on the 45-Tactical. With her free hand, she waved at the robber. "Hey, dude. Chill for a sec. If you wanna see what we're holding, it's in the trunk. You name it, we got it."

"Why'd you just tell me the trunk was empty, bitch?" He pulled back the hammer on his Saturday-Night Special.

"If you were riding on the stash we've got, you'd lie about it, too." Laura put her hand between the gun barrel and her face.

Matthias pulled over, put the car in park, and popped the trunk. Laura locked eyes with the hitchhiker.

"Get out and see for yourself," she offered.

"What, you think I'm some kinda dumbass? I'm guessin' your mama told you not to pick up hitchhikers, didn't she?" He thrust the business end of his pistol into Laura's palm. "What's in the trunk? Answer me, bitch!"

"I'll get out with you."

"Damn right you will. You, and that motherfucker behind the wheel. We all get out together. No bullshit."

As Jason slipped out of the back seat, Matthias and Laura opened their doors. Laura tumbled out with the .45 pistol in hand and aimed it over the roof at the robber, who dropped his own pistol in surprise. Matthias, still silent, stepped onto the road to block him in.

"Goddamn! Alright, I fucked up!" Jason raised his hands and shook his head. "What can we do here to put this behind us? You know, let bygones be bygones an' shit?"

"Get your fucking pack out and put it on!" Laura held the 45-Tactical with perfect trigger discipline. "You reach for that gun and my boyfriend over there's gonna snap your fucking neck!"

Trembling, the drifter pulled out his pack and slung it over his shoulders.

"Now, leave everything you took from us on the back seat!"

"Not a problem. Not a problem." Jason pitched the wallet back into the idling car. "Want me to shut the door?"

"Yeah."

Jason did as he was told and remained with his hands in the air. "So what now?"

"Start walking." Laura gestured with the handgun. "Go on."

"Yo. Thanks for lettin' me go. I swear to fuck I won't say a word to *anybody*, yo. Seriously."

"Who said anything about letting you go?" Matthias finally broke his silence. Jason spun to face him. "We're just giving you a head start."

Jason wavered for a moment as Laura kept the pistol trained on her mark. He panicked, and cut around the car to head into the woods.

"Laura," Matthias said. "Take him down."

Although her hunger had been tempered from two nights of feeding, the rage was still inside her. Her fury was rekindled by the audacity of Jason Halleck's botched carjacking attempt. She set out after him as he pushed through deadfall and low-lying branches. She could hear his panting as he loosened his backpack and let it fall to the ground. Free from the extra weight, Halleck took off at a faster clip, but Laura closed the distance and hurdled

251

the abandoned knapsack. She tapped the laser sight mounted beneath the barrel, and let it dance off the trees around her prey before lining up a shot.

As Halleck sprung ahead, Laura fired a shot that clipped his shoulder. Jason cried out and fell forward into the underbrush.

Laura sprinted ahead to catch up. She towered over the robber and kicked him hard with her boot. Jason rolled onto his back and held up his hands to ward her away. "Please..." he managed. "I'm sorry...just let me go."

Laura tilted her head as she stared down at the helpless drifter. The copper smell of his blood sent a shiver of excitement up her spine.

"You're a liar," she whispered. "You were about to do the same thing to us."

"No," Jason groaned and clutched at his shoulder. "I swear. I ain't no killer!"

Laura squeezed the trigger without compunction. The large-caliber round tore through his throat and severed his carotid artery. The blood came in dark, viscous waves.

Halleck could no longer speak. He coughed as the blood gushed from his throat. His wide eyes gazed up at her in terror.

The vampire bent toward the gaping wound. She straddled the hitchhiker's prone form, digging her knees into the wet leaves. As she inched forward, a small silver crucifix slipped out from under his shirt. The sight of the holy symbol took Laura by surprise and she cringed in revulsion. She reached forward to snatch the charm from its chain, but the cross burned the tips of her fingers. With a grunt, she tore the necklace off, and hurled it into a nearby thicket.

Halleck had lost consciousness. Much of his blood had already spoiled the ground beneath them, so she wasted no more time. She licked a probing tongue across the wound and found the tear in his artery. Her lips locked on the thick blood vessel. Crimson liquid spilled into Laura's mouth, accompanied by a euphoric rush of power. The fledgling vampire was so enraptured that she failed to hear Matthias approach from behind. He dropped a shovel, a pickaxe, and Halleck's backpack beside the prostrate body.

When she finished, Laura glanced up and wiped her bloody chin on the dead man's filthy coat. "I didn't leave any for you." She swallowed hard. "I'm sorry. I—"

"He was your prey. You took him down on your own, so you feed until you are sated." Matthias leaned over and grabbed the pickaxe. After kicking some leaves aside, he began to break up the ground with the sharp tool. "You handled yourself well, even before the takedown. But I'm curious. Why did you cry out a moment ago?"

"He wore a crucifix." She held up a blistered palm. "I had no idea it would be so...I don't know...*hot*? It was fucking weird."

"I told you those symbols were potent," he reminded her. "Never underestimate your prey. Remember this feeling."

She glowered at Matthias. "I don't think I'll forget anytime soon."

As he brought the pickaxe down, sparks flew as the steel head struck a stone.

"Matthias." She leaned back, too glutted with blood to help him dig. "I know there's more good than evil left in you."

"Why do you say that?"

"You still love the memory of your wife. Music. You know, what we did here tonight—"

"I'm not doing anything but digging a grave."

"Hear me out," Laura pled. "We could feed on criminals. Low-life assholes like this guy." She waited for a reaction from Matthias, but he kept swinging the pickaxe. "We could hunt rapists, murderers, degenerates. I don't know, fuckin' politicians. We could do some good."

Matthias paused and stood upright. The handle of the tool slid through his slackened fingers and the steel head thumped against the ground. "You are suggesting we become vigilantes?"

"It's just an idea. You don't have to—"

"Why do we hunt?"

"To survive. But couldn't we—"

"I've been doing this for decades. I sought to kill every man who executed my comrades because I thought it would quiet the beast inside. A few days before I met you, the last of those men died of old age before I could take his life. Vengeance is just sport, and for us, killing is not a game."

"I know that."

"Then as you mature, you will learn to leave no trace of your existence. The best way to do that is to choose your victims at random." He pitched the entrenching tool aside and picked up the shovel to deepen the makeshift grave. "Sometimes you get lucky. Like tonight. But there is no need to risk everything to prove something to yourself. Who do we have to answer to? Traditional concepts of good or evil don't apply to us."

"Except when someone pulls out a cross, right? Then we know which side we're playing for."

"Well, when you put it that way..." Matthias trailed off. "I guess you're right."

Laura felt a twinge of her waning conscience. "Right. So if we're gonna do this. If we *have* to do this to survive, then there's no rule against killing those who deserve to die."

"And what gives you the right to decide who lives or dies?" Matthias pitched soil from the hole over his shoulder. He continued to turn the earth until the collapsing hole became a shallow grave. Finally, Laura spoke.

"All I'm saying is we have this *power*. There's no reason to kill innocent people when there are others out there who deserve to be punished." She kicked Jason Halleck's corpse into its ignominious resting place. "Maybe there's someone who mocked you once, or dragged your name through the mud and sullied your reputation."

"You think people should be punished for simply mocking you? Wouldn't you say death is a stiff penalty for such a petty transgression?"

"OK, fine. Someone that hurt you or hurt someone you love."

"I told you," Matthias replied through clenched teeth. "All my enemies are dead now. And I have nothing to show for it. It sounds like you already have a few people in mind. Perhaps some suitor who broke your heart? A beautiful woman that made you jealous?" He narrowed his eyes as he gripped the shovel handle. "Or maybe a professor that gave you a poor mark?"

"That's enough," Laura said. "Let me help you bury—"

"Although you'll never admit it, you will relish the power." Matthias pushed his fledgling further. "But I learned the hard way. To kill with vengeance is to kill with blindness."

He began to cover the body. "If you don't stop this line of thinking, the contradictions of our existence will wear you down. We kill to live. Anything beyond that and you will lose yourself completely."

"This is a fate I didn't choose," Laura stated with contempt. "But I can choose how I act."

"One day you might," Matthias said. "But if you want to survive long enough to earn the privilege of choice, you will do as I say."

"And live like a brute? Scavenging like a goddamn animal?"

Matthias leaned on the shovel handle. When he spoke, his native accent grew more pronounced. "Who are you to lecture me on brutality? When

I was in the *Wehrmacht,* we moved through White Russia and destroyed villages suspected of harboring Red Partisans. One day, an SS officer with an *Einsatzgruppen* detachment came through our ranks." Matthias stared off into the darkness. "It turned out they barricaded eighty or ninety Russian Jews and suspected partisans in a barn with a thatched roof. They were civilians. Men, women, children. All were shut up inside. This SS officer asked for volunteers to help burn down the barn. And what do you think happened?"

Laura shrugged and avoided his stare. She knew she had no right to question him, and felt embarrassed of her sheltered life. Matthias spat on the dead man as he recalled the unpleasant memory.

"About half the regular soldiers milling around after the fight fell in to assist the officer with the mass execution. They weren't fanatical Nazis or SS men. Most were army conscripts fresh off the troop trains. They didn't *need* to kill those prisoners. They *wanted* to see that barn burn down and hear the screams from inside."

"What's your point, Matthias?" Laura countered. "There are things like that throughout the entire history of the human race. It's no secret how despicable we...I mean, *they* are. That's my whole point!"

"I was there!" Matthias sneered at her. A lock of his hair fell alongside his frigid blue eyes. "I saw these men laugh and joke as they went off to do the deed, then come back to eat dinner like nothing happened. Still laughing, still joking."

Matthias dumped a pile of earth on Jason Halleck's face. "You and I were mortals. And there's nothing we can do that's more brutal or ruthless than what living men and women have done and continue to do every day. At least we have a reason to kill." He swung the shovel again. "You can't tell who is or is not *evil* by just looking at them."

"I'm not gonna argue with you anymore." Laura shook her head and began to pace again. "I pretty much agree with you anyway."

"Then help me get this body in the ground so we can leave."

Laura kicked a clod of dirt into the grave. "Are you mad at me?"

"Not at all," Matthias replied. "I just don't want you to make the same mistakes I made. Now come on. We need to finish up here."

43

LAURA AWOKE IN THE MASTER BEDROOM OF THE SAFE-HOUSE. She couldn't tell if it was night or day, as the cabin windows were also obscured with cardboard and duct tape. From another room, she could hear the soft strains of Baroque music.

Although she was familiar with a lot of classical, she couldn't place this particular work. It sounded as though two orchestras were playing in tandem, and their combined efforts were breaking apart instrument by instrument.

Laura rolled off the mattress and stood. She knew Matthias was somewhere nearby, and couldn't resist the compulsion to follow the music and find him. She opened the bedroom door and stole down a short carpeted hallway. Cobwebs wafted along the ceiling as the music began to swell into an undulating and grievous melody. As she emerged into the nearly empty living room, Laura spied Matthias unpacking boxes and large plastic bags. A stack of broken and scratched jewel cases had been laid out on the floor before him.

"What time is it?"

"Midnight," he answered without looking up. "You slept past sundown." He dusted his hands on his shirt as he took a step back.

"What's all this?" She raised her voice as the music got louder.

"I cleaned out the last apartment," he replied. "The one where I first took you. Now there's only this safe-house."

"And you went shopping?" Laura nodded at the bags.

"I bought more duct tape." He held up a roll. "Aluminum foil. Plastic sheeting. A couple heavy tarps." He pushed the heavy bags aside with his arm. "Went to three different hardware stores to avoid suspicion. Paid cash, just like you'll learn to do for everything."

"What's in there?" Laura pointed to another small bag beside the others.

"New clothes," he explained, gesturing for her to come closer. "For you."

Matthias tossed the plastic bag to her. Laura scanned through the bag to find two solid black t-shirts, a few pairs of black socks, and a three-pack of cotton panties.

Laura felt embarrassed when she saw the underwear, but was grateful that he had been so thoughtful. She was too caught up in the whirlwind of strange events to have noticed the state of her clothes.

"There's a shower in the back," Matthias told her as the music continued to blare from the small stereo. "The water pressure is weak but it should suffice."

"Great. Thanks."

Matthias continued to sift through his belongings. The lilting melody on the portable stereo erupted into a grand chorus. Laura found the sudden outpouring of grief to be comforting.

"What is this piece?" Laura asked.

"Bach," the vampire answered. *"Matthäus-Passion.* Final chorus."

She remembered seeing the title on an old record her grandfather once owned. The irony of Matthias' song choice wasn't lost on her.

"So austere," she ventured. "It definitely suits you."

Matthias spoke above the melancholic piece. *"Wir setzen uns mit Tränen nieder."* He was careful to enunciate each syllable.

"I don't speak German." Laura reminded him. "What's that mean?"

"We sit down in tears." Matthias bent down to adjust the volume of the stereo. "That's the name of the final chorus."

Laura nodded. She watched as the vampire put his sorting tasks aside and reached into his coat pocket.

"I've been holding onto this. But it's yours, not mine."

Matthias tossed Laura's cell phone in her direction. She caught it, and looked it over.

"I meant to give it back to you earlier." He turned to rummage through yet another box. "Even though you broke my cello."

"I'm sorry I did that."

"Like I said, petty revenge only leads to regret." Matthias closed the box lid. Laura turned on her cell phone and waited for the device to load.

"Before you review your messages, I need to talk to you about something."

Laura scowled. "I'm not gonna call the cops if that's what you're afraid of."

"Not at all," he said. "I trust you. Do you trust me?"

"You're growing on me." Laura sat down on the floor and folded her legs. "So what's up?"

"I listened to your voice mail." The vampire rose to his full height and leaned against the living room wall. "You really should have a lock or password on that device."

"I never had a problem with nosy sidekicks before," she quipped. "So what's going on?"

"You have a lot of missed calls on there," he explained. "Several of which appear to be from that Veronica Upham woman." He paused to let his words sink in. "It seems like your friends are still looking for you." He stopped to correct himself. "Well...your old professor seems more interested in finding *me.*"

With the phone pressed against her ear, Laura raised a finger to hush the vampire before he spoke again. Her eyes grew wide as she listened to Veronica's most recent message.

"This is definitely an interesting turn of events," she muttered.

"When I took you," Matthias continued as Laura lowered the phone into her lap. "I thought they would realize how foolish it was to hunt me."

"No." Laura shook her head. "That's not how Raymer works. I'm not really surprised by any of this, I guess. What's funny is that woman and I are like oil and water. She's a total flake. But she's harmless." Laura swallowed. "I didn't think she'd be willing to risk her life for Raymer and stay in the middle of all this. She's flighty, but she's not stupid."

Laura fell silent as Matthias looked on with a concerned scowl. He began to pace across the room with his hands locked behind his back. Laura glanced up and brushed a lock of hair from her eyes.

"I don't think Raymer's gonna call off his dogs." She tapped her fingers on the edge of her knee. "I guess we're gonna have to find a way to deal with this after all. They're determined to find us."

"They never will," Matthias insisted. "Tomorrow's our last night in Williamsport. And we're not coming back."

"That won't stop him." She stretched out her legs and was about to push her way up from the floor when the vampire leaned over to assist her.

"He'll follow us," she said. "This man's obsessed with killing you. Or killing anyone like *us*. I told you before. It's his life's work."

"Well, it doesn't sound like they have any solid leads," Matthias replied. "We have been careful. And the plan is to leave town after sundown tomorrow. Like you said before, we can't kill them. Too high profile. And I don't think you're ready to do what needs to be done anyhow."

"And what's that supposed to mean?" Laura snapped and pursed her lips. "You don't think I'm ready?"

"I don't think you're ready to confront someone that was close to you," Matthias clarified. "You said this Veronica woman is harmless. But if she's working with the other professor, how can you be so sure?"

"I can handle her."

"I have no doubt you can *overpower* her. But when the time comes, will you hesitate if she poses a threat? Our weaknesses are no longer the things of myth and legend in this age."

"I told you, I can handle her."

"What about the older man?" Matthias sneered as the name escaped his lips. "Luttrell?"

"I'll leave him to you." Laura folded her arms across her chest. "So you can finish what you started."

"No." Matthias shook his head as he continued to reflect. "No good can come of this. I don't think you are ready."

"Can we just fucking drop this?" Laura shouted. She cast an icy glance at Matthias. "I guess we'll run. Like cowards."

"I didn't say that. I simply don't believe you are ready for this conflict. Not yet. And it doesn't appear as though the threat is immediate. If they pursue us, we will confront them in the future."

"Are we hunting tonight?" Laura interrupted. She was determined to change the subject. "It's still early. And I think I need to get the fuck outta here."

"I wasn't planning on it." Matthias wrinkled his brow and returned to the boxes on the floor. "Besides, you don't need to. You should be fine after last night."

"What if I *want* to?" Laura remained persistent.

"Then I'd say you need to keep your desires in check." Matthias crossed his arms and provoked his progeny with a wary eye. "You kill to survive. Not because you are throwing a tantrum."

"Well, I sure as fuck don't want to stand around here while you pack a bunch of boxes!"

"The keys to the car are in my pocket," he told her. "Come get them." He rattled the keychain in his jacket pocket and taunted her.

"Fuck you!" Laura spat. "I'm not playing these fucking games."

"Then prove to me that you can handle yourself."

Laura roared in frustration and rushed forward to tackle her mentor. The elder vampire stepped to the side and grasped Laura by her right arm. He spun her in a circle and pulled her against his chest, his strong hand clutching her throat.

"Not good enough," he whispered in her ear.

With another harsh grunt, Laura snapped her neck back to smash Matthias in his jaw. Caught off guard, the elder vampire bit hard into his lower lip. Dark blood began to stream down his chin.

Matthias laughed and brushed a lock of slick hair from his gleaming eyes. "Much better." He dabbed his fingers along his chin and rubbed the back of his hand along his mouth.

"I fuckin' thought so," Laura shot back. Her entire body tingled with the thrill of the fight.

But before she could revel too long in her victory, she was staring up at the low ceiling of the cabin. Matthias had taken her down by surprise. The back of her head—which already throbbed from its impact with Matthias' chin—had hit the floor hard in the fall. A cold blade was pressed tight against her throat, and Matthias stared into her eyes.

"Never underestimate your enemy!" Matthias warned and let his grip go slack. Within seconds the vampire was on his feet, and once again extended his hand to his fledgling. He handed her the large serrated blade, along with a leather sheath.

"You may not be ready for your friends," Matthias said. "But I think you're ready to get some blood on your hands."

44

MATTHIAS EASED THE CAR TO A STOP AFTER TRAVELING the length of a weed-infested dirt road.

"Doesn't look like anyone's been down here for years." Laura studied her reflection against the high sheen of the massive knife. After a quick shower and a change of clothes, she felt refreshed and ready for another night out. "When you said we were hunting in the city, I thought we'd be around other people and—"

"Look through the woods there." Through the window and a copse of trees, she could see porch lights in a neat row. Across the railroad tracks to their left, cars streamed across a concrete overpass. "We are closer to civilization than you think."

Laura's expression soured. "Just like that bike path where you—"

"Don't dwell on the past."

"You're one to talk," Laura shot back. "I mean—"

"You can reminisce all you want once you've dispatched your prey, but these moments before you attempt a kill, you take in your surroundings and prepare for everything that could possibly go wrong."

"Look." Laura flung open the passenger door and addressed him in a curt tone. "I'm a quick study. I think I've proven that, haven't I? You point me in the direction I need to go, and I'll do what we came here to do."

Matthias got out to address her over the roof of the car. "Keep your voice down and your senses up," he hissed. "I won't tell you where to go. Use your senses. *Listen!*" He pointed to his ear. "Your hearing is much more acute than any living being." Matthias dropped his fingers to tap the bridge

261

of his nose. "You can smell the blood of your victims. Close your eyes, and you can trace it coursing through their veins."

Laura closed the door. She shoved the sheathed knife into her waistband and broke off into the woods on her side of the car. Matthias stepped forward to follow her as she led them away from the distant lights. When he caught up, she whispered in his direction. "Back at the country house, when you were packing...you...you never said where we're going?"

"Now is not the time to discuss this." Matthias clutched her arm. "Stay focused—"

"Trust me," Laura interrupted. "I'm doing everything you've taught me. So what's the ultimate plan?"

"If you're having second thoughts, you don't have to stay with me forever." He shoved his hands into his jacket pockets. "For now, I think it best we stick together. At least until we figure out what to do about Raymer and the others."

"Is that the only reason?"

"No," he admitted. "I hoped that you would want to continue to learn a bit longer. Then, you can go off on your own if you choose."

"Is that what you want?"

Matthias didn't answer. He stepped over a rotting log. In the distance, he could see the outline of a derelict train station and its lower platform. "I've got a responsibility to you. When I became what I am, I had no one to teach me. No one to turn to for questions, or for help. But once my obligation to you has been fulfilled, I've no intention of keeping you prisoner."

"That's not the point, and you know it." Laura touched his wrist, but he withdrew his hand. "What do you want from me, Matthias?"

"You figured it out right away, remember? But what I want and what *you* want may not be—"

"You're making an assumption about me." She darted ahead to descend a steep grade and called back to him. "Don't assume anything."

By the time she reached the lower platform of the desolate building, Matthias was halfway down the hill. Laura moved into the shadows and let her senses guide her. She stopped before the charred remains of a door that had been burned for heat. The crumbling platform was littered with beer cans, broken glass, and spent syringes. Behind the brick wall to which she clung, Laura smelled the distinct odor of a living being.

She heard Matthias cross the platform behind her as she ducked into the gutted remains of the train station's lower level. There was a vast open waiting room filled with debris. Wooden benches were piled in all four corners, and she noticed the dim glow of a trashcan fire beside one of the empty doorways. The scent of burning wood couldn't mask the enticing aroma of pulsing blood.

Laura pulled the knife from its sheath and let it hang by her thigh. As she ducked behind a pile of refuse, she spotted a woman in her early forties by a smoldering oil drum. The orange embers cast odd shadows on her pockmarked face. Her bare arms were covered in track marks. Puss oozed from two abscessed needle-holes in her left forearm. A piece of cloth rolled around her upper arm hung loose, and Laura assumed the rag had helped the junkie raise one of her many collapsed veins.

As Laura approached the woman, she felt Matthias' presence behind her. She stole a glimpse over her shoulder. Matthias stood in the doorway, arms across his chest as usual, and gave her a single nod to urge her forward.

Take the kill.

As she moved closer, the addict stirred and muttered something unintelligible. Laura fell to a crouch beside the junkie, who was propped against the brick wall. A halo of graffiti tags surrounded her frail body as she turned over and opened her eyes.

"Hey," the junkie rasped. "What the fuck are you—"

Laura slashed the long blade across her victim's neck. For a split second, the vampire thought she'd missed. Yet her cut had been precise, and the blood began to flow despite the initial delay. The addict twitched as a torrent of blood spilled from the cut to stain her shirt. Her victim raised a trembling hand to stop the bleeding, but Laura batted it away and pushed the woman's head backwards.

They always reach for their throats. Always.

The vampire shoved her lips over the wound and let the blood fill her waiting mouth. She heard Matthias move closer. A rotted board snapped beneath his weight, but Laura wasn't startled. Her head spun with euphoria as the final draught splashed over her tongue.

On all fours, Laura crawled back with the hilt of the knife pressed to the grimy floor. As she raised the blade to lick it clean, she noticed a figure standing before her. How Matthias had managed to get around her didn't quite register, until she realized the filthy khaki trousers and beat-up tennis shoes in her field of view weren't his.

"Laura!" Matthias shouted from behind.

Blade in hand, the blood-drunk vampire glanced up to see the gaunt form of an old black man, with wild white hair and a beard framing his angry face. His eyes were obsidian pools, and she could smell no living blood in his body. His heart didn't beat, and there was no sign of breath condensing in the air before him.

"This is my fuckin' territory!" he bellowed.

Matthias' boots shuffled behind her. "I've seen you." A guttural growl rumbled in his throat. "On the bus. The other night."

"Yeah," the strange vampire snarled. "An' I didn't tread on your huntin' ground, so what the fuck you doin' on mine?"

Laura felt caged between them. She rose, with her eyes riveted to the wild-eyed old man. She clutched the Bowie knife at her side. The vampire turned his attention to her, and pointed a gnarled finger at the corpse slumped by the smoldering oil drum.

"She was my kill." The older vampire in tattered clothes edged a single step closer to Laura. "Now, you gonna pay me for what you took!"

"Back away from him and give me the knife!" Matthias ordered.

Laura shook her head and noticed her vision constrict until her sole focus was on her new enemy. She held up the glistening blade and let out a frenzied roar.

The white-haired vampire charged at Laura. Before she could defend herself, he slammed into her with his bony shoulder. Laura was hit with such force that she tumbled backwards. She skidded across the floor and collided with an overturned bench.

Matthias vaulted over her to position himself between Laura and her attacker. Matthias attempted to mollify the enemy. "You made your point. Now let's call it even. You won't see us down here again. You have my word."

"Fuck you!" The vampire lunged at Matthias, who side-stepped his attack and picked up a plank of wood. Laura watched as Matthias slammed the heavy beam against the enraged vampire's back. He cried out as a cluster of nails pierced his skin. The beam, however, had splintered from the collision. Matthias dropped the useless board as the frenzied vampire recovered.

"Matthias!" Laura leapt to her feet. "That fucker's mine! Back the hell off!"

Before her mentor could reply, Laura plowed into the enemy vampire and jabbed the knife into his chest. Even with her narrow vision, she saw Matthias step over the junkie's body to stand next to the burning oil drum.

The vampire bellowed and shoved Laura aside. As she fell upon a pile of bricks, she maintained her grip on the hilt of the knife. The once-shiny blade was now darkened with dead blood.

The old vampire, now bleeding from a gash in his right side, lumbered over the debris. Matthias stepped forward to block his charge and absorb the brunt of the assault. As Laura fought to rally, she watched the marauding vampire fall backward after smashing against Matthias' chest. His knees buckled under the raw force, but he remained standing. As Matthias converged on the enemy, Laura yelled out once again for him to stop.

"I'll take him!"

Matthias pressed the heel of his boot against the vampire's chest. Dead blood oozed from the knife wound and slicked the floor.

"Then get over here and finish him! Drive that knife into his heart and pin him to the floor!"

Matthias released the vampire as Laura scrambled to bring the knife down again. In spite of his injury, the elder vampire dodged the arc of the blade by rolling on his side. Laura drove the tip of the Bowie knife into the rotten floorboards. As she struggled to pull it out, the other vampire leapt to his feet. Matthias struck with the heel of his palm, but he deflected the blow and threw his weight at Matthias. Still on her knees, Laura managed to slash the vampire's lower left leg.

The cut barely slowed his movement as he charged toward Matthias again. The two vampires were deadlocked as Laura rose to her feet and plunged the knife into the enemy's back. He lurched forward against Matthias, who trapped him in a bear hug. As Laura withdrew the blade, the crippled vampire turned to face her.

Matthias nodded to Laura over the enemy's shoulder and released his stranglehold.

"Fuckin' bitch!" The white-haired creature roared and stumbled forward, flailing his arms.

Laura bared her teeth and rushed forward with the blade. But her stronger opponent smashed a tight fist against her forearm and she dropped the knife. Before she could duck down, her attacker wrapped his fingers around her neck and lifted her off her feet. With one arm aloft, he held Laura toward the high ceiling.

Matthias made no move to help her as the attacker bent down and fumbled for the knife. As his attention turned to picking up the blade, Laura landed a sharp kick to his face, smashing his nose and upper jaw. He cried out, but the pain seemed only to renew his sense of purpose. He spit out two teeth as a stream of black blood trickled over his lips and stained his beard. With the blade now firmly in hand, he stabbed Laura and then dragged the knife across her chest.

Matthias plowed into the elder vampire's back. He groaned but managed to thrust the blade deeper into Laura's belly. He relinquished his grip on her as Matthias pulled their desperate enemy backward. With inhuman force, he wrapped his arms around the attacker and pushed inward. After crushing several of the creature's ribs, Matthias forced him to the ground.

The wounds that would've killed Laura as a mortal barely slowed her down. She picked up the knife and drove it through her assailant's heart. She leaned on the blade until she felt the tip puncture the wooden floor beneath him. Laura kept pushing down until the hilt was against the writhing vampire's bony chest.

"I get up and I'll fuckin' kill you. You hear me you fuckin' whore? I'll rip your heart out your chest and—"

Matthias brought the heel of his boot down on the vampire's mouth with enough force to break his jawbone. Teeth and sinew sprayed into the air as Matthias withdrew his heel and brought it down again.

While the knife had pinned the vampire to the ground, the blade possessed no occult properties. The enemy—still far from paralyzed—twisted back and forth, hoping to work himself free. His ruined jaw hung open, although most of his teeth were gone.

Matthias helped Laura to her feet and took two steps backward. Blood seeped through her t-shirt and wool jacket. She held one hand over the wound as she locked eyes with her attacker.

"You need to act now, Laura!" Matthias commanded. "Look around you. How can you finish him?"

"I could take the knife—"

"Don't explain yourself!" Matthias slapped his hands around her upper arms and pulled her aside. "Just remember. How do you kill one of us?"

She gave him a blank stare and held up her blackened hands.

"Look for something in this room to finish the bastard off!" Matthias raised a finger to point at the glowing embers in the oil drum.

Laura spun around and raced toward the rusty barrel. She placed her slick hands on the scorching rim and dragged it across the floor. Lifting it into the air, she heaved its flaming contents onto her pinned enemy, who was desperately trying to pull the knife from his chest. A cascade of hot coals covered the old vampire's damaged face and body. It only took a moment for the searing embers to catch the attacker's clothing on fire. He cried out and gnawed his split lips as a raging inferno engulfed him.

"Stand back!" Matthias yanked Laura to safety as the dark flesh of the vampire began to boil. The flames rose higher and oily smoke drifted to the ceiling.

The pair watched in silence until their enemy no longer thrashed or wailed. Where there was once flesh, a charred figure remained. Choking smoke grew thick and acrid with an indescribable fetor. The flames were dying, and the waiting room had filled with a sickening gray vapor.

Matthias stormed past Laura and stomped out the flames. The monster's now-brittle bones cracked beneath his heavy boots. While he ground the vampire's remains to ash, Laura opened her coat and lifted her shirt. Her belly and chest were lacerated, and she staggered back in shock. "Matthias, I...I thought we were invulnerable?"

"No. That's why I wanted you to watch him die. So you remember we are *not* immortal." He surveyed the bleeding slits on her bare skin. "Right now you're injured, but the fresh blood in your veins and a day of sleep will heal you." Before she slipped to the floor, Matthias braced her. "Trust me. You will be fine."

They crossed the platform and stepped down into the grass. With the sudden descent, Laura winced as the pain of her wounds became evident.

"It hurts."

"Stay quiet." Matthias led her up the incline and into the woods. "Save your strength until we get back to the car."

"I can still talk, y'know." She closed her eyes and grit her teeth. "Did we just do what I think we did?"

"No, you did it." Matthias tightened his grip around her shoulder. "You killed one of our own."

"You said you'd seen him before?"

"Once." Matthias helped her onto a familiar footpath. "But just for a second. He was one tough son of a bitch. Probably a hundred...maybe two hundred years old."

"And I took him out?"

"You did. You've learned so much. And so fast," Matthias said.

"If you hadn't been there, he would've killed me. Don't pretend—"

"No, Laura." The white car came into view through the low lying shrubs. "He was your kill. Maybe I was wrong back at the cabin."

"What do you mean?"

"Clearly, you can handle yourself," Matthias reflected. "So maybe you won't have any trouble taking care of your old friends after all?"

"I don't know about that." Laura replied. "You're the one that pointed out the oil barrel. I still don't think I could've done it without you."

"If you continue to second guess yourself," Matthias warned, "you will get nowhere. Doubt will be the death of you. If you keep your wits about you, you will be fine."

"I guess so."

Matthias leaned her against the car as he opened the passenger door. With difficulty, Laura bent down and eased herself into the seat. Matthias closed the door behind her, passed around the front of the vehicle, and took his place behind the steering wheel.

"Back at the cabin..." Laura clutched her midsection and grimaced. "You said I needed to get my hands dirty or something like that."

"I did." Matthias was careful to avoid her gaze. "So?"

"You knew about this guy, didn't you?"

Matthias hesitated and then fastened his seatbelt with a click. "I had my suspicions."

"Mother of fuck!" Laura began to laugh. "You coulda gotten me killed!"

"Then it's a damn good thing you are already dead," he replied with a humorless smile.

"Still!" She felt a sense of pride that he had so much faith in her. "Seriously though. How many more of us are out there?"

"I don't know. There could be hundreds, maybe more. Until now, I've never crossed paths with any since I was in Germany." Matthias cranked the engine, backed up, and swung the car around.

Laura sat in silence, replaying the evening's events over in her mind. Although Matthias had stressed that they were not invulnerable, she felt completely invincible.

As Matthias turned onto an unused city street and drove towards a distant stoplight, Laura broached a subject that had been weighing on her since they left the cabin.

"I wanna go with you."

Matthias glanced over at her and nodded. "That's the plan."

"No, I mean I wanna stay with you. Even after..." Laura thought uneasily of Raymer and the others. "After whatever happens when we leave here."

"Are you sure?" Matthias cleared his throat and shifted in the driver's seat. "You might change your mind after a few more weeks."

Laura bit her lower lip. "I doubt it."

They drove in silence for several minutes. After a few miles, Matthias turned on the car stereo. He reached across Laura's lap and retrieved a CD from the glove compartment. Matthias removed the disc from the plastic tray and slipped it into the stereo. The opening phrases of Schubert's *Der Tod und das Mädchen* quartet galloped from the speakers.

Laura recognized the famous quartet at once, but Matthias reached to advance the CD to the darker and more introspective second movement.

As Matthias moved to return his right hand to the wheel, Laura clasped it with her left hand and gently guided it to rest on her thigh. He squeezed her fingers as she looked away. The trees on Route 619 sped past as they neared the long driveway to the safe-house. In the east, the first rays of dawn discolored the night sky as the rising sun crossed the Virginia landscape.

45

"GET THE HELL OFF MY PROPERTY!" THE OLD WOMAN slammed her screen door on Edison Raymer and Junior Luttrell as they stood on her rickety wooden porch.

Raymer was still holding up the picture of Matthias Bartsch he'd printed from his computer. Junior balled his hand into a fist and punched the doorframe. "Yeah, fuck you too!"

He stomped past Raymer and towards the SUV, where Veronica sat behind the steering wheel. After removing his spectacles, Raymer stepped off the porch and into the sun. He shoved the folded picture into his coat pocket and fished out a handkerchief. As he climbed into the passenger seat and wiped his smudged lenses, he noticed Veronica put her cell phone away with a guilty look. Raymer squinted at her as he donned his glasses.

"Guess that could've gone better." She gestured to the dilapidated house on the side of the road.

"Why did you hide the phone?"

"What're you talking about?"

He nodded at her loose hand as it hovered over her jacket pocket. "Are you keeping something from me?"

"No." Veronica seemed wounded. "I still have a job and responsibilities at the college. I was just checking my voice mail to see—"

"Goddammit!" Junior interrupted. "We've spent the whole day out here with nothin' to show for it. Goin' house to house like a buncha Jehovah's Witnesses 'cause she found this garbage on that damn computer!"

From the backseat of the SUV, Junior pitched the paper-clipped article at Edison Raymer. It landed face up in his lap. The headline read 'BIZARRE INCIDENTS ON STATE ROUTE 619.' There were several unexplained occurrences along this back road that made for an interesting, if not sensationalist, newspaper article. A recent trailer fire and the disappearance of a tow truck driver—along with his vehicle—were two incidents that caught Raymer's attention. He had decided they should canvas the country lane in search of clues, as he was running out of leads to pursue. The trio had spent the day going from door to door along the sparsely populated road, asking the same futile questions at every house.

The people they'd spoken to had ranged from confused to apathetic to downright belligerent. Raymer fought to keep his cool as Junior continued his tirade. Veronica pulled onto the road and accelerated up a low hill as the early evening sun set in the west.

"I mean, why the hell don't you just come out an' admit you got nothin' on Bartsch?" Junior leaned in between the front seats and directed his ire at Raymer. "You two thought you had all these leads a couple days ago and they didn't amount to shit. We went to all them soup kitchens last night. Not a single bum's seen him. All the chatter on the police scanner and nobody said nothin'. It's like the cops dropped the whole damn case."

He sat back and crossed his arms. Raymer looked over at Veronica, who kept her eyes on the road. The silence was short-lived, however, as Junior wasn't finished complaining.

"Now we're out here in the middle of nowhere because of some bullshit newspaper story? I'll bet—"

"Mr. Luttrell," Raymer said in a calm voice. "You claim you've wanted revenge on this vampire since he killed your father. What's a few more days of searching in the grand scheme of things?"

"It's a goddamn waste of time, that's what it is." Junior leaned forward again. "I'll tell you what. You get one more night outta me. That's it!"

"Then what?" The professor peered over his shoulder at the irate man. "What do you plan to do with yourself? Give up the search and go back to work at the shipyard like none of this ever happened?"

"Hell, no!" Junior Luttrell struck the passenger seat headrest with the flat of his palm. "I'm gonna take my .44 and go hunt that son of a bitch myself!"

Raymer rubbed his forehead and clenched his eyes shut. Finally, he looked back at Junior with as much sincerity as he could muster. "And how exactly do you plan to find him?"

"I'll come up with a better plan than this!"

"Really?" Raymer said. "What's your grand scheme? I'm all ears."

"Well, I sure as *fuck* ain't gonna—"

"Stop it!" Veronica interjected. "As usual, we're all tired. We're frustrated. Let's just drop it."

Raymer refused to back down.

"What evidence do you have to work with that I didn't already provide you?" He ignored a nasty look from Veronica. "Tell me! What are *you* going to do that's so radically different to catch Matthias Bartsch and destroy him?"

"Like I said, one more night." Junior lowered his voice. "Then I walk and take matters into my own hands."

The professor turned in disgust. As they crossed a long concrete bridge over a lake, Raymer stared out at an abandoned boat launch. He began to rap his knuckles against the window as Junior and Veronica remained quiet. It wasn't long before Raymer broke the tension in the SUV with another observation.

"I don't think either one of you understand the purpose of my diligence here. At this point, we're doing what any detective worth his salt would do. Chase down any and every lead."

"Oh, spare me!" Veronica rolled her eyes. "This is a hunch, not a lead, Edison! The cops ruled the trailer fire a murder-suicide. The wife shot the husband, turned on the gas, and blew her brains out. As for the tow truck driver—"

Raymer picked up the article and tapped two fingers against the front page. "The towing company's dispatcher reported that he was sent out there to pick up a gray sedan. That driver was never heard from or seen again. Does that sound like a coincidence?" He nodded at the choppy waters beyond the bridge. "For all we know, Bartsch got him and dumped his truck in this lake. There could be a whole graveyard of missing vehicles resting on the bottom—"

"Edison, I've had about enough of this!" Veronica clenched the steering wheel. "One out of every ten cars in this goddamn county are gray and have four doors. The article said the plates were from Pennsylvania. That doesn't match what we have on video from Thursday night."

To calm herself, she drew in a deep breath.

"Remember all those puzzle pieces we talked about?" Raymer asked. "This is the last one we have. We need to make our search count or we're back to square one with nothing to show for it."

"And you're just realizin' this?" Junior chimed in from the backseat. "What the hell have I been sayin' all along?"

"Ed, you need to face facts." Veronica could no longer disguise the irritation in her voice. "Matthias Bartsch is smarter than you. Than all of us. Did you think you were gonna catch this guy just because you're Edison fucking Raymer? Because you refuse to admit defeat? Because you can't face—"

"You're goddamn right we're gonna catch him!" Raymer bellowed. "And the only way we're gonna do it is to keep up this search. See that mailbox up ahead?"

Veronica nodded and gripped the steering wheel.

"You're gonna slow down, pull over there, and I'm gonna go knock on the door. And we'll keep doing this until I'm satisfied we've exhausted all avenues."

"No, I'm not." Veronica took a hand off the wheel to gesture at the approaching driveway. "You wanna know why?"

"Look, I told you to stop so—"

"Let me finish! We're not stopping because we've already been there! That's where we started our little house-to-house search at eight o'clock this fucking morning!"

Raymer sighed as they passed the house and he realized she was right. Yet he remained undaunted. "There were a few houses that we skipped, so I think we need to double back—"

"Edison, I agree with Junior. If you can't come up with a better plan tonight, you'll have to find someone else to run your goddamn camera."

"Really?" Raymer bristled as Veronica put the gas pedal to the floor.

"Really." Veronica shifted in her seat. "And tomorrow, I'm going to the police to file a missing persons report."

"You made a promise." He couldn't bring himself to look at her. "Laura made a promise. And now, you think you can just sever the ties and act the concerned citizen? The first thing those detectives will do is ask why you didn't report Laura's disappearance *Friday morning*. Then, you'll be in a mad dash to cover your tracks."

"I don't care anymore, Ed."

"You will when they sit you down in a windowless room and start interrogating you. How long do you think you can hide the truth before the cops break you?"

"Did you not fucking hear me?" Veronica raised her voice. "I don't give a shit about covering my tracks, or finding Bartsch, or any of it! You're so selfish! You've got your head so far up your ass you don't even care that Laura's gone."

"What else am I supposed to do, Veronica?" Raymer shouted. "I'm trying to find her. That's what we're doing here!"

"No, you're looking for *Bartsch.*" She glanced back at Junior in the rear-view mirror. "Both of you. That's all either of you care about. And I've had it. Enough with this fucking vampire shit. We're never gonna find them. And if we do, this guy's gonna kill us. Whether he's a goddamn monster or not."

"Look, I'm real sorry for what happened to Laura," Junior admitted. "We shoulda seen that comin' a mile away. Especially you two! All those fuckin' degrees an' not a lick a common sense between ya. But I still wanna nail that son of a bitch. We need to do *somethin'* before the bastard does this again!"

Raymer pressed his lips into a scowl and stared out the window. The pointlessness of the argument and the sarcastic criticism of his plan had pushed him to a breaking point.

"Edison?" Veronica cocked her head at Raymer. "Don't you have some pompous remark ready for us?"

"I'm done." Raymer unbuckled his safety belt. The professor braced his hand against the glove compartment. "Pull over and let me out. Right here."

"Are you serious?" Veronica laughed in disbelief. "Quit being so melodramatic. If you can't handle—"

"I said pull over." Edison Raymer didn't raise his voice. His face showed little emotion at all.

Veronica spun the wheel and drifted onto the shoulder. Before she could bring the SUV to a complete stop, Raymer flung open the passenger door and leapt out. The professor slammed the door and cut around the front of the idling vehicle. Veronica put the window down as a gust of wind blew through the trees and across the desolate road.

"Edison, this is ridiculous! What the hell do you want me to do with your—"

"I don't give a *fuck* what you do!" The wind tore at Raymer's long black coat as he plowed through the tall grass, jumped an overgrown drainage ditch, and ascended a ridge toward the tree line. His colleague behind the wheel yelled something out to him, but between the howling October wind and his pulse pounding in his ears, Raymer heard nothing.

He ducked under a few low hanging branches and found himself in a copse of tall trees. As he pushed forward, stepping on pine saplings that stood in his path, the cell phone in his coat pocket vibrated.

Raymer didn't bother to look. He knew exactly who it was. The wind died down enough for him to notice the sound of a departing vehicle. After a few moments, the phone began to hum again. He worked his way down a ridge and stepped across a puddle. The professor picked up a dead branch and used it as a makeshift club to forge a path through the underbrush.

With every step, Raymer walked deeper into the murky forest. Only dim light filtered down to guide his path. His shiny black dress shoes were now scratched and covered with mud. He stomped over piles of deadfall and through briar patches.

After walking for an indeterminate amount of time, he noticed two things. The phone had stopped ringing, and he was alone in the unfamiliar forest as the last rays of the sun winked out in the distance. Raymer pulled his long coat tighter and entered a clearing. At the edge of another tree line was an old barn. The metal roof had oxidized to an orange-brown color, and it was clear from the rotting boards that no one had used the structure in years. Nonetheless, he approached it, and tore open a heavy door. He stepped inside and walked into a spider web.

In the dying light he could make out an abandoned tractor covered in scaling green paint. As Raymer backed out, he waved his stick back and forth to knock down more tangled webs. When he stepped outside, he noticed something tiny moving up his sleeve. He brushed the spider away, and as it fell towards the ground on a strand from its swollen abdomen, the professor noticed the angry red hourglass on its underbelly.

Raymer crushed the black widow beneath a shoe as he changed direction. He passed the barn, and in his mind's eye, was walking parallel to the road he had left behind.

He left the clearing and began to swing his branch at the undergrowth of the dense forest ahead. The embattled professor wandered through the trees and thick shrubbery. Raymer began to feel the sting of futility and regret.

How the fuck am I gonna catch this bastard?

He swung the branch like a baseball bat, cracking a decaying log that blocked his path. Above him, the moon faded into view in the eerie hues of twilight. Another gust of wind assailed him, so he stopped to button his overcoat.

Raymer stepped out of the trees and into an overgrown yard. The outline of an A-frame cabin loomed in the distance. He adjusted his glasses to inspect the back of the cottage. Every visible window was blocked off with torn pieces of cardboard and duct tape. His sharp mind made a startling connection, and he scrambled to duck behind a corrugated potting shed.

The windows. Exactly like the apartment on Saturday.

Raymer took a divergent path back into the woods, then hooked around so he was parallel to the alpine-style cabin. He slowed his breathing and his pace, treading carefully as he stalked through the shadows. An early '90s model white car sat parked beside the front door at the end of a long gravel driveway. The windows in the front were covered in the same fashion, proof enough to Raymer that the house was not abandoned.

Sit down and wait a while. If you just stumbled across the monster's den, it will show itself soon enough.

Just like one of Veronica's penny dreadfuls.

In the waning light, Raymer ducked behind a tree. He was far enough away to remain concealed, but had a clear vantage point to watch both the car and the front door.

Raymer silenced his cell phone and noted the time on his wristwatch. He kept his eyes on the front door as the last light melded with the oncoming darkness of early evening. The cold wind nipped at his face, and his bladder began to fill. Yet Edison Raymer didn't move a muscle. He was convinced that the vampire who'd evaded him lurked somewhere behind that door. He had no weapons with which to fight it, but he could at least confirm that he had found the demon's lair.

He waited.

An hour. Almost two.

Finally, the front door creaked open. Matthias Bartsch stepped into the moonlight. Raymer trembled as he saw his nemesis in the flesh for the first time. The match to the photograph was identical. With his angular features, distinctive hair, and muscular neck, Bartsch looked like he had somehow stepped out of an old military propaganda poster. The vampire was clad in black from head to toe, and his heavy boots drummed a cadence on the gravel driveway. To Raymer's surprise, Laura McCoy followed. A shudder overcame the otherwise-stalwart professor as he noticed her bloodstained wool jacket.

Bartsch wasn't leading her by force. She didn't stagger along like a prisoner in defeat. She moved with the same vitality and purpose as the decades-old vampire. Raymer recalled Veronica's wild story about blood along the footpath, and could only assume that Laura had been turned. He was now observing not one, but two vampires climbing into the car without speaking.

Raymer shifted his position so he was hugging the damp ground. His heart thundered in his chest. The car's engine sputtered to life, and a pair of headlights cut the darkness above his head as Bartsch swung the vehicle around. Raymer carefully parted the tall grass blocking his view to watch the car spin out and charge down the gravel drive. Bald tires left a cloud of chalky dust in the car's wake.

The professor could hardly contain himself. He checked his watch again, and waited a few minutes before springing to his feet. He remained among the trees as he followed the snaking driveway down to meet State Route 619. A battered mailbox, which they must have overlooked earlier that day, read SAUNDERS. Raymer darted back into a shadowy thicket of pine trees. He dug through his pocket, removed his cell phone, and returned Veronica's last call.

"Edison? Where the fuck—"

"Both of you need to get everything together and get yourselves back out to 619 right now. Don't waste any time."

"I don't understand what you're—"

"Shut up and listen," Raymer managed. "I found him." He shifted the phone to his other ear. "And I found Laura, too."

46

LAURA WATCHED IN SILENCE AS MATTHIAS PUSHED THE sedan into the murky water of the drainage pond. Together, they stood in the moonlight to watch the car sink. They had just fed off the blood of a vagrant Matthias picked up from a truck stop on the interstate.

"Do you think anyone'll find it? Or the body inside?" Laura pitched the keys into the dark water. "I mean, what if the water's too shallow?"

"It's not." Matthias gestured at the disappearing taillights and bumper. "Besides, if anyone pulls that car out, it won't matter. We will be long gone." The light from the waning moon shone against the pockmarked surface of his dog tag, which had slipped from beneath his shirt. "We should go. It's already getting late and I have one more thing to do before we go back to the cabin."

Matthias pulled open the door of the white utility van he had hotwired an hour after sundown. The idling vehicle would take them somewhere far from Williamsport. Laura leaned against it to watch the thick carpet of algae close around the sunken car. A fine mist arose from the pond in the late October chill. "Of all possible things, you had to steal a white van." She slapped an open palm against the hood. "You have any idea how conspicuous this is?"

"No." Matthias put a booted foot inside and hung on the open door. "Why do you say that?"

Laura rolled her eyes. "Remember those two mass murderers up in Northern Virginia a few years back? The first bit of information released was something about them driving around and shooting from a white van."

"So?" the German replied. "What difference does it make? I see vans like this one on the road all the time."

"You're missing my point." Laura crossed her arms. "Appearances are everything, and this hunk of shit you drove off in is the very definition of suspicious."

Matthias pointed to her bloodstained wool jacket. "You're one to lecture me about looking suspicious. Anyway, if the van bothers you that much, we'll leave it after a couple days on the road. Now get in."

Matthias adjusted his seat and the angle of the steering wheel as Laura slammed the passenger door behind her. The sound echoed throughout the empty vehicle. "About this van." She pressed her hands between her legs and looked over her shoulder. "How are we gonna block out the sun if we have to hide inside?"

"That's why I bought the tin foil and duct tape." Matthias fumbled with two hanging wires beneath the steering column. Sparks flew and the smell of ozone wafted around them. He revved the engine. "You see what I just did there?"

"Yeah. I think so."

"Good." Matthias sat up and shifted the van into drive. "We can cover the front and back windows in under five minutes if we need to. We can also hang the tarp I bought across this utility cage for extra protection." He reached over his shoulder to rattle the barrier behind them. "It's good to prepare, but the route we're taking has a motel or two in every town. Once we cross the state line, we can hide out in one of those places before sunrise."

"You sure about that?"

"Relax." Matthias eased the van onto the dirt trail and turned on the headlights. "Everything's gonna be fine. Once we're done at the cabin tonight, we won't have any problems getting underway. I promised I'd look out for you as long as you need me."

"Thanks," she said. "So what's this other thing you still gotta do?"

"A personal obligation."

A sly smile tugged at Laura's lips. "One last enemy to dispatch?"

"Nothing like that." Matthias turned onto a paved road. "I have to pay a visit to someone."

"So it's not the sort of visit where we feed?"

"Not that kind of visit."

"Then this so-called obligation…what's it all about? I thought you were a lone wolf around here."

"I am." Matthias shifted the van into gear. "You'll see soon enough."

"Fine." Laura pouted. She tapped her fingers on the armrest between the seats. "So is the plan to still head southwest?"

"Yeah. Las Cruces to be precise."

"I've never seen New Mexico." Laura sighed. "And I guess I never will in the daytime."

"The sky is brighter and clearer at night. The land is vast and beautiful in the dark."

"So that's it then?" Laura opened the glove compartment. Matthias had stashed the 45-Tactical inside. "We're gonna work our way west, leaving a trail of unsolved murders and disappearances in our wake?"

"Possibly." Matthias kept his eyes on the winding road ahead. Several minutes passed before he spoke again. "I've been meaning to ask you something."

"Yeah?"

"Besides that woman, I noticed there were no calls from friends or family on your voice mail. Is there no one close to you that might be concerned about—"

"Matthias, I'm twenty-seven. Not a teenager." Laura ran her fingers through her straight blonde hair. "Anyway, I keep to myself. All my old friends either got married, knocked up, or both. I've been in college for almost a decade, so time goes on for the rest of the world while I'm locked away in my own head. The life of a scholar…" Laura trailed off with another sigh. "When it comes to family, I never knew my father, and my mother passed away three years ago."

"Any brothers or sisters?"

"Nope. Only child." Laura tugged on her seatbelt. "I mean, I have a few distant relatives, but they're all out in Illinois, Iowa. Places like that."

"Is that where you're from? You never mentioned where you grew up."

"Cairo, Illinois. Pronounced like the syrup. Complete shithole. I couldn't wait to get out of that town." Laura slumped further into the seat as her tone grew pensive. "Seems like I've always been looking for a way out."

"Is that why you went to college all the way out here?"

"Mostly." Laura turned to the vampire with a look of uncertainty. "What's with all the questions?"

"Just curious." Ignoring a stop sign, Matthias swung the van into a sharp turn. They were now on Route 619. "Well, do you have any important obligations to wrap up at school?" he asked. "Maybe we should change our travel plans so you can tie up some loose ends?"

"We don't need to," she replied. "I can handle it over the phone."

"Don't you think it'd be better if you withdrew in person rather than—"

"No, people drop out of Annandale all the time. In fact, most people do it through email. Really, it doesn't matter."

"What were you studying there?"

"Parapsychology and criminology."

Matthias laughed. "Well, I guess it all makes sense now."

"What makes sense?"

"How easily you adjusted to things. You were already a believer in the supernatural."

"No," she answered. "To be honest with you, I'm a skeptic. Well, I *was* a skeptic. But I've always been fascinated by the supernatural and the occult. Ever since I was a kid."

Matthias nodded. As they left the woods behind, the van passed South Williamsport Elementary School. They were on their way to a distant intersection where stoplights glowed red.

"I suppose I owe a lot of my academic success to Dr. Raymer." Laura took a short pause to choose her words with care. "If it weren't for him, I never would've found a way to pursue my interests professionally. He was the first person I ever met that took the occult seriously. He studied it. Believed in it."

"And because of that, his friends and colleagues dismissed him?"

"Well, partially," Laura noted. "He's not exactly the easiest person to get along with. He's very stubborn." She braced herself as Matthias brought the van to a complete stop. "But he was right. All this time he believed vampires were real. And here we are."

"So when you say parapsychology, do you mean haunted houses? Telepathy? Those kinds of things?"

"Yeah. I dabbled with a little bit of everything," she confirmed. "But for my dissertation, I was following a group of exorcists and observed three Church-sanctioned exorcisms."

"Really?"

"Yeah, well I was basically tagging along with them so I could discredit them," Laura confessed. "They didn't know that, but they didn't need to know. The likelihood of encountering genuine demonic possession decreases with every new exorcism movie that comes out. It's no longer some obscure rite in the Catholic Church. It's a cultural phenomenon. I believe possession is just a psychological or psychosomatic response to a specific set of stimuli, which I argue is the rite of exorcism itself."

The stoplight turned green and Matthias hung a left. "So you don't believe in demons? Or any of that?"

"Well, now I don't know what to believe." Laura shrugged her shoulders. "I'm riding shotgun with an undead soldier from World War II, I'm allergic to sunlight, and I've killed and drunk the blood of what, *five* people now?" She laughed out loud. "Yeah. Let me get back to you on that."

Matthias smiled and turned the wheel to avoid a pothole. "There are indeed many wonders in this world..."

The unlikely pair fell into another awkward silence. Laura twisted a lock of hair around her finger. "So, I've told you about me. There's still so much I don't know about you."

"There's not much more to tell," he replied.

"Oh, come on!" Laura persisted. "You've been a vampire since the 1940s! You were around for the War, and then what? What else do you remember? The Cuban Missile Crisis? The Kennedy assassinations? Vietnam?" She spoke faster as her excitement got the best of her. "What about the moon landing? Or when they tore down the wall between East and West Germany?"

"I never paid much attention to politics or world events. It's always the same conflict wrapped up in some new disguise. That's one thing I can tell you. Human history repeats itself."

"So why'd you come to America?" Laura asked. "Were you looking for the vampires that killed you?"

"No," Matthias corrected her. "I came to the United States to track down a group of American soldiers. The ones that shot me and left me for dead."

"Oh, that's right," Laura recalled. The vampire had only mentioned his death and transformation in vague terms. "So what exactly happened?"

"Do you know about the Battle of the Bulge?"

"Sure." Laura gestured to her moth-nipped Ike jacket. "My great-grandfather was in it."

"Well, my unit was part of the offensive. We were on some Belgian backroad when American soldiers ambushed our armored column. The fight didn't last long. Our commanding officer surrendered the remnants of our unit. At the time, I was treating the wounded, but a couple American soldiers put me in line with our combatants."

Matthias maneuvered the van onto an unfamiliar street before continuing.

"They burned our pay books and took our tags so our bodies couldn't be identified. Then, your countrymen stood in a line and shot us down. And in case his son neglected to mention it, Fenton Luttrell's father was one of the soldiers that shot me."

"So that's why you killed him?"

"I don't know what he told you about his father, but that man won a Silver Star for executing prisoners of war."

"I didn't know that," she responded. "And I don't think Junior knows either."

"It doesn't matter."

Laura could tell that Matthias was uncomfortable discussing the war, yet curiosity spurred her to ask more questions.

"So then how did you become a vampire?"

"When they shot me, I fell face-forward so the executioners couldn't see my breath. They left before dark, and I don't think anyone but me survived before sundown. Not long after that, two vampires came out of the woods. They fed on me, and then they turned me."

"And you said they were all deformed?"

"Very much so," he nodded. "They were feeding on the dead. Like scavengers. They must have migrated from the east to take advantage of the war and the bodies left in its wake."

"And you never saw them again?"

"Never."

"That's pretty fucked up."

Matthias didn't reply. To fill the silence, Laura tapped her fingers against the window and tried to change the subject.

"So what year were you actually born?"

"1918."

She ran the numbers. "So you were twenty-six when you were turned? That makes me older than you."

"In a way, I suppose it does."

"But you never aged," she responded. "So I guess I'll also be like this forever?"

"It seems that way. As long as we feed, the body is sustained and remains unchanged." Matthias glanced at Laura with a slight gleam in his eye. "And before you ask, I don't know why. I have no idea how to account for any of the mysteries of what we are."

"Well, that's one thing that ain't so bad." A half-smile spread over Laura's lips as she drifted into contemplation. Afraid to let the conversation lag, she asked the vampire another pointed question. "So what else do you remember from before the war?"

"I remember music," he said softly. "My father had a phonograph and he would play records. Brahms. Schubert. Schumann. I was drawn to the cello early and began lessons at the age of six. I entered the conservatory shortly before my country invaded Poland, which started the Second World War. But before that, music was everything. Music is what brought me to Anna."

"Do you remember the last time you saw her?"

"I was granted leave in May of 1944. This was right before the Allies landed at Normandy." Matthias paused in remembrance. "We had two short days together in Darmstadt, my hometown, before I was sent back to France."

As Matthias slowed to make yet another turn, he clenched his jaw and brushed away an errant lock of hair.

"I remember we had a fight about how the war had hardened me. We didn't part on good terms. She wrote in August to tell me she was pregnant. In September, I learned she was dead." The vampire paused. "In a way, I'm thankful for that."

"What?" Laura was shocked by his response. "Why would you say something like—"

"I'm glad she never had to see me like this," Matthias interrupted. "I would've taken her and made her like me."

"Oh, I see." Blood rushed to Laura's temples. "So this was too horrible a curse for Anna, but you had no problem doing it to me?"

"Anna couldn't have handled this," Matthias insisted. "She was a faithful Catholic. Gentle. Loving. All those things would have doomed her as a vampire. She couldn't kill. There was no real darkness in her. She would've despaired, and would never have forgiven me."

"But I'm supposed to forgive you, aren't I?" Laura kicked the glove compartment with a booted foot. "You know, I was starting to like you. Maybe even admire you. And now you pull this shit!"

"You are *not* Anna!" Matthias shouted. "I've known that from the start. You are stronger. I sensed that when I passed you on the street that night. *You* put yourself out there. Whether you knew it or not, you came looking for answers. Now you have them. There was an emptiness inside you which the gift has filled."

"The gift?" She cradled her head in her hands. "Please! Cut the pretentious bullshit, Matthias. It doesn't suit you."

Matthias gripped the steering wheel but offered no reply. He turned the van into a private driveway. As he killed the headlights, Laura noticed an illuminated brick sign with ornate black letters. The sign read ROSEMONT MEMORIAL PARK.

Laura braced herself against the dashboard and looked around in confusion. "What the fuck are we doing in a cemetery? Do you really think it's a good idea to be surrounded by headstones shaped like crosses?"

"You don't have to worry about that. Look at the ground." He waved a finger at a rolling hill. "There. Out the window. Nothing but flat markers. The plaques show names and dates." He stopped for a moment to reflect. "Seems like most cemeteries are becoming like this. They are more convenient for the living to maintain."

"So why the hell are we here?" She was still irritated by his comments about Anna.

Matthias refused to answer, which further incensed Laura. They drove around a maze of one-lane roads and bland fields of neatly trimmed grass. "This won't take more than five minutes. If you want to wait I'll be—"

"No," Laura said as she tugged on the door handle. "I wanna see what's so damned important about this place."

Matthias parked the van and jerked the door open. Despite her burning ire, Laura was intrigued by the vampire's mysterious task. She scrambled out and ran to catch up, as he was already several yards ahead of her.

Matthias dug into his pocket, and then stopped to kneel at a particular grave. The soil beneath his knees was freshly turned, as if a casket had been recently placed in the ground. A neat row of smooth stones was lined up along the edge of the bronze plaque, which was attached to a meager slab of marble. In the moonlight, Laura read the inscription.

"Who's Gretl Fleischmann?" She tried to capture Matthias' attention, but his mind was elsewhere.

In his palm, he held a stone, which he rolled into his fingers and began to turn over. "Her own son and his family won't come to visit her here. That row of stones on her grave never gets any longer unless I add to it."

"She was Jewish, right? How'd you know this woman?" Laura clenched Matthias' muscular arm. "Was it someone from the war?"

He ignored the question. "She suffered so much in life. At the hands of my people when she was young. Then she raised a son that left her to rot in a nursing home."

"Did you kill her, Matthias?"

"Only because she asked me to. I took no blood from her and put her to rest without pain."

"Why?"

"She wanted to die. She begged me to die. I saw the numbers tattooed on her arm. She was at Birkenau. A place built by the country I served. As bad as the war was for me, I could never in a million years conceive of the pain and suffering she endured at the hands of my government. My people who knew those camps were there and turned a blind eye. When I took her life, I felt guilt and shame for the first time in decades." He added the stone to the end of the row. "Then the visions began. And they kept getting worse."

"What visions?" Laura eyed him with suspicion. "What are you talking about?"

"Every waking moment I only saw Anna. I had to quiet my mind. It's why I tried to take the girl." He rose to face her. "It's why I took you."

"And you made it clear I'm a worthy successor to your precious Anna!" Laura put her hand on her hip. "This night just keeps getting more and more interesting. I'm not sure I really *want* to know anything else about you."

"Then stop asking."

Laura stepped back to face him again. "I know what you're doing here to remember this woman. The Jews call it a *Mitzvah*. A good thing. A kindness."

"I know. And I'm sorry I—"

"Save your fucking apologies!" Laura kicked the stones across the wet grass. "What the fuck are you doing here? You've got no right to honor the dead!"

Matthias looked away as Laura continued to vent her frustration.

"So you kill this woman and then come back to decorate her grave? You're a fucking contradiction! You tell me we're supposed to be cold-blooded predators. And now here you are, brooding over the grave of one of your victims!"

Matthias glared at Laura. His eyes were cold and his stance imposing. Yet the vampire failed to mask his regret. "You have no right to question what I do."

Laura stormed forward and poked her finger into his chest. "Don't forget what you are. And don't forget what you made me!"

She retreated to the van as Matthias crouched to collect the stones. When he had replaced them, he walked slowly toward the vehicle and slipped behind the wheel.

She had already hotwired the engine for him.

They didn't speak to each other on the drive back to the small A-frame cottage. Matthias parked the van and cut the engine at the end of the driveway.

After she removed the pistol from the glove compartment, Laura put her hand on his.

"I'm sorry for what I did back there," she said.

"Everything you said is true." Matthias shrugged.

"I just feel so...I don't know. Fucked up inside. My emotions are all out of whack. Sometimes I feel so angry, and I just start saying shit without thinking first."

He stared ahead. "It's the hunger inside you."

"That's a convenient excuse." Laura rapped her knuckles on the cold glass window. "Truth is, I've always been kinda like this. So I'm not sure anything's really that different. It's just more intense."

"Try to think of it like this," Matthias explained. "Humans are ill-tempered. They are easily angered, and they let their emotions dictate their actions." Matthias rubbed the back of his neck. "We need to be colder and more calculating. So we surrender our humanity to the bloodlust. But keep something in mind," he warned. "Every mistake I've made since I was turned has been due to human weakness. It always sneaks back in, and it will be the hardest struggle you face. So you have to do everything in your power to sublimate those lingering desires, or you'll—"

"I know that's what you've tried to teach me, but is that really what you believe?" Laura turned to face him.

"It's not as simple as I thought it was," he admitted.

"Well, I think it *is* simple. At least for me. I'm not who I was, and I can never go back." She gave his hand another squeeze. "So I go with you."

Matthias opened his door and put one foot on the gravel. Laura tightened her grasp on his hand. She pursed her lips as if she wanted to speak, then changed her mind. Matthias forced a smile.

"We don't have much time if we wanna make it to North Carolina before sunrise. Come on, let's get our things—"

But the vampire turned his attention to the front door of the cabin. As Laura let go of his hand, he focused on a small area around the doorknob. There was a sliver of wood missing where the lock was—as if someone had used a crowbar to break in. The wind died down for a moment, and he stepped aside to shut the van door. Somewhere close, he smelled blood. He could hear human hearts pounding as he took a few cautious steps forward.

"Laura!" He spun to face her, but she had already started for the front door.

47

BEFORE LAURA COULD HEED MATTHIAS' WARNING, THE cabin door burst open. A blinding muzzle flash, followed by a sharp *crack,* erupted from the darkness inside. Junior Luttrell shouldered his way out of the cabin, the smoking barrel of his .44 trained on Matthias. He moved with the determination of a much younger man as he lined up another shot.

Laura staggered backward and caught a glimpse of Matthias. He clutched his chest as dead blood dripped through his long fingers. "Silver!" he cried out in surprise. His cold eyes gleamed with fury.

As Matthias trudged forward on unsteady legs, Edison Raymer rushed to stand beside Luttrell. He didn't advance past the gunman's line of fire. Instead, he brandished a large silver crucifix in one hand and a blinding flashlight in the other. Veronica Upham slid along the exterior wall of the cabin—in the opposite direction of the others. A shiny silver cross swung from a chain around her neck as she aimed Raymer's digital camera in Matthias' direction.

The mere sight of the crucifixes paralyzed Laura. In desperation, she threw her hands up to shield herself from the debilitating symbols. Through her fingers, Laura saw Matthias cut right to place himself between her and their enemies. Junior, who stood parallel to the open door, led his target with the chromed handgun and took another shot. The round tore into Matthias' chest, and he roared in agony. Wisps of smoke drifted from his bullet-riddled torso.

"Now flank his worthless ass!" Junior commanded in a loud, frenzied voice. "The crosses, goddammit! Surround him with the fuckin' crosses!"

Laura watched Raymer break away from the group to box in Matthias. Veronica didn't move a muscle. She pressed herself against the wooden boards of the cabin, kept the camera on Matthias, and held up the small cross around her neck with her free hand. Over the enticing aroma of Veronica's blood, Laura could sense her fear and confusion.

Matthias reeled as Raymer closed in on him. Luttrell took a tentative step forward, the pistol still leveled at the vampire. Everywhere Laura looked, there were crucifixes. Dangling from chains around their necks. Clasped in their clammy hands. Shoved into their belts. Matthias spun to his left and then to his right, but the hateful image of the cross surrounded him on all sides.

Matthias glanced over his shoulder. "Run!" he commanded. "Go, Laura! Now!"

Junior took the opportunity to line up his mark and squeezed the pistol's trigger once again. A large caliber round struck Matthias beneath his collarbone. The wiry man recovered and took his fourth shot. Black blood exploded from the wound as Luttrell's bullet grazed the vampire's neck.

The silver round traced the scar left by a Russian marksman at Stalingrad over seventy years ago. Matthias collapsed. He began to writhe on a carpet of wet leaves as he clutched his chest. He cursed his assailants. *"Ich werde dich und jeden von euch töten!"*

"Fucking bastard!" Laura wailed at Junior. Her fury was, for a moment, stronger than the repugnant crosses. She bolted toward Luttrell, who executed a flawless pivot on the heel of his snakeskin boot.

Junior took a shot at Laura, who ducked as she moved, and the round spun past her.

Before he could empty the cylinder, Laura struck Junior Luttrell beneath the chin with the heel of her palm. The force of the impact instantly broke the older man's neck.

Luttrell's mouth went slack as his limbs failed him. His legs buckled, and the smoking pistol dropped from his hands. Junior then fell face-first to the ground.

Laura heard Raymer shouting at Matthias. The injured vampire struggled to stand, but slipped back to the ground, clutching his wounds. Laura plowed across the muddy yard. She lunged at Veronica Upham and felt the professor's crucifix brush her arm. With a well-placed swing, Laura knocked the digital camera from Veronica's hand. It sailed through the air and hit the windshield of the van. The camera shattered along with the safety glass.

"No!" Raymer yelled from somewhere behind them. Laura ignored him. She seized the hapless professor by her neck and tore into her throat before she could scream.

Raymer diverted his attention from the broken camera and his struggling prey to intervene in Laura's swift attack. He thrust his crucifix in front of his flashlight's beam. The crude shadow of a cross spread upon the wall of the cabin. Laura surrendered her prey and recoiled in frustration. Veronica sank to the ground in shock. Blood pooled between her thin fingers and stained the front of her blouse.

As Raymer moved to aid Veronica, Matthias managed to knock him off-balance with a weak yet unexpected kick. The professor dropped his flashlight to the ground.

Unfortunately for Laura's partner, Raymer now had a free hand. Ignoring his wounded colleague, Raymer reached into the satchel over his shoulder and removed a vial of holy water. As Laura found her resolve, Raymer spun around, thumbed the cork, and splashed the sacred water onto Matthias.

"You piece of filth!" the professor bellowed. He stepped forward and lifted the glass vial over his shoulder.

"*In nomine Patris...*" He flicked his wrist to make the sign of the cross. "*Et Filli, et Spiritus Sancti!*"

Matthias screamed in pain as the holy water singed his exposed flesh.

"In the name of our Lord Jesus Christ!"

Laura tore across the close space between them and leveled her shoulder to strike Raymer, who continued his potent invocation.

"It is He who commands you! He who spurns you! He who rebukes—"

Laura hit the muscular man with enough force to topple him, but Raymer stood firm. He swung his crucifix into her line of sight and Laura was compelled to back away.

"I told you to run!" Matthias cast his cold eyes up at her. "Get the fuck out of here!"

Raymer leaned over and thrust the head of his crucifix into a bullet wound on Matthias' chest. The professor pushed it deep into the vampire's flesh. Matthias arched his back and screamed as the silver cross did its damage.

291

"You!" Laura sneered at Raymer, who stood upright and splashed holy water in her direction. She sidestepped the potent liquid. "I'm gonna make you suffer in ways you never thought possible!"

Raymer took another step toward her. He thrust the crucifix forward, forcing Laura to retreat still further. "Back off!"

Laura turned and ran toward the van for cover. She swung herself around using the open passenger door to fetch the 45-Tactical from the open glove box.

Raymer returned his attention to Matthias. He repeatedly kicked the vampire in his ribs. After landing several blows, he paused to pour a stream of holy water onto one of Matthias' gunshot wounds.

Stepping around the van, Laura took aim and fired a single round. The bullet clipped her former professor's left arm. Although the wound was superficial, he cried out and dropped the vial of consecrated water.

"Edison!" Veronica shouted.

Laura turned the gun on Veronica, who was slumped on the ground with her back against the cottage. She continued to clutch the wound on her neck. When she sensed that Laura's spiteful gaze was upon her, the English professor frantically grabbed for the bloody cross around her neck. With trembling hands, she lifted the charm and held it outward.

"Stay...stay the hell away from me!"

"Fuck!" Laura spun away from the odious symbol. She lowered the gun and lifted her eyes to see Raymer approaching from her left. Despite his wounded arm, he continued to wield the crucifix with a steady and unwavering hand.

"That's right, bitch," he said. "We've got you!"

She turned back to Veronica. The professor's face was ghastly in the moonlight. She sat with her knees drawn up to her chest, her back still pressed against the cabin wall. Although panting heavily and unable to catch her breath, Veronica continued to hold her cross high above her head and in Laura's line of vision.

The vampire feared her only chance of escape was to dash past Luttrell, who was lying motionless in the grass, and make her way into the woods.

Against her instincts, Laura lunged in the direction of Raymer. The professor smiled and took another step forward. He held the cross aloft, forcing her to cast her eyes first to the ground, and then to the sky in anger.

Laura clenched her jaw. A feral groan issued from her throat. She felt nauseous. Her eyes burned. Her arms were numb. Her legs threatened to collapse beneath her.

"This isn't over, fucker!"

She raised the heavy pistol and blindly fired at Raymer. But the frenzied vampire had missed her mark by several inches.

With the report from the .45 still ringing in his ears, Edison Raymer watched as Laura sprinted across the lawn and toward the shadows of the nearby forest. He cursed under his breath and tucked the crucifix under his wounded arm.

"Get up, Veronica!" He shouted. Raymer clasped his free hand over the wound in his arm and made his way back to Matthias. "I need you over here!"

"I c-can't, Ed!" She tried to push herself to her feet but failed to muster the strength. Her quaking hand found its way back to the gleaming cross hanging from her neck.

Raymer procured another container of holy water from the satchel, then kicked Matthias onto his back. The professor emptied the contents of the entire glass vial onto the vampire's face, neck, and chest.

"*Es brennt! Es brennt!*" Matthias wailed in agony. "*Verdammt!*"

Veronica turned away as her colleague tortured the incapacitated vampire. Raymer looked on in triumph as the skin beneath Matthias' shirt began to sear and smoke again. The pungent stench of burning flesh stung the professor's nostrils. He bent down close to Matthias and whispered contemptuously into his ear.

"*Quid stas, et resistis, cum scias, Christum Dóminum vias tuas pérdere?*"

Matthias snarled and struggled to turn away. Raymer stretched his arm forward and pressed the crucifix against the vampire's chest.

"*Timete eum!*" Raymer shouted. "*Timete nomen sanctum!*" He knelt beside the vampire and tightened his grip upon the handle of the crucifix. Raymer thrust the head of the cross into another of Matthias' wounds. Using the palm of his hand, Raymer jammed the cross deeper into the vampire's shoulder. "Fear me!" he threatened through clenched teeth. Matthias screamed in pain.

Veronica forced herself away from the cabin wall. She began to crawl across the yard to where Junior lay. When her fingers slid across the barrel of his gun, she fumbled to pick it up but it slipped from her hand.

With his eyes locked on Matthias, Raymer called to Veronica over his shoulder. "Get Junior's jacket off, tear up his shirt, and wrap the pieces around your neck! Do it now!"

Veronica attempted to follow his instructions. She tugged on the dead man's coat with an unsteady hand. After two unsuccessful attempts, she managed to pull the jacket off. With trembling hands, she began to shred the material of Luttrell's shirt. Veronica crumpled the fabric into a loose ball and held it against her bleeding neck.

Ignoring the sting of his own wound, Raymer bent forward to address his foe.

"It's time, Bartsch."

"Was machst du?" Matthias dug his booted feet into the muddy ground.

After kicking the crucifix from the vampire's chest, Raymer pushed apart the lapels of his coat and retrieved a stake from the leather bandolier across his chest. Matthias continued to twitch involuntarily, his motorcycle jacket creaking with each contortion of his body.

"You know what I'm about to do, don't you?" Raymer taunted the crippled vampire. "I'm going to give you one final gift." Raymer pressed the tip of the stake against Matthias' pale cheek. "You get to see the sun rise after seventy years of darkness."

"Nein!" Matthias gnashed his teeth. *"Fick dich!"*

"Your threats are useless." Raymer pulled the heavy hammer from his waist-belt. "You'll be a pile of ash and bone in no time."

Veronica knelt in the grass at the edge of the driveway. Her neck was now girded by a makeshift bandage crafted from the scraps of Junior's shirt. "Edison! Junior's dead. And we...we need to get help. I feel—"

"No, you need to help *me*. That's the only reason you're out here." Raymer averted his gaze from Matthias to face her. "You were supposed to protect the camera at all costs. You couldn't even do that right. Now, there's no record of—"

"Fuck you, Edison!" Her angry retort instigated a short coughing fit. "You're more of a monster than he is!"

"Sticks and stones, Veronica." He gestured to her again. "Now get over here. And bring your cross."

Matthias had managed to turn on his side, but Raymer flipped him over to pin his back to the ground. With a low moan, Veronica struggled to her feet. Still woozy from the loss of blood, she swayed from side to side but took careful steps forward.

"Hurry up!" Raymer shouted.

As she inched closer, she stared in horror at the mangled creature in the grass. She thrust her cross forward but turned her head away from the gory spectacle.

"Look at it!" Raymer screamed at the vampire. Veronica trembled but held the cross as steady as she was capable. Matthias groaned and threw a weak arm over his scarred face.

Raymer gripped the hammer in one hand and placed the tip of the stake against Matthias' chest. The silver began to singe the vampire's flesh, and he made a weak attempt to swat the stake away. Edison Raymer raised the hammer in his right hand. He clenched his teeth and the veins strained along his temples and neck.

With a guttural roar, Edison Raymer swung the hammer down. Sparks flew as steel met the silver head of the stake. His hand stung upon impact as the sharp implement sunk a few inches into the vampire's chest.

Veronica shrieked. She bent forward and clutched her stomach. As she lowered the cross to her side, she began to hyperventilate.

"Keep that cross on him," Raymer snapped. "And don't turn your head away!"

Matthias howled, his half-ruined face a rictus of pain. Dead blood poured from the wound to drench his soiled shirt. It flooded over the leather of his jacket and began to seep into the ground beneath him.

Raymer swung the hammer down again, the stake slipping through his grasp. It was now imbedded between the vampire's ribs, protruding only two or three inches from his chest. Raymer stood up and leaned back with the heavy hammer at his side. His hands dripped with Matthias' dark blood as he admired his murderous handiwork.

"Ich werde dich in der Hölle sehen!" Bartsch's voice was savage and otherworldly. Raymer leaned back and delivered another blow. The force of the strike drove the stake through the vampire's back and into the blood-soaked ground. Matthias' arms and legs stiffened. His mouth hung opened, and his jagged teeth glistened with blood and saliva.

Veronica gripped her crucifix and took a hesitant step forward. The ghastly sight of the immobilized creature appalled her. The holy water had blistered and scarred the vampire's flesh like acid. His face was stained with gore. Raymer looked on with curiosity as Veronica knelt beside the vampire. She lifted the cross in her trembling hands.

Matthias spat in Veronica's face. She recoiled and wiped her cheek, then slid backward across the mud and leaves.

Raymer took the hammer in both hands, leaned back at the waist and brought the implement down a final time. The last hit drove the stake deeper into the blood-drenched earth.

Matthias' arms jerked toward Raymer, but the professor stepped away and dropped the hammer at his feet. With smug satisfaction, he glanced at his wristwatch and addressed Matthias again.

"You have less than an hour, Bartsch, before you see the sun. My work here is finished, and so are you."

Matthias did not hear the professor's words. The vampire whispered a flurry of unfamiliar words in German. He flailed his head from side to side as his eyes swept the horizon.

Raymer assumed the vampire was hallucinating. As Bartsch slipped into oblivion, Raymer felt cheated that the creature's mind was eroding, and wouldn't be conscious of its fate.

"Fernhalten!" the vampire shouted. *"Schwanzlutscher!"* Matthias thrashed upon the ground. He clutched at the head of the submerged stake, but his fingers were seared by the silver rod pinning him to the earth.

Raymer crouched again. "What do you see, Bartsch? Your victims? The dozens you've killed coming back to take you apart? Or do you think you see Anna with her open arms?"

"Shut up!" Veronica shouted. "You've won! Leave him the fuck alone! All you have to do now is wait for the goddamned sun, and he's finished." She stared into Raymer's eyes, and saw nothing but rancor. "What the hell are we gonna do about Junior?"

"We'll bury him," Raymer replied as he looked past Veronica into the trees. "But not until I've seen this monster burn."

He picked up the half-empty vial of holy water and flung fresh streams of the clear liquid onto the vampire's body. Matthias had no strength left to cry out for mercy. Raymer deliberately poured the rest of the holy water around the head of the sunken stake.

"Stop it, Edison, you sick fuck!" Tears streamed down Veronica's bloodstained cheeks as Matthias groaned. "You don't need to torture him anymore! You've won! You beat him. What you're doing is vile, and I can't—"

"What *you* can do is sit back, shut up, and wait for sunrise!" He held a finger towards the sky, which was growing red like the embers of a dying fire.

Veronica began to pace alongside Matthias' twitching body. As she adjusted the ragged t-shirt around her neck, she glanced at the sky above. A muted shade of light fell across the forest, the yard, and the cottage.

"So that's it, then?" she asked. "We just sit back and watch the poor bastard burn?"

"Yes." Raymer nodded once, then continued. "This didn't go as I planned, and I want to make sure we're ready the next time we encounter them. It's only a matter of time before Laura comes looking for revenge, and who knows how many more there are besides her."

"You can forget about that, Edison!" Veronica's voice was hoarse, but her anger was palpable. "I'm through with all of this."

Raymer's features remained stoic. "What makes you think Laura is through with *you?* Because she spared you a bullet? You crossed the line here. And whether you like it or not, there's no turning back now."

The vampire behind them groaned again, aroused by the onset of daylight. Matthias tried to speak, but he failed to form any intelligible words. He clenched his fists as the first rays of the rising sun fell across his legs.

Raymer took two steps back as the flesh beneath the creature's clothing began to burn. Soon, Matthias' entire body was convulsing. He slapped his palms against the ground and dug furrows in the soil with his boot-heels. He raised his head and slammed it backward, over and over.

With a blinding flash, Matthias caught fire. Raymer crossed his arms and watched as clouds of black, roiling smoke filled the air. The dying vampire was fully ablaze.

"Oh, God!" Veronica covered her mouth and nose with a blood-stained hand.

The smell of dead flesh and dormant innards commingled with the stench of the vampire's clothing. Raymer studied the skeletal visage of his victim's face. The skin peeled and shriveled to blackened strips. Matthias' head collapsed inward, the jaw opening to reveal his pointed teeth. The surrounding gum line began to boil, and a fetid burst of smoke emerged from the vampire's gaping maw.

Unmoved, Raymer watched as Matthias Bartsch was reduced to ashes. Cinders from the still-burning bones eddied across the open ground. Almost as quickly as they started, the flames consuming Matthias' body died out.

Raymer drove his shoe into the charred vampire's skull. It crumbled into a fine gray powder.

The professor trampled on the brittle pile of bones until there was nothing left of Matthias Bartsch. All that remained among the ashes was the tarnished silver stake and a scorched aluminum disk. With his heel, Raymer pushed the stake all the way into the ground.

Professor Upham reached down and probed at the flat oval, which the vampire had been wearing around his neck. It was still warm, but not too hot for her to pick up. She scraped the black coating from the object's surface and squinted to read the markings.

3. KP./15.PZ.GREN...1207 A.

She showed it to Raymer, who was now looking over the gray dust at his feet. "Any idea what this means?" she asked.

"I assume it was his military identification disk. I'm not an expert on Third Reich history. Give it to me, and I'll put it with the box I took from inside the cabin."

"What are you gonna do with all the money you found in there?"

"I'm unemployed. Remember?" Raymer stamped the pile of ash as smoldering cinders drifted around his legs. "So I think I'll keep that cash, if you have no objections."

Veronica turned around. "So that's it, then?"

"Yes," Raymer answered. "He's gone. Forever."

"And Laura?"

"I already told you. She'll come looking for her pound of flesh from both of us." A bemused smile crossed his lips. "But I'll be ready for her. You can count on that."

48

IN THE BACK OF THE STOLEN VAN WERE TWO SHOVELS AND A pickaxe. Raymer slid the tools out, one by one, and set them against the bumper. Veronica stood a few steps behind him, her hand still pressed against her neck. The improvised bandage had stopped the bleeding, but the wound was still painful to the touch.

Raymer surveyed the head of the pickaxe and the fresh earth that clung to the iron surface. "Well, now we know how they were disposing of bodies."

"What do you mean *they?*"

"Are you naïve enough to think Laura has no blood on her hands?" Raymer replied. "She's been with him for days. You saw how quickly she came to his defense. And let's not forget what she did to Junior."

"Fine." Veronica fired back. "But I know there's still some part of her left in there. She hesitated. She fucking *ran*, Edison!"

"Don't be sentimental." Raymer hefted the axe. "Besides, you're forgetting something else."

"And what's that?"

"Your position as a distinguished faculty member at Williamsport College. It's one thing for them to kill a few homeless vagrants or patients in a nursing home. But they weren't going to risk their anonymity by murdering a tenured professor."

"So how do *you* explain what happened? What about the German? He sure as fuck wasn't gonna let us get away."

"We caught them off guard and forced their hand," Raymer explained. "They didn't have a choice. But Bartsch likely warned her beforehand not to kill us. And that's the only reason Laura hesitated. That, and the crosses seemed to have affected her."

Veronica was silent as she considered her colleague's rationale. Before she could raise any further questions, Raymer spoke up again.

"But now, she doesn't have anyone to guide her. She'll be lost without him, and as ironic as it is, she'll be blinded by vengeance. She'll make her move," he nodded. "I know her better than you do. She's always been impulsive. And when her judgment is this clouded, she'll be careless, too."

"As usual, you sound so certain of yourself."

"Never mind that right now." Raymer extended the shovel toward Veronica. "We need to put Luttrell in the ground and get the hell out of here."

Veronica marched across the yard to wrench the shovel from Raymer's grasp. "Our goddamn fingerprints are gonna be all over these tools."

"That's why I asked you to bring *everything*. Including work gloves." Raymer sighed. "But that's neither here nor there. We'll take these with us and I'll get rid of them later."

Raymer slipped past Veronica and began to look for a patch of soft ground in an inconspicuous place. She followed a few steps behind him.

He stopped before a spot of bare earth. No grass or leaves covered the blighted ground at the edge of the side yard. There was already a slight depression, and water pooled in the narrow rut. He raised the pickaxe and went to work.

Veronica leaned on the shovel. She winced as she twisted her neck slightly. "Both of us need medical attention. We need to get to the hospital as soon as we're done here."

"Hospital?" Raymer didn't look up as he loosened the dirt. "Here's how this is going to work. I'm dropping you off at your house. You're gonna dowse your neck in peroxide, put a real bandage on your neck, take two aspirin, and go to bed."

"You're such an asshole." Veronica stuck out her lower lip. "Why do I even bother?"

"You tell me." Raymer knocked a clump of wet soil off the flat head of the pick.

"Edison, I've let you fuck up my life for years. But I'm not going down because of this crazy bullshit!"

"Then I highly suggest you avoid going to the emergency room." Raymer nodded at his left arm. "I got shot. Do you hear me complaining?"

"That bullet just grazed you."

"Trust me, Veronica, you'll live," Raymer said. "And just in case the thought crosses your mind, you're not going to wake up a vampire tomorrow night just because she bit you. Now hand me the shovel."

She wandered forward through the tall grass to hand him the long-handled tool. Raymer flung the pickaxe aside and began to dig.

"What I'm saying, if you even care to hear it, is that it's over. All of it."

"Suits me," Raymer said and carried on with his work.

"I'll bet it does. You've been looking for a reason to end things between us for a long time, haven't you? And you have the gall to do it here." Veronica waved her arm in the direction of the cottage and van. She stormed around Edison to retrieve the pickaxe. "Hell, I don't think you *ever* cared, did you?"

Raymer stopped, shrugged, then cleaved the soil again.

"You just kept me around because I was useful, didn't you?"

"Yeah, that's it." Raymer shook his head. "You were *real* useful out here tonight, just like you're being real useful right now."

"You know what I mean." Veronica scowled. "I was the woman on your arm to complete the veneer of normalcy. You were the middle-aged college professor, unflappable in his convictions, who was secretly *getting it on* with his colleague. Yeah, that was and is the extent of our relationship. You never took me seriously, yet I proved to be a suitable sounding board for your obsessions, didn't I?"

"Veronica, this isn't the time."

"Why not?" she asked as she watched the hole in the ground grow deeper. "I mean, look at you. This is your moment of triumph. You killed a vampire! You were right, and I was the blinkered skeptic who just wanted to go back to my amateur séances and parlor games. Your words paraphrased, remember?"

"*We* may be finished," Raymer replied, "but you and I are literally partners in crime. We're ditching a body right now, and I plan to take that gun. There's one round left in the chamber, and when the time comes, I intend to make it count. We're linked forever, whether I'm in the picture or not."

Veronica stood by in silence.

"But I'm in total agreement with you," he continued. "After I drop you off at your house, you won't see me again. So don't call me if Laura McCoy shows up at your house tonight. You're on your own."

Veronica shot Raymer a puzzled glance. "I thought they had to be invited in. Isn't that—"

"And you invited her!" Raymer looked up at her. "We both did! Before she became what she is."

"But—"

"She can come and go as she pleases. It probably doesn't matter whether she's living or dead when the invitation was offered." He paused to consider his words. "Perhaps *undead* is the correct term, as cliché as it sounds."

"So what should I do?" Veronica's voice quavered.

"Hope and pray Laura comes to me first." Raymer stopped digging and laid the shovel down. The grave was knee high. "I think this will do."

"What if someone heard Junior's pistol and called the cops. They'll—"

"It's hunting season. Even if anyone lived nearby, they wouldn't call the police this time of year for early morning gunshots."

"Oh, yeah? And what about the fire?"

"It lasted all of three minutes, maybe less." Raymer climbed out of the grave. "Now you think you can help me drag his body over here and put the man to rest?"

Veronica turned away and walked back to the cabin as Raymer followed. Working quickly, they dragged Junior Luttrell's body to the grave and dumped him in. Raymer jogged back and returned with the dead man's blood-soaked jean jacket and the remnants of his torn shirt. He laid them over Luttrell's face and upper body.

"Do you want to say anything before I cover him up?" Raymer dusted his hands on his black trousers.

Veronica knelt by the grave. She reached down and folded the dead man's slender arms across his chest. After a moment of silence, she uttered the only words that came to mind. "I'm sorry you didn't live to see your father avenged."

Edison Raymer stood behind her with the shovel. He had stowed Junior Luttrell's revolver in the waistband of his pants. "Are you done?"

Veronica fought back a wave of tears as she stood to face him. "I've never understood you. How you can have no compassion for anyone. No regrets for the mistakes you've made, and let me assure you, there've been quite a few recently. For one, people are dead because of you and the foolish decisions you made!"

"No." Raymer dropped a shovelful of clay across Junior Luttrell's body. "They were adults who decided to take part in this hunt. I never said or did anything to deceive them. They knew this would be dangerous."

"Have you ever felt an ounce of remorse for anything or anyone?"

"At the moment, no."

"Did you ever even love *me,* Edison?"

He shifted more dirt onto the corpse. "What we had amounted to something akin to lust. From time to time, we shared mutual interests and a grudging respect for one another. But all you usually left me with was an empty liquor cabinet or a series of migraines."

Veronica stooped to take up the pickaxe. "I don't even know what to say to you right now."

"Don't say anything," Raymer replied. "I'll leave an offer on the table for you. Consider it an olive branch of sorts, for this offer will stand indefinitely."

Veronica looked at the ground. She kicked a rough stone and waited for him to continue.

"One day, you'll realize the significance of what we did here." Raymer dumped more dirt over Luttrell's body. "You've seen something that will stay with you for the rest of your life. Nothing else is going to matter. Everything has changed," he insisted. "But when you're ready to step up to the plate again and play in the big leagues, you'll know where to find me."

"Only a man as pompous and as arrogant as you could say something like that and think of it as a fucking olive branch." Veronica turned her head away. "And *I'll know where to find you?* What the fuck does that mean?"

"You're not stupid, Veronica. You'll figure it out."

"You know, right now I'm only sure of two things." She spoke in a low whisper. "First, that you're the biggest fucking prick I've ever had the misfortune of sharing a bed with."

"Should I brace myself for the second?"

Veronica shouldered the pickaxe and turned her back to him. "That vampires really do exist," she admitted. "Congratulations on your momentous discovery, Edison. Maybe one day, *you'll* realize the significance of what *we* witnessed tonight. Beyond your own selfish obsessions."

Dr. Upham made her way toward the rear of the cottage where they'd hidden the SUV. Raymer shook his head and continued to fill the shallow grave.

49

WITH AN EYEDROPPER FULL OF HYDROGEN PEROXIDE IN hand, Edison Raymer sat on the edge of the toilet seat and positioned his left arm to face the bathroom mirror. In the glass, he could see the furrow left by the bullet. The professor squeezed the antiseptic onto the wound and grimaced as the laceration began to foam. He stood and put the peroxide bottle away, and paced around the bathroom until the pain became a dull ache.

Raymer was dressed in khaki pants, a clean pair of shoes, and a ribbed tank-top. A crisp dress shirt hung on his bedroom door, but he had no intention of slipping his arms through either of its carefully pressed sleeves.

When the professor returned to his townhouse earlier that morning, he hadn't parked in his driveway, but on the other side of the narrow street. All the items pilfered from Bartsch's cabin and van remained in the vehicle's cargo space. The townhouse beside his was vacant, and the occupants of the third and final home in the row—the Pulaskis—appeared to be out for the day.

After a double dose of Ibuprofen, Raymer packed an overnight bag with several days' worth of clothes and an extra pair of shoes. So as not to arouse suspicion, he made three isolated trips to his vehicle to ferry the bag and load two boxes of carefully selected books.

Around four o'clock that afternoon, a woman walking her dog passed him as he hefted a box into the backseat. She stopped and tried to make small talk. "Sellin' off some old books?"

304

"Something like that." His reply had been curt as he hurried across the street and disappeared through his front door.

Between the searing pain in his left arm and the anticipation building inside, he forced himself to cook a light dinner and eat. As he sat at the table, the sun faded outside his kitchen window. In his mind's eye, Raymer had gone over various permutations of his plan numerous times. Upon finishing his supper, a strange sense of calm had washed over him.

He knew Laura was coming for him. The professor hadn't bothered to check his wristwatch, but it had been dark outside for hours. Raymer stopped to glance in the spotless mirror, and picked up Junior Luttrell's revolver from the countertop. He polished the tarnished chrome with a hand towel and shoved the gun in between his belt and trousers. A smile tugged at his lips as he studied his chiseled upper body, close-cropped hair, and bearded face in the mirror.

You always play to win, Edison.

He extinguished the bathroom light and padded down the stairs. Out of instinct, his hand dropped to the grip of the handgun. He knew his enemy was stealthy, and could be waiting around any corner. He relaxed when he found the front door shut and the foyer empty. Raymer moved into the living room to take a seat in his leather wingback chair.

On the side table was his last vial of holy water, his hammer, and a single silver stake. Only the ghostly moonlight filtered in through the living room curtains as he withdrew the .44 Magnum and admired its craftsmanship. The cylinder of Luttrell's pistol had one silver bullet left, and Raymer double-checked the chambers to make sure the round was exactly where he wanted it. One careful squeeze of the trigger, and the silver slug would sear through its mark in a blaze.

As the minutes turned to hours, he considered pouring himself a shot or two of scotch. Yet the voice in his head that had guided him to victory against Matthias Bartsch warned him not to dull his senses. His opponent would be counting on his exhaustion, weakness, and frailty to aid in his defeat.

He had no plans to grant her that wish.

In the heavy stillness of his townhouse, Edison Raymer reflected on his life since the incidents at the Aston house. He had spent the intervening years in pursuit of a singular purpose, and it hadn't been an easy road. Yet he had persevered in honing his body, sharpening his wits, and filling his expansive mind with every bit of vampire lore he could unearth. The distractions of his career, the facile relationships with his peers, and even his failed attempt at intimacy with Veronica Upham had all been necessary evils to throw off accusations and innuendo. He knew if anyone discovered his true purpose, his professionalism, credibility, and sanity would be questioned.

But in the destruction of his foe, he had been reborn. All the grueling preparation Raymer had undergone for nearly three decades led him to the capture and staking of Matthias Bartsch. He was now a hunter, and for the rest of his life, he would be compelled to seek out his prey. This meant thinking and living like them. Moving from place to place like the proverbial thief in the night.

Like the ruthless creatures he yearned to hunt, Raymer had transcended his humanity. The vampires roaming the world would learn to fear him and speak his name with revulsion. Every night would be a new vigil, every day a preparation for the next attack. He had traded the tedium of academia for unadulterated power. A life of normalcy was a luxury he could no longer afford.

There was no turning back, and Raymer regretted nothing. He was eager for his next fight. With diligence, he checked the long pull of the handgun's trigger, the keen point of the stake, and the heft of his hammer.

And he waited.

When the knob of the front door rattled once, Raymer secured his weapons and eased his tense body back into the chair. A gust of wind blew dead leaves into the foyer as the slow approach of booted feet echoed from the front hall. He gently cocked the hammer of the revolver for a single-action shot. He recalled that his opponent was armed as well, and he had to act first. He would leave her no time to react whatsoever.

The shadow of his enemy fell across his feet as the front door creaked shut of its own accord. Although Raymer's face was hidden in the darkness, he could see the vampire as she moved to stand before his chair.

"Laura," he greeted her in a low voice.

Her teeth were clenched as she replied. "I've come to finish what you started." She dropped a hand to tighten the suppressor on her semi-automatic pistol. "This time, Raymer, I'm not gonna graze you. And when you're dying in that chair, I'm gonna drain every last drop of your blood for what you did to him, do you under—"

Edison Raymer leveled the .44 Magnum and squeezed the trigger. The muzzle flash lit the living room, and the deafening *boom* resounded throughout every corner. The silver bullet hit Laura square in the chest. She glanced down at the dark stain spreading across her closed wool jacket.

"You—"

The stunned vampire's legs gave out and she collapsed to the hardwood floor. Raymer cast the pistol aside, took up his hammer and stake, and darted forward. Laura thrashed on the floor as the silver spread its poison through her bloodstream.

"Son...of a bitch..."

Before she could react, her opponent had already subdued her. Raymer straddled her, placing his full weight upon her. "I can't believe you fell for the same trap!" He provoked her. "I thought you'd be smarter, Laura. I actually thought you might've been a challenge."

As Laura fought to sit up, Raymer drove the sharp point of the stake through her ribs and into her heart with a single swing of his hammer. The infusion of silver and the force of the blow knocked her flat on her back. Dark blood splashed across his face as he raised the hammer again, and brought it down a second time.

"With this, I bring you from shadow into light!" His voice thundered. *"Ex umbra in lucem!"*

Through the smudged lenses of his spectacles, he locked eyes with his prey. She glared back with malice and confusion—as if she never expected her reviled enemy could act with such precision and decisive fury.

The professor bit into his lip as he continued to smash the blunt end of the hammer against the protruding head of the stake. The vampire opened and closed her mouth as if to scream, but she could not utter a sound. Deep in the throes of agony, Laura continued to lash out in Raymer's direction, but her futile blows decreased in frequency and force. The tip of the stake pierced the hardwood under her back. Laura McCoy's arms went slack, and her legs slid out straight across the lacquered floor.

Raymer stood and hit the stake's flat head one final time with his hammer. He felt stinging up and down his bare arms where Laura had scratched him as he tossed the hammer into the fireplace. The professor stepped back, picked up the smoking revolver, and shoved it into his belt.

Laura cocked her head to face him. She bared her teeth. "When I pull out this stake...and get up...from this floor..."

Raymer took the vial of holy water in hand and opened it. With a flick of his wrist, he splashed Laura's face with the blessed liquid. Her pale skin began to singe and blister. Smoke commingled with the stench of the silver burning her chest.

"You and every one of your kind will learn to fear me!" He flung the vial to the floor by her head. The thick glass shattered and the consecrated water ran in rivulets across the floorboards.

He moved around the living room to open the curtains. Laura howled a curse in his direction, but Raymer ignored her. He stopped at his liquor cabinet and opened his best bottle of single malt scotch. After taking a hard swig, he approached the vampire and set the whiskey bottle down next to her.

Laura's face was now bisected with a hideous, frothing scar. She gnashed her teeth as Raymer bent down and patted her jacket pocket. Without speaking, he removed her crumpled box of cigarettes and her steel lighter.

"Fucking let me up!" she begged. "Just pull out the stake and I'll leave."

"You lie." Raymer shoved the cigarette box into his pants' pocket. "You're here because I killed him. And you won't leave until you've had your revenge."

"None of this is my fault. You called me and I came down here to help, you son of a bitch!"

"And you turned on me."

He twirled the lighter in his hand as he watched the holy water seep around her head. Raymer dropped to one knee and dabbed his fingers into the exposed flesh around her heart. The professor smeared black ash from Laura's scorched skin onto his face and neck. He wiped his fingers across his undershirt.

Before he rose, he took the whiskey bottle in his free hand. As he stood astride the paralyzed vampire, Raymer poured the contents of the bottle onto her legs, chest, and face. He flipped open the lighter.

"I'm not even going to wait for the sun to finish you. That gunshot probably woke the entire neighborhood, and I'm sure someone's already called the police."

"What are they gonna find when they kick down your door, Edison?" Laura asked. "That you nailed a woman to the floor of your living room? Shot and tortured her? How you gonna bullshit your way outta this one?" Her tone grew bolder and she managed a strained laugh. "You didn't think this through, did you?"

"Believe me, Miss McCoy," He raised the roll of silver duct tape he had taken from Matthias' van. "I thought of everything."

"What are you doing?"

Raymer tore a thick piece of tape from the roll and squatted down beside her. "Any last words?"

Laura met his gaze with a look of defiant resignation. "You don't deserve victory."

Raymer smiled as he fastened the tape over the vampire's mouth. "Whether I deserve it or not is inconsequential." After sparking the lighter, he bent forward and held it against Laura's alcohol drenched boot. A rolling blue flame shot up her leg and across her chest.

"I won." He rose and extinguished the lighter. "Twice."

Laura's eyes grew wide as the flames engulfed her. Although Raymer was denied the pleasure of hearing her screams, he relished the look of terror that flashed in her eyes.

With little time to spare, Edison Raymer sprinted to the foyer and retrieved his black coat from the rack. After he slid it on, he stepped into the kitchen. After lifting the stovetop, he snuffed out the pilot lights and opened the oven door. A deep breath through his nose confirmed the fragrant odor of natural gas filling the room.

Raymer spun on his heel and walked out the front door. He noticed lights on in the houses around him, heard dogs barking in nearby yards, and could discern the distant wail of sirens. Mrs. Pulaski in the townhouse at the end of the row leaned out her open bedroom window. She yelled something in his direction, but he ignored her.

Raymer crossed the street, opened the rear door of his SUV, and slipped the pistol out from under his coat. He jammed it under the passenger seat, closed the door gently, and sat down on the cold curb across from his townhouse. Thick smoke began to pour out the front door, which he had left half open.

As he palmed one of Laura's remaining cigarettes, he imagined her flesh peeling as she strained and pulled at the silver rod pinning her to the floor. Raymer lit the cigarette with her lighter and took a short drag. He coughed and pounded a fist against his chest as he clutched the Indonesian *kretek* between his lips.

Mr. and Mrs. Pulaski scurried across their lawn and they tied their bathrobes closed to ward off the cold. They were shouting at Raymer, but he kept his eyes on his townhouse.

He took another drag on the clove as a police car spun around a corner and charged down the narrow street. It pulled to a stop at the curb and two officers emerged with boxy handguns drawn. He recognized the passenger. It was the Latina cop who once told Laura to clear off from the bus stop. He had watched the video footage of their first hunt enough times that the officer's face was unmistakable.

Raymer sat in silence and feigned a degree of shock as the police approached him.

"Sir?" The male officer pointed his pistol at the ground. "Is that your house over there?"

Raymer exchanged glances with both of them. He opened his mouth to let the cigarette hang precariously from his lower lip, but didn't say a word.

"We received a report of a loud noise, possibly a gunshot, from this neighborhood. Do you know anything about that?" The female cop approached him with less trepidation than her partner. She slipped her pistol back into its holster. Raymer looked up at her silver badge and her nametag, which read PEREZ. "The fire department is on the way, but in the meantime, you need to start answering our questions!"

"I..." Raymer reached a trembling hand to his mouth and clutched the cigarette between two fingers.

"Go on, sir! Tell me what happened."

The other officer sprinted toward the neighbors, warning them not to get any closer to the burning building or the man on the curb.

"I was asleep." Raymer stared past the stocky officer as she moved closer. "There was a loud noise downstairs. Like a firecracker exploding. I think it came from my kitchen. Then I..."

He trailed off again as the officer's radio squawked on her duty belt. She held the transceiver clipped to her epaulet and responded in fashion. Raymer didn't pay attention to what she said, and took another drag from the cigarette.

Before he could blink, her attention was back on him. "Sir, you need to keep talking to me. Do you need medical attention?" Officer Perez was donning latex gloves as she spoke.

"No." Raymer coughed. "I think I made it out in time." He pretended to struggle with his words. "Not sure, but I think I smelled gas...you know, from the stove."

Perez leaned in closer. "You been drinking tonight, sir?"

Before he could answer, another police car pulled up to block a perpendicular street. More uniformed officers rushed across the blacktop.

"Just...just a shot of whiskey before bed. A nightcap." Raymer's voice clutched in his throat. "But that was hours ago."

"I can still smell it on your breath. Are you sure—"

The gas explosion across the street blew out every glass window of Raymer's townhouse. Roiling bolts of white-hot flame blew out of every opening. The front door shot off its hinges and tumbled across the grass. Raymer shut his eyes to avoid the blinding flash. Perez ducked beside the rear of the professor's SUV to brace for an oncoming blast. Searing heat rushed around them as police officers stumbled and fell to the pavement.

Within minutes of the explosion, the vacant townhouse beside his was caught in the conflagration. Fire trucks arrived, followed by paramedics. The street suddenly teemed with first responders and emergency workers.

Officer Perez was led away by an EMT while Raymer sat unfazed before the flickering light of his collapsing home. Firefighters had tapped a nearby hydrant, and swept two snaking hoses along the base of the roaring inferno.

Strange faces continued to appear in Raymer's field of vision. He sat motionless the entire time. Finally, someone he recognized stood to block his view of the fiery townhome.

"Dr. Raymer." Rudy Pettit nursed a tall cup of coffee. "The vampire expert. As I live and breathe."

"Detective." Raymer lit McCoy's last cigarette.

Pettit scowled. "I didn't know you smoked. I don't recall seein' any ashtrays in your livin' room."

With a limp hand, Raymer withdrew the *kretek*. "It's a dirty habit, so I usually smoke outside." He looked over the detective's shoulder at the charred remains of his gutted house as cinders drifted into the lightening sky. "Guess it would be more appropriate to say I used to smoke outside, seeing as I'm now homeless."

"Listen." Pettit adjusted the tweed hat on his balding head. "They called me down here because you still had a 'person of interest' flag on your file. I meant to take it off but I forgot." Pettit stopped to look at the smoldering remains of the professor's house. "Man, you got shit for luck, don't ya? First, you lose your job, then your house burns down." Pettit flipped up his collar as the wind blew down the street. "So what are we gonna find when we sift through those ashes?"

"Not much of anything." Raymer took another drag on the cigarette. "Several hundred...no, several *thousand* dollars in rare books just...just *gone*.

All my lecture notes and research. Gone." Raymer pressed his hand against his soot-streaked forehead.

"The initial report said there was a gunshot in this neighborhood. You don't own a gun, do you?"

Raymer glanced up at the frowning detective. "My house is collapsing in front of me and you're asking me about a goddamn gunshot? I already told half the Williamsport police force I heard a loud report from my kitchen, and woke up to the smell of gas and smoke."

"Hey, just doin' my job here," Pettit replied as he sipped his hot coffee. Behind him, two police cruisers sped away on another call as firefighters moved across Raymer's lawn to pick through the embers. "You need a ride to the E.R.? I mean, you don't look so hot right now. You ain't gonna throw up, are ya?"

"I'm fine, detective." Raymer grit his teeth and clutched his wounded arm. "I made it out before things got bad in there."

"Yeah, looks like you even had time to get dressed." Pettit furrowed his brows.

Raymer pulled open his coat to reveal his stained undershirt. The black blood looked like soot in the dying light of the inferno. Raymer closed the lapels of his coat. "I must've fell asleep with my shoes and trousers on. It's been a long week."

"Fair enough." Pettit shrugged his shoulders in the early light of dawn. "Hey, listen. The fire marshal's gotta pick through everything. See if your story checks out. In the meantime..." Pettit was distracted by a sudden burst of flame from the house. "Damn, I hope you got good insurance."

"I'll be fine." Raymer stomped out the cigarette beneath the heel of his shoe. "You were saying something?"

"Oh, yeah. Don't stray too far. You know, don't leave town or anything. Dependin' on what the fire inspector finds, this might get ruled an arson, and then you and I will be talkin' again. I mean, you take an out of work professor, funds dryin' up, doesn't wanna sell any of his books or anything. The guy decides to torch his place and collect a six or seven figure check. Not only arson but fraud to boot."

Raymer stood and dug into his coat pocket for the key to his SUV. "One flaw in your logic, Pettit."

"Pray tell."

"If I didn't want to sell my books or valuables, then why the hell would I burn them up?"

Pettit waved a finger at Raymer. "You're good, you know that? I think you missed your callin'. With a sharp mind for detail like yours, you should've been a police detective. Or a criminal mastermind. Either way, I'll be retirin' in a couple days if you're still lookin' for a job."

"I'm fifty-four, Pettit. A little late to be getting in the game, wouldn't you say?" Raymer held up his keys. "Anyway, I guess I'm going to go check into a hotel for now. Not sure how much use I can be here. Is that OK with you?"

"Sure." Pettit backed toward his unmarked cruiser. "Just remember what I said. Don't leave town and keep your cell phone on."

Raymer nodded as Pettit wandered away. The professor unlocked his SUV and slid behind the steering wheel. He glanced at his townhouse, which was nothing more than a flaming pile of debris.

With enough digging, investigators might find a silver stake among the wreckage. Maybe they'd uncover the melted frame of Laura's polymer hand-gun. But considering how easily Matthias Bartsch's skeleton had crumbled beneath Raymer's shoes, they wouldn't find any trace of human remains.

What he killed in there wasn't human.

Edison Raymer slipped his key into the ignition and started the SUV. Pettit hadn't noticed the mud-caked tires, nor had he bothered to peer through the tinted windows at the items packed inside.

Raymer glanced over his shoulder at the boxes of priceless occult books—some dating back to the Renaissance. He remembered the pistol under the seat, the remaining silver stake in the cargo space, and Bartsch's worn bag full of cash.

Before he released the parking brake, Raymer tapped his fingers against the steering wheel as a sly grin spread across his face.

"I won."

EPILOGUE

THE HEAVY SUN WAS SINKING BELOW THE HORIZON. TYLER Marshall ran beneath the streetlamps at the edge of the playground. They flickered on with a low and steady hum. He slipped past the chain-link fence and into the forest surrounding South Williamsport Elementary School. He tottered along swiftly, indifferent to the cold and the shadows lengthening around him. Tyler was a brave boy, and he relished these weekday afternoons when his mother would take him to the playground. He didn't even mind returning to school, because his mother was more fun than Miss Larson, his first-grade teacher. She let him climb up the metal stairs and go down the big kids' slide, and would catch him when he landed.

"Tyler!" His mother's voice called out in the twilight. He heard the hiss of air brakes and the roar of an empty school bus as it left the parking lot next to the gymnasium. "Where are you, honey?"

Mommy wants to play Hide-n-Seek, Tyler thought with increasing delight.

The boy bounded through the thicket of dark trees. Although short of breath, he plunged deeper into the murky recesses of the woods, smiling broadly. He was pleased with his plan to outsmart his mother, and he knew she would be proud of him as well. He could tell she wanted to play, because her voice seemed to grow more excited as he ran deeper into the forest.

Determined to find the perfect hiding place, Tyler darted from the winding dirt path and found himself venturing further into the heart of the woods. As he raced breathless through the forest, the young boy failed to see a large cluster of tangled roots protruding from the path. He fell to

314

the hard ground, skinning his knee. When he stood up, the seven-year old paused and felt a sudden pang of anxiety. He had become disoriented from the fall. The path he thought he had taken looked unfamiliar, and the other directions were foreign and uninviting. As the light dimmed around him, the landscape of the forest seemed to shift and change before his eyes. It was as if the underbrush had grown fuller, and the trees had grown taller and crowded closer together. The frightened child also realized that he was no longer within earshot of his mother's panicked cries.

Tyler heard a faint rustling to his left, and turned to face the swaying trees. He noticed a vague silhouette moving among the shadows. He felt a sense of relief, and assumed a grown-up was nearby. The adult would help him find his way back to the playground. Yet when the figure emerged from the woods, the child froze in confusion and terror.

The lady that came from the woods was very dirty and strange. She wore a black, tattered, old-fashioned dress, like in the movies he sometimes saw on the black and white TV channel. Her hair was wild and there were pieces of grass and other dirty things tangled in it. The lady's hair was an ugly yellow color, and to Tyler it almost looked white. But her face was even whiter. She stretched a gnarled arm toward him, tilting her head as if she could see him better if she were sideways. Her back was bent as she crouched low along the grass, her ripped skirt catching in the brown and yellow leaves.

"William?" she whispered. Her eyes were glassy as she inched her grimy face closer with every hunched and labored step. Tyler felt a sick and nervous feeling welling up from his stomach. He didn't like the way the lady's voice sounded, nor did he like the way her clothes seemed all wrong and tore up—like she was in some kind of bad accident. As the lady came closer, she tilted her head to the other side. The young boy hated the way the lady was looking at him. Her eyes seemed to get darker, and she looked like she was hurting really badly.

The lady muttered something about the other little boy she was searching for. When he saw the lady's sharp brown teeth, he hadn't enough time to scream or cry out for his mother. The weird woman's eyes went black, and she lunged at him through the darkness. With a ferocious roar, she locked her jaws upon the tiny throat of Tyler Marshall and dragged him into the quiet, enveloping shadows of the forest.

APPENDIX

CHAPTER 1

Das verstehe ich nicht.
I do not understand.

Mein Englisch ist nicht so gut.
I do not speak English very well.

Steh auf!
Stand up! (Arise!)

Wie heißt du?
What is your name?

Ich bin ein Sanitäter.
I am a medic.

Hast du in Russland gekämpft?
Did you fight in Russia?

Wie hast du das verdient?
How did you earn this?

Ist das deine Frau?
Is that your wife?

Sie werden uns erschießen!
They are going to shoot us!

Schau mal was sie mit unserem Soldbücher tun!
Look what they are doing with our paybooks!

317

CHAPTER 2

Hilf mir!
Help me!

Bitte! Ich bin noch am Leben! Hilf mir!
Please! I'm still alive! Help me!

Schau mal weg! Mein Gott, nein! Schau sie nicht an!
Look away! My God, no! Do not look at them!

Čo je to?
What is it?

Tento ešte žije. Čo by sme mali robiť s ním?
This one lives. What do we do with him?

Dajte mu dar!
Give him the Gift.

CHAPTER 3

Hände hoch!
Hands up!

Auf die knie!
On your knees!

Hände auf den kopf!
Hands on your head!

Kannst du mich hören?
Can you hear me?

Suchst du diese Leute? Amerikaner?
Are you looking for these people? Americans?

CHAPTER 4

Jetzt erinnere ich mich.
I remember now.

Ich tat es.
I did it.

Das Sonnenlicht!
The sunlight!

Lauf!
Run!

CHAPTER 7

Guten abend, Herr Bartsch.
Good evening, Mr. Bartsch

Hitler-Jugend
Hitler Youth

Juden raus!
Jews out!

Judenhäuser
Jewish houses

Es tut mir leid.
I am sorry.

CHAPTER 12

Aussteigen!
Get out!

Rette mich! Rette unsere kinder!
Save me! Save our child!

Heraus!
Out!

Halte mich!
Hold me!

Es tut mir leid
I'm sorry

CHAPTER 30

Liebst du mich, Matti?
Do you love me, Matti?

Ich liebe dich
I love you

Du wirst viele Leben retten!
You will save many lives!

Mein tapferer Matti! Ein Sanitäter!
My brave Matti! A medic!

Wirst du auf mich warten?
Will you wait for me?

Ich bin deine Frau. Ich werde ewig warten!
I am your wife. I will wait forever!

CHAPTER 38

Ex umbra in lucem
From darkness into light

CHAPTER 47

Ich werde dich und jeden von euch töten!
I will kill each and every one of you!

Es brennt! Es brennt! Verdammt!
It burns! It burns! Dammit!

Quid stas, et resistis, cum scias, Christum Dóminum vias tuas pérdere?
Why, then, do you stand and resist, knowing as you must that Christ the Lord brings your plans to nothing?

Timete eum!
Fear Him!

Timete nomen sanctum!
Fear His holy name!

Was machst du?
What are you doing?

Fick dich!
Fuck you!

Ich werde dich in der Hölle sehen!
I'll see you in hell!

Fernhalten!
Keep away!

Schwanzlutscher!
Cocksucker!

CHAPTER 49

Ex umbra in lucem!
From darkness into light!

We want to hear from you! Please visit our website for more information about new releases, author updates, special offers, and more!

www.StygianPress.com

Lightning Source UK Ltd.
Milton Keynes UK
UKHW041836010221
378065UK00003B/3/J